# STARVE

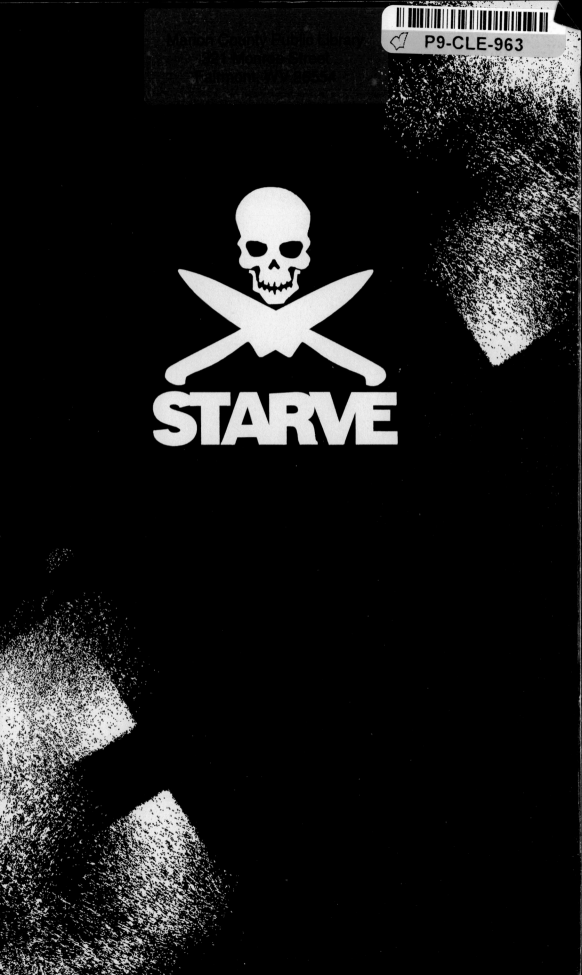

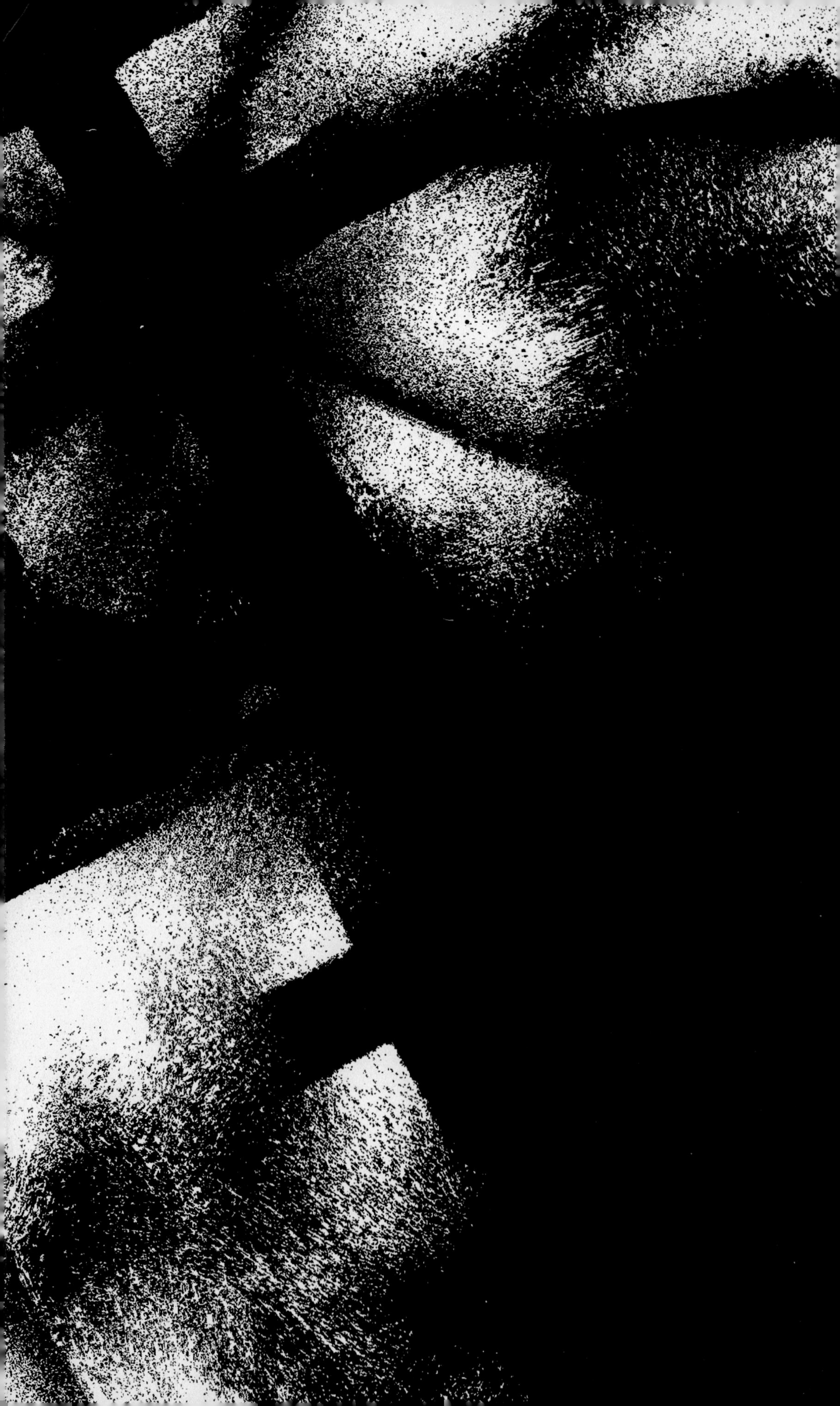

# STARVE

**CREATED BY** BRIAN WOOD, DANIJEL ZEZELJ, AND DAVE STEWART

**LETTERING BY** STEVE WANDS AND CLAYTON COWLES (ISSUE #1)

**PRODUCTION AND DESIGN BY** BRENNAN THOME

## IMAGE COMICS, INC.

Robert Kirkman – Chief Operating Officer
Erik Larsen – Chief Financial Officer
Todd McFarlane – President
Marc Silvestri – Chief Executive Officer
Jim Valentino – Vice-President

Eric Stephenson – Publisher
Corey Murphy – Director of Sales
Jeff Boison – Director of Publishing Planning & Book Trade Sales
Jeremy Sullivan – Director of Digital Sales
Kat Salazar – Director of PR & Marketing
Emily Miller – Director of Operations
Branwyn Bigglestone – Senior Accounts Manager
Sarah Mello – Accounts Manager
Drew Gill – Art Director
Jonathan Chan – Production Manager
Meredith Wallace – Print Manager
Briah Skelly – Publicity Assistant
Randy Okamura – Marketing Production Designer
David Brothers – Branding Manager
Ally Power – Content Manager
Addison Duke – Production Artist
Vincent Kukua – Production Artist
Sasha Head – Production Artist
Tricia Ramos – Production Artist

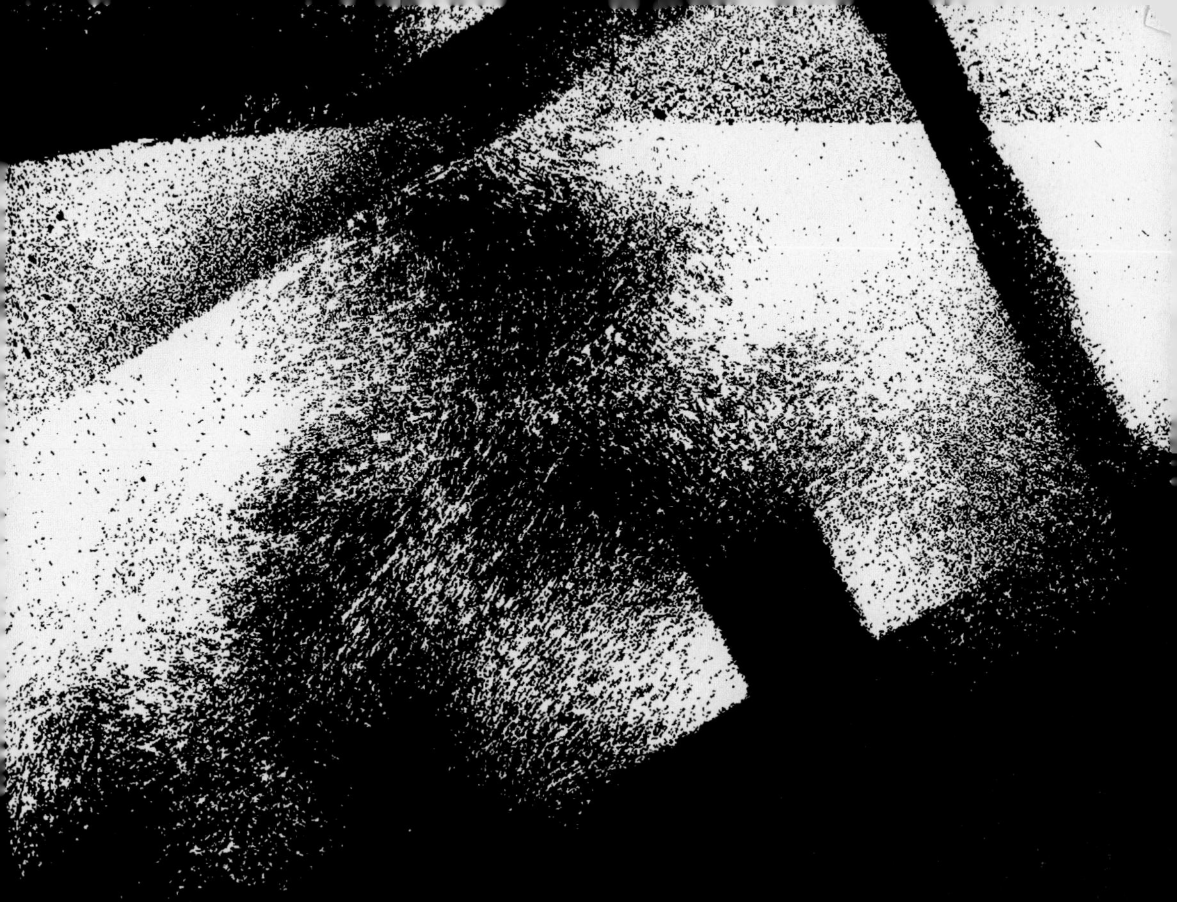

# TABLE OF CONTENTS

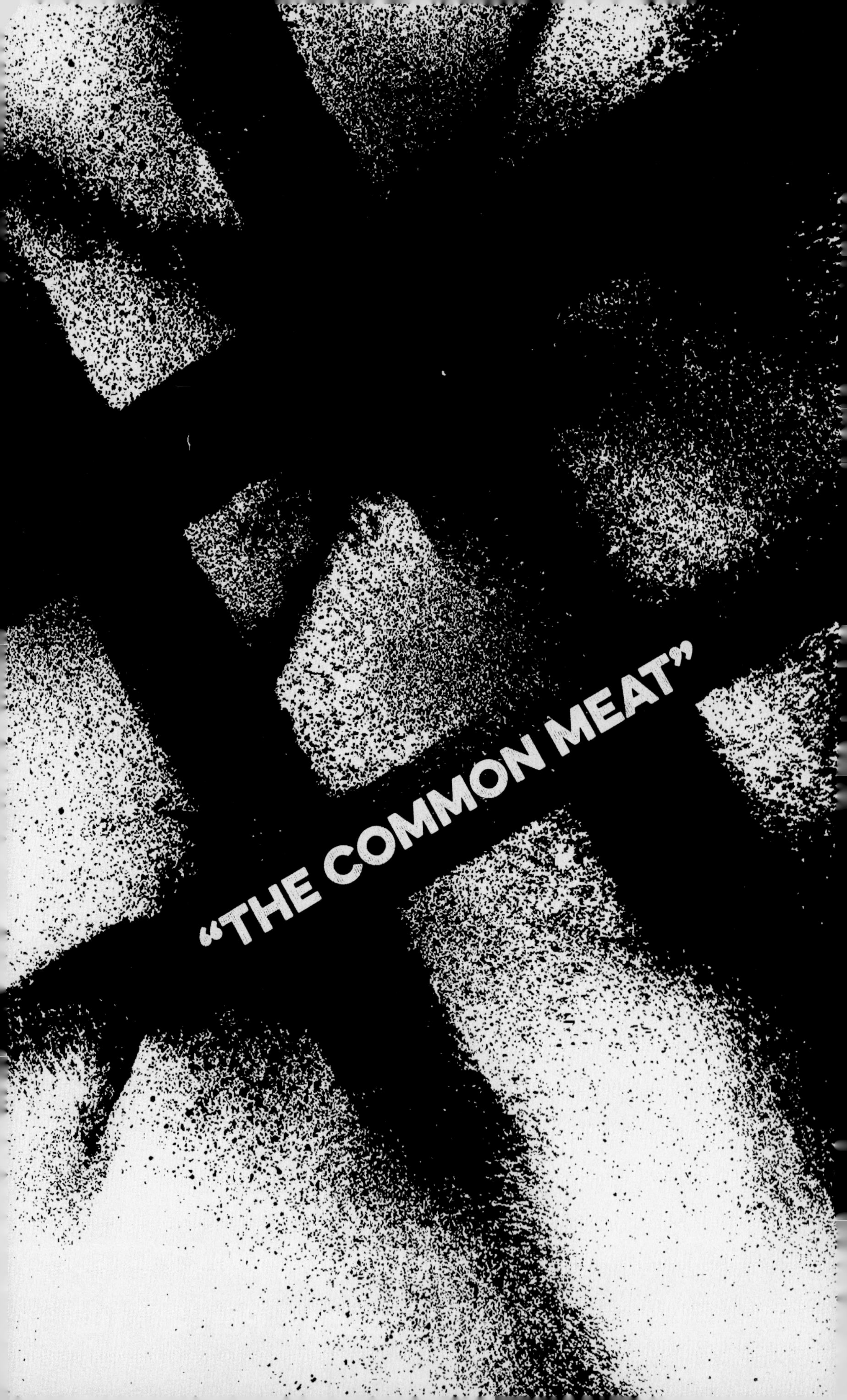
"THE COMMON MEAT"

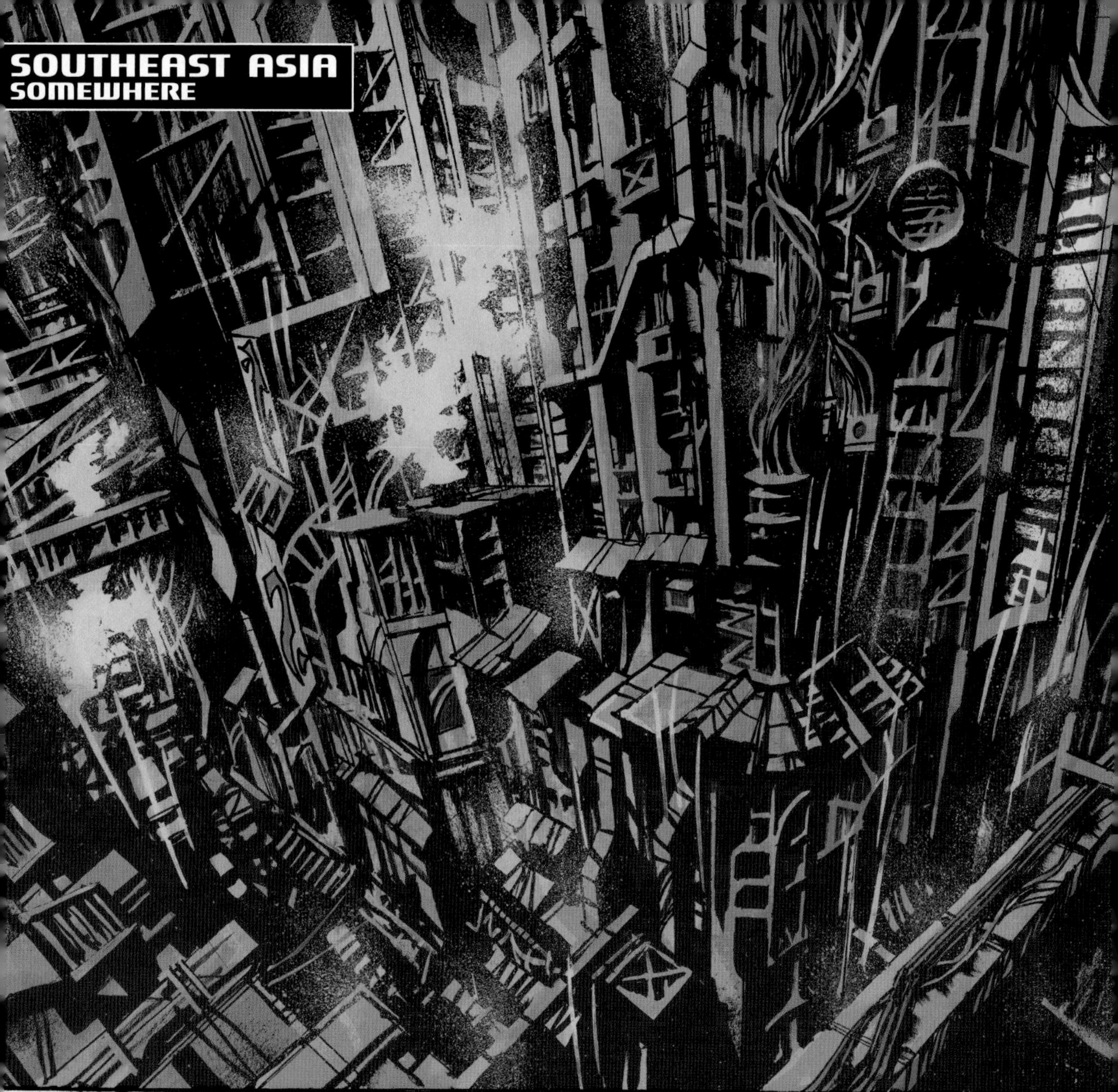
SOUTHEAST ASIA
SOMEWHERE

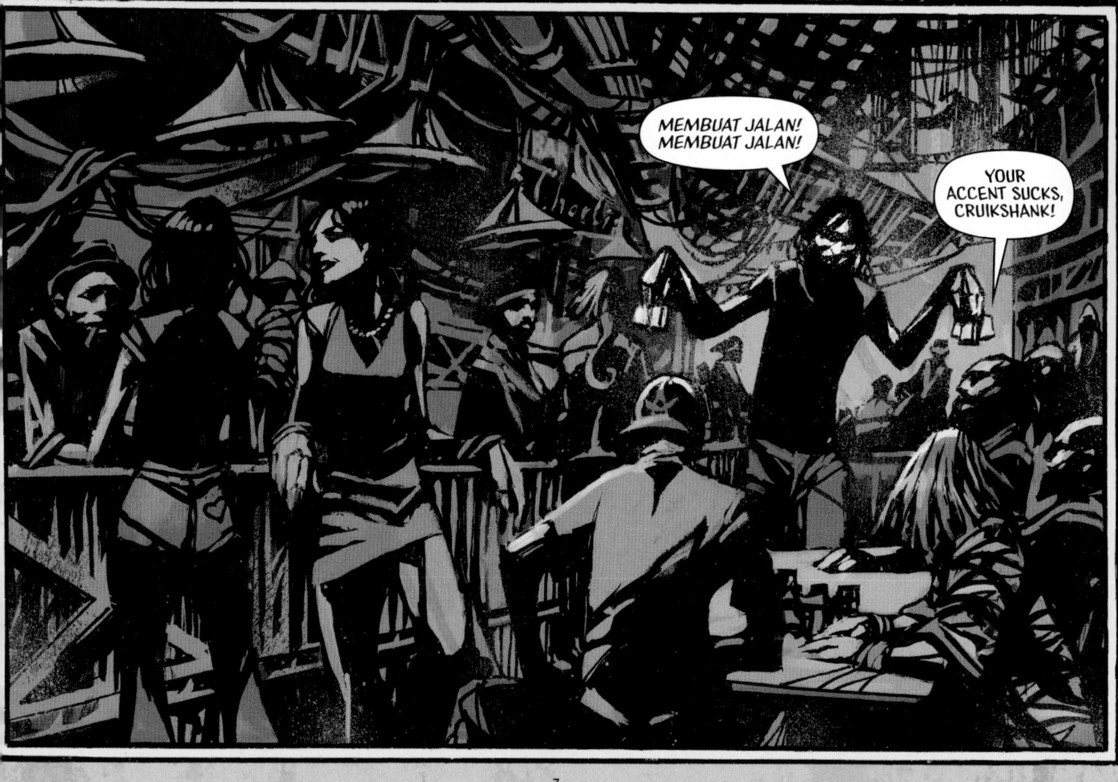
MEMBUAT JALAN! MEMBUAT JALAN!
YOUR ACCENT SUCKS, CRUIKSHANK!

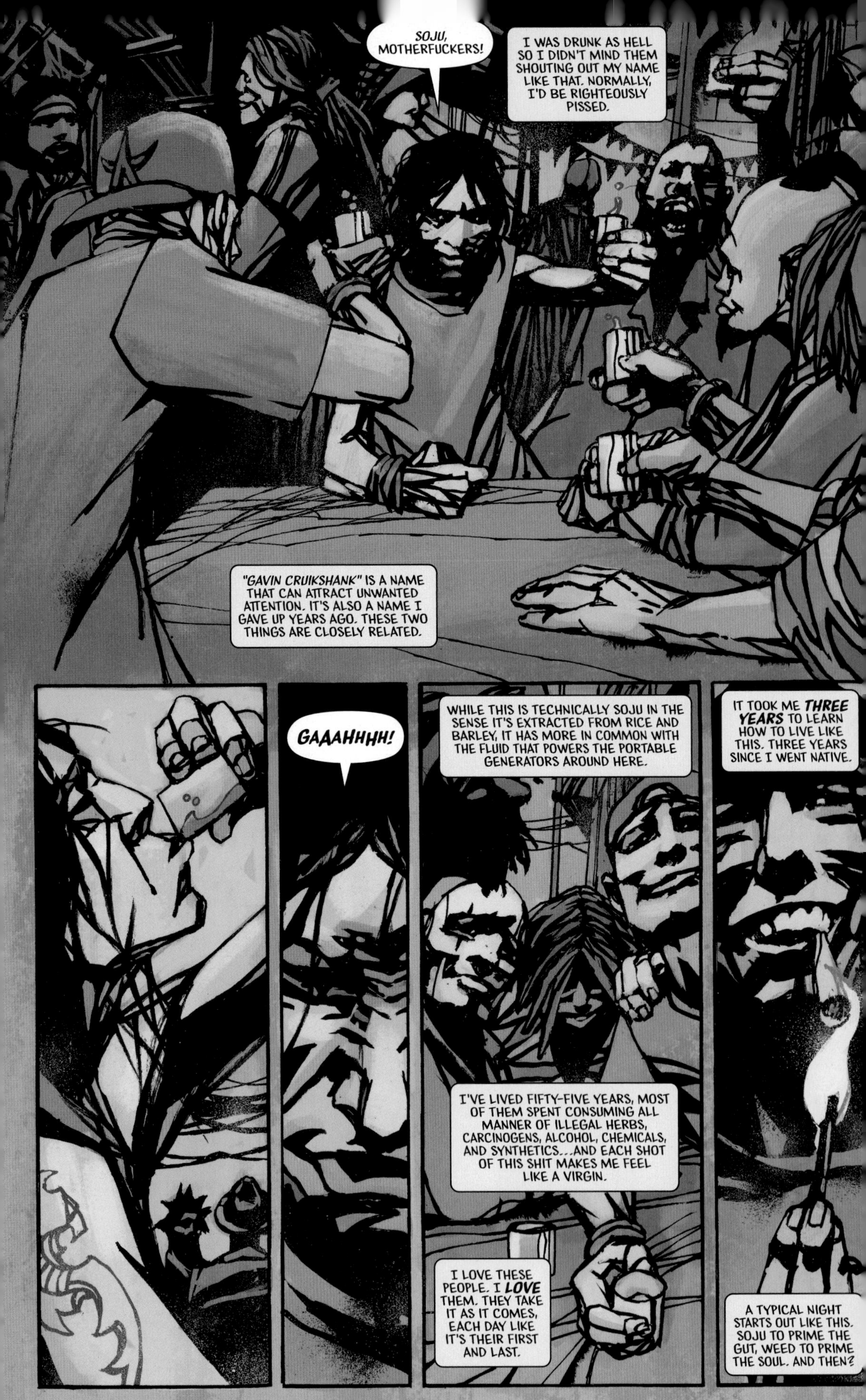

SOJU, MOTHERFUCKERS!
I WAS DRUNK AS HELL SO I DIDN'T MIND THEM SHOUTING OUT MY NAME LIKE THAT. NORMALLY, I'D BE RIGHTEOUSLY PISSED.
"GAVIN CRUIKSHANK" IS A NAME THAT CAN ATTRACT UNWANTED ATTENTION. IT'S ALSO A NAME I GAVE UP YEARS AGO. THESE TWO THINGS ARE CLOSELY RELATED.
GAAAHHHH!
WHILE THIS IS TECHNICALLY SOJU IN THE SENSE IT'S EXTRACTED FROM RICE AND BARLEY, IT HAS MORE IN COMMON WITH THE FLUID THAT POWERS THE PORTABLE GENERATORS AROUND HERE.
I'VE LIVED FIFTY-FIVE YEARS, MOST OF THEM SPENT CONSUMING ALL MANNER OF ILLEGAL HERBS, CARCINOGENS, ALCOHOL, CHEMICALS, AND SYNTHETICS...AND EACH SHOT OF THIS SHIT MAKES ME FEEL LIKE A VIRGIN.
I LOVE THESE PEOPLE. I LOVE THEM. THEY TAKE IT AS IT COMES, EACH DAY LIKE IT'S THEIR FIRST AND LAST.
IT TOOK ME THREE YEARS TO LEARN HOW TO LIVE LIKE THIS. THREE YEARS SINCE I WENT NATIVE.
A TYPICAL NIGHT STARTS OUT LIKE THIS. SOJU TO PRIME THE GUT, WEED TO PRIME THE SOUL. AND THEN?

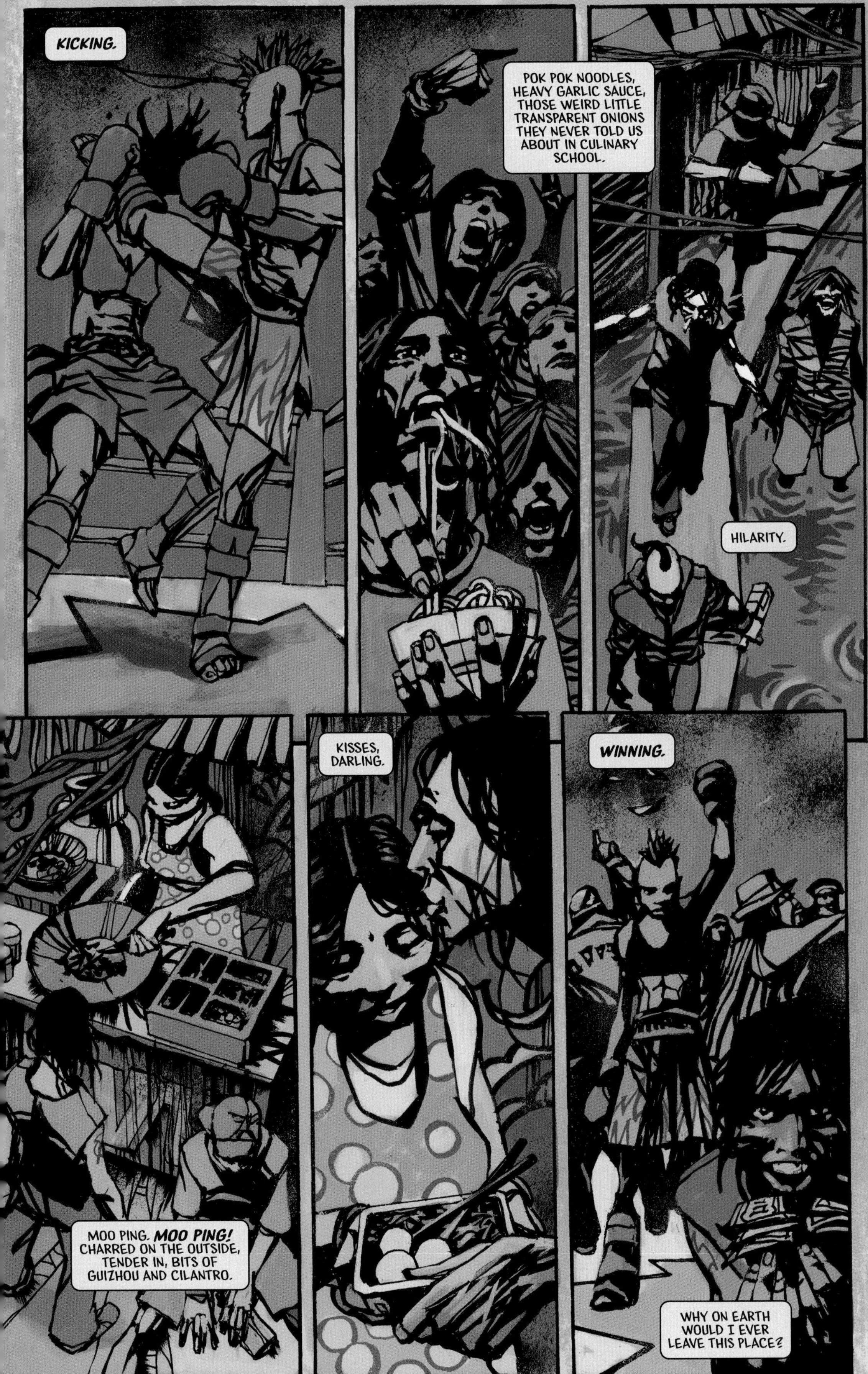
KICKING.
POK POK NOODLES, HEAVY GARLIC SAUCE, THOSE WEIRD LITTLE TRANSPARENT ONIONS THEY NEVER TOLD US ABOUT IN CULINARY SCHOOL.
HILARITY.
MOO PING. MOO PING! CHARRED ON THE OUTSIDE, TENDER IN, BITS OF GUIZHOU AND CILANTRO.
KISSES, DARLING.
WINNING.
WHY ON EARTH WOULD I EVER LEAVE THIS PLACE?

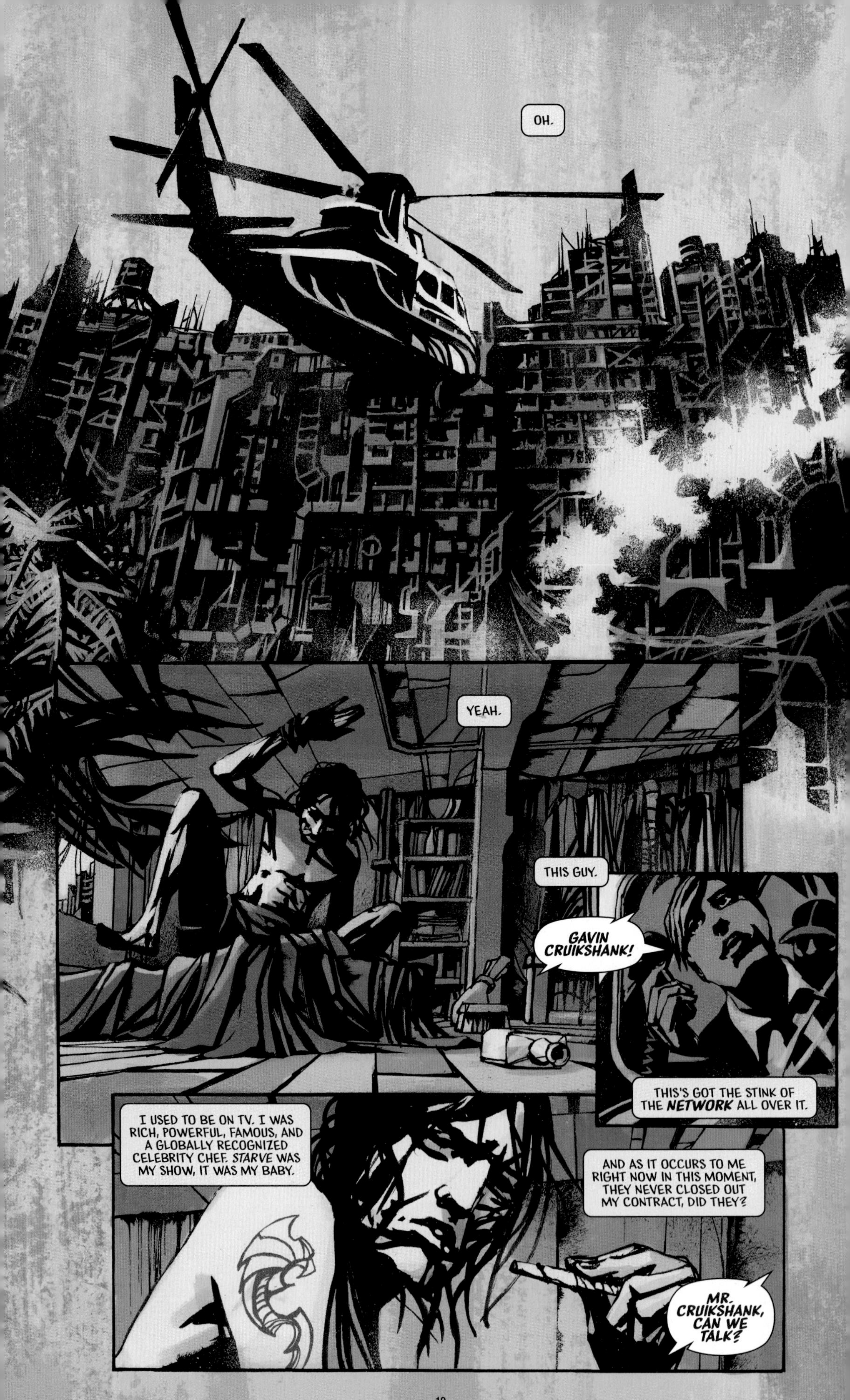

OH.
YEAH.
THIS GUY.
GAVIN CRUIKSHANK!
THIS'S GOT THE STINK OF THE NETWORK ALL OVER IT.
I USED TO BE ON TV. I WAS RICH, POWERFUL, FAMOUS, AND A GLOBALLY RECOGNIZED CELEBRITY CHEF. STARVE WAS MY SHOW, IT WAS MY BABY.
AND AS IT OCCURS TO ME RIGHT NOW IN THIS MOMENT, THEY NEVER CLOSED OUT MY CONTRACT, DID THEY?
MR. CRUIKSHANK, CAN WE TALK?

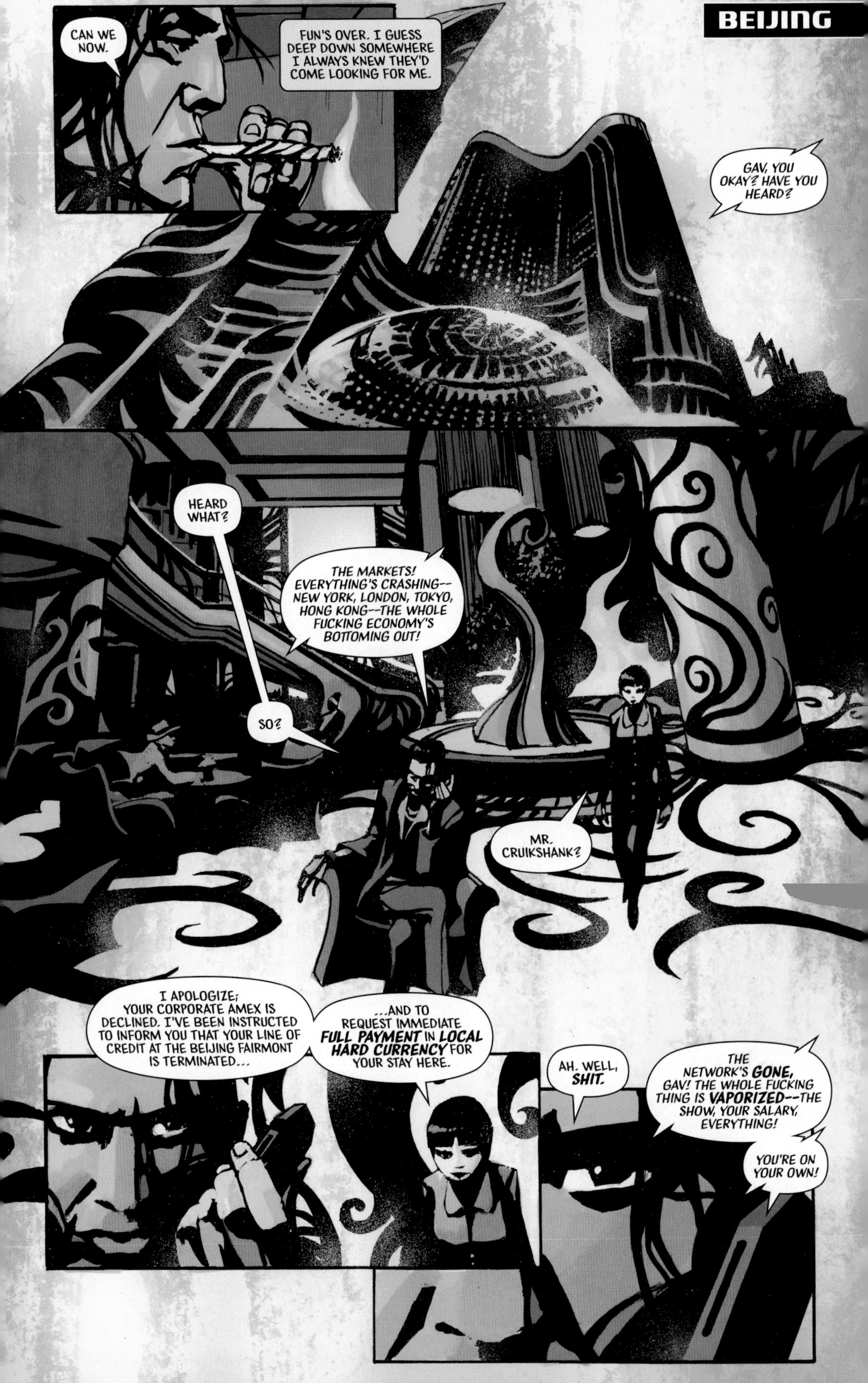
BEIJING
CAN WE NOW.
FUN'S OVER. I GUESS DEEP DOWN SOMEWHERE I ALWAYS KNEW THEY'D COME LOOKING FOR ME.
GAV, YOU OKAY? HAVE YOU HEARD?
HEARD WHAT?
THE MARKETS! EVERYTHING'S CRASHING-- NEW YORK, LONDON, TOKYO, HONG KONG--THE WHOLE FUCKING ECONOMY'S BOTTOMING OUT!
SO?
MR. CRUIKSHANK?
I APOLOGIZE; YOUR CORPORATE AMEX IS DECLINED. I'VE BEEN INSTRUCTED TO INFORM YOU THAT YOUR LINE OF CREDIT AT THE BEIJING FAIRMONT IS TERMINATED...
...AND TO REQUEST IMMEDIATE FULL PAYMENT IN LOCAL HARD CURRENCY FOR YOUR STAY HERE.
AH. WELL, SHIT.
THE NETWORK'S GONE, GAV! THE WHOLE FUCKING THING IS VAPORIZED--THE SHOW, YOUR SALARY, EVERYTHING!
YOU'RE ON YOUR OWN!

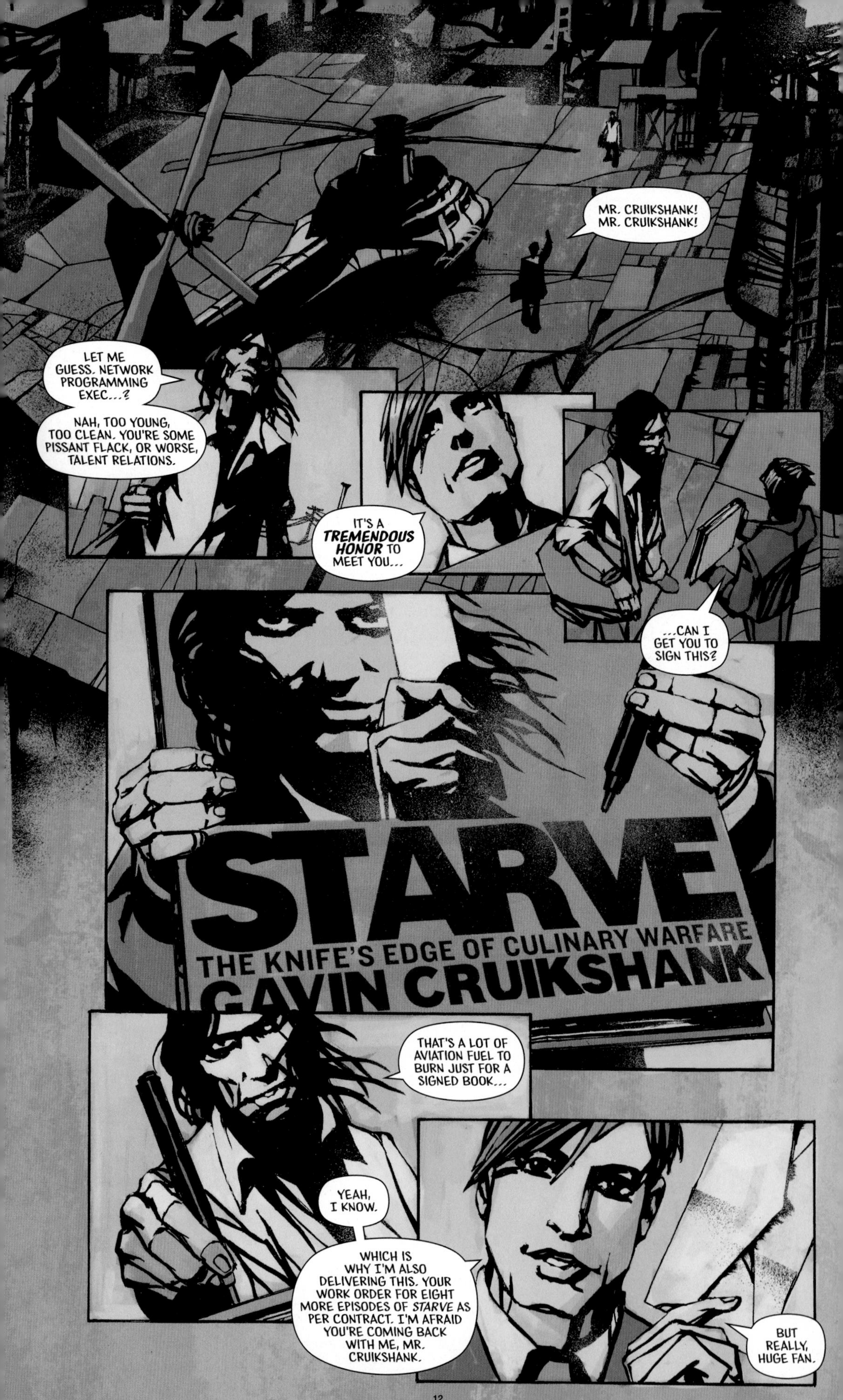

MR. CRUIKSHANK! MR. CRUIKSHANK!
LET ME GUESS. NETWORK PROGRAMMING EXEC...?
NAH, TOO YOUNG, TOO CLEAN. YOU'RE SOME PISSANT FLACK, OR WORSE, TALENT RELATIONS.
IT'S A TREMENDOUS HONOR TO MEET YOU...
...CAN I GET YOU TO SIGN THIS?
STARVE
THE KNIFE'S EDGE OF CULINARY WARFARE
GAVIN CRUIKSHANK
THAT'S A LOT OF AVIATION FUEL TO BURN JUST FOR A SIGNED BOOK...
YEAH, I KNOW.
WHICH IS WHY I'M ALSO DELIVERING THIS. YOUR WORK ORDER FOR EIGHT MORE EPISODES OF STARVE AS PER CONTRACT. I'M AFRAID YOU'RE COMING BACK WITH ME, MR. CRUIKSHANK.
BUT REALLY, HUGE FAN.

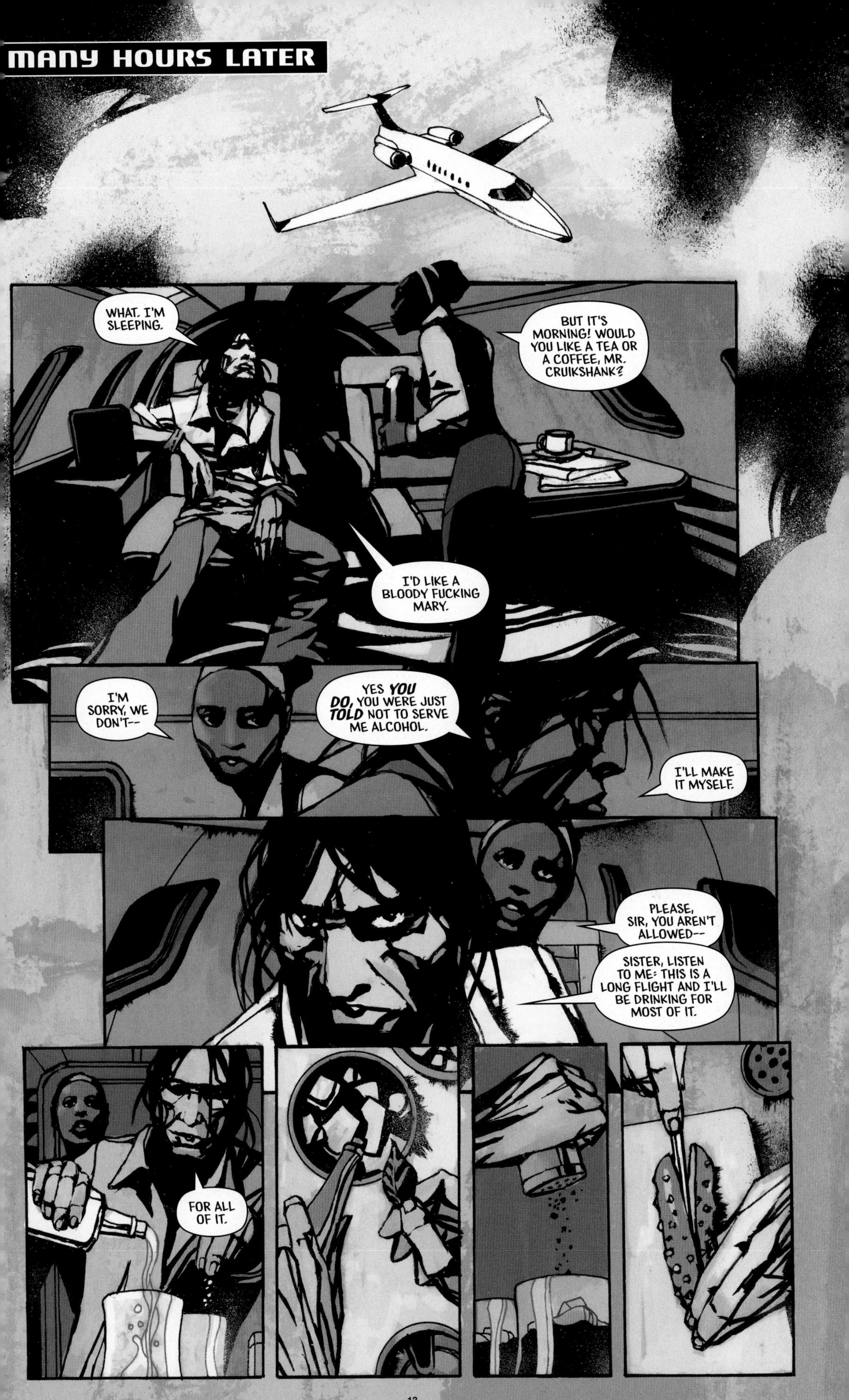

MANY HOURS LATER
WHAT. I'M SLEEPING.
BUT IT'S MORNING! WOULD YOU LIKE A TEA OR A COFFEE, MR. CRUIKSHANK?
I'D LIKE A BLOODY FUCKING MARY.
I'M SORRY, WE DON'T--
YES YOU DO, YOU WERE JUST TOLD NOT TO SERVE ME ALCOHOL.
I'LL MAKE IT MYSELF.
PLEASE, SIR, YOU AREN'T ALLOWED--
SISTER, LISTEN TO ME: THIS IS A LONG FLIGHT AND I'LL BE DRINKING FOR MOST OF IT.
FOR ALL OF IT.

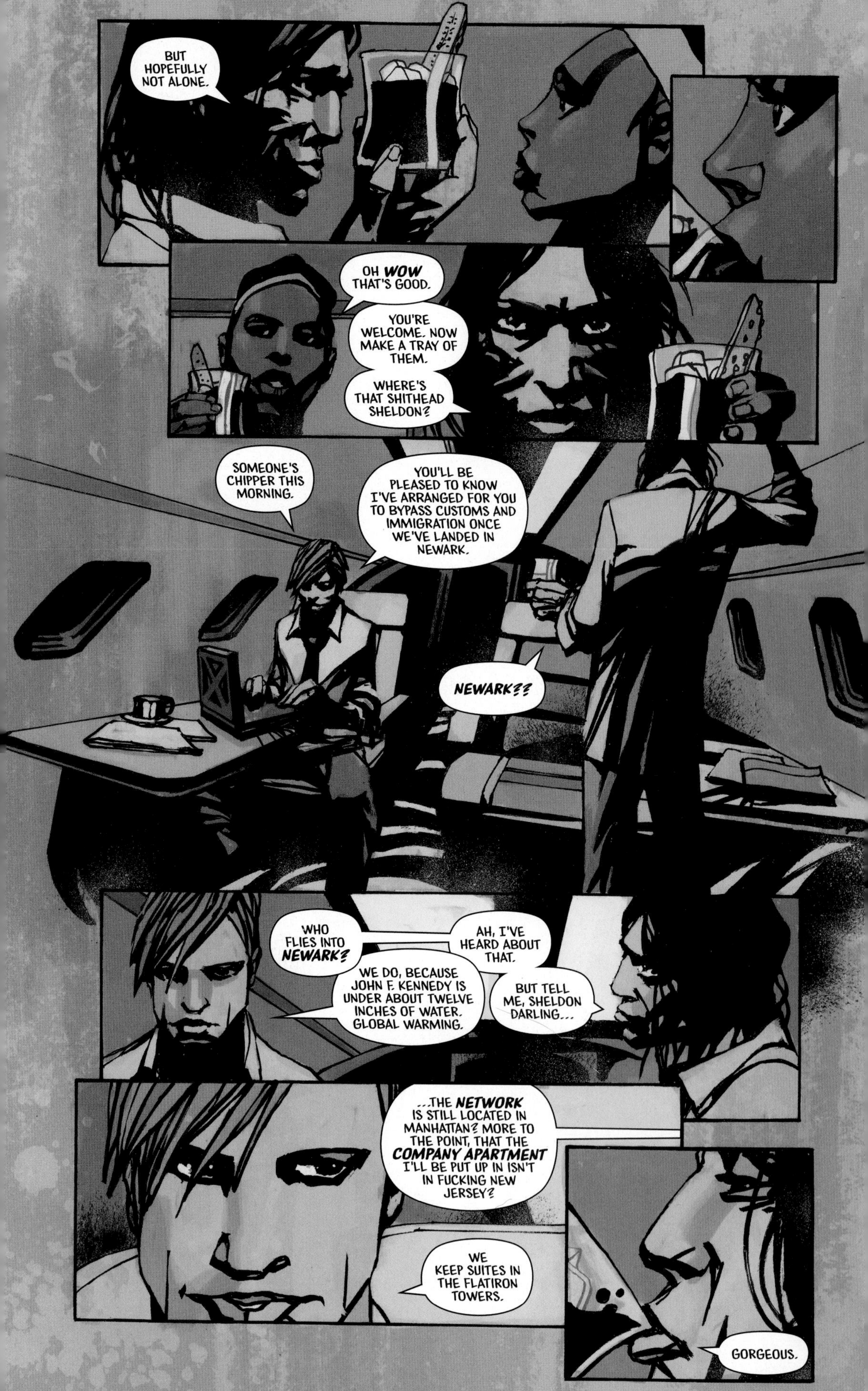
BUT HOPEFULLY NOT ALONE.
OH WOW THAT'S GOOD.
YOU'RE WELCOME. NOW MAKE A TRAY OF THEM.
WHERE'S THAT SHITHEAD SHELDON?
SOMEONE'S CHIPPER THIS MORNING.
YOU'LL BE PLEASED TO KNOW I'VE ARRANGED FOR YOU TO BYPASS CUSTOMS AND IMMIGRATION ONCE WE'VE LANDED IN NEWARK.
NEWARK??
WHO FLIES INTO NEWARK?
WE DO, BECAUSE JOHN F. KENNEDY IS UNDER ABOUT TWELVE INCHES OF WATER. GLOBAL WARMING.
AH, I'VE HEARD ABOUT THAT.
BUT TELL ME, SHELDON DARLING...
...THE NETWORK IS STILL LOCATED IN MANHATTAN? MORE TO THE POINT, THAT THE COMPANY APARTMENT I'LL BE PUT UP IN ISN'T IN FUCKING NEW JERSEY?
WE KEEP SUITES IN THE FLATIRON TOWERS.
GORGEOUS.

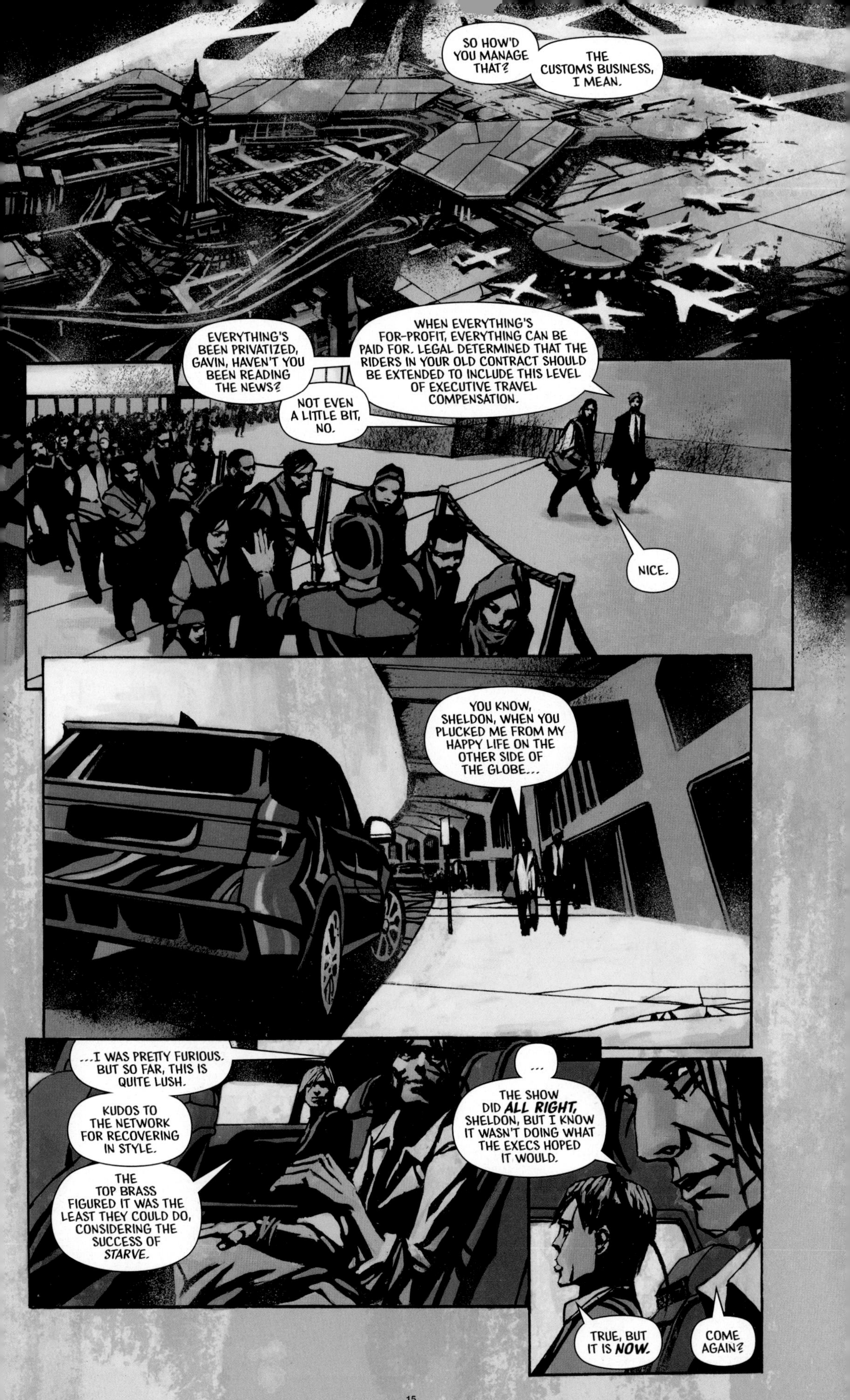
SO HOW'D YOU MANAGE THAT?
THE CUSTOMS BUSINESS, I MEAN.
EVERYTHING'S BEEN PRIVATIZED, GAVIN, HAVEN'T YOU BEEN READING THE NEWS?
NOT EVEN A LITTLE BIT, NO.
WHEN EVERYTHING'S FOR-PROFIT, EVERYTHING CAN BE PAID FOR. LEGAL DETERMINED THAT THE RIDERS IN YOUR OLD CONTRACT SHOULD BE EXTENDED TO INCLUDE THIS LEVEL OF EXECUTIVE TRAVEL COMPENSATION.
NICE.
YOU KNOW, SHELDON, WHEN YOU PLUCKED ME FROM MY HAPPY LIFE ON THE OTHER SIDE OF THE GLOBE...
...I WAS PRETTY FURIOUS. BUT SO FAR, THIS IS QUITE LUSH.
KUDOS TO THE NETWORK FOR RECOVERING IN STYLE.
THE TOP BRASS FIGURED IT WAS THE LEAST THEY COULD DO, CONSIDERING THE SUCCESS OF *STARVE*.
...
THE SHOW DID **ALL RIGHT,** SHELDON, BUT I KNOW IT WASN'T DOING WHAT THE EXECS HOPED IT WOULD.
TRUE, BUT IT IS **NOW.**
COME AGAIN?

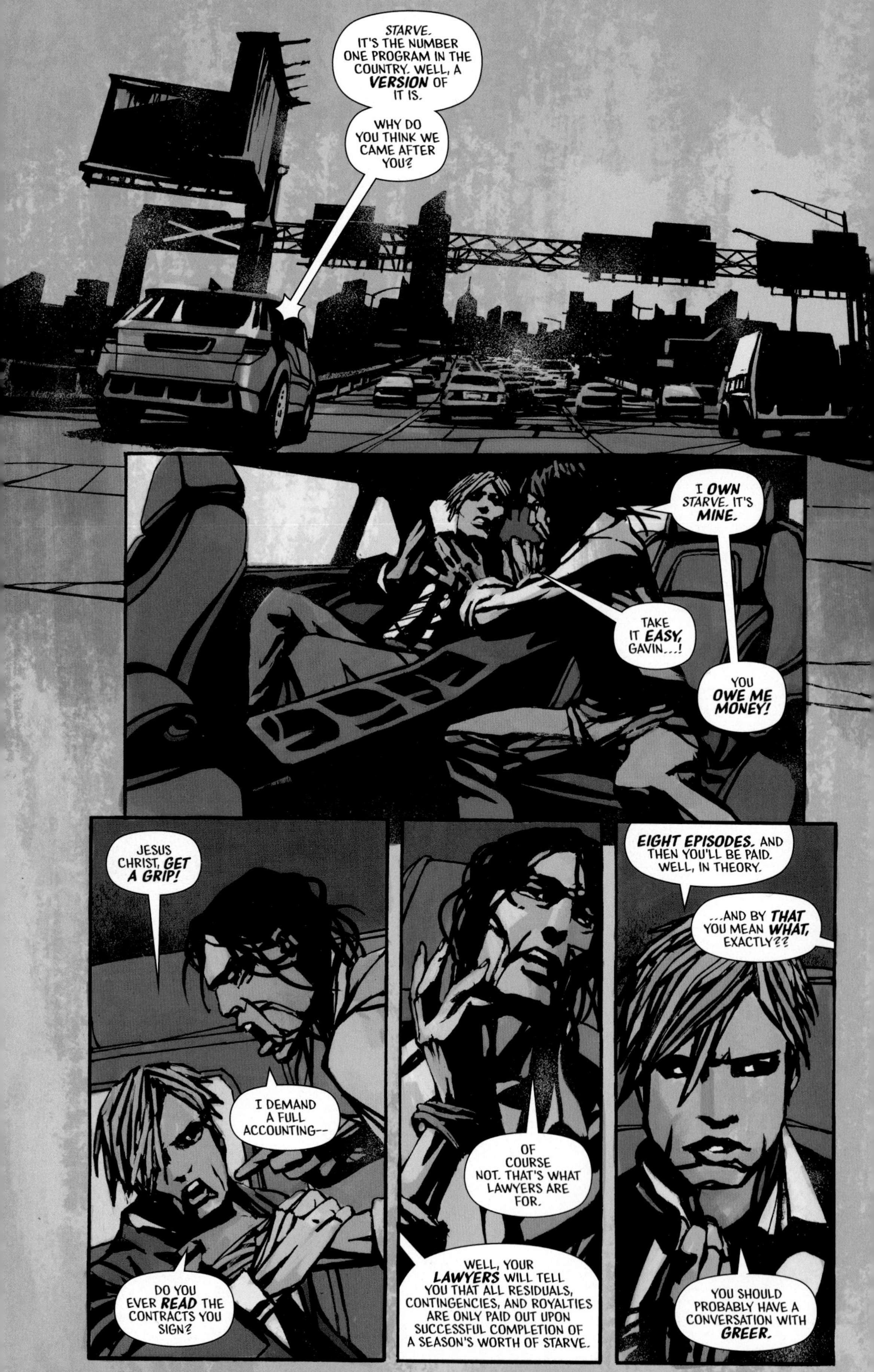

STARVE. IT'S THE NUMBER ONE PROGRAM IN THE COUNTRY. WELL, A VERSION OF IT IS.
WHY DO YOU THINK WE CAME AFTER YOU?
I OWN STARVE. IT'S MINE.
TAKE IT EASY, GAVIN...!
YOU OWE ME MONEY!
JESUS CHRIST, GET A GRIP!
I DEMAND A FULL ACCOUNTING--
DO YOU EVER READ THE CONTRACTS YOU SIGN?
OF COURSE NOT. THAT'S WHAT LAWYERS ARE FOR.
WELL, YOUR LAWYERS WILL TELL YOU THAT ALL RESIDUALS, CONTINGENCIES, AND ROYALTIES ARE ONLY PAID OUT UPON SUCCESSFUL COMPLETION OF A SEASON'S WORTH OF STARVE.
EIGHT EPISODES. AND THEN YOU'LL BE PAID. WELL, IN THEORY.
...AND BY THAT YOU MEAN WHAT, EXACTLY??
YOU SHOULD PROBABLY HAVE A CONVERSATION WITH GREER.

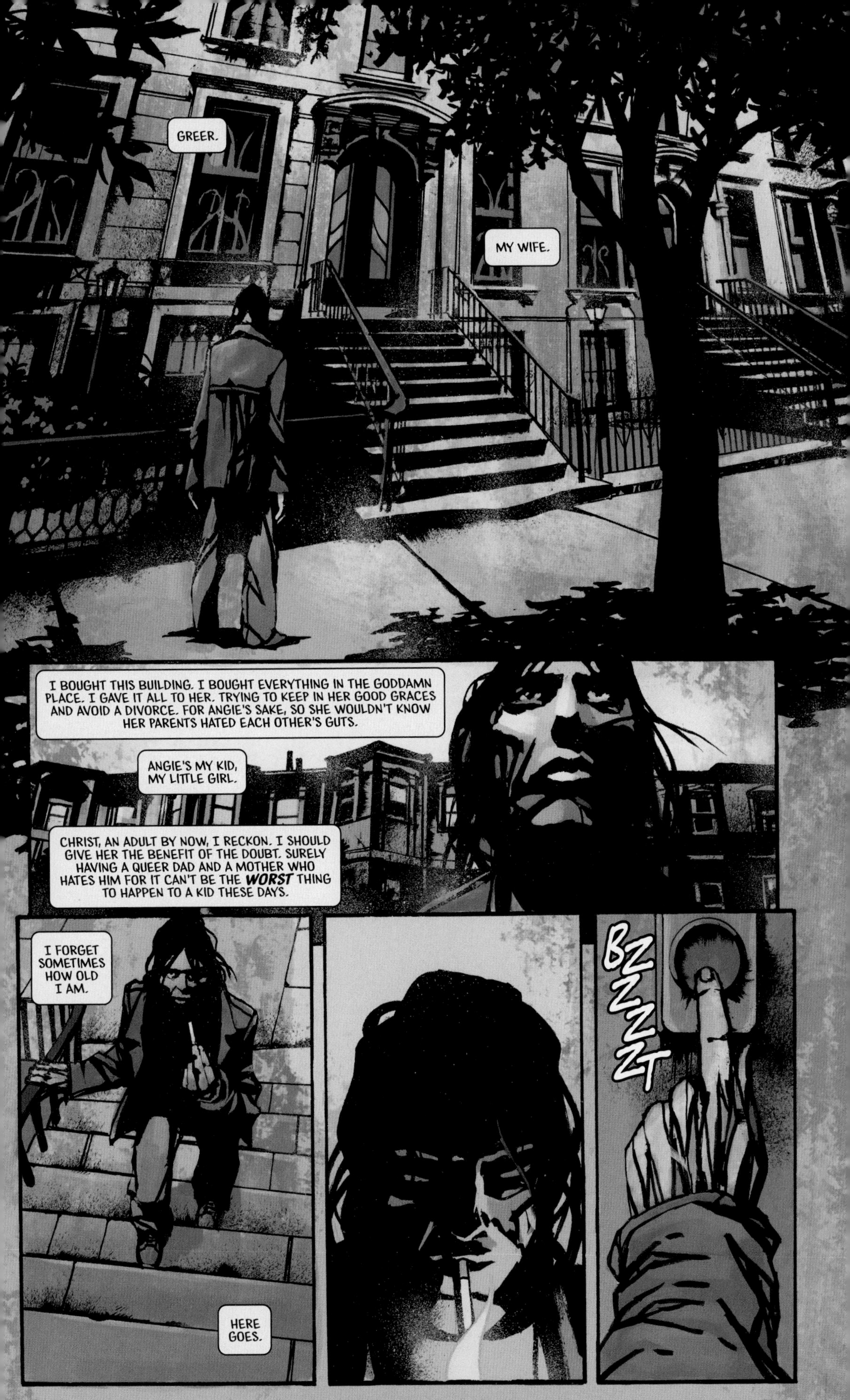
GREER.
MY WIFE.
I BOUGHT THIS BUILDING. I BOUGHT EVERYTHING IN THE GODDAMN PLACE. I GAVE IT ALL TO HER. TRYING TO KEEP IN HER GOOD GRACES AND AVOID A DIVORCE. FOR ANGIE'S SAKE, SO SHE WOULDN'T KNOW HER PARENTS HATED EACH OTHER'S GUTS.
ANGIE'S MY KID, MY LITTLE GIRL.
CHRIST, AN ADULT BY NOW, I RECKON. I SHOULD GIVE HER THE BENEFIT OF THE DOUBT. SURELY HAVING A QUEER DAD AND A MOTHER WHO HATES HIM FOR IT CAN'T BE THE WORST THING TO HAPPEN TO A KID THESE DAYS.
I FORGET SOMETIMES HOW OLD I AM.
HERE GOES.
BZZZZT

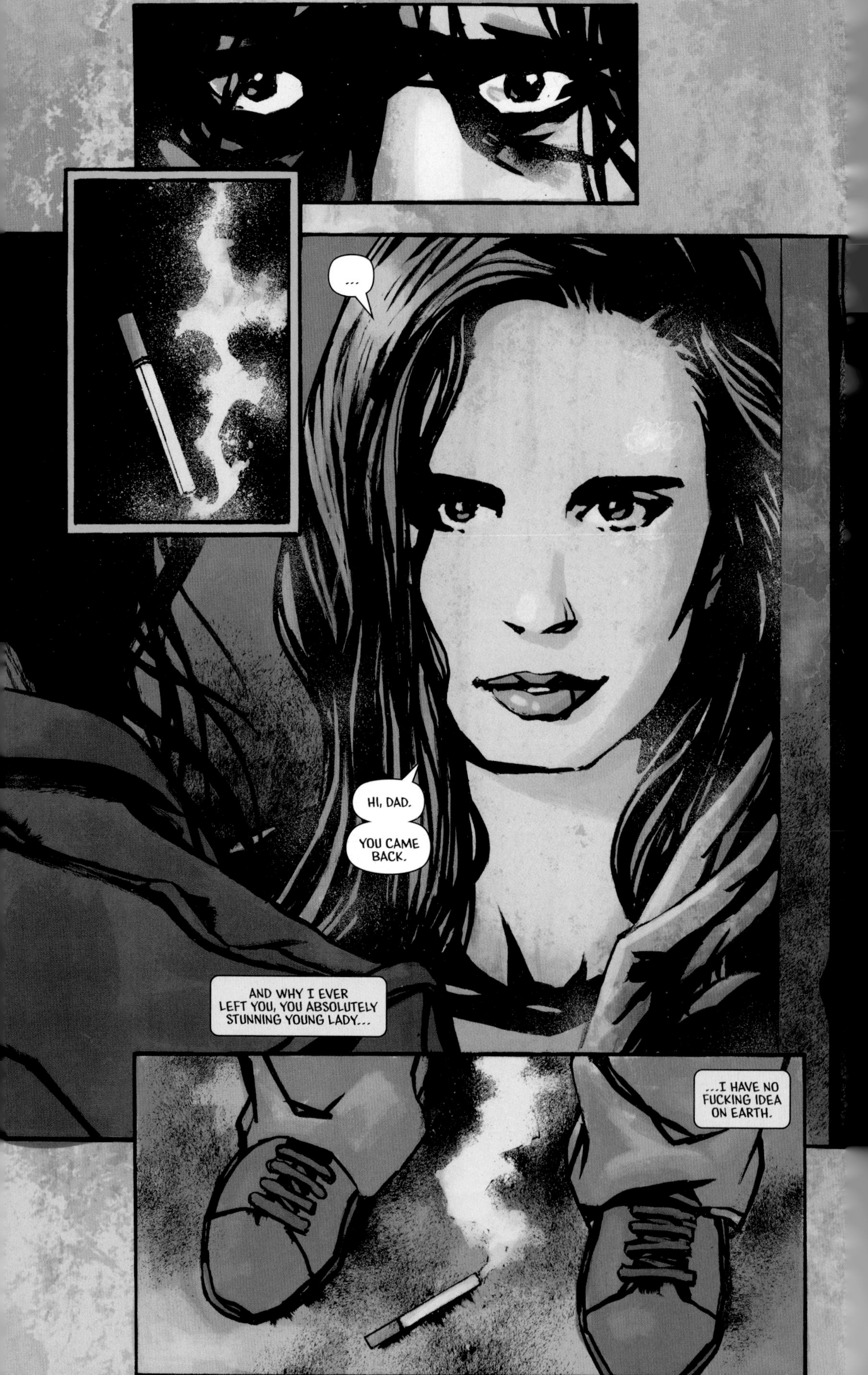
...
HI, DAD.
YOU CAME BACK.
AND WHY I EVER LEFT YOU, YOU ABSOLUTELY STUNNING YOUNG LADY...
...I HAVE NO FUCKING IDEA ON EARTH.

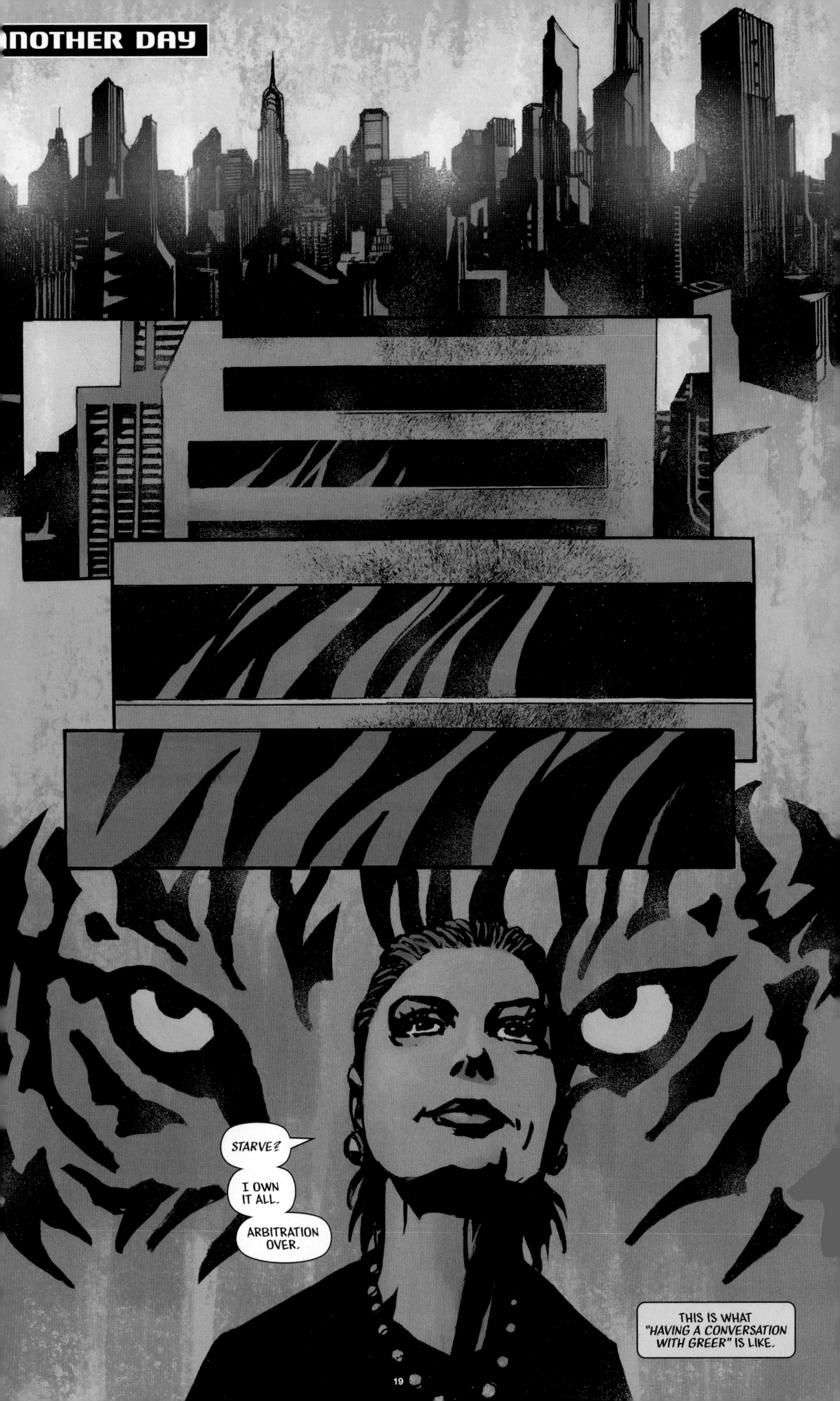
NOTHER DAY
STARVE?
I OWN IT ALL.
ARBITRATION OVER.
THIS IS WHAT "HAVING A CONVERSATION WITH GREER" IS LIKE.

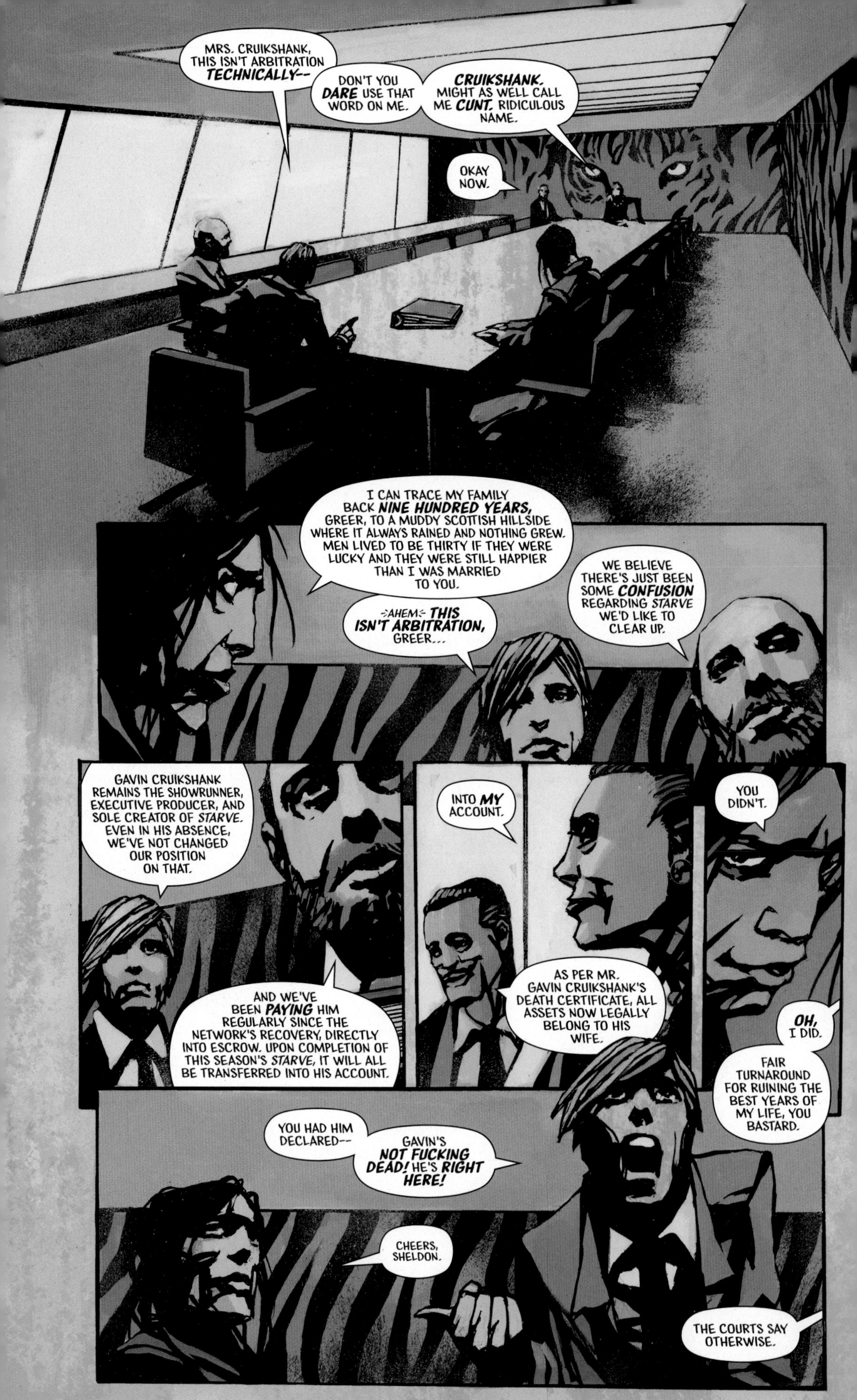

MRS. CRUIKSHANK, THIS ISN'T ARBITRATION ***TECHNICALLY--***
DON'T YOU ***DARE*** USE THAT WORD ON ME.
***CRUIKSHANK.*** MIGHT AS WELL CALL ME ***CUNT.*** RIDICULOUS NAME.
OKAY NOW.
I CAN TRACE MY FAMILY BACK ***NINE HUNDRED YEARS,*** GREER, TO A MUDDY SCOTTISH HILLSIDE WHERE IT ALWAYS RAINED AND NOTHING GREW. MEN LIVED TO BE THIRTY IF THEY WERE LUCKY AND THEY WERE STILL HAPPIER THAN I WAS MARRIED TO YOU.
*AHEM* ***THIS ISN'T ARBITRATION,*** GREER...
WE BELIEVE THERE'S JUST BEEN SOME ***CONFUSION*** REGARDING *STARVE* WE'D LIKE TO CLEAR UP.
GAVIN CRUIKSHANK REMAINS THE SHOWRUNNER, EXECUTIVE PRODUCER, AND SOLE CREATOR OF *STARVE.* EVEN IN HIS ABSENCE, WE'VE NOT CHANGED OUR POSITION ON THAT.
AND WE'VE BEEN ***PAYING*** HIM REGULARLY SINCE THE NETWORK'S RECOVERY, DIRECTLY INTO ESCROW. UPON COMPLETION OF THIS SEASON'S *STARVE,* IT WILL ALL BE TRANSFERRED INTO HIS ACCOUNT.
INTO ***MY*** ACCOUNT.
AS PER MR. GAVIN CRUIKSHANK'S DEATH CERTIFICATE, ALL ASSETS NOW LEGALLY BELONG TO HIS WIFE.
YOU DIDN'T.
***OH,*** I DID.
FAIR TURNAROUND FOR RUINING THE BEST YEARS OF MY LIFE, YOU BASTARD.
YOU HAD HIM DECLARED--
GAVIN'S ***NOT FUCKING DEAD!*** HE'S ***RIGHT HERE!***
CHEERS, SHELDON.
THE COURTS SAY OTHERWISE.

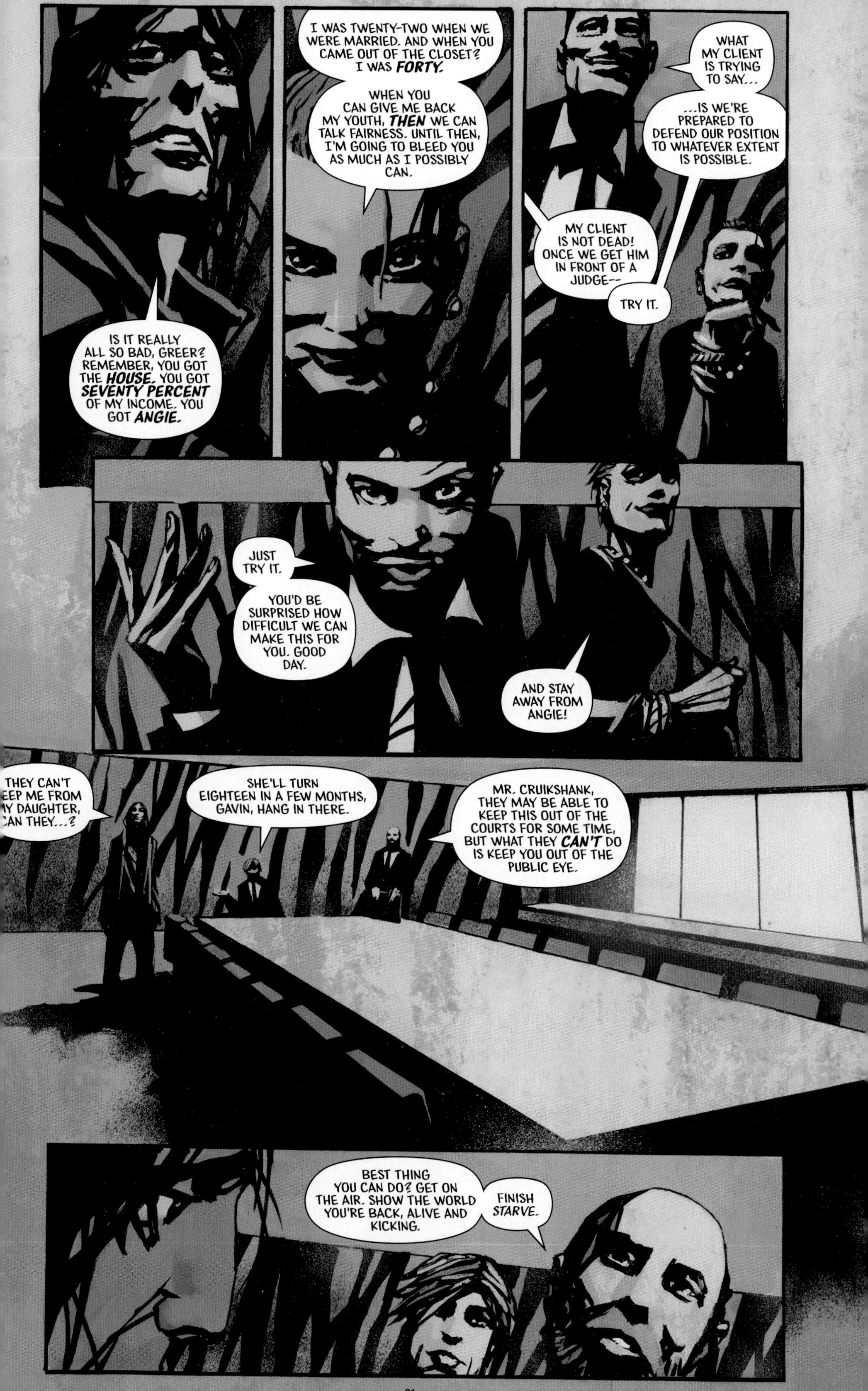
IS IT REALLY ALL SO BAD, GREER? REMEMBER, YOU GOT THE HOUSE. YOU GOT SEVENTY PERCENT OF MY INCOME. YOU GOT ANGIE.
I WAS TWENTY-TWO WHEN WE WERE MARRIED. AND WHEN YOU CAME OUT OF THE CLOSET? I WAS FORTY.
WHEN YOU CAN GIVE ME BACK MY YOUTH, THEN WE CAN TALK FAIRNESS. UNTIL THEN, I'M GOING TO BLEED YOU AS MUCH AS I POSSIBLY CAN.
WHAT MY CLIENT IS TRYING TO SAY...
...IS WE'RE PREPARED TO DEFEND OUR POSITION TO WHATEVER EXTENT IS POSSIBLE.
MY CLIENT IS NOT DEAD! ONCE WE GET HIM IN FRONT OF A JUDGE--
TRY IT.
JUST TRY IT.
YOU'D BE SURPRISED HOW DIFFICULT WE CAN MAKE THIS FOR YOU. GOOD DAY.
AND STAY AWAY FROM ANGIE!
THEY CAN'T KEEP ME FROM MY DAUGHTER, CAN THEY...?
SHE'LL TURN EIGHTEEN IN A FEW MONTHS, GAVIN, HANG IN THERE.
MR. CRUIKSHANK, THEY MAY BE ABLE TO KEEP THIS OUT OF THE COURTS FOR SOME TIME, BUT WHAT THEY CAN'T DO IS KEEP YOU OUT OF THE PUBLIC EYE.
BEST THING YOU CAN DO? GET ON THE AIR. SHOW THE WORLD YOU'RE BACK, ALIVE AND KICKING.
FINISH STARVE.

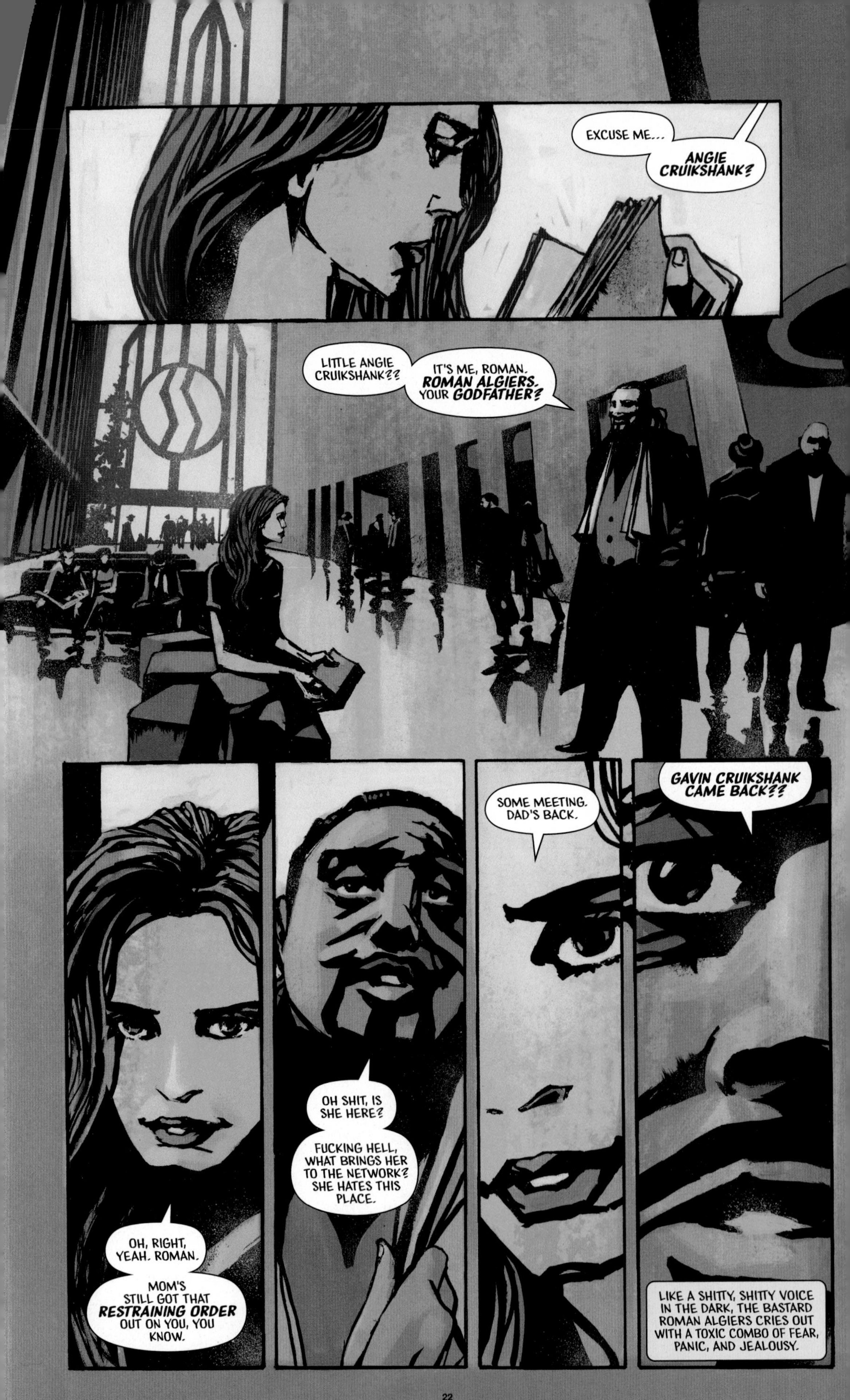
EXCUSE ME...
ANGIE CRUIKSHANK?
LITTLE ANGIE CRUIKSHANK??
IT'S ME, ROMAN. ROMAN ALGIERS. YOUR GODFATHER?
OH, RIGHT, YEAH. ROMAN.
MOM'S STILL GOT THAT RESTRAINING ORDER OUT ON YOU, YOU KNOW.
OH SHIT, IS SHE HERE?
FUCKING HELL, WHAT BRINGS HER TO THE NETWORK? SHE HATES THIS PLACE.
SOME MEETING. DAD'S BACK.
GAVIN CRUIKSHANK CAME BACK??
LIKE A SHITTY, SHITTY VOICE IN THE DARK, THE BASTARD ROMAN ALGIERS CRIES OUT WITH A TOXIC COMBO OF FEAR, PANIC, AND JEALOUSY.

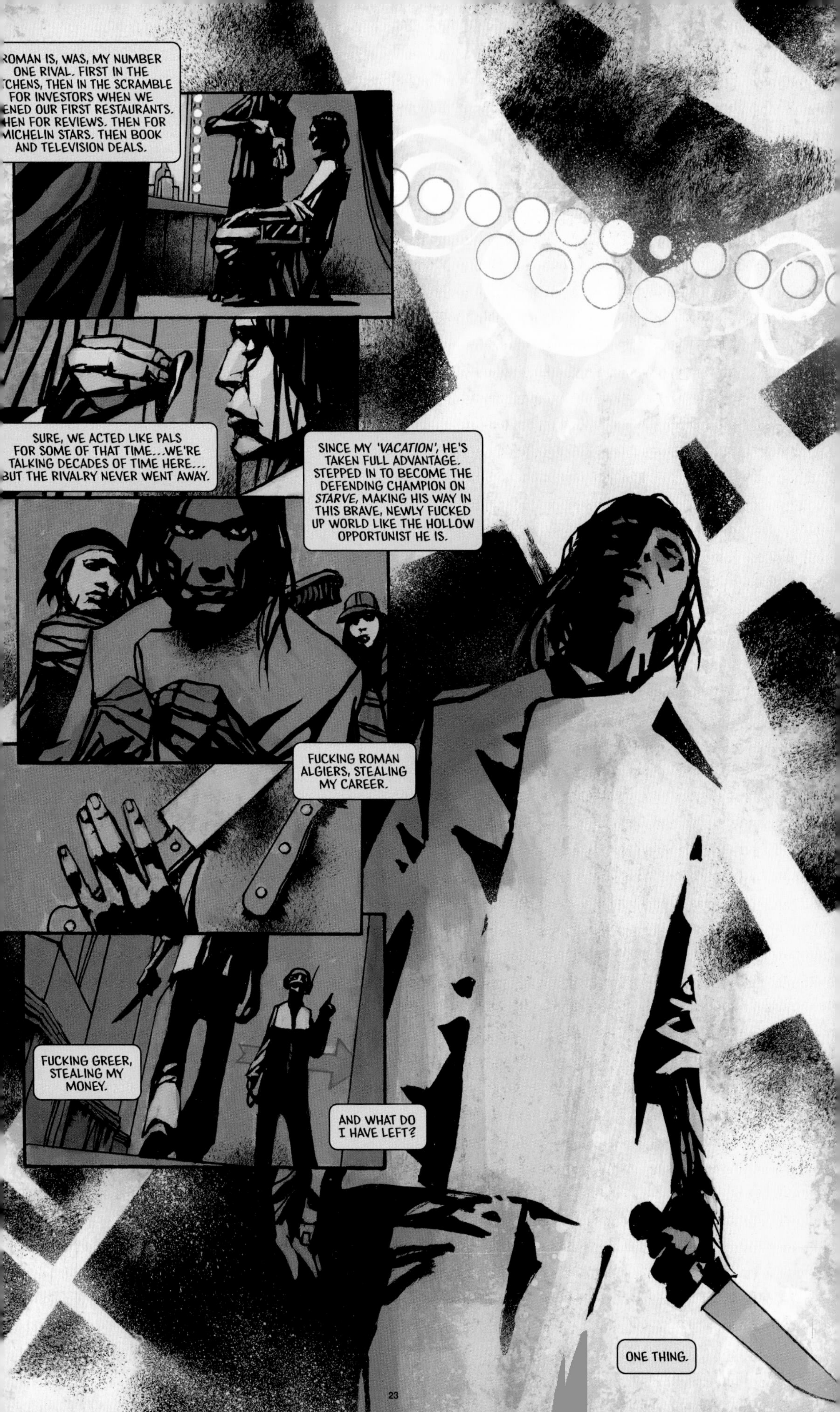
ROMAN IS, WAS, MY NUMBER ONE RIVAL. FIRST IN THE KITCHENS, THEN IN THE SCRAMBLE FOR INVESTORS WHEN WE OPENED OUR FIRST RESTAURANTS. THEN FOR REVIEWS. THEN FOR MICHELIN STARS. THEN BOOK AND TELEVISION DEALS.
SURE, WE ACTED LIKE PALS FOR SOME OF THAT TIME... WE'RE TALKING DECADES OF TIME HERE... BUT THE RIVALRY NEVER WENT AWAY.
SINCE MY 'VACATION', HE'S TAKEN FULL ADVANTAGE. STEPPED IN TO BECOME THE DEFENDING CHAMPION ON STARVE, MAKING HIS WAY IN THIS BRAVE, NEWLY FUCKED UP WORLD LIKE THE HOLLOW OPPORTUNIST HE IS.
FUCKING ROMAN ALGIERS, STEALING MY CAREER.
FUCKING GREER, STEALING MY MONEY.
AND WHAT DO I HAVE LEFT?
ONE THING.

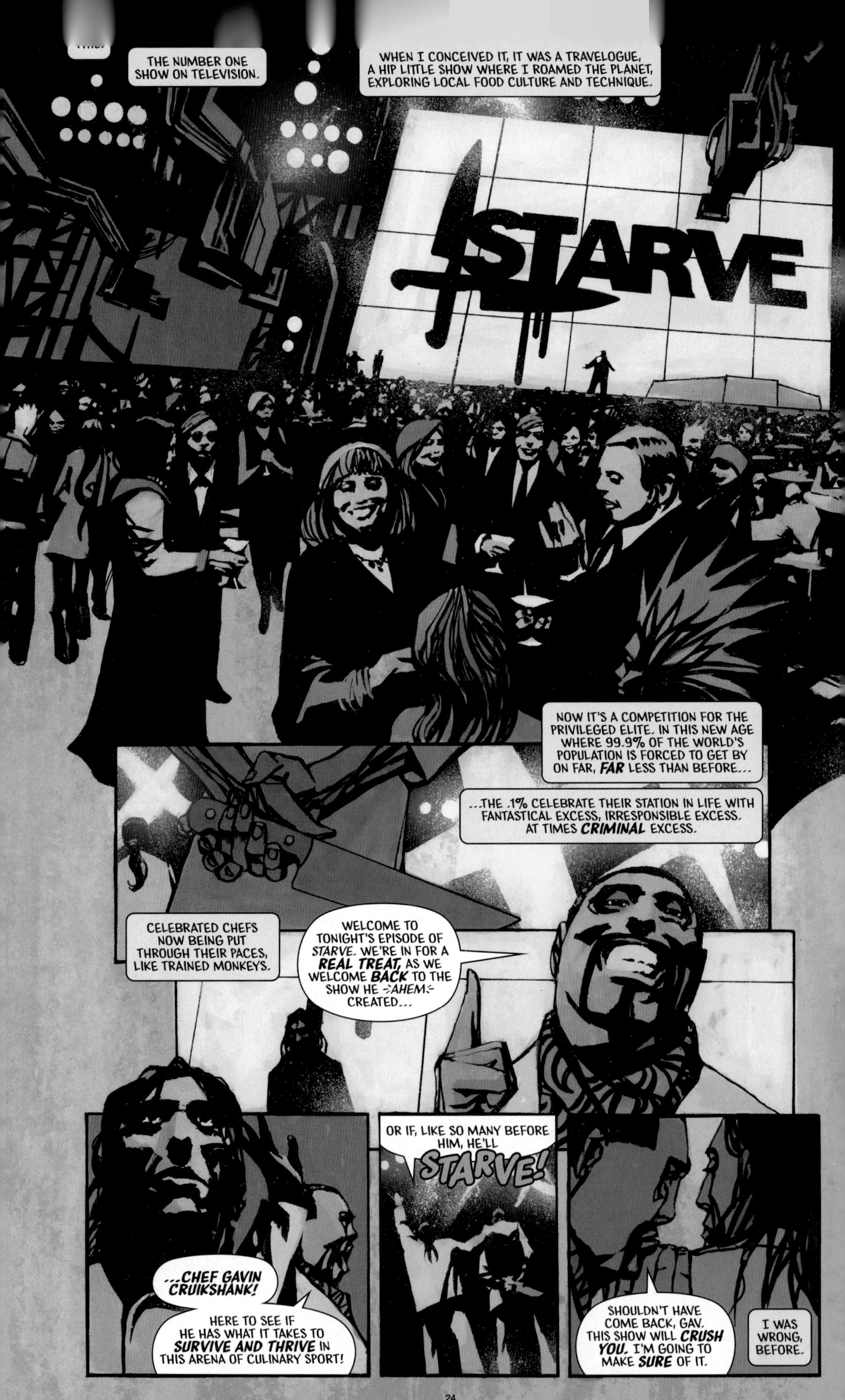

THE NUMBER ONE SHOW ON TELEVISION.
WHEN I CONCEIVED IT, IT WAS A TRAVELOGUE, A HIP LITTLE SHOW WHERE I ROAMED THE PLANET, EXPLORING LOCAL FOOD CULTURE AND TECHNIQUE.
STARVE
NOW IT'S A COMPETITION FOR THE PRIVILEGED ELITE. IN THIS NEW AGE WHERE 99.9% OF THE WORLD'S POPULATION IS FORCED TO GET BY ON FAR, FAR LESS THAN BEFORE...
...THE .1% CELEBRATE THEIR STATION IN LIFE WITH FANTASTICAL EXCESS, IRRESPONSIBLE EXCESS. AT TIMES CRIMINAL EXCESS.
CELEBRATED CHEFS NOW BEING PUT THROUGH THEIR PACES, LIKE TRAINED MONKEYS.
WELCOME TO TONIGHT'S EPISODE OF STARVE. WE'RE IN FOR A REAL TREAT, AS WE WELCOME BACK TO THE SHOW HE -AHEM- CREATED...
...CHEF GAVIN CRUIKSHANK!
HERE TO SEE IF HE HAS WHAT IT TAKES TO SURVIVE AND THRIVE IN THIS ARENA OF CULINARY SPORT!
OR IF, LIKE SO MANY BEFORE HIM, HE'LL STARVE!
SHOULDN'T HAVE COME BACK, GAV. THIS SHOW WILL CRUSH YOU. I'M GOING TO MAKE SURE OF IT.
I WAS WRONG, BEFORE.

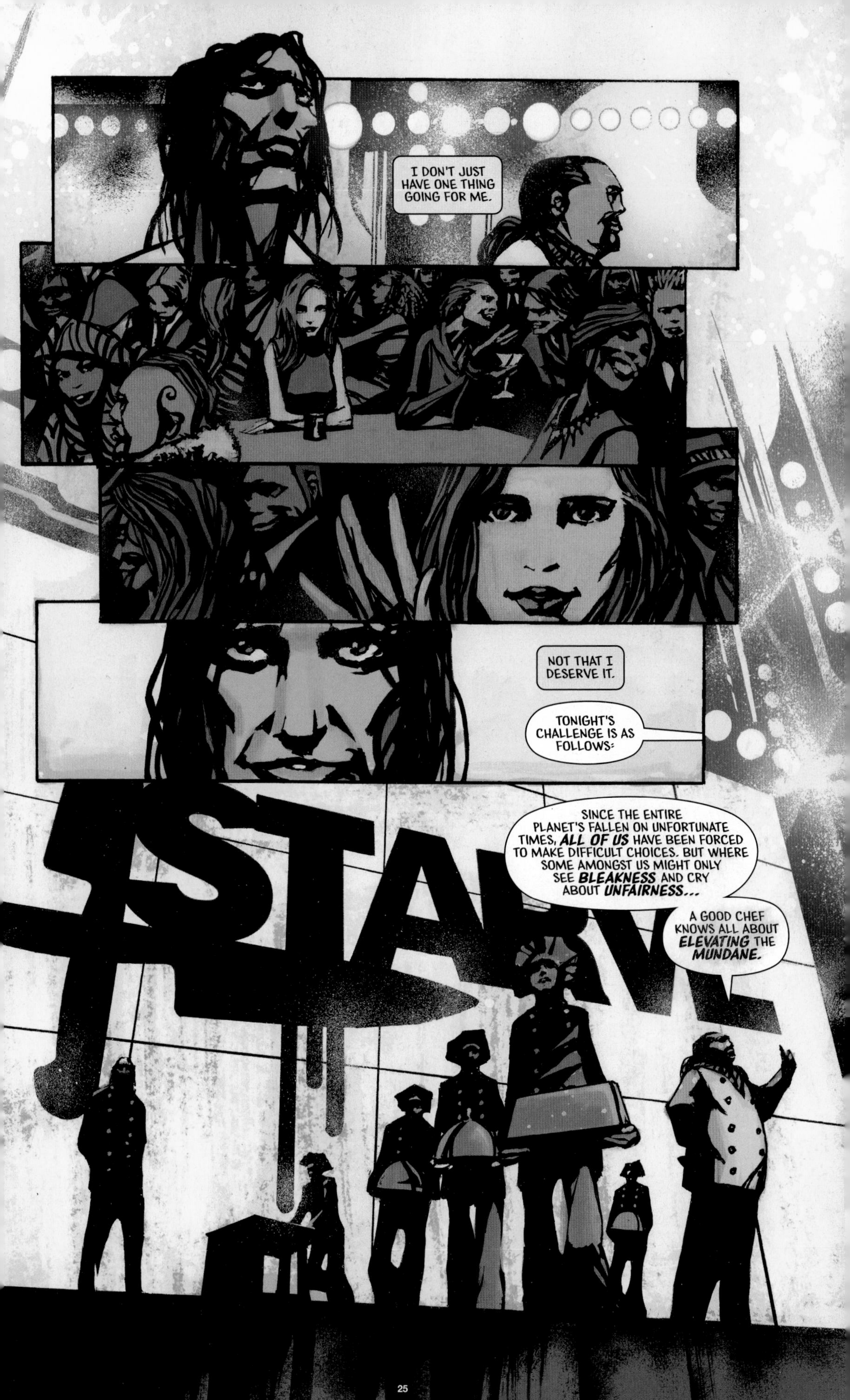

I DON'T JUST HAVE ONE THING GOING FOR ME.
NOT THAT I DESERVE IT.
TONIGHT'S CHALLENGE IS AS FOLLOWS:
SINCE THE ENTIRE PLANET'S FALLEN ON UNFORTUNATE TIMES, ALL OF US HAVE BEEN FORCED TO MAKE DIFFICULT CHOICES. BUT WHERE SOME AMONGST US MIGHT ONLY SEE BLEAKNESS AND CRY ABOUT UNFAIRNESS...
A GOOD CHEF KNOWS ALL ABOUT ELEVATING THE MUNDANE.

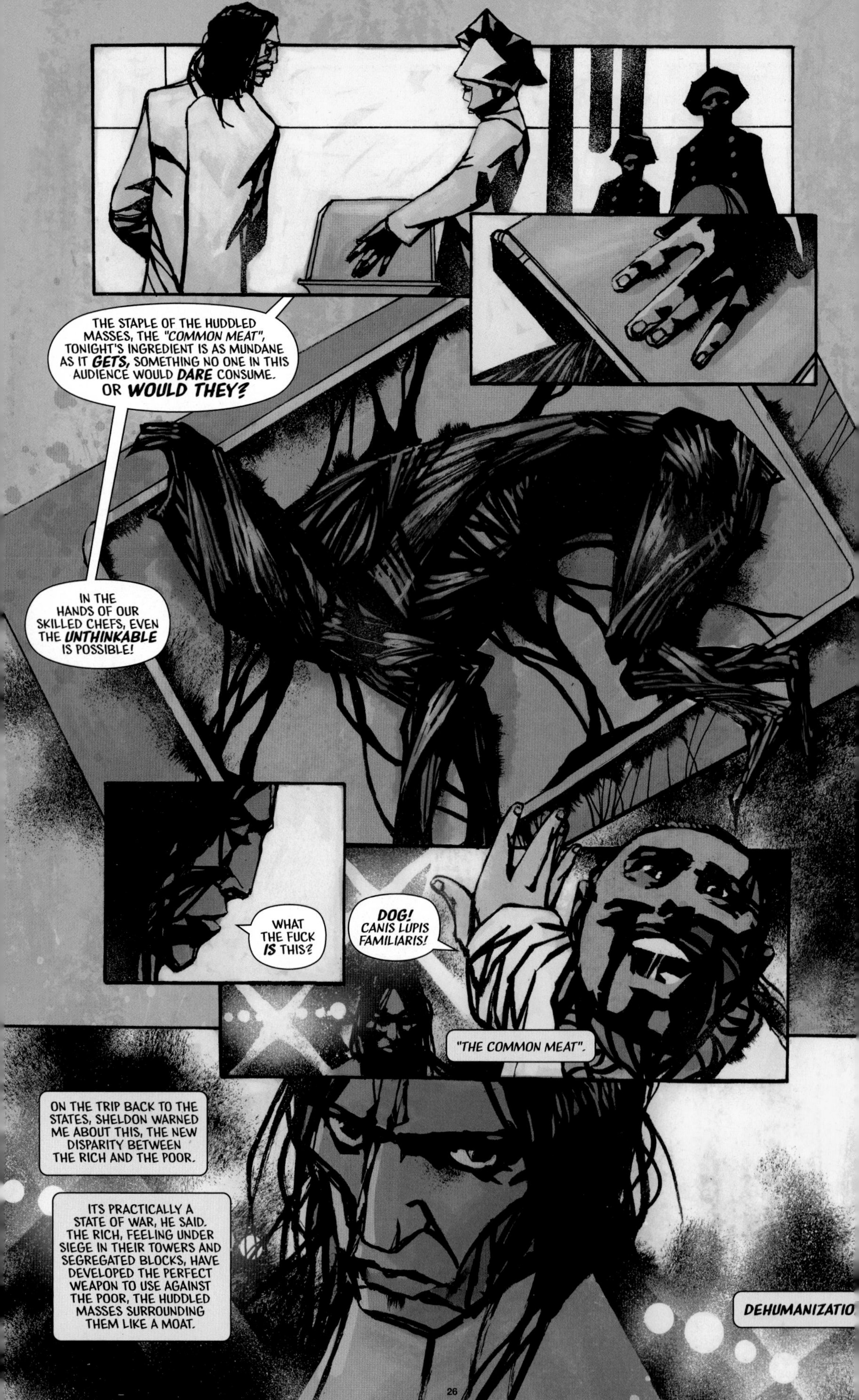

THE STAPLE OF THE HUDDLED MASSES, THE "COMMON MEAT", TONIGHT'S INGREDIENT IS AS MUNDANE AS IT GETS, SOMETHING NO ONE IN THIS AUDIENCE WOULD DARE CONSUME. OR WOULD THEY?
IN THE HANDS OF OUR SKILLED CHEFS, EVEN THE UNTHINKABLE IS POSSIBLE!
WHAT THE FUCK IS THIS?
DOG! CANIS LUPIS FAMILIARIS!
"THE COMMON MEAT".
ON THE TRIP BACK TO THE STATES, SHELDON WARNED ME ABOUT THIS, THE NEW DISPARITY BETWEEN THE RICH AND THE POOR.
ITS PRACTICALLY A STATE OF WAR, HE SAID. THE RICH, FEELING UNDER SIEGE IN THEIR TOWERS AND SEGREGATED BLOCKS, HAVE DEVELOPED THE PERFECT WEAPON TO USE AGAINST THE POOR, THE HUDDLED MASSES SURROUNDING THEM LIKE A MOAT.
DEHUMANIZATIO

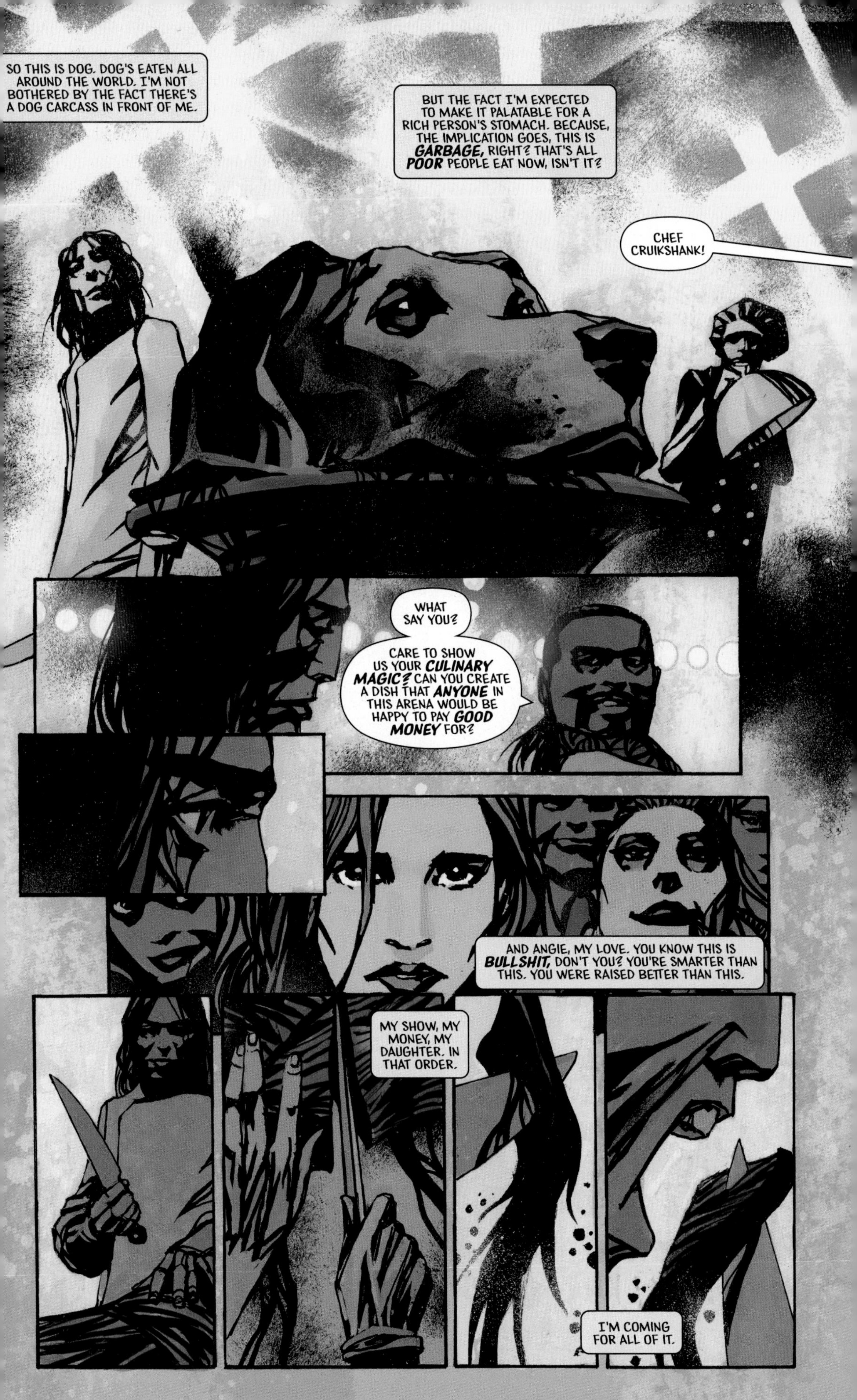
SO THIS IS DOG. DOG'S EATEN ALL AROUND THE WORLD. I'M NOT BOTHERED BY THE FACT THERE'S A DOG CARCASS IN FRONT OF ME.
BUT THE FACT I'M EXPECTED TO MAKE IT PALATABLE FOR A RICH PERSON'S STOMACH. BECAUSE, THE IMPLICATION GOES, THIS IS **GARBAGE,** RIGHT? THAT'S ALL **POOR** PEOPLE EAT NOW, ISN'T IT?
CHEF CRUIKSHANK!
WHAT SAY YOU?
CARE TO SHOW US YOUR **CULINARY MAGIC?** CAN YOU CREATE A DISH THAT **ANYONE** IN THIS ARENA WOULD BE HAPPY TO PAY **GOOD MONEY** FOR?
AND ANGIE, MY LOVE. YOU KNOW THIS IS **BULLSHIT,** DON'T YOU? YOU'RE SMARTER THAN THIS. YOU WERE RAISED BETTER THAN THIS.
MY SHOW, MY MONEY, MY DAUGHTER. IN THAT ORDER.
I'M COMING FOR ALL OF IT.

BUT I WON'T PLAY THE GAME THEY WANT ME TO PLAY.
THIS IS MY FUCKING SHOW.
I'M GOING TO DO MY EIGHT EPISODES AND BURN THIS WHOLE PLACE TO THE GROUND.
WATCH.

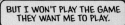

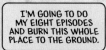

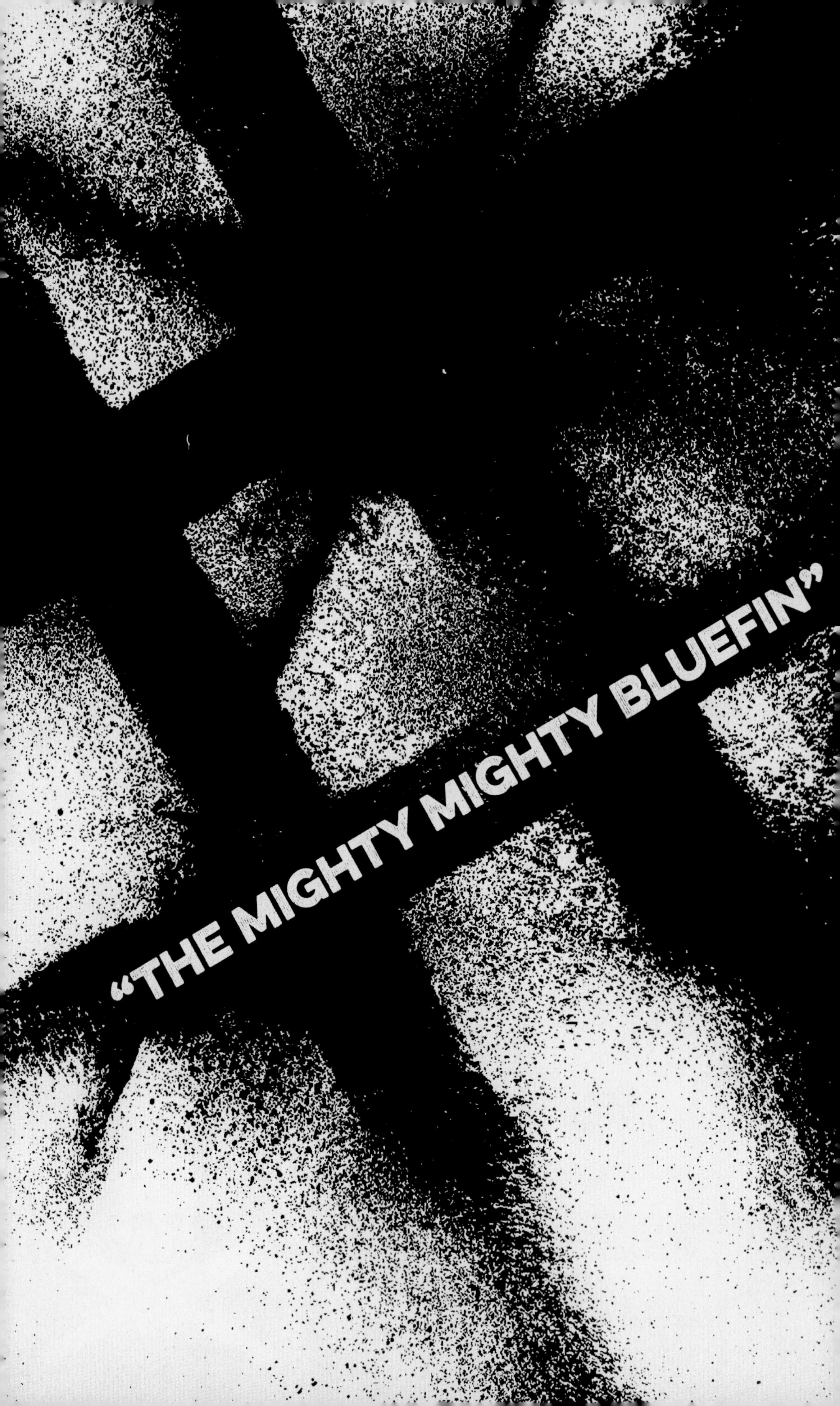
"THE MIGHTY MIGHTY BLUEFIN"

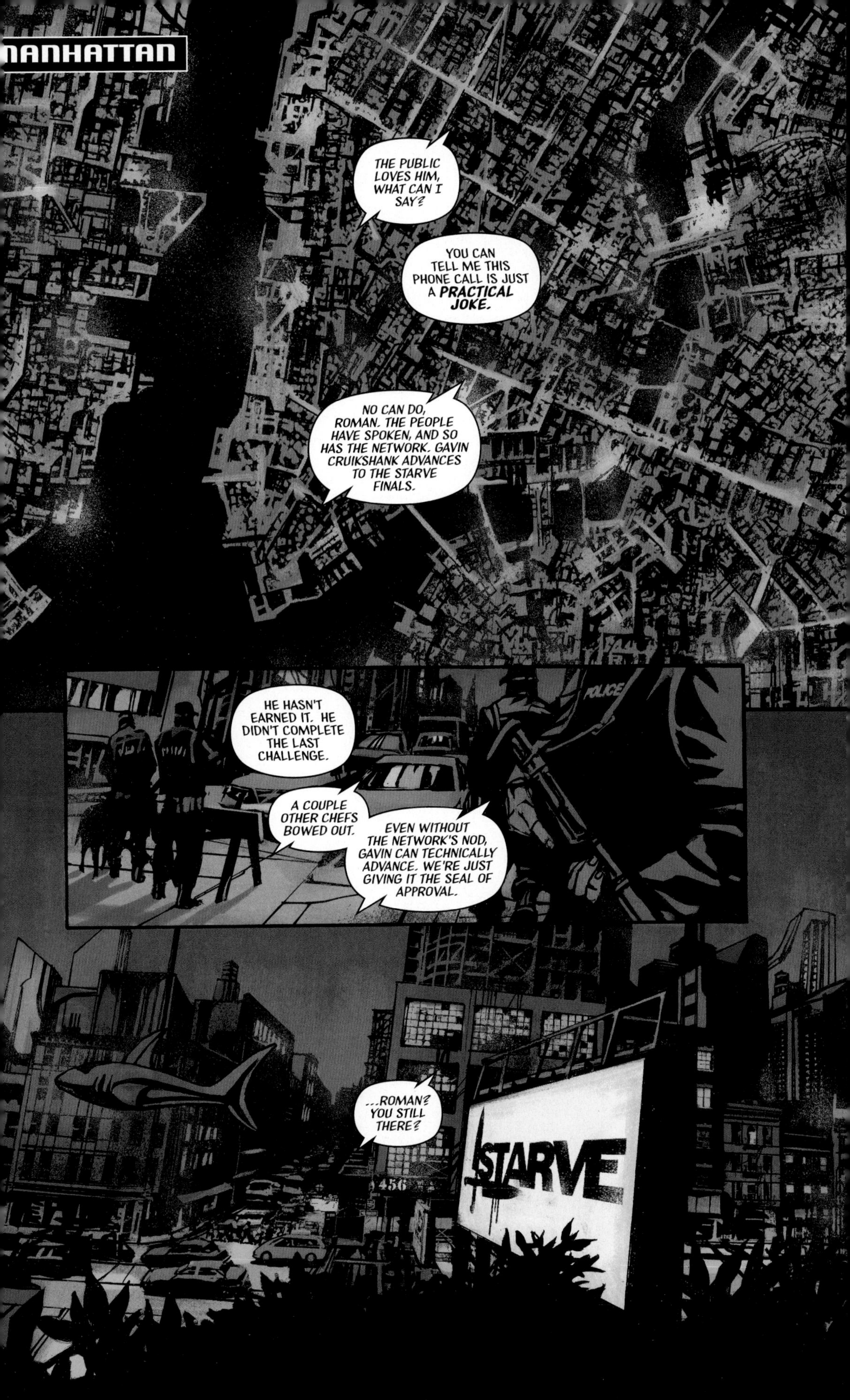
MANHATTAN
THE PUBLIC LOVES HIM, WHAT CAN I SAY?
YOU CAN TELL ME THIS PHONE CALL IS JUST A PRACTICAL JOKE.
NO CAN DO, ROMAN. THE PEOPLE HAVE SPOKEN, AND SO HAS THE NETWORK. GAVIN CRUIKSHANK ADVANCES TO THE STARVE FINALS.
POLICE
HE HASN'T EARNED IT. HE DIDN'T COMPLETE THE LAST CHALLENGE.
A COUPLE OTHER CHEFS BOWED OUT.
EVEN WITHOUT THE NETWORK'S NOD, GAVIN CAN TECHNICALLY ADVANCE. WE'RE JUST GIVING IT THE SEAL OF APPROVAL.
...ROMAN? YOU STILL THERE?
456
STARVE

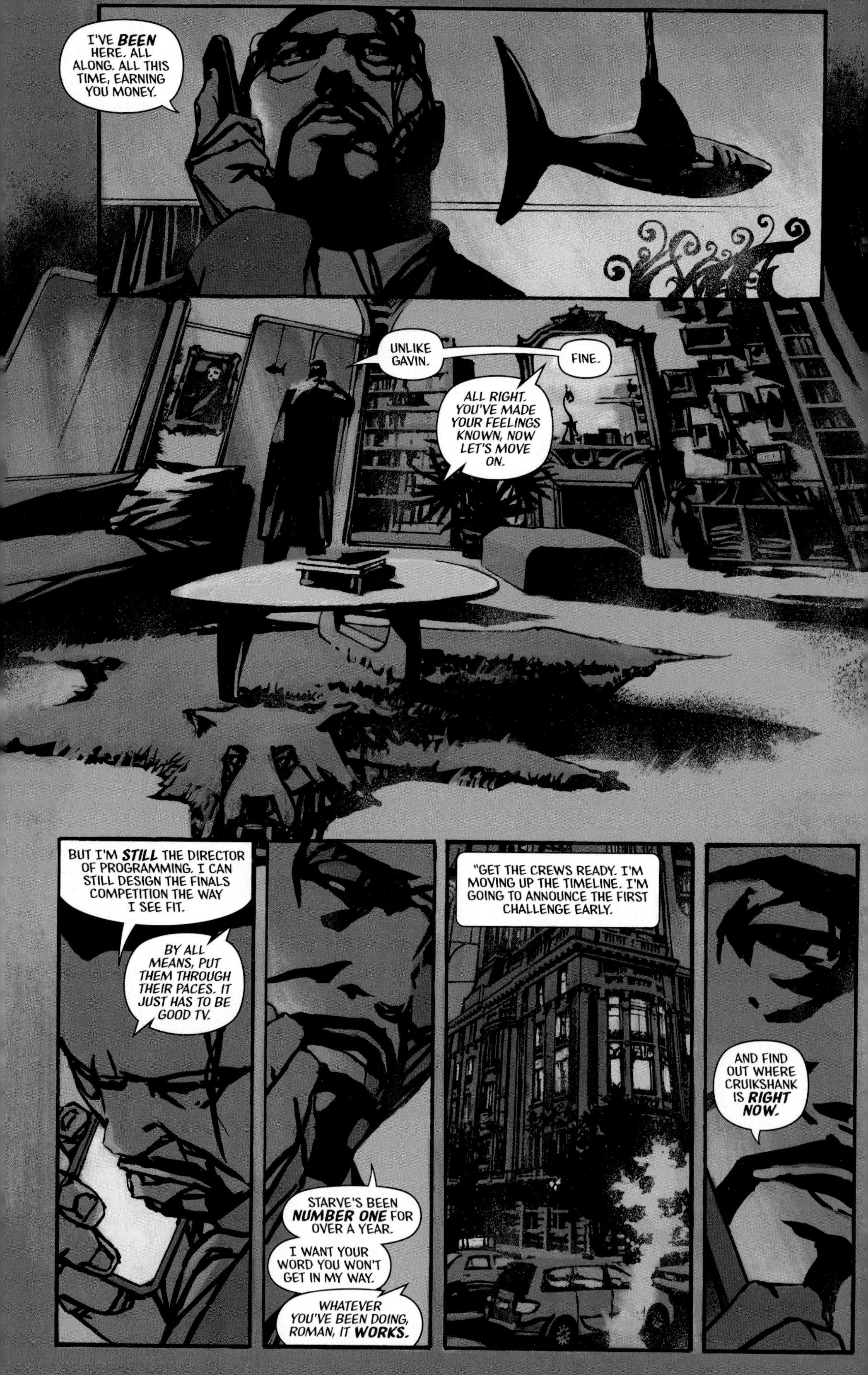
I'VE **BEEN** HERE. ALL ALONG. ALL THIS TIME, EARNING YOU MONEY.
UNLIKE GAVIN.
FINE.
ALL RIGHT. YOU'VE MADE YOUR FEELINGS KNOWN, NOW LET'S MOVE ON.
BUT I'M **STILL** THE DIRECTOR OF PROGRAMMING. I CAN STILL DESIGN THE FINALS COMPETITION THE WAY I SEE FIT.
BY ALL MEANS, PUT THEM THROUGH THEIR PACES. IT JUST HAS TO BE GOOD TV.
STARVE'S BEEN **NUMBER ONE** FOR OVER A YEAR.
I WANT YOUR WORD YOU WON'T GET IN MY WAY.
WHATEVER YOU'VE BEEN DOING, ROMAN, IT **WORKS.**
"GET THE CREWS READY. I'M MOVING UP THE TIMELINE. I'M GOING TO ANNOUNCE THE FIRST CHALLENGE EARLY.
AND FIND OUT WHERE CRUIKSHANK IS **RIGHT NOW.**

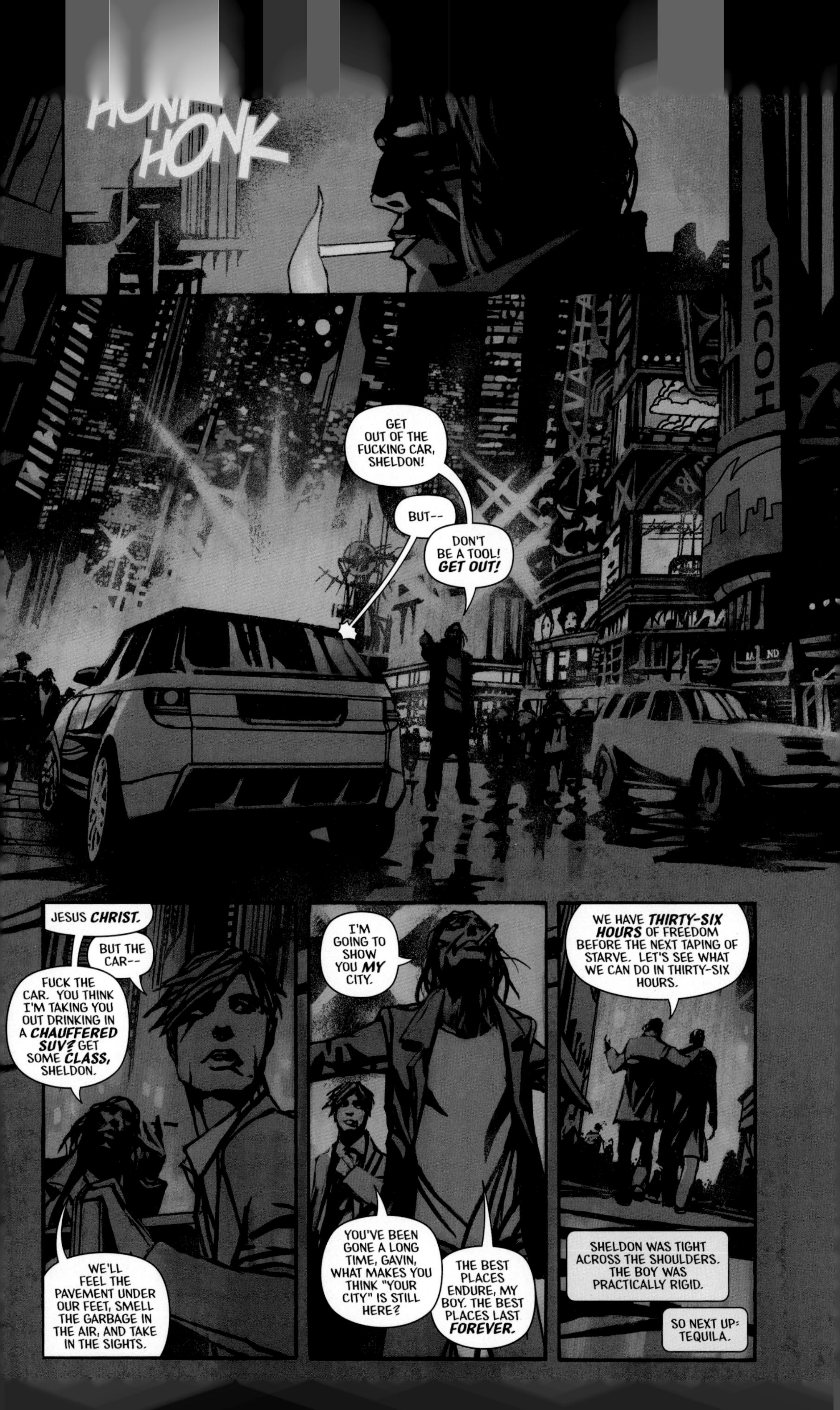
HONK
HONK
GET OUT OF THE FUCKING CAR, SHELDON!
BUT--
DON'T BE A TOOL! GET OUT!
JESUS CHRIST.
BUT THE CAR--
FUCK THE CAR. YOU THINK I'M TAKING YOU OUT DRINKING IN A CHAUFFERED SUV? GET SOME CLASS, SHELDON.
WE'LL FEEL THE PAVEMENT UNDER OUR FEET, SMELL THE GARBAGE IN THE AIR, AND TAKE IN THE SIGHTS.
I'M GOING TO SHOW YOU MY CITY.
YOU'VE BEEN GONE A LONG TIME, GAVIN. WHAT MAKES YOU THINK "YOUR CITY" IS STILL HERE?
THE BEST PLACES ENDURE, MY BOY. THE BEST PLACES LAST FOREVER.
WE HAVE THIRTY-SIX HOURS OF FREEDOM BEFORE THE NEXT TAPING OF STARVE. LET'S SEE WHAT WE CAN DO IN THIRTY-SIX HOURS.
SHELDON WAS TIGHT ACROSS THE SHOULDERS. THE BOY WAS PRACTICALLY RIGID.
SO NEXT UP: TEQUILA.

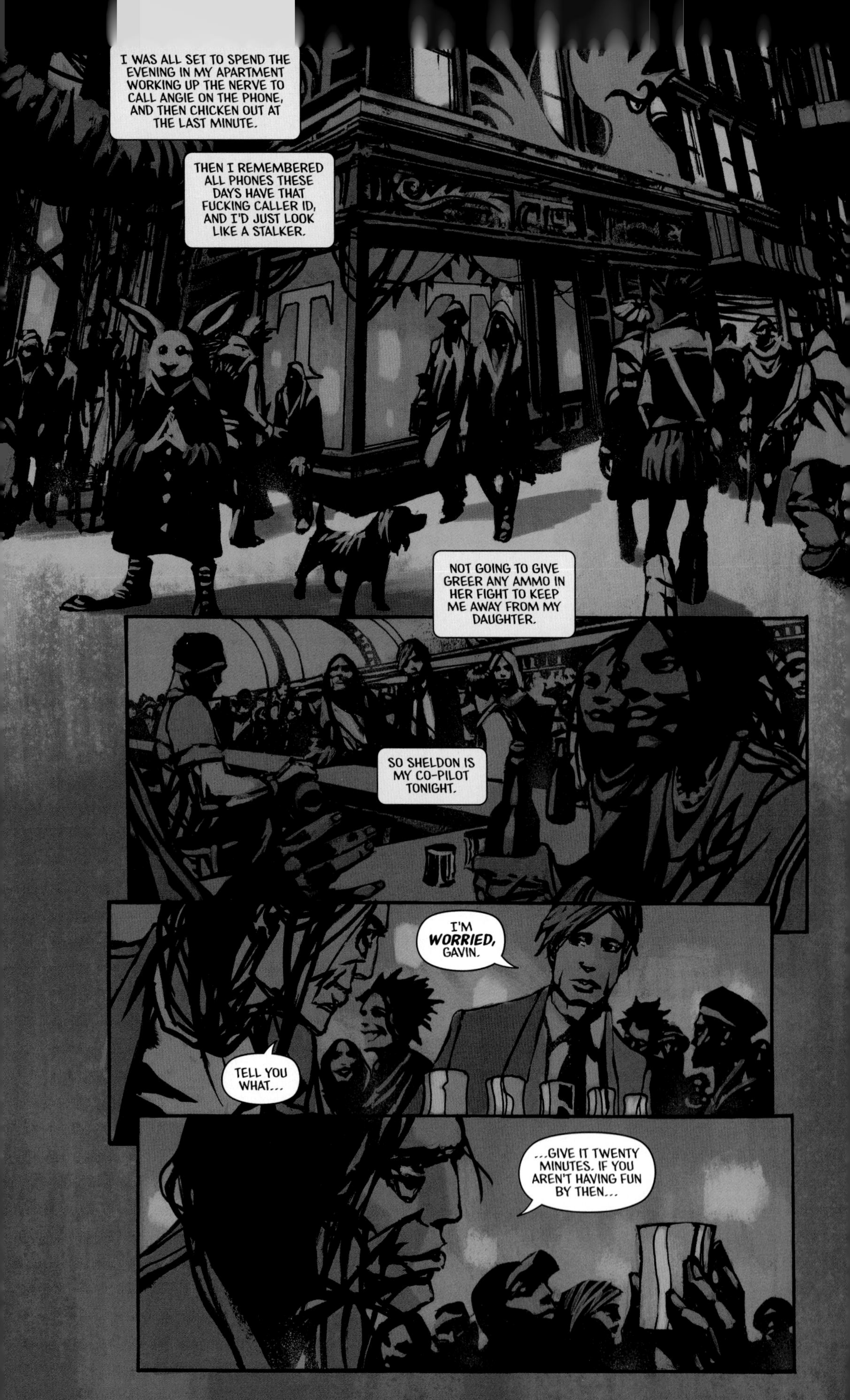
I WAS ALL SET TO SPEND THE EVENING IN MY APARTMENT WORKING UP THE NERVE TO CALL ANGIE ON THE PHONE, AND THEN CHICKEN OUT AT THE LAST MINUTE.
THEN I REMEMBERED ALL PHONES THESE DAYS HAVE THAT FUCKING CALLER ID, AND I'D JUST LOOK LIKE A STALKER.
NOT GOING TO GIVE GREER ANY AMMO IN HER FIGHT TO KEEP ME AWAY FROM MY DAUGHTER.
SO SHELDON IS MY CO-PILOT TONIGHT.
I'M *WORRIED,* GAVIN.
TELL YOU WHAT...
...GIVE IT TWENTY MINUTES. IF YOU AREN'T HAVING FUN BY THEN...

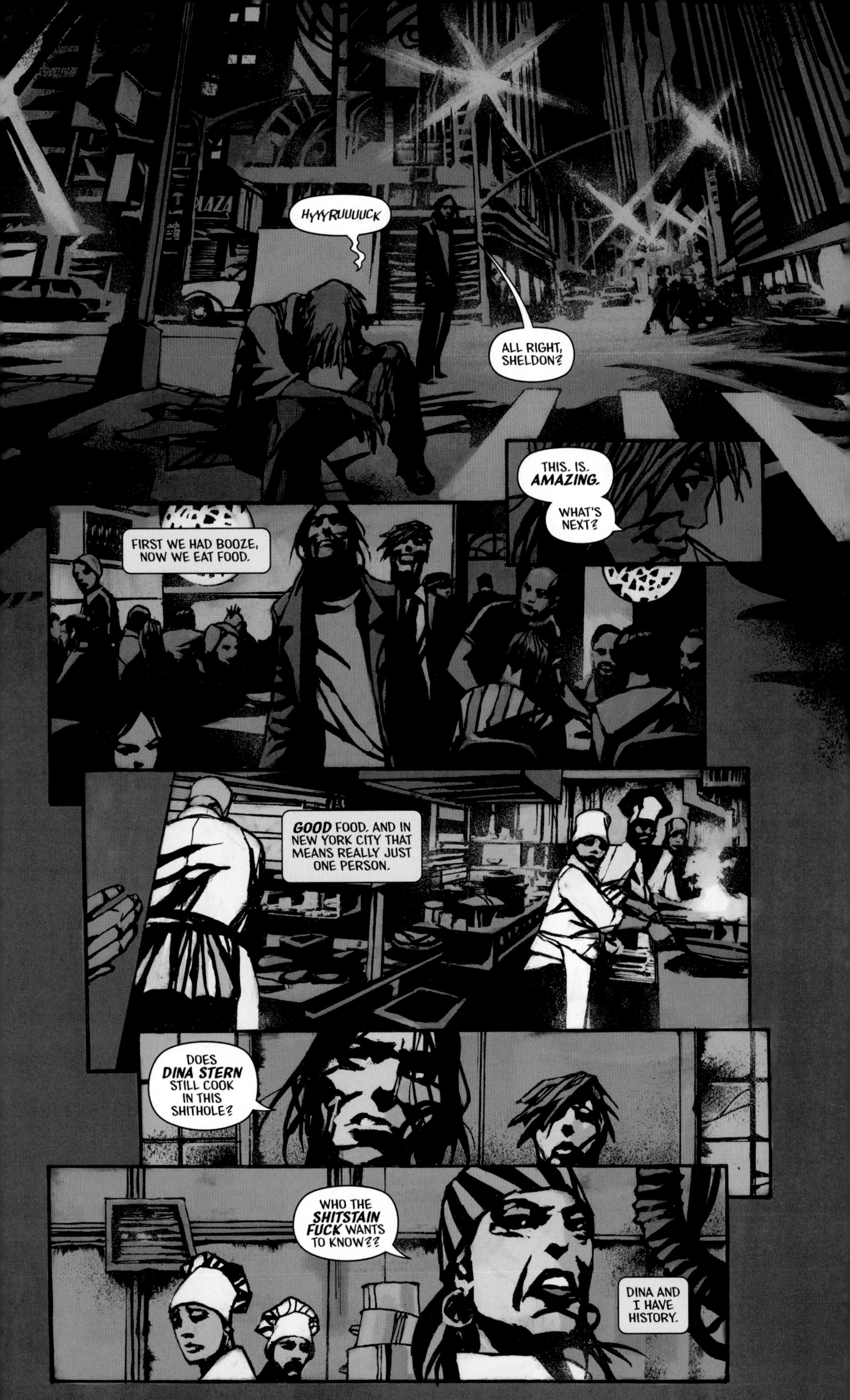
HYYYRUUUUCK
ALL RIGHT, SHELDON?
THIS. IS. AMAZING.
WHAT'S NEXT?
FIRST WE HAD BOOZE, NOW WE EAT FOOD.
GOOD FOOD. AND IN NEW YORK CITY THAT MEANS REALLY JUST ONE PERSON.
DOES DINA STERN STILL COOK IN THIS SHITHOLE?
WHO THE SHITSTAIN FUCK WANTS TO KNOW??
DINA AND I HAVE HISTORY.

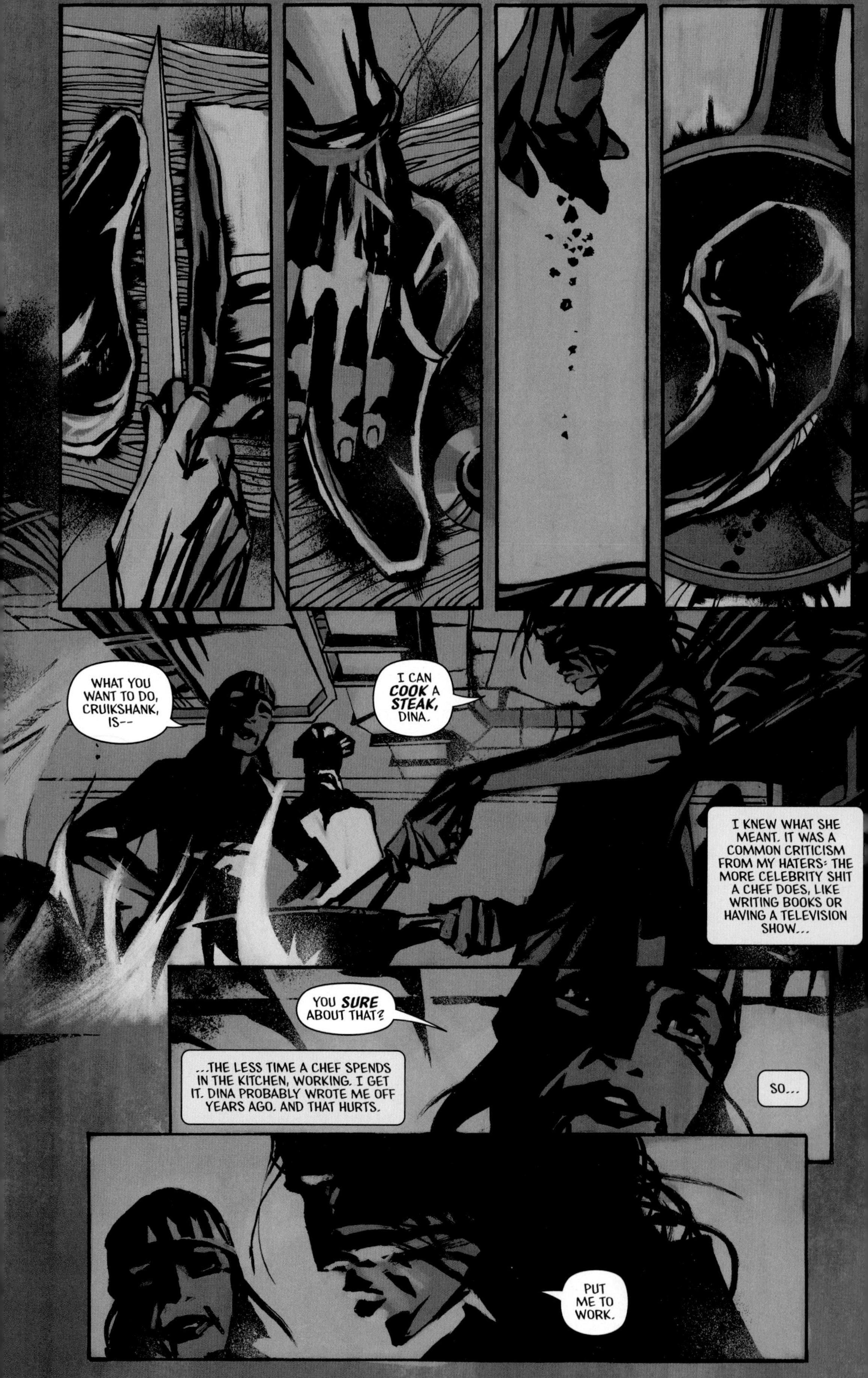
WHAT YOU WANT TO DO, CRUIKSHANK, IS--
I CAN COOK A STEAK, DINA.
I KNEW WHAT SHE MEANT. IT WAS A COMMON CRITICISM FROM MY HATERS: THE MORE CELEBRITY SHIT A CHEF DOES, LIKE WRITING BOOKS OR HAVING A TELEVISION SHOW...
YOU SURE ABOUT THAT?
...THE LESS TIME A CHEF SPENDS IN THE KITCHEN, WORKING. I GET IT. DINA PROBABLY WROTE ME OFF YEARS AGO. AND THAT HURTS.
SO...
PUT ME TO WORK.

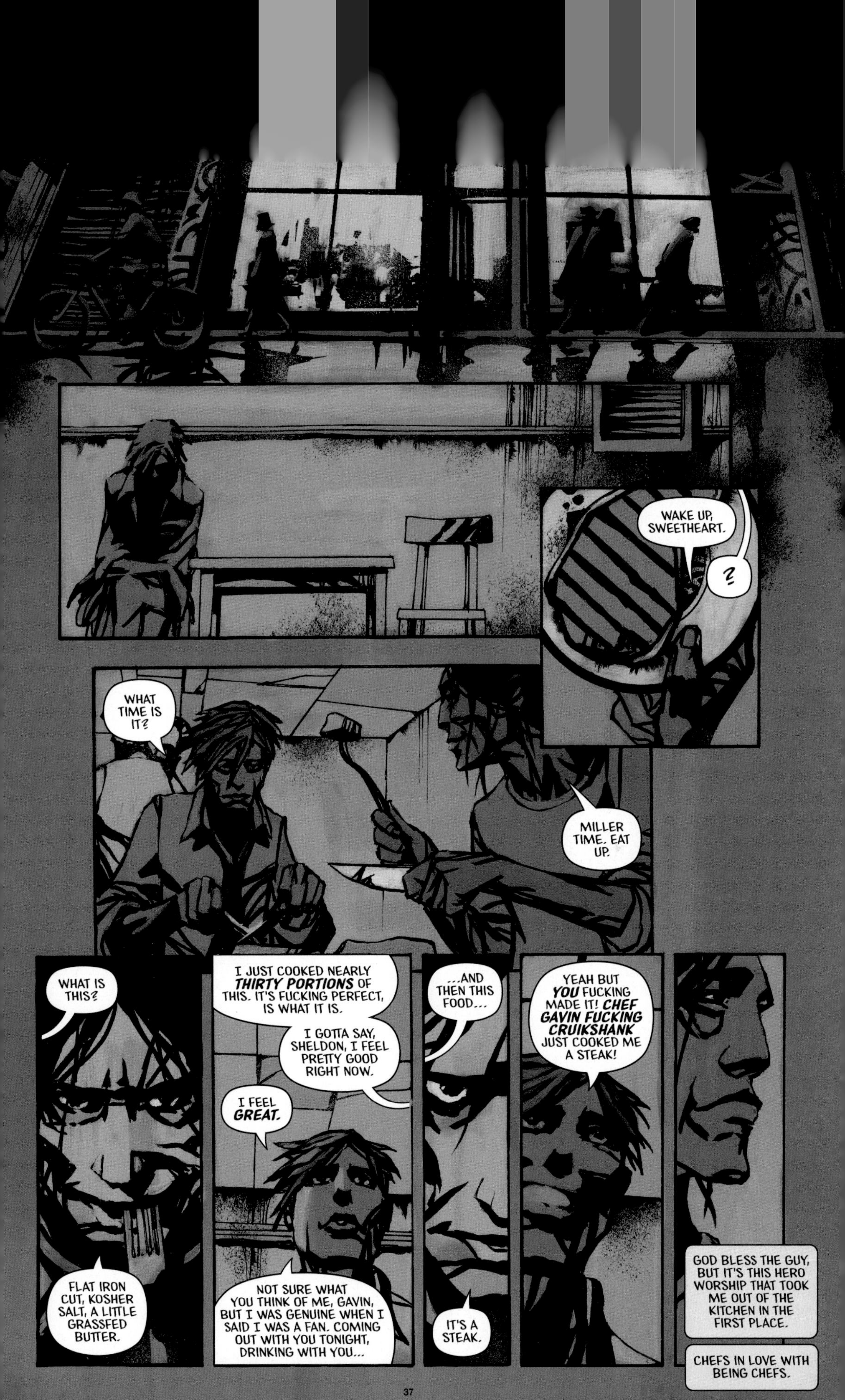
WAKE UP, SWEETHEART.
?
WHAT TIME IS IT?
MILLER TIME. EAT UP.
WHAT IS THIS?
FLAT IRON CUT, KOSHER SALT, A LITTLE GRASSFED BUTTER.
I JUST COOKED NEARLY THIRTY PORTIONS OF THIS. IT'S FUCKING PERFECT, IS WHAT IT IS.
I GOTTA SAY, SHELDON, I FEEL PRETTY GOOD RIGHT NOW.
I FEEL GREAT.
NOT SURE WHAT YOU THINK OF ME, GAVIN, BUT I WAS GENUINE WHEN I SAID I WAS A FAN. COMING OUT WITH YOU TONIGHT, DRINKING WITH YOU...
...AND THEN THIS FOOD...
IT'S A STEAK.
YEAH BUT YOU FUCKING MADE IT! CHEF GAVIN FUCKING CRUIKSHANK JUST COOKED ME A STEAK!
GOD BLESS THE GUY, BUT IT'S THIS HERO WORSHIP THAT TOOK ME OUT OF THE KITCHEN IN THE FIRST PLACE.
CHEFS IN LOVE WITH BEING CHEFS.

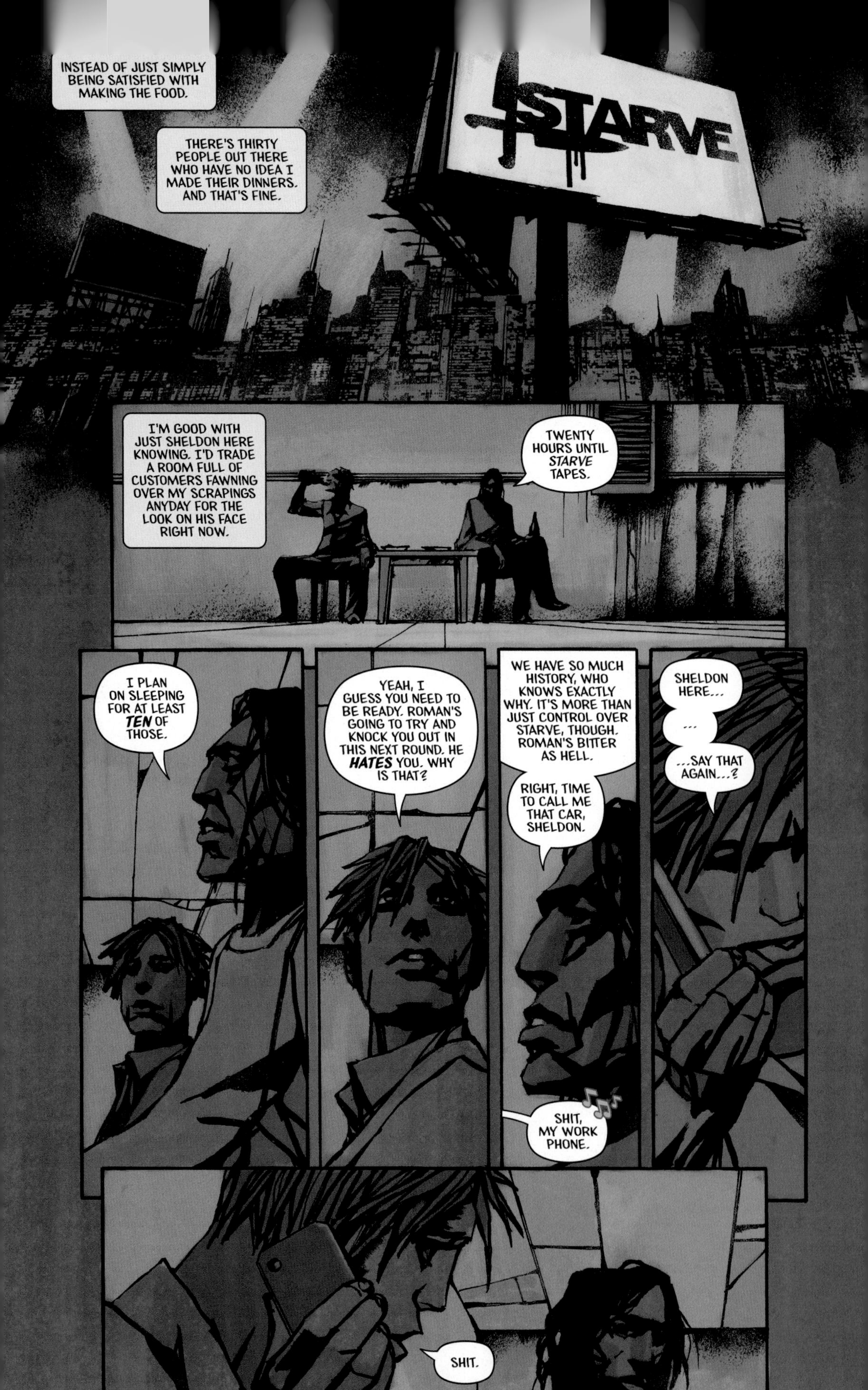
INSTEAD OF JUST SIMPLY BEING SATISFIED WITH MAKING THE FOOD.
STARVE
THERE'S THIRTY PEOPLE OUT THERE WHO HAVE NO IDEA I MADE THEIR DINNERS. AND THAT'S FINE.
I'M GOOD WITH JUST SHELDON HERE KNOWING. I'D TRADE A ROOM FULL OF CUSTOMERS FAWNING OVER MY SCRAPINGS ANYDAY FOR THE LOOK ON HIS FACE RIGHT NOW.
TWENTY HOURS UNTIL *STARVE* TAPES.
I PLAN ON SLEEPING FOR AT LEAST ***TEN*** OF THOSE.
YEAH, I GUESS YOU NEED TO BE READY. ROMAN'S GOING TO TRY AND KNOCK YOU OUT IN THIS NEXT ROUND. HE ***HATES*** YOU. WHY IS THAT?
WE HAVE SO MUCH HISTORY, WHO KNOWS EXACTLY WHY. IT'S MORE THAN JUST CONTROL OVER STARVE, THOUGH. ROMAN'S BITTER AS HELL.
RIGHT, TIME TO CALL ME THAT CAR, SHELDON.
SHIT, MY WORK PHONE.
SHELDON HERE...
...
...SAY THAT AGAIN...?
SHIT.

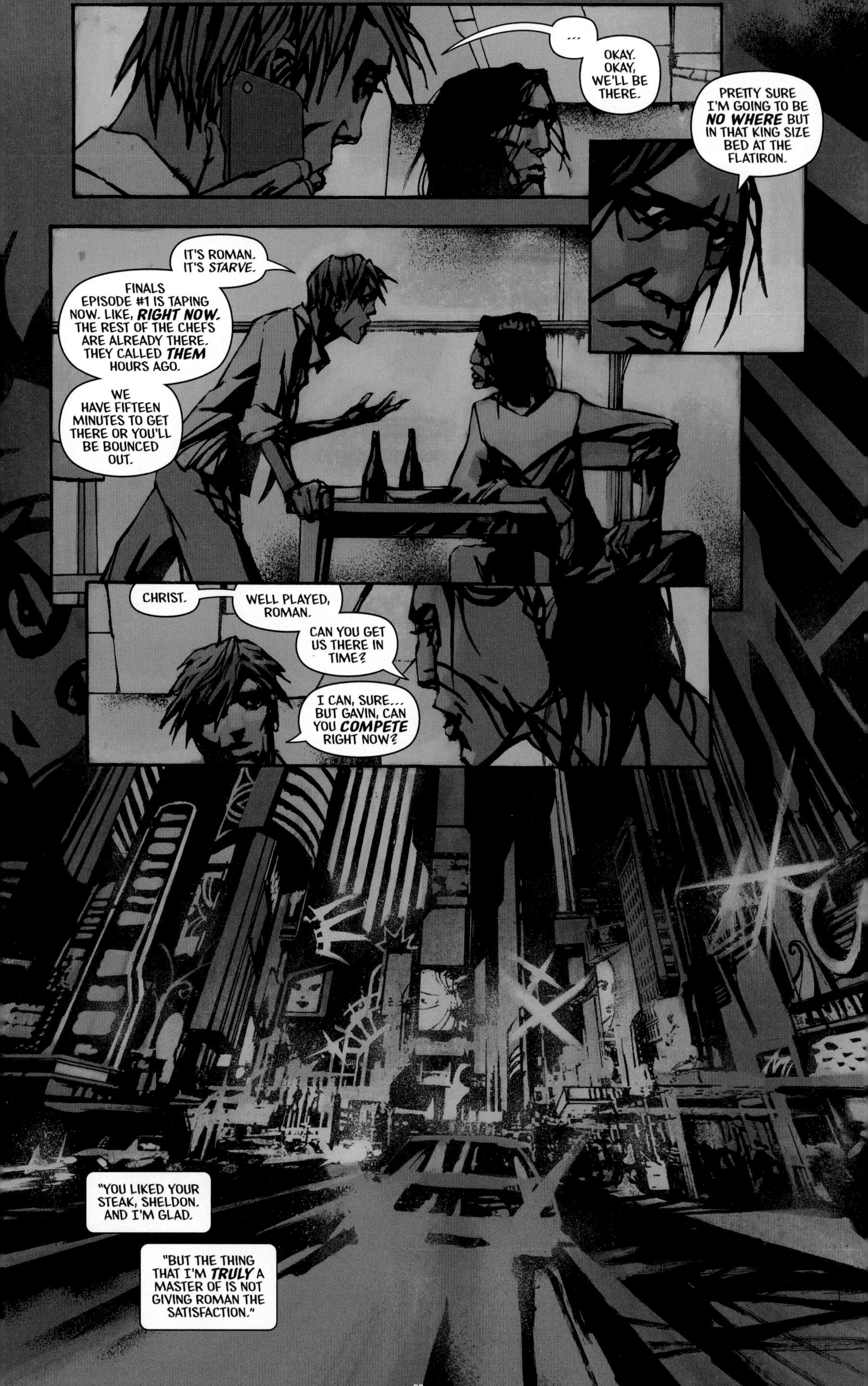
...
OKAY. OKAY, WE'LL BE THERE.
PRETTY SURE I'M GOING TO BE NO WHERE BUT IN THAT KING SIZE BED AT THE FLATIRON.
IT'S ROMAN. IT'S STARVE.
FINALS EPISODE #1 IS TAPING NOW. LIKE, RIGHT NOW. THE REST OF THE CHEFS ARE ALREADY THERE. THEY CALLED THEM HOURS AGO.
WE HAVE FIFTEEN MINUTES TO GET THERE OR YOU'LL BE BOUNCED OUT.
CHRIST.
WELL PLAYED, ROMAN.
CAN YOU GET US THERE IN TIME?
I CAN, SURE... BUT GAVIN, CAN YOU COMPETE RIGHT NOW?
"YOU LIKED YOUR STEAK, SHELDON. AND I'M GLAD.
"BUT THE THING THAT I'M TRULY A MASTER OF IS NOT GIVING ROMAN THE SATISFACTION."

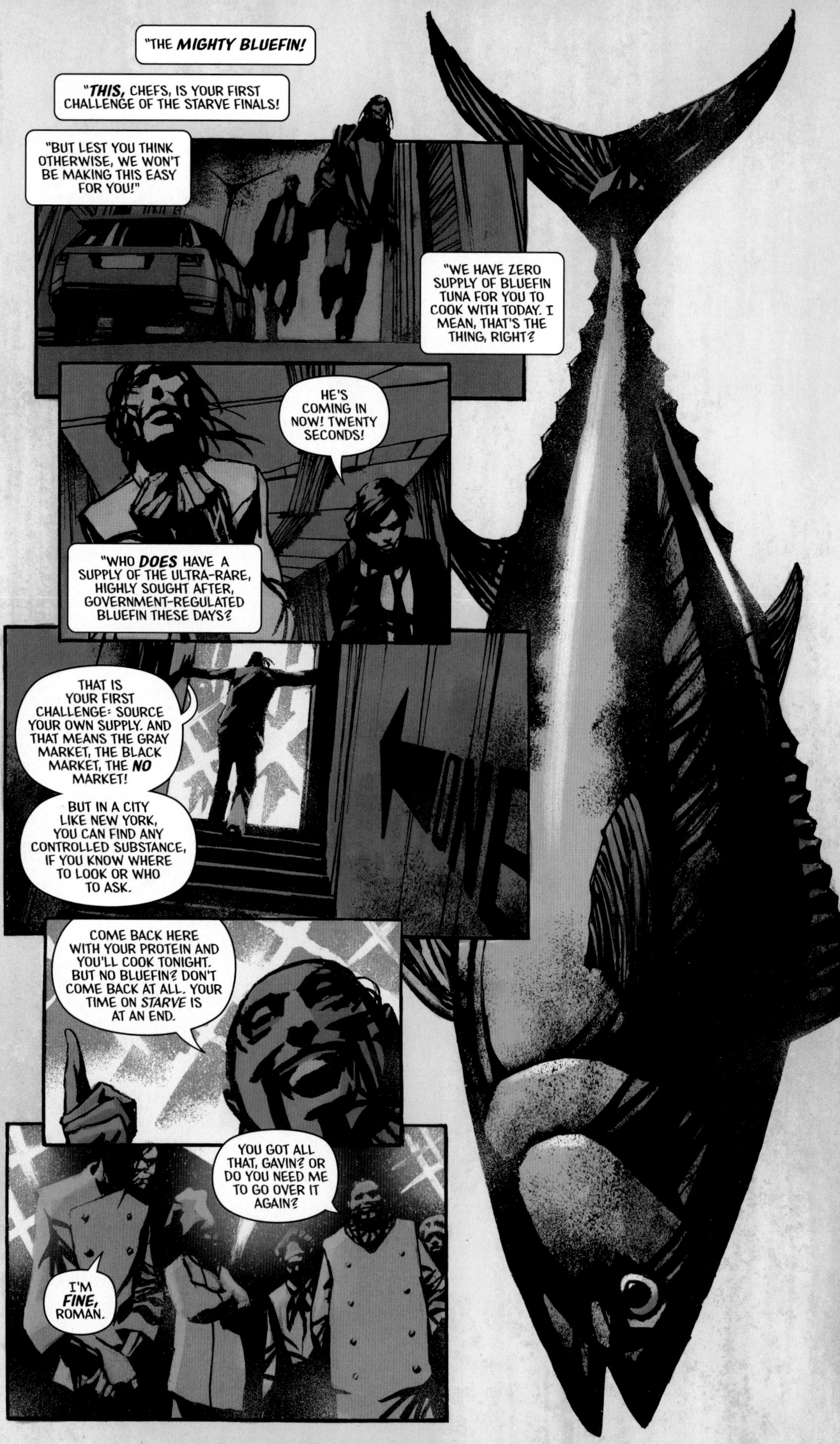
"THE MIGHTY BLUEFIN!
"THIS, CHEFS, IS YOUR FIRST CHALLENGE OF THE STARVE FINALS!
"BUT LEST YOU THINK OTHERWISE, WE WON'T BE MAKING THIS EASY FOR YOU!"
"WE HAVE ZERO SUPPLY OF BLUEFIN TUNA FOR YOU TO COOK WITH TODAY. I MEAN, THAT'S THE THING, RIGHT?
HE'S COMING IN NOW! TWENTY SECONDS!
"WHO DOES HAVE A SUPPLY OF THE ULTRA-RARE, HIGHLY SOUGHT AFTER, GOVERNMENT-REGULATED BLUEFIN THESE DAYS?
THAT IS YOUR FIRST CHALLENGE: SOURCE YOUR OWN SUPPLY. AND THAT MEANS THE GRAY MARKET, THE BLACK MARKET, THE NO MARKET!
BUT IN A CITY LIKE NEW YORK, YOU CAN FIND ANY CONTROLLED SUBSTANCE, IF YOU KNOW WHERE TO LOOK OR WHO TO ASK.
COME BACK HERE WITH YOUR PROTEIN AND YOU'LL COOK TONIGHT. BUT NO BLUEFIN? DON'T COME BACK AT ALL. YOUR TIME ON STARVE IS AT AN END.
YOU GOT ALL THAT, GAVIN? OR DO YOU NEED ME TO GO OVER IT AGAIN?
I'M FINE, ROMAN.

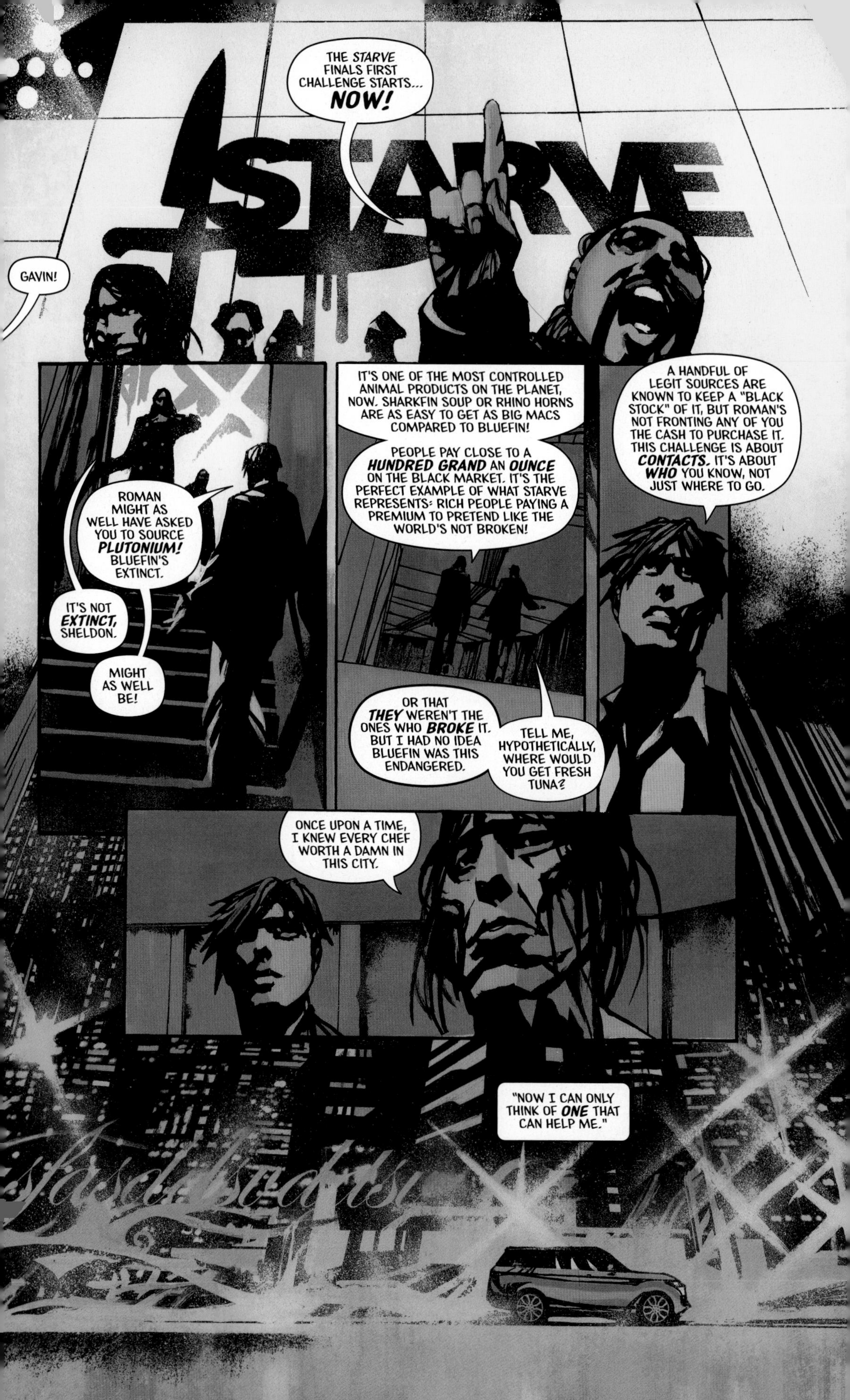
THE *STARVE* FINALS FIRST CHALLENGE STARTS... **NOW!**
STARVE
GAVIN!
ROMAN MIGHT AS WELL HAVE ASKED YOU TO SOURCE ***PLUTONIUM!*** BLUEFIN'S EXTINCT.
IT'S NOT ***EXTINCT,*** SHELDON.
MIGHT AS WELL BE!
IT'S ONE OF THE MOST CONTROLLED ANIMAL PRODUCTS ON THE PLANET, NOW. SHARKFIN SOUP OR RHINO HORNS ARE AS EASY TO GET AS BIG MACS COMPARED TO BLUEFIN!
PEOPLE PAY CLOSE TO A ***HUNDRED GRAND*** AN ***OUNCE*** ON THE BLACK MARKET. IT'S THE PERFECT EXAMPLE OF WHAT STARVE REPRESENTS: RICH PEOPLE PAYING A PREMIUM TO PRETEND LIKE THE WORLD'S NOT BROKEN!
OR THAT ***THEY*** WEREN'T THE ONES WHO ***BROKE*** IT. BUT I HAD NO IDEA BLUEFIN WAS THIS ENDANGERED.
TELL ME, HYPOTHETICALLY, WHERE WOULD YOU GET FRESH TUNA?
A HANDFUL OF LEGIT SOURCES ARE KNOWN TO KEEP A "BLACK STOCK" OF IT, BUT ROMAN'S NOT FRONTING ANY OF YOU THE CASH TO PURCHASE IT. THIS CHALLENGE IS ABOUT ***CONTACTS.*** IT'S ABOUT ***WHO*** YOU KNOW, NOT JUST WHERE TO GO.
ONCE UPON A TIME, I KNEW EVERY CHEF WORTH A DAMN IN THIS CITY.
"NOW I CAN ONLY THINK OF ***ONE*** THAT CAN HELP ME."

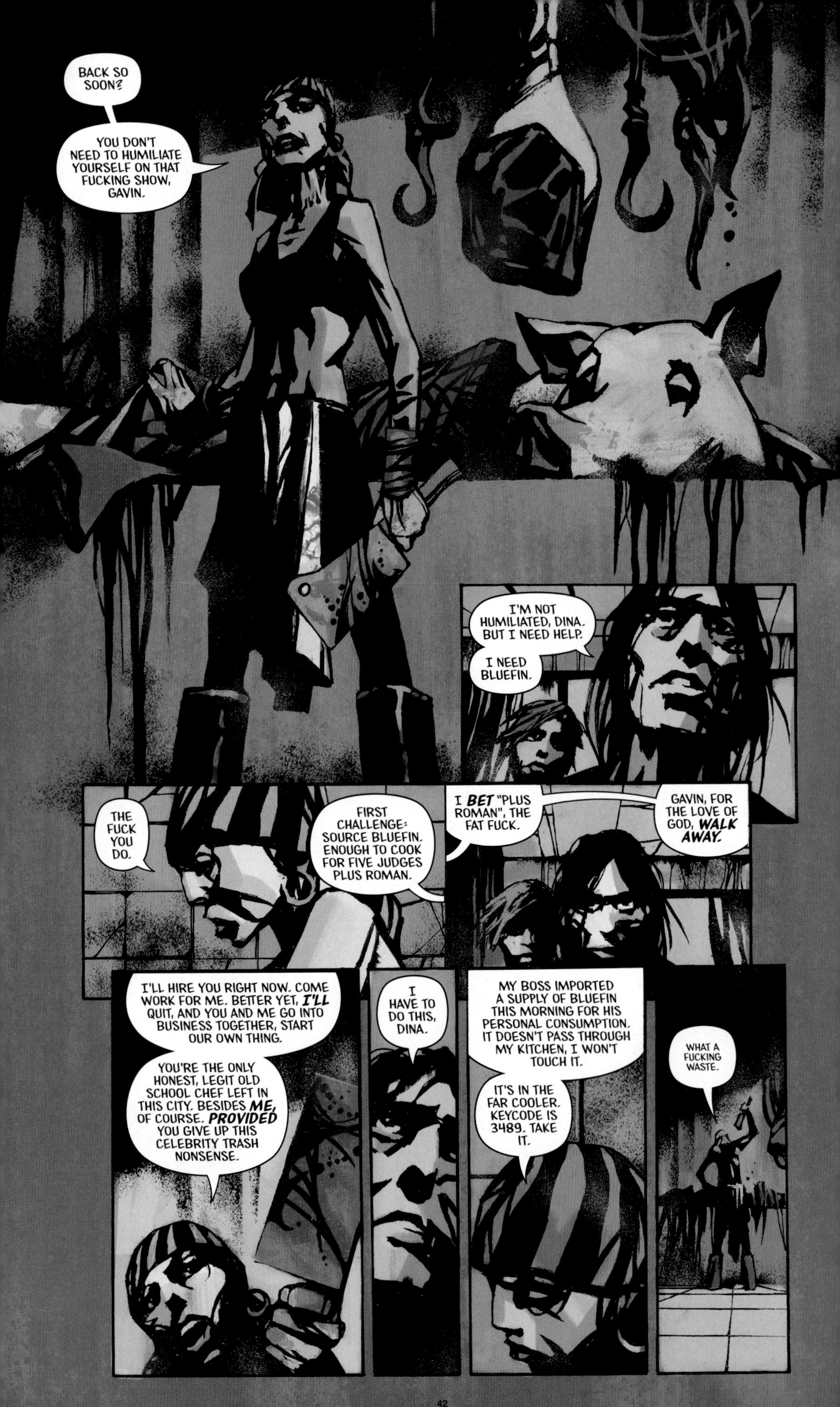
BACK SO SOON?
YOU DON'T NEED TO HUMILIATE YOURSELF ON THAT FUCKING SHOW, GAVIN.
I'M NOT HUMILIATED, DINA. BUT I NEED HELP.
I NEED BLUEFIN.
THE FUCK YOU DO.
FIRST CHALLENGE: SOURCE BLUEFIN. ENOUGH TO COOK FOR FIVE JUDGES PLUS ROMAN.
I **BET** "PLUS ROMAN", THE FAT FUCK.
GAVIN, FOR THE LOVE OF GOD, **WALK AWAY.**
I'LL HIRE YOU RIGHT NOW. COME WORK FOR ME. BETTER YET, ***I'LL*** QUIT, AND YOU AND ME GO INTO BUSINESS TOGETHER, START OUR OWN THING.
YOU'RE THE ONLY HONEST, LEGIT OLD SCHOOL CHEF LEFT IN THIS CITY. BESIDES ***ME,*** OF COURSE. ***PROVIDED*** YOU GIVE UP THIS CELEBRITY TRASH NONSENSE.
I HAVE TO DO THIS, DINA.
MY BOSS IMPORTED A SUPPLY OF BLUEFIN THIS MORNING FOR HIS PERSONAL CONSUMPTION. IT DOESN'T PASS THROUGH MY KITCHEN, I WON'T TOUCH IT.
IT'S IN THE FAR COOLER. KEYCODE IS 3489. TAKE IT.
WHAT A FUCKING WASTE.

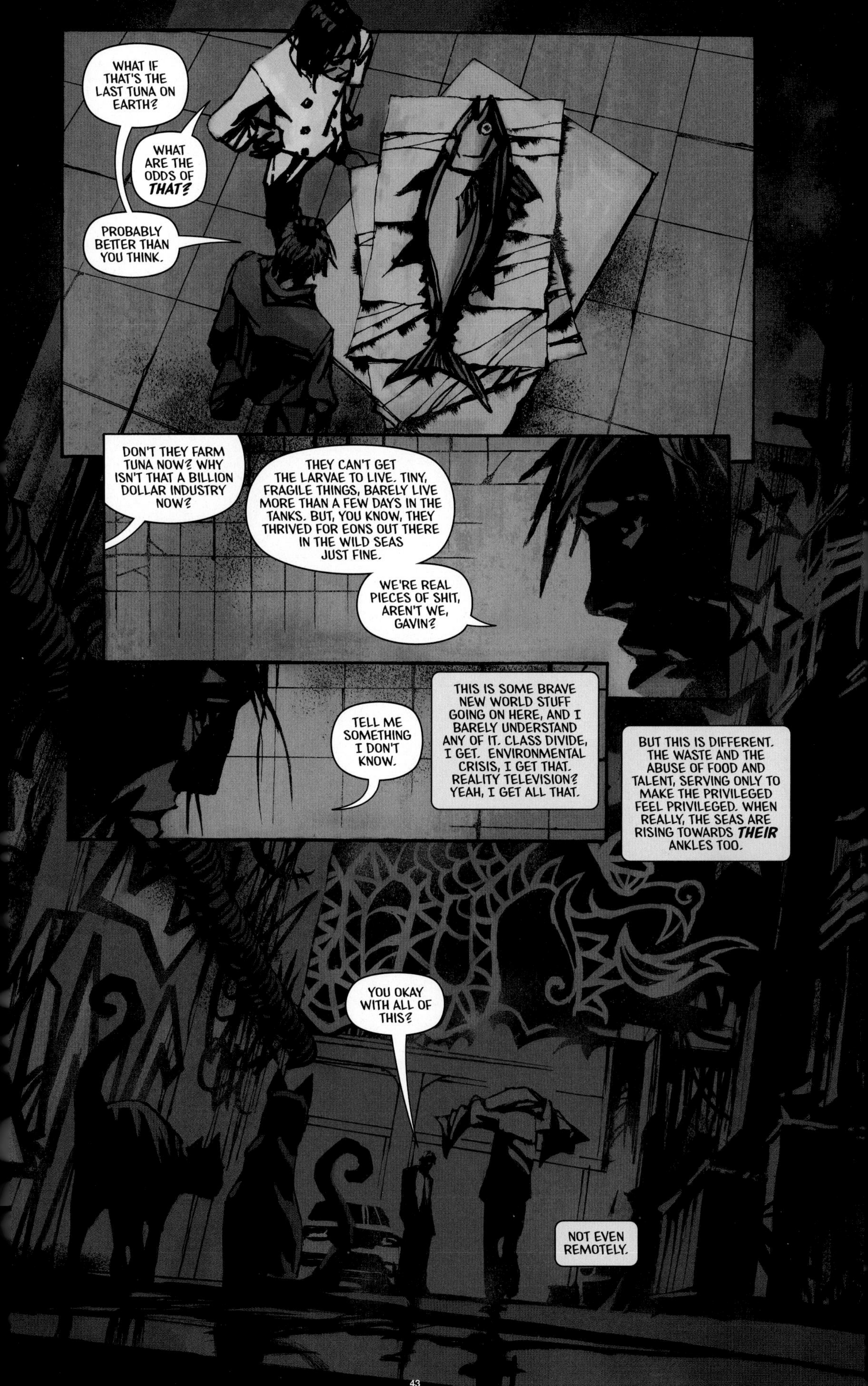
WHAT IF THAT'S THE LAST TUNA ON EARTH?
WHAT ARE THE ODDS OF THAT?
PROBABLY BETTER THAN YOU THINK.
DON'T THEY FARM TUNA NOW? WHY ISN'T THAT A BILLION DOLLAR INDUSTRY NOW?
THEY CAN'T GET THE LARVAE TO LIVE. TINY, FRAGILE THINGS, BARELY LIVE MORE THAN A FEW DAYS IN THE TANKS. BUT, YOU KNOW, THEY THRIVED FOR EONS OUT THERE IN THE WILD SEAS JUST FINE.
WE'RE REAL PIECES OF SHIT, AREN'T WE, GAVIN?
TELL ME SOMETHING I DON'T KNOW.
THIS IS SOME BRAVE NEW WORLD STUFF GOING ON HERE, AND I BARELY UNDERSTAND ANY OF IT. CLASS DIVIDE, I GET. ENVIRONMENTAL CRISIS, I GET THAT. REALITY TELEVISION? YEAH, I GET ALL THAT.
BUT THIS IS DIFFERENT. THE WASTE AND THE ABUSE OF FOOD AND TALENT, SERVING ONLY TO MAKE THE PRIVILEGED FEEL PRIVILEGED. WHEN REALLY, THE SEAS ARE RISING TOWARDS THEIR ANKLES TOO.
YOU OKAY WITH ALL OF THIS?
NOT EVEN REMOTELY.

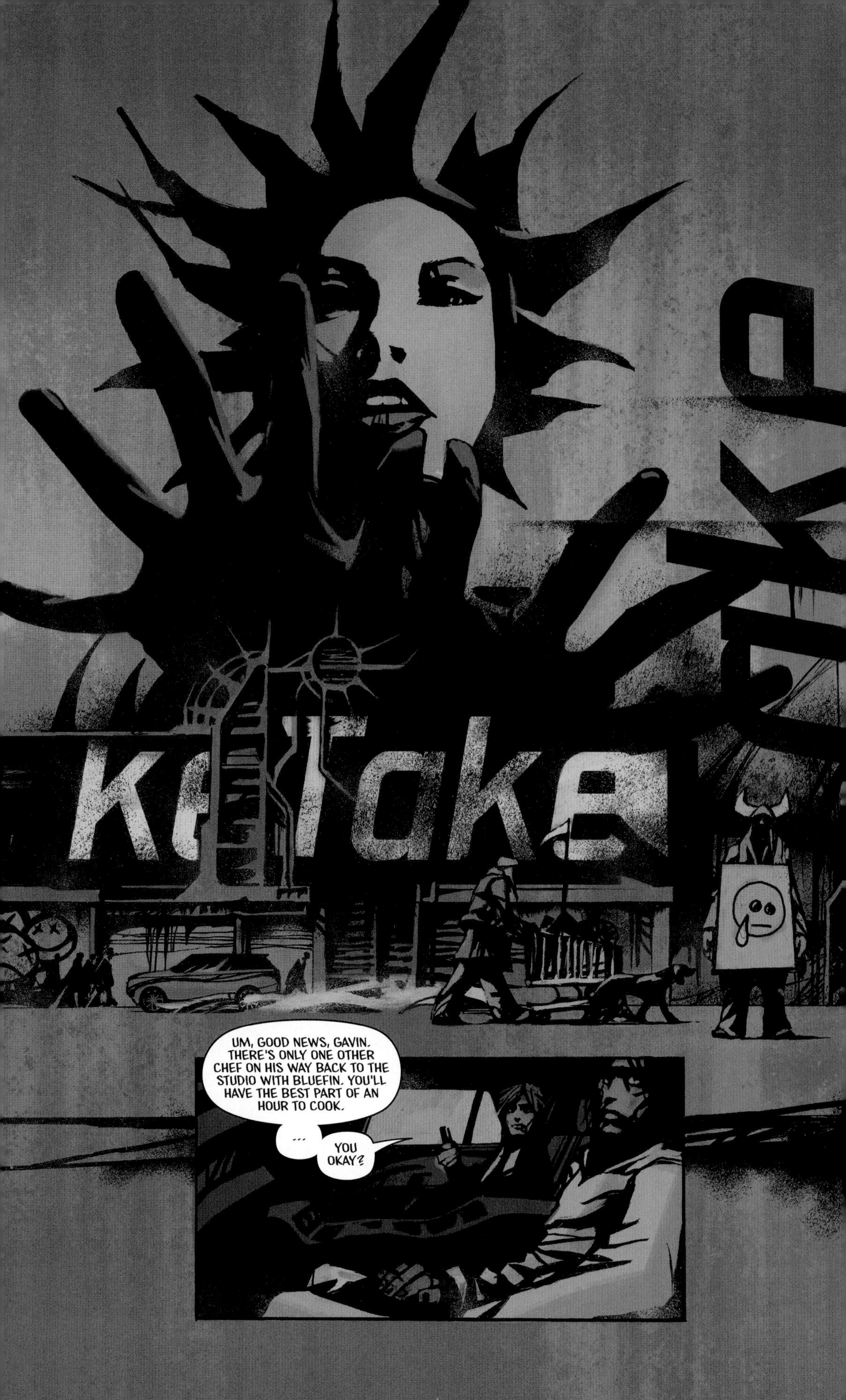
UM, GOOD NEWS, GAVIN. THERE'S ONLY ONE OTHER CHEF ON HIS WAY BACK TO THE STUDIO WITH BLUEFIN. YOU'LL HAVE THE BEST PART OF AN HOUR TO COOK.
...
YOU OKAY?

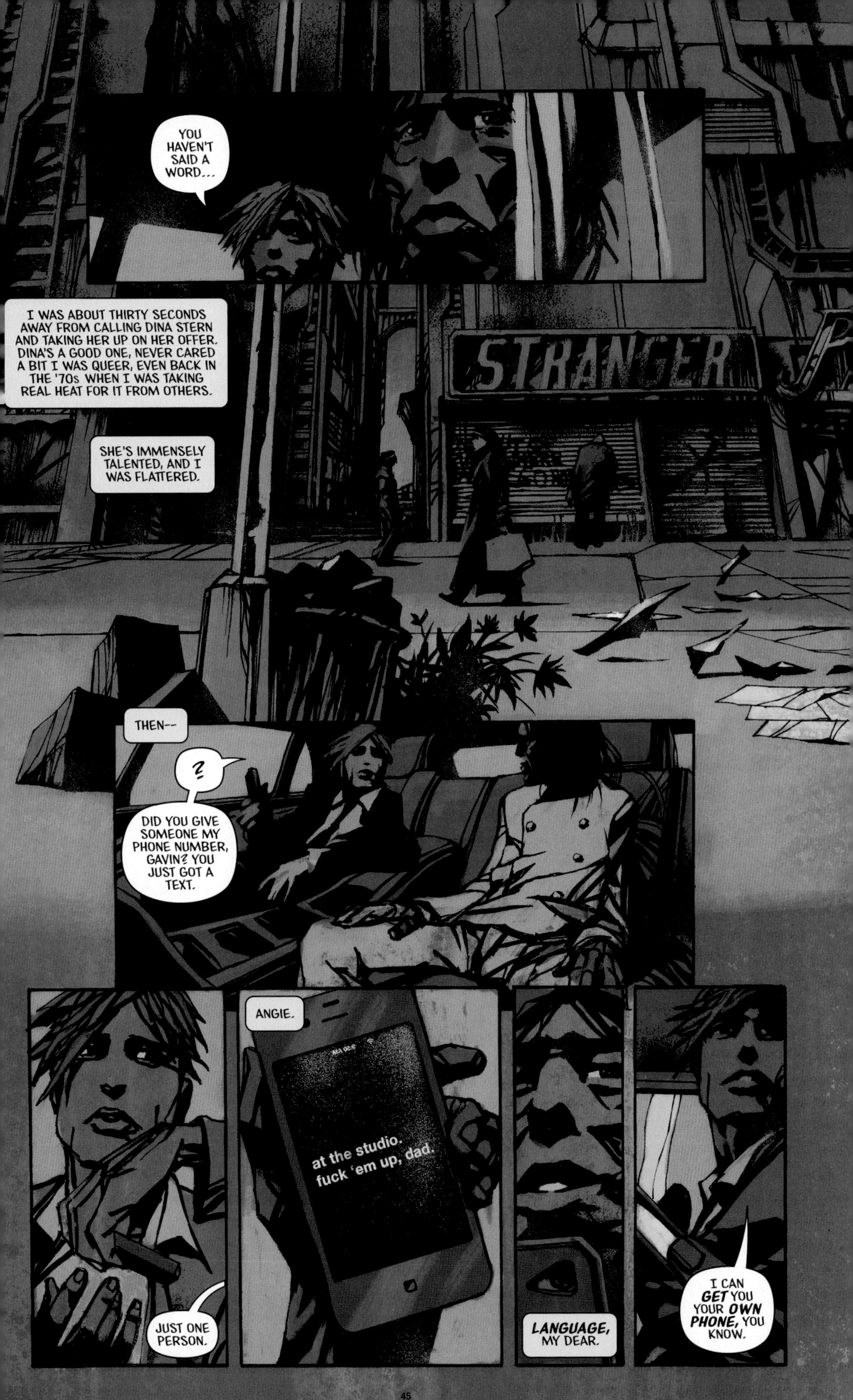
YOU HAVEN'T SAID A WORD...
I WAS ABOUT THIRTY SECONDS AWAY FROM CALLING DINA STERN AND TAKING HER UP ON HER OFFER. DINA'S A GOOD ONE, NEVER CARED A BIT I WAS QUEER, EVEN BACK IN THE '70s WHEN I WAS TAKING REAL HEAT FOR IT FROM OTHERS.
SHE'S IMMENSELY TALENTED, AND I WAS FLATTERED.
STRANGER
THEN--
?
DID YOU GIVE SOMEONE MY PHONE NUMBER, GAVIN? YOU JUST GOT A TEXT.
JUST ONE PERSON.
ANGIE.
at the studio. fuck 'em up, dad.
LANGUAGE, MY DEAR.
I CAN GET YOU YOUR OWN PHONE, YOU KNOW.

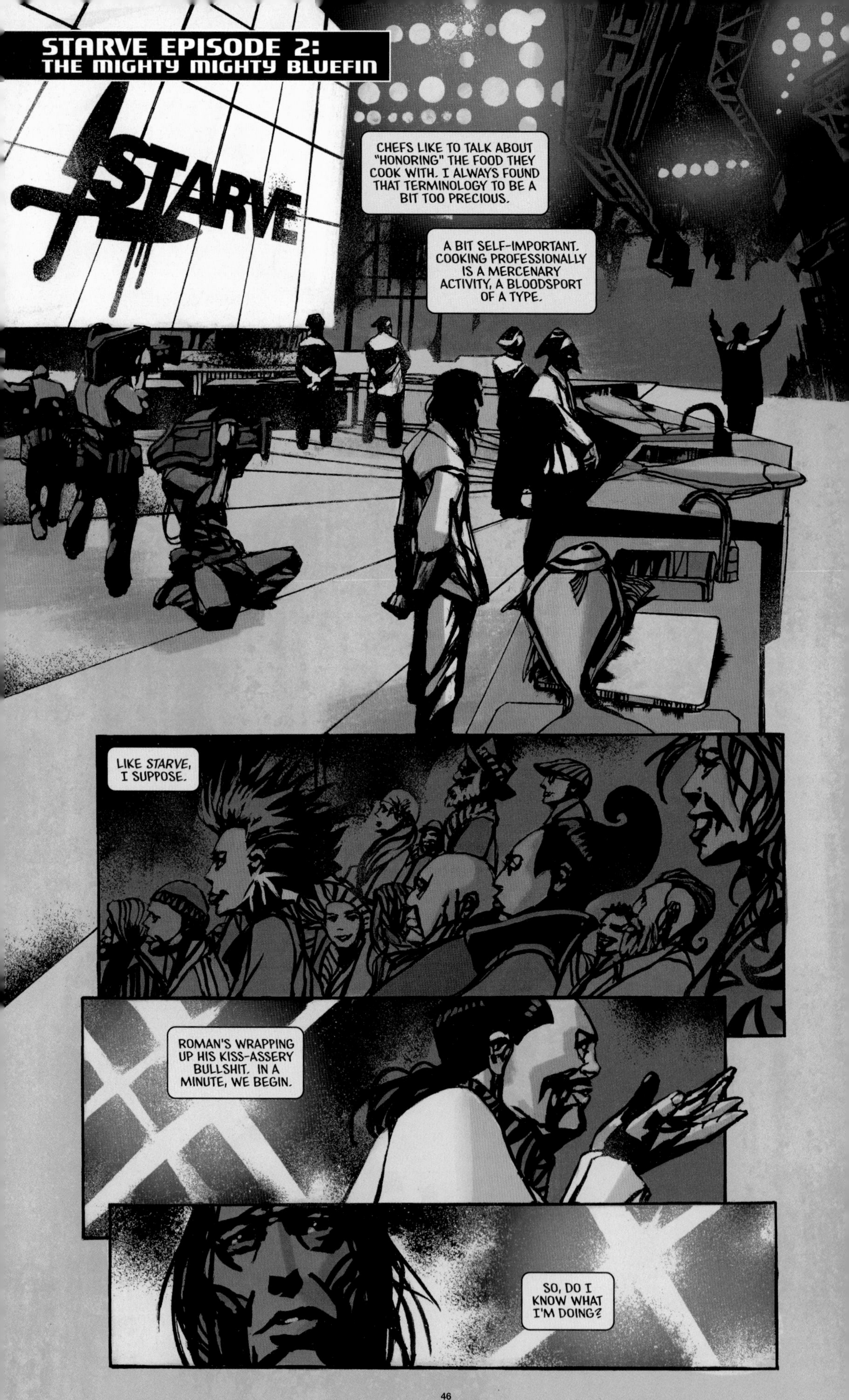
STARVE EPISODE 2:
THE MIGHTY MIGHTY BLUEFIN
STARVE
CHEFS LIKE TO TALK ABOUT "HONORING" THE FOOD THEY COOK WITH. I ALWAYS FOUND THAT TERMINOLOGY TO BE A BIT TOO PRECIOUS.
A BIT SELF-IMPORTANT. COOKING PROFESSIONALLY IS A MERCENARY ACTIVITY, A BLOODSPORT OF A TYPE.
LIKE *STARVE*, I SUPPOSE.
ROMAN'S WRAPPING UP HIS KISS-ASSERY BULLSHIT. IN A MINUTE, WE BEGIN.
SO, DO I KNOW WHAT I'M DOING?

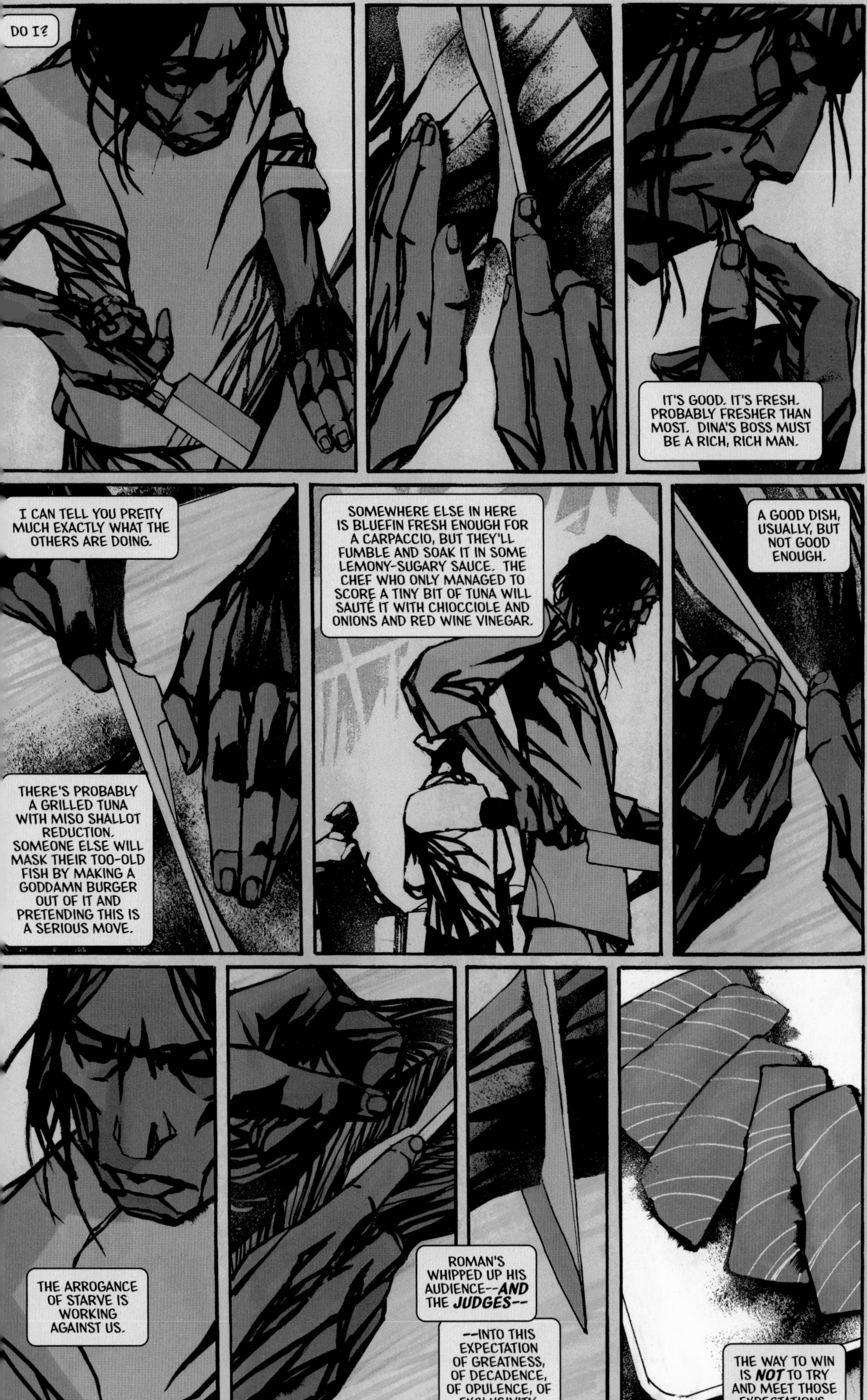
DO I?
IT'S GOOD. IT'S FRESH. PROBABLY FRESHER THAN MOST. DINA'S BOSS MUST BE A RICH, RICH MAN.
I CAN TELL YOU PRETTY MUCH EXACTLY WHAT THE OTHERS ARE DOING.
THERE'S PROBABLY A GRILLED TUNA WITH MISO SHALLOT REDUCTION. SOMEONE ELSE WILL MASK THEIR TOO-OLD FISH BY MAKING A GODDAMN BURGER OUT OF IT AND PRETENDING THIS IS A SERIOUS MOVE.
SOMEWHERE ELSE IN HERE IS BLUEFIN FRESH ENOUGH FOR A CARPACCIO, BUT THEY'LL FUMBLE AND SOAK IT IN SOME LEMONY-SUGARY SAUCE. THE CHEF WHO ONLY MANAGED TO SCORE A TINY BIT OF TUNA WILL SAUTÉ IT WITH CHIOCCIOLE AND ONIONS AND RED WINE VINEGAR.
A GOOD DISH, USUALLY, BUT NOT GOOD ENOUGH.
THE ARROGANCE OF STARVE IS WORKING AGAINST US.
ROMAN'S WHIPPED UP HIS AUDIENCE--*AND* THE *JUDGES*--
--INTO THIS EXPECTATION OF GREATNESS, OF DECADENCE, OF OPULENCE, OF EXCLUSIVITY.
THE WAY TO WIN IS ***NOT*** TO TRY AND MEET THOSE EXPECTATIONS.

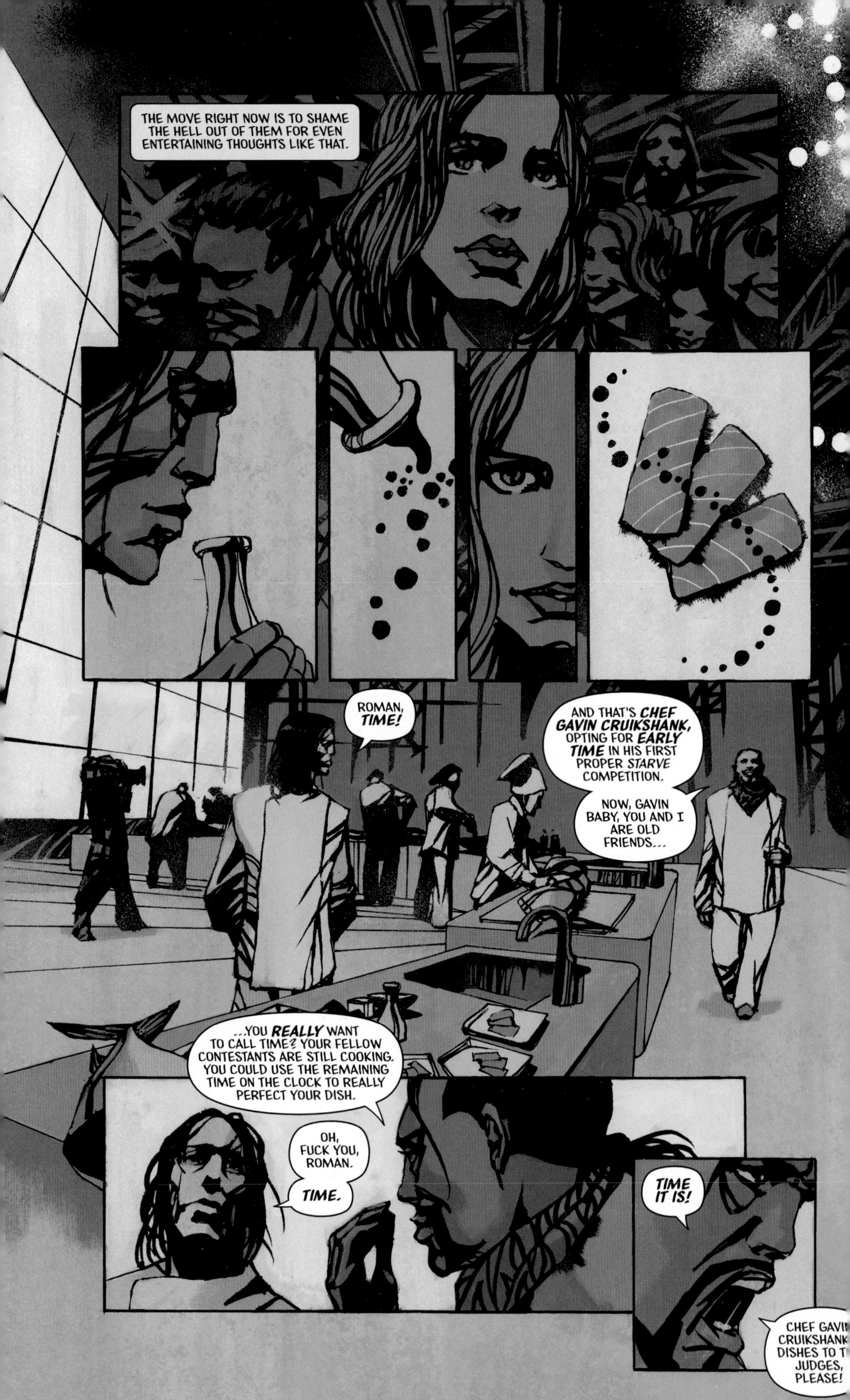
THE MOVE RIGHT NOW IS TO SHAME THE HELL OUT OF THEM FOR EVEN ENTERTAINING THOUGHTS LIKE THAT.
ROMAN, TIME!
AND THAT'S CHEF GAVIN CRUIKSHANK, OPTING FOR EARLY TIME IN HIS FIRST PROPER STARVE COMPETITION.
NOW, GAVIN BABY, YOU AND I ARE OLD FRIENDS...
...YOU REALLY WANT TO CALL TIME? YOUR FELLOW CONTESTANTS ARE STILL COOKING. YOU COULD USE THE REMAINING TIME ON THE CLOCK TO REALLY PERFECT YOUR DISH.
OH, FUCK YOU, ROMAN.
TIME.
TIME IT IS!
CHEF GAVI CRUIKSHANK DISHES TO T JUDGES, PLEASE!

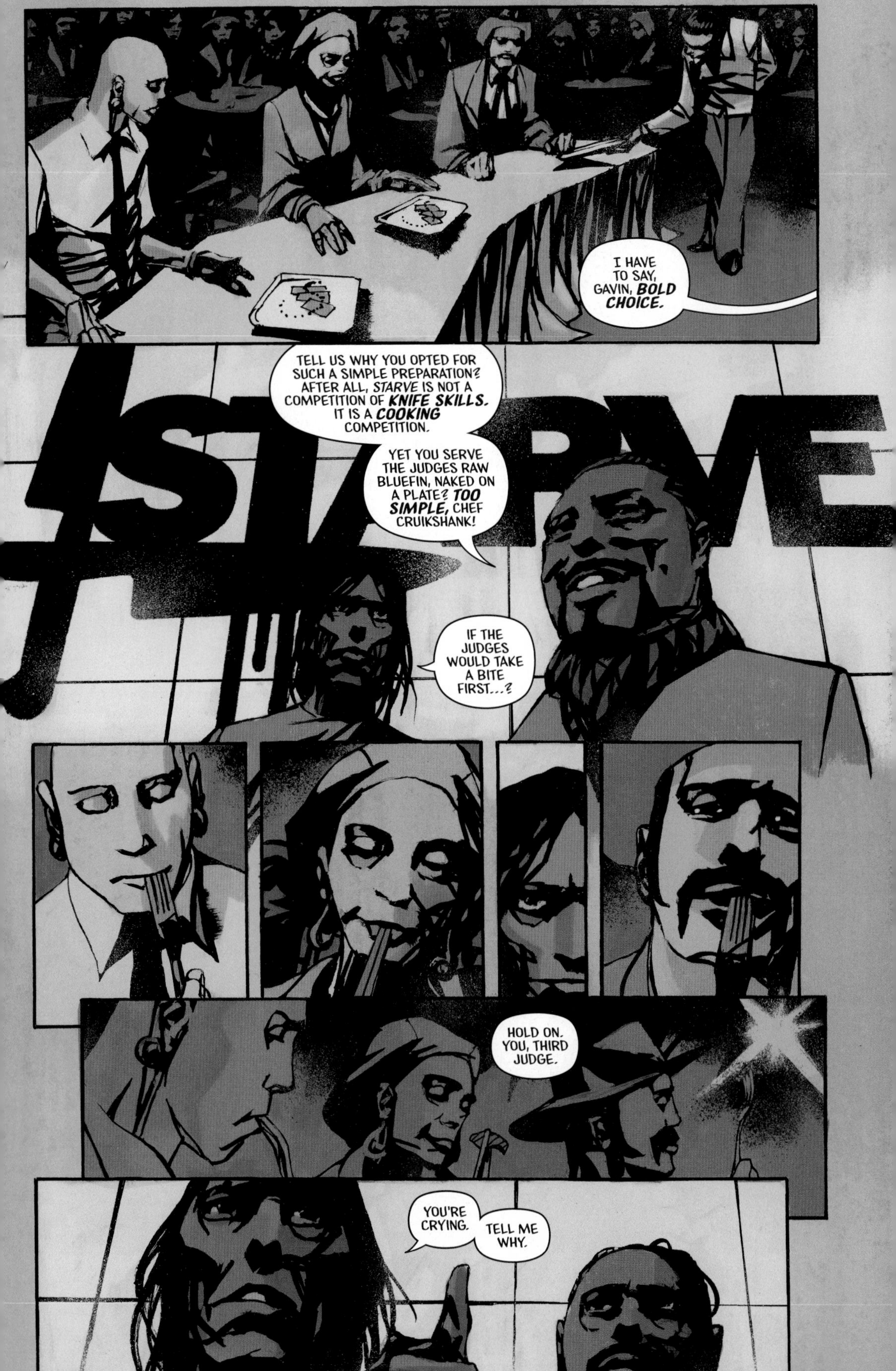
I HAVE TO SAY, GAVIN, BOLD CHOICE.
TELL US WHY YOU OPTED FOR SUCH A SIMPLE PREPARATION? AFTER ALL, STARVE IS NOT A COMPETITION OF KNIFE SKILLS. IT IS A COOKING COMPETITION.
YET YOU SERVE THE JUDGES RAW BLUEFIN, NAKED ON A PLATE? TOO SIMPLE, CHEF CRUIKSHANK!
#STARVE
IF THE JUDGES WOULD TAKE A BITE FIRST...?
HOLD ON. YOU, THIRD JUDGE.
YOU'RE CRYING.
TELL ME WHY.

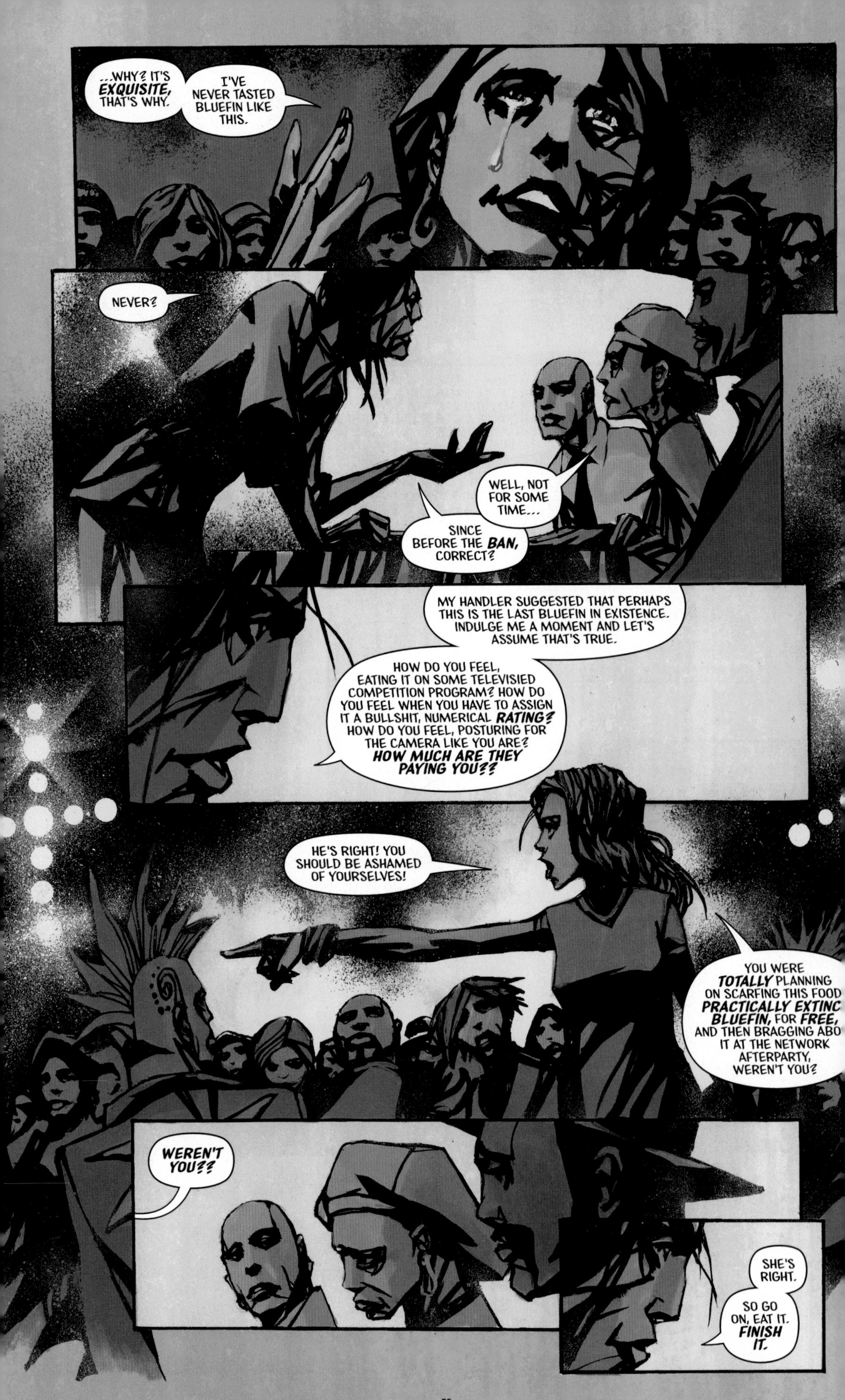
...WHY? IT'S EXQUISITE, THAT'S WHY.
I'VE NEVER TASTED BLUEFIN LIKE THIS.
NEVER?
WELL, NOT FOR SOME TIME...
SINCE BEFORE THE BAN, CORRECT?
MY HANDLER SUGGESTED THAT PERHAPS THIS IS THE LAST BLUEFIN IN EXISTENCE. INDULGE ME A MOMENT AND LET'S ASSUME THAT'S TRUE.
HOW DO YOU FEEL, EATING IT ON SOME TELEVISIED COMPETITION PROGRAM? HOW DO YOU FEEL WHEN YOU HAVE TO ASSIGN IT A BULLSHIT, NUMERICAL RATING? HOW DO YOU FEEL, POSTURING FOR THE CAMERA LIKE YOU ARE? HOW MUCH ARE THEY PAYING YOU??
HE'S RIGHT! YOU SHOULD BE ASHAMED OF YOURSELVES!
YOU WERE TOTALLY PLANNING ON SCARFING THIS FOOD PRACTICALLY EXTINC BLUEFIN, FOR FREE, AND THEN BRAGGING ABO IT AT THE NETWORK AFTERPARTY, WEREN'T YOU?
WEREN'T YOU??
SHE'S RIGHT.
SO GO ON, EAT IT. FINISH IT.

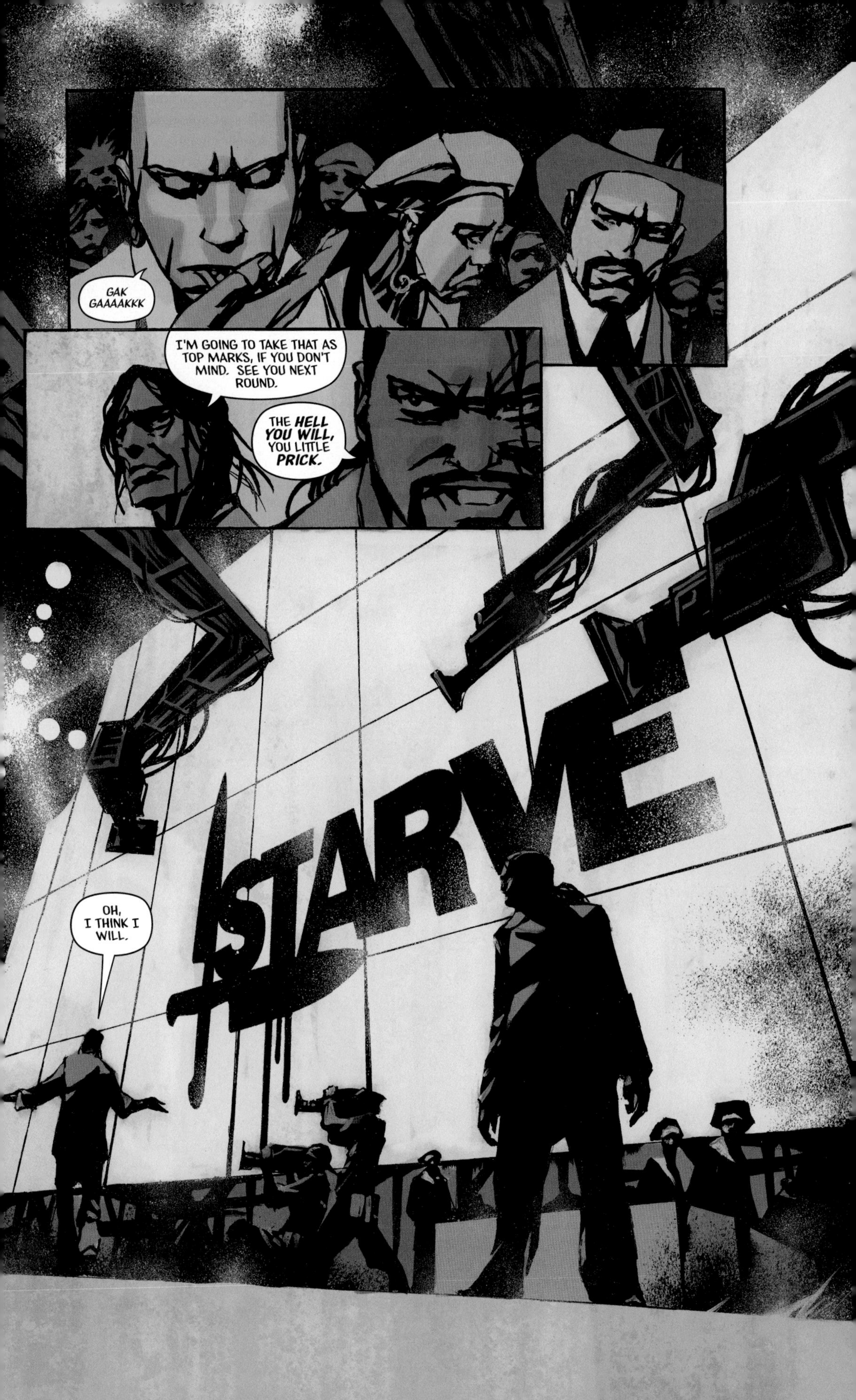
GAK GAAAAKKK
I'M GOING TO TAKE THAT AS TOP MARKS, IF YOU DON'T MIND. SEE YOU NEXT ROUND.
THE HELL YOU WILL, YOU LITTLE PRICK.
STARVE
OH, I THINK I WILL.

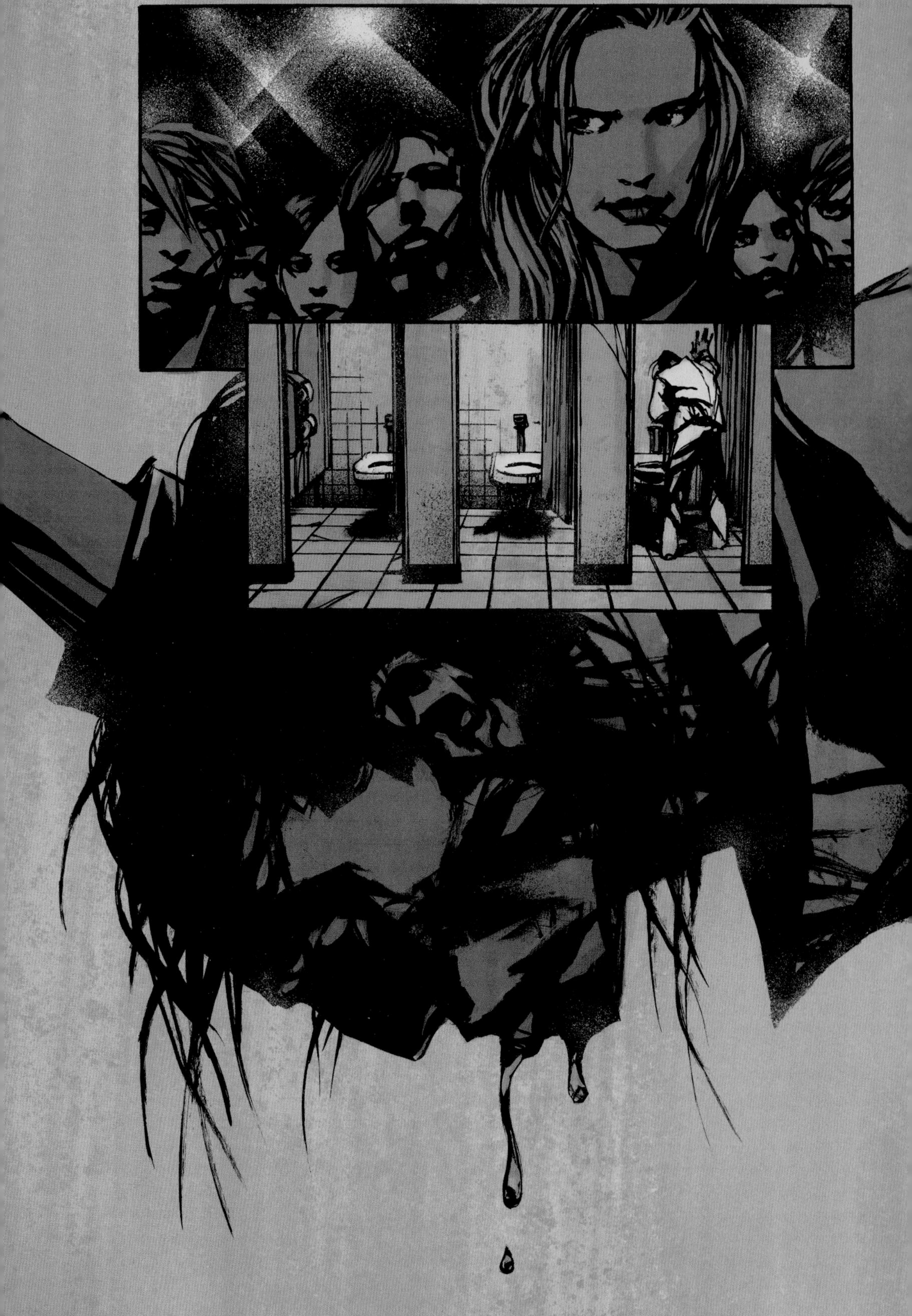
"THIS IS **GOOD TV,** ISN'T IT?"

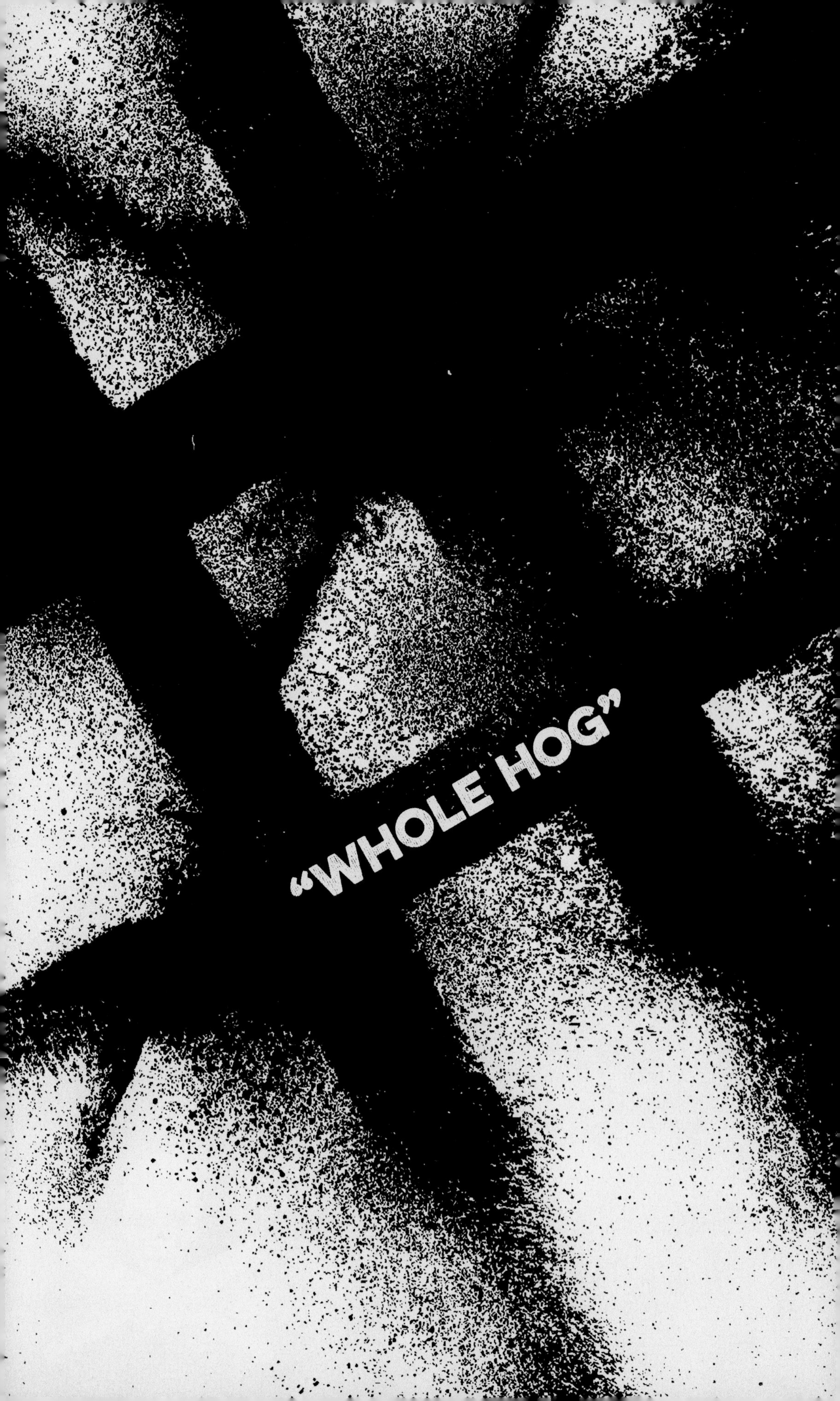
“WHOLE HOG”

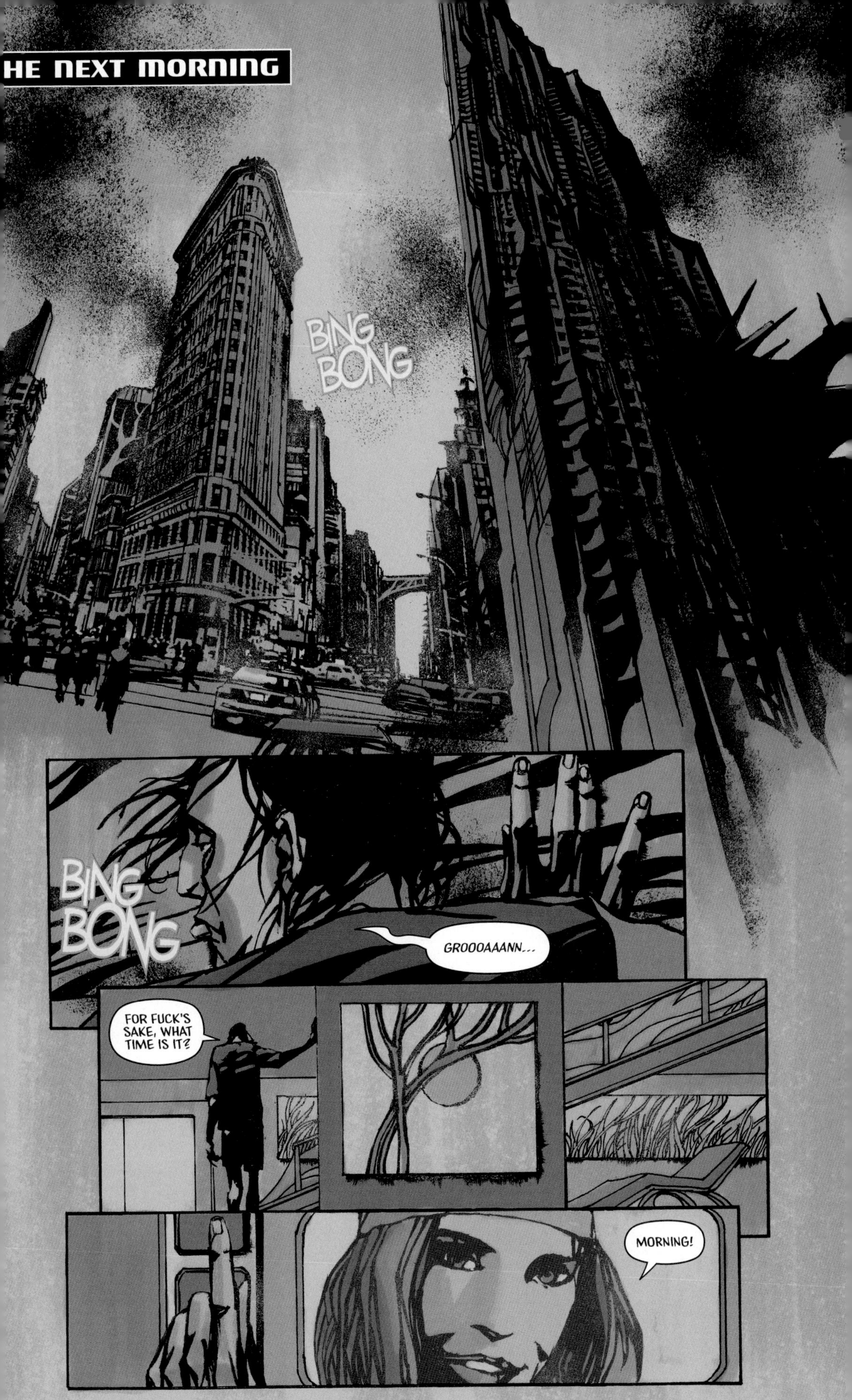
HE NEXT MORNING
BING BONG
BING BONG
GROOOAAANN...
FOR FUCK'S SAKE, WHAT TIME IS IT?
MORNING!

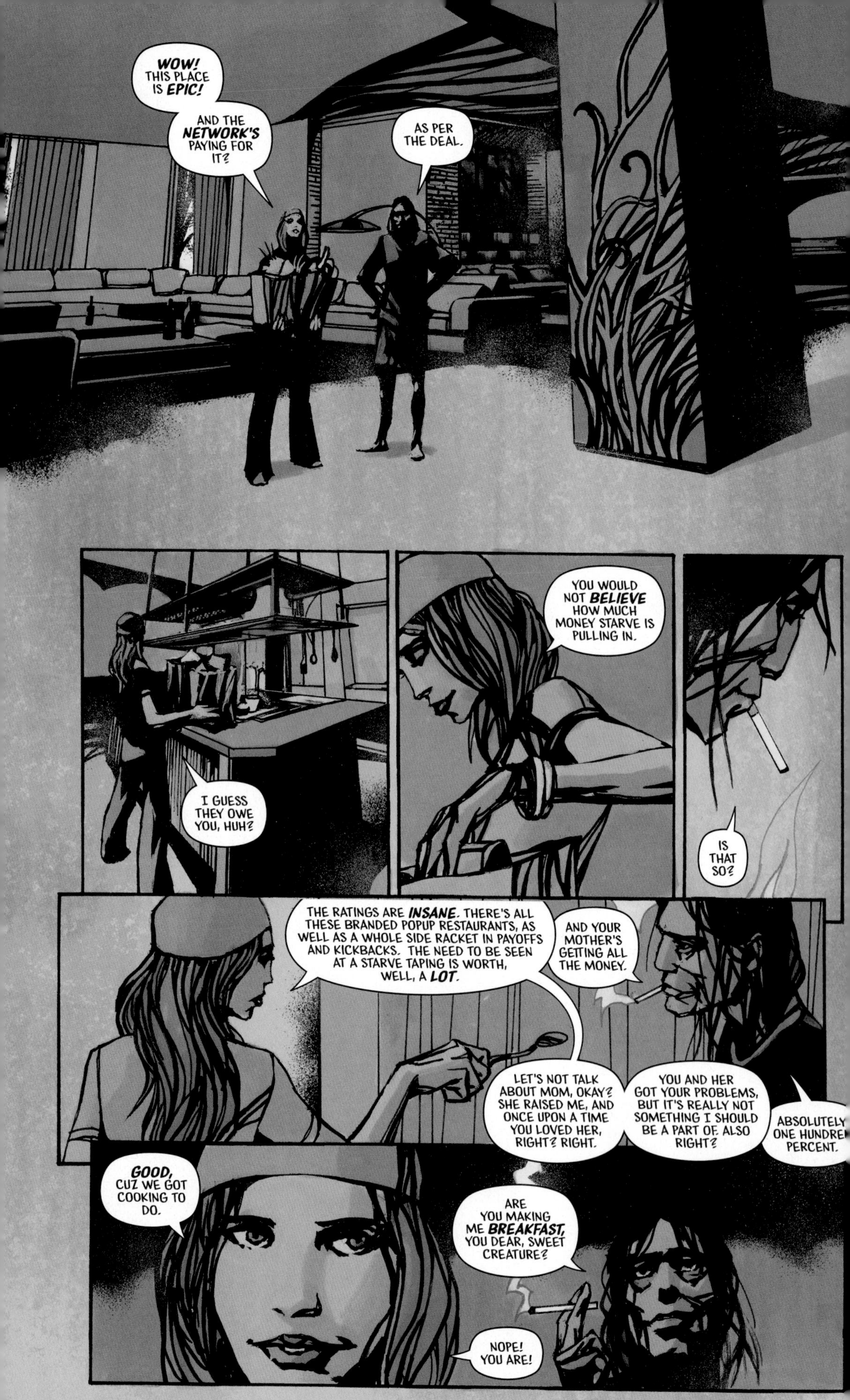

WOW! THIS PLACE IS EPIC!
AND THE NETWORK'S PAYING FOR IT?
AS PER THE DEAL.
I GUESS THEY OWE YOU, HUH?
YOU WOULD NOT BELIEVE HOW MUCH MONEY STARVE IS PULLING IN.
IS THAT SO?
THE RATINGS ARE INSANE. THERE'S ALL THESE BRANDED POPUP RESTAURANTS, AS WELL AS A WHOLE SIDE RACKET IN PAYOFFS AND KICKBACKS. THE NEED TO BE SEEN AT A STARVE TAPING IS WORTH, WELL, A LOT.
AND YOUR MOTHER'S GETTING ALL THE MONEY.
LET'S NOT TALK ABOUT MOM, OKAY? SHE RAISED ME, AND ONCE UPON A TIME YOU LOVED HER, RIGHT? RIGHT.
YOU AND HER GOT YOUR PROBLEMS, BUT IT'S REALLY NOT SOMETHING I SHOULD BE A PART OF. ALSO RIGHT?
ABSOLUTELY ONE HUNDRE PERCENT.
GOOD, CUZ WE GOT COOKING TO DO.
ARE YOU MAKING ME BREAKFAST, YOU DEAR, SWEET CREATURE?
NOPE! YOU ARE!

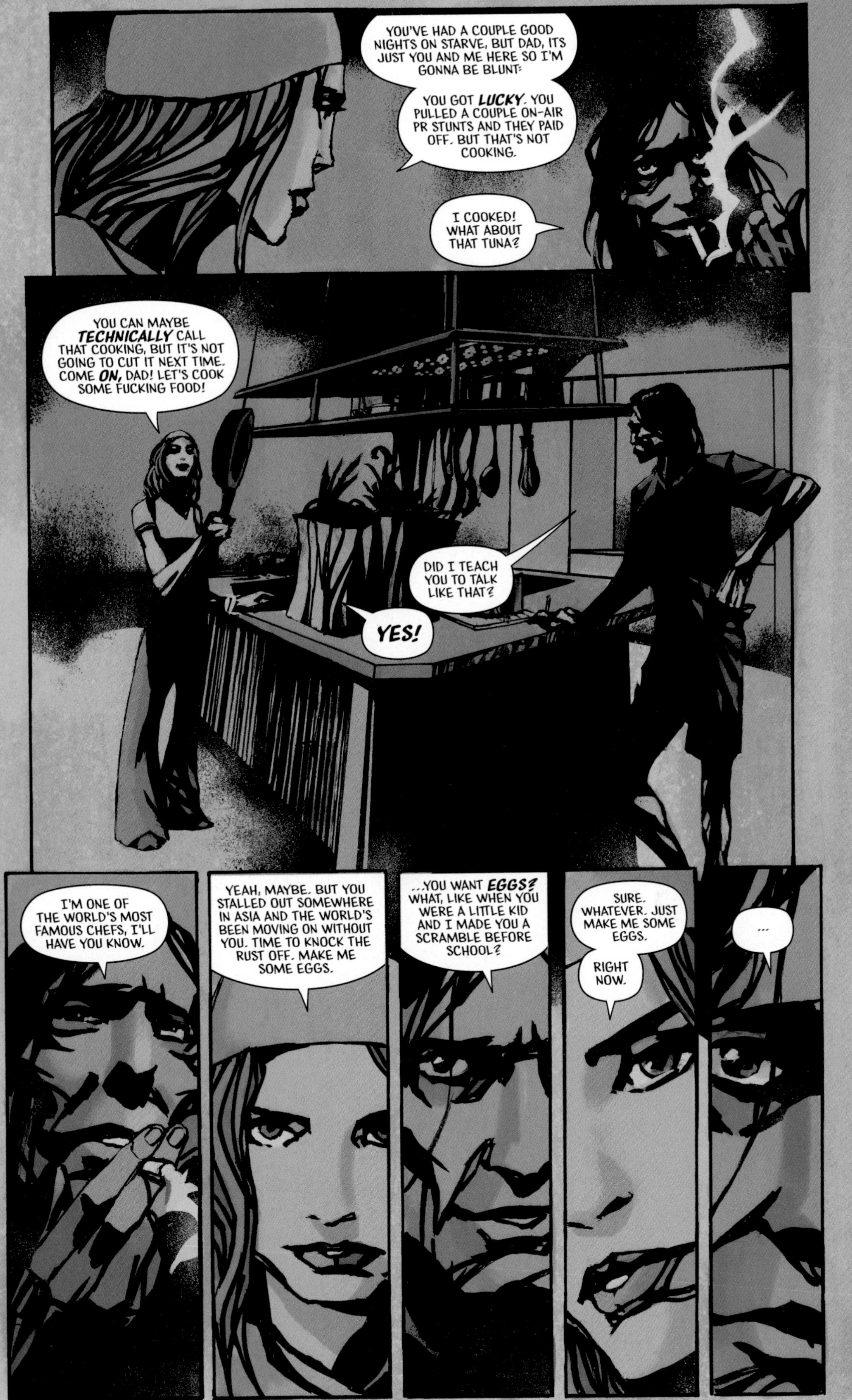
YOU'VE HAD A COUPLE GOOD NIGHTS ON STARVE, BUT DAD, ITS JUST YOU AND ME HERE SO I'M GONNA BE BLUNT:
YOU GOT LUCKY. YOU PULLED A COUPLE ON-AIR PR STUNTS AND THEY PAID OFF. BUT THAT'S NOT COOKING.
I COOKED! WHAT ABOUT THAT TUNA?
YOU CAN MAYBE TECHNICALLY CALL THAT COOKING, BUT IT'S NOT GOING TO CUT IT NEXT TIME. COME ON, DAD! LET'S COOK SOME FUCKING FOOD!
DID I TEACH YOU TO TALK LIKE THAT?
YES!
I'M ONE OF THE WORLD'S MOST FAMOUS CHEFS, I'LL HAVE YOU KNOW.
YEAH, MAYBE. BUT YOU STALLED OUT SOMEWHERE IN ASIA AND THE WORLD'S BEEN MOVING ON WITHOUT YOU. TIME TO KNOCK THE RUST OFF. MAKE ME SOME EGGS.
...YOU WANT EGGS? WHAT, LIKE WHEN YOU WERE A LITTLE KID AND I MADE YOU A SCRAMBLE BEFORE SCHOOL?
SURE. WHATEVER. JUST MAKE ME SOME EGGS.
RIGHT NOW.
...

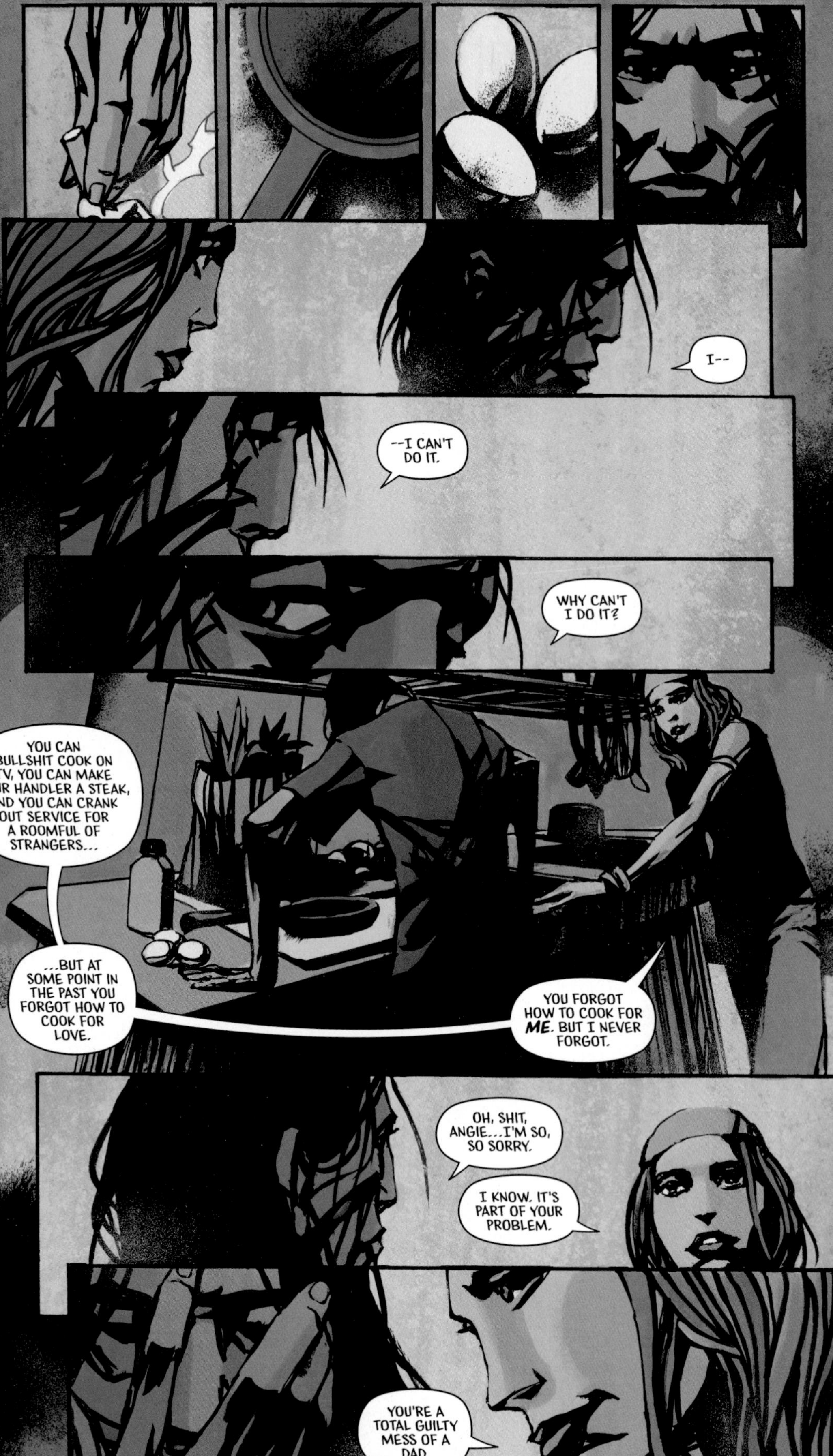
I--
--I CAN'T DO IT.
WHY CAN'T I DO IT?
YOU CAN BULLSHIT COOK ON TV, YOU CAN MAKE YOUR HANDLER A STEAK, AND YOU CAN CRANK OUT SERVICE FOR A ROOMFUL OF STRANGERS...
...BUT AT SOME POINT IN THE PAST YOU FORGOT HOW TO COOK FOR LOVE.
YOU FORGOT HOW TO COOK FOR ME. BUT I NEVER FORGOT.
OH, SHIT, ANGIE...I'M SO, SO SORRY.
I KNOW. IT'S PART OF YOUR PROBLEM.
YOU'RE A TOTAL GUILTY MESS OF A DAD.

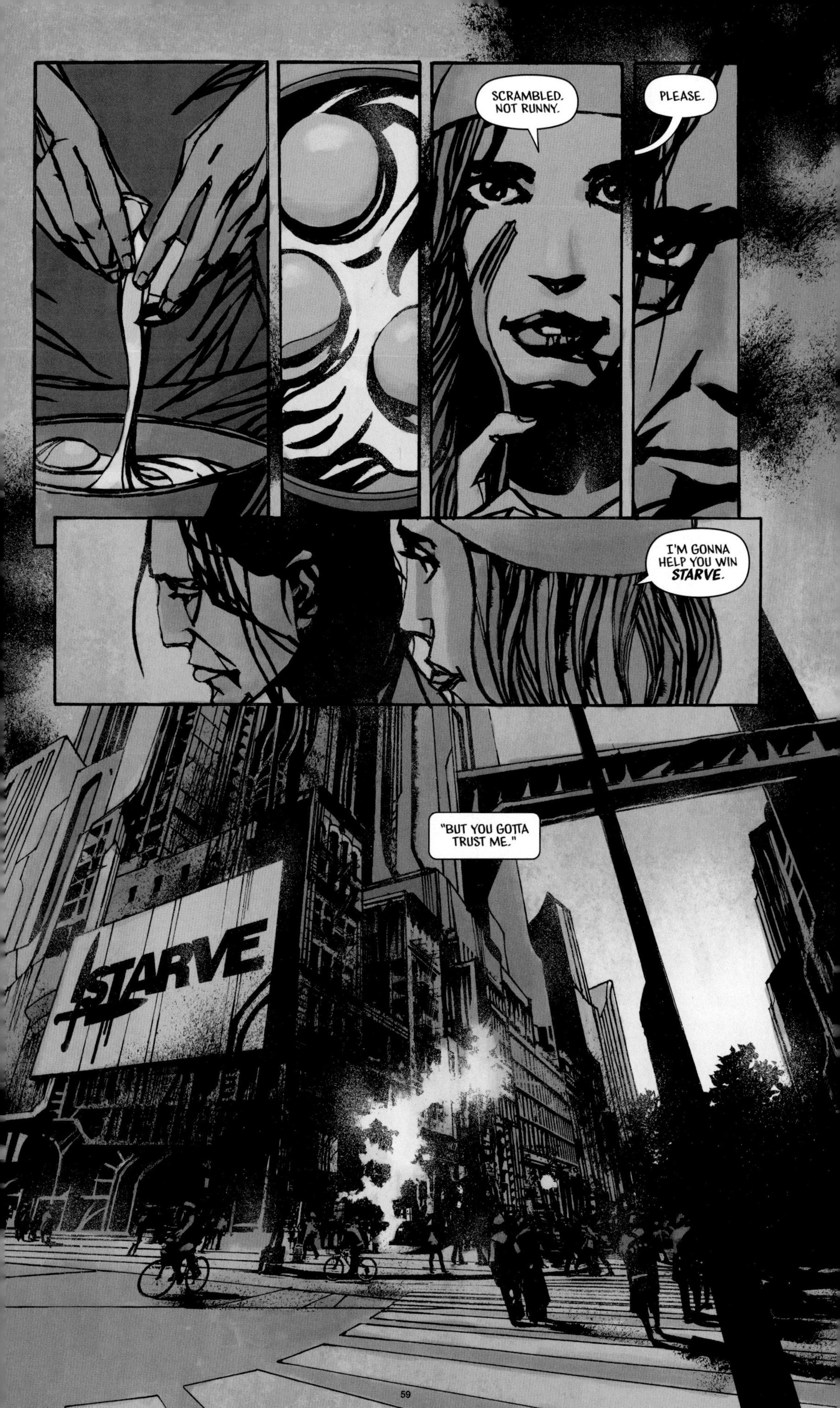
SCRAMBLED. NOT RUNNY.
PLEASE.
I'M GONNA HELP YOU WIN STARVE.
"BUT YOU GOTTA TRUST ME."
STARVE

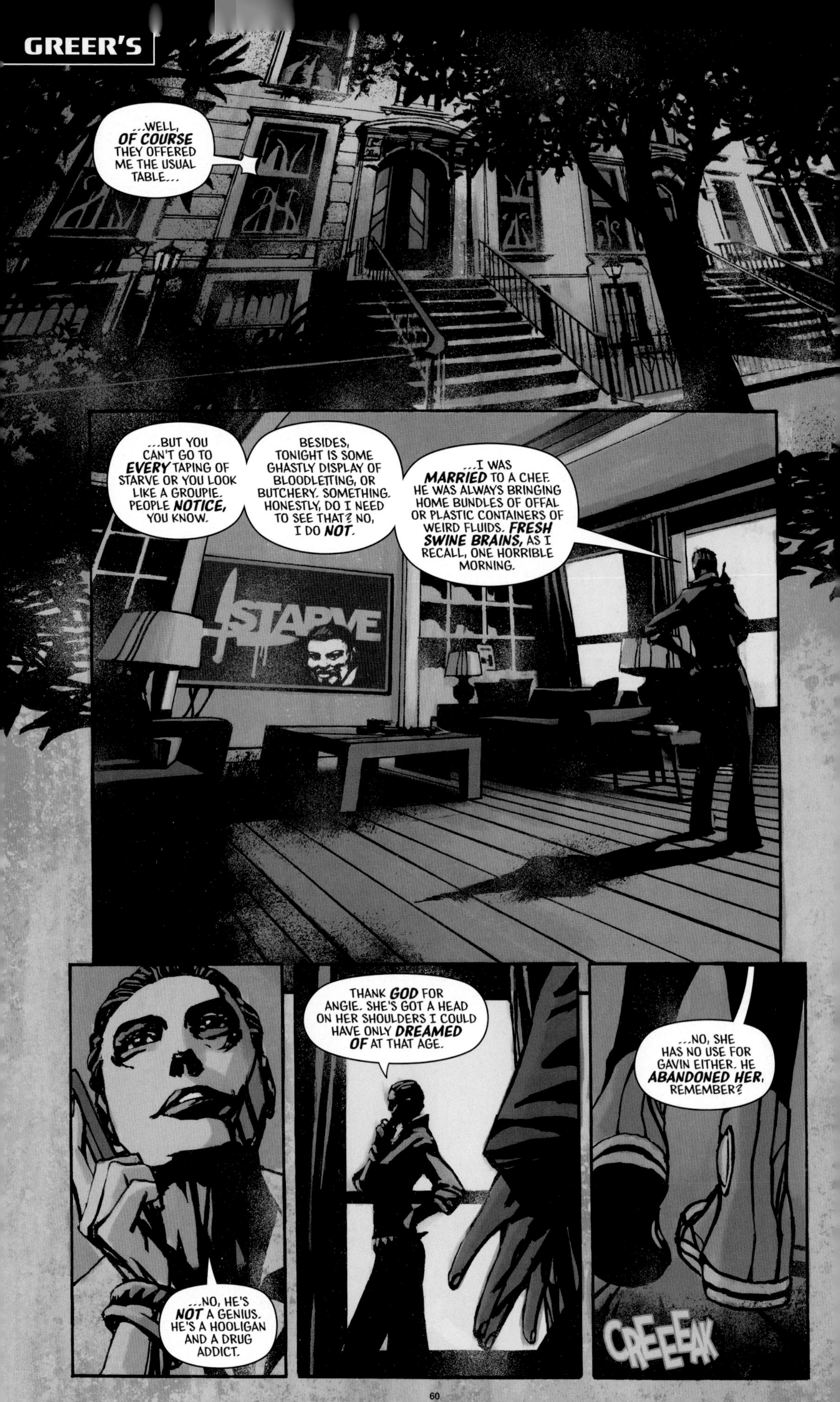
GREER'S
...WELL, OF COURSE THEY OFFERED ME THE USUAL TABLE...
...BUT YOU CAN'T GO TO EVERY TAPING OF STARVE OR YOU LOOK LIKE A GROUPIE. PEOPLE NOTICE, YOU KNOW.
BESIDES, TONIGHT IS SOME GHASTLY DISPLAY OF BLOODLETTING, OR BUTCHERY. SOMETHING. HONESTLY, DO I NEED TO SEE THAT? NO, I DO NOT.
...I WAS MARRIED TO A CHEF. HE WAS ALWAYS BRINGING HOME BUNDLES OF OFFAL OR PLASTIC CONTAINERS OF WEIRD FLUIDS. FRESH SWINE BRAINS, AS I RECALL, ONE HORRIBLE MORNING.
STARVE
...NO, HE'S NOT A GENIUS. HE'S A HOOLIGAN AND A DRUG ADDICT.
THANK GOD FOR ANGIE. SHE'S GOT A HEAD ON HER SHOULDERS I COULD HAVE ONLY DREAMED OF AT THAT AGE.
...NO, SHE HAS NO USE FOR GAVIN EITHER. HE ABANDONED HER, REMEMBER?
CREEEAK

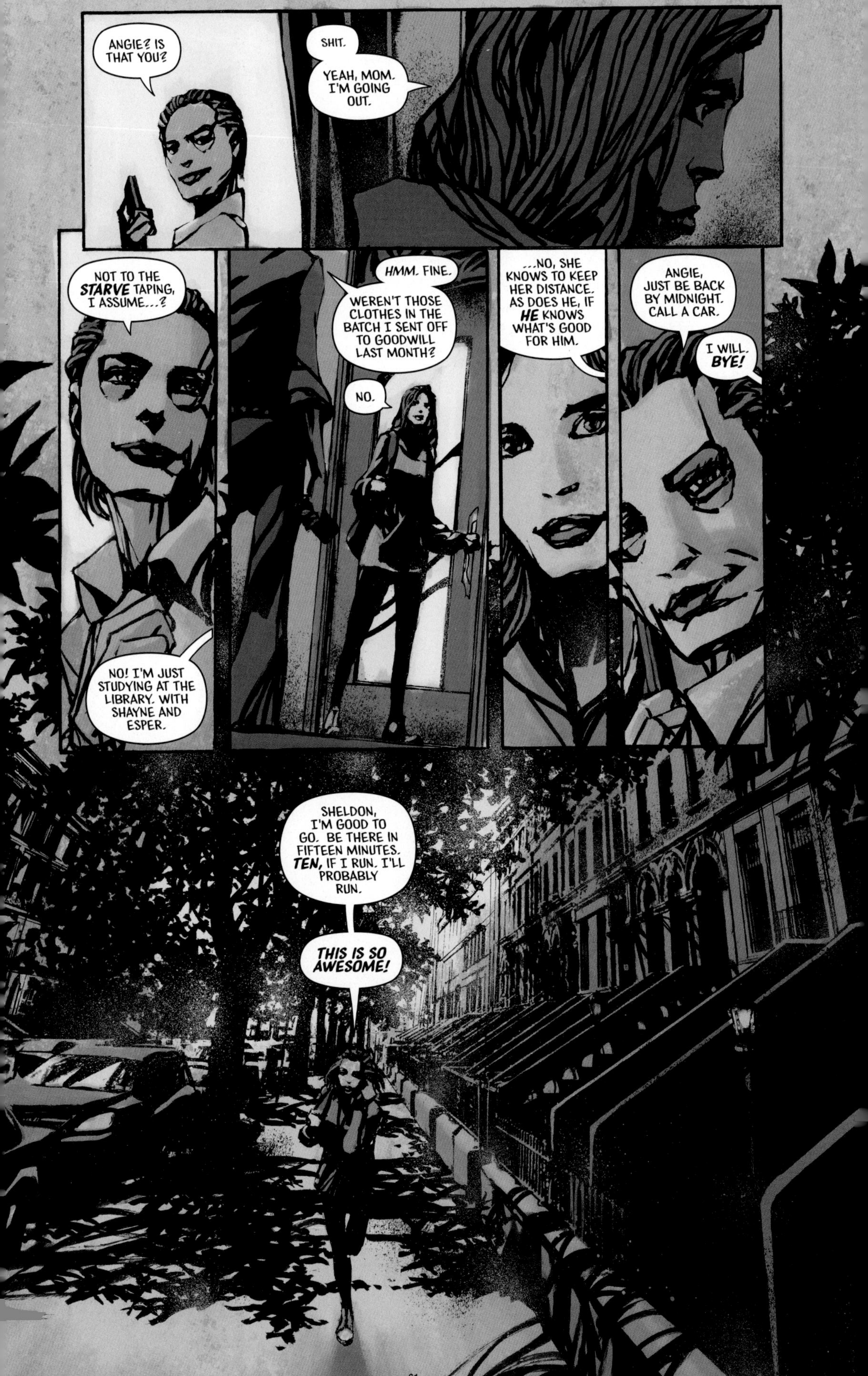

ANGIE? IS THAT YOU?
SHIT.
YEAH, MOM. I'M GOING OUT.
NOT TO THE STARVE TAPING, I ASSUME...?
NO! I'M JUST STUDYING AT THE LIBRARY. WITH SHAYNE AND ESPER.
HMM. FINE.
WEREN'T THOSE CLOTHES IN THE BATCH I SENT OFF TO GOODWILL LAST MONTH?
NO.
...NO, SHE KNOWS TO KEEP HER DISTANCE. AS DOES HE, IF HE KNOWS WHAT'S GOOD FOR HIM.
ANGIE, JUST BE BACK BY MIDNIGHT. CALL A CAR.
I WILL. BYE!
SHELDON, I'M GOOD TO GO. BE THERE IN FIFTEEN MINUTES. TEN, IF I RUN. I'LL PROBABLY RUN.
THIS IS SO AWESOME!

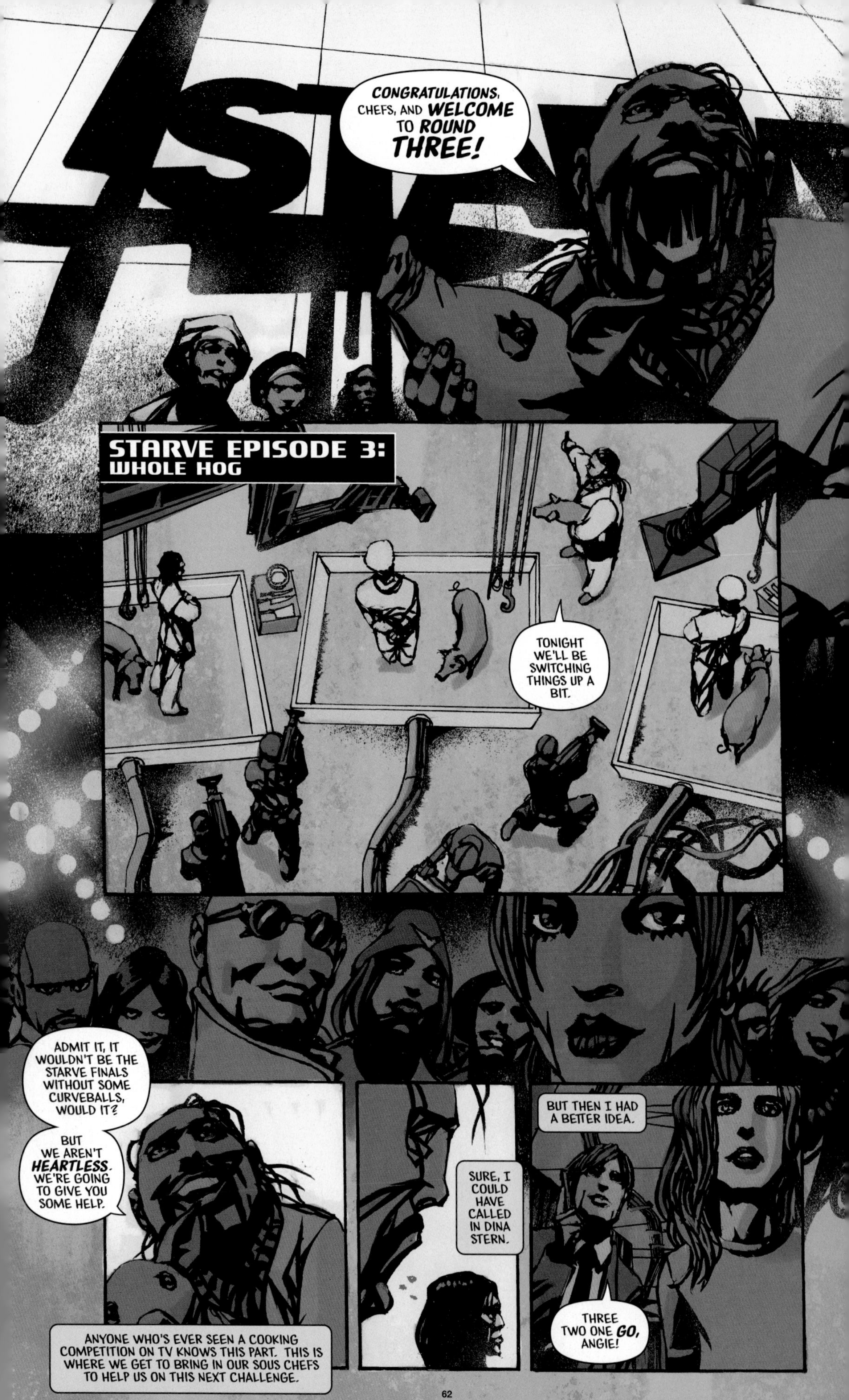

CONGRATULATIONS, CHEFS, AND WELCOME TO ROUND THREE!
STARVE EPISODE 3: WHOLE HOG
TONIGHT WE'LL BE SWITCHING THINGS UP A BIT.
ADMIT IT, IT WOULDN'T BE THE STARVE FINALS WITHOUT SOME CURVEBALLS, WOULD IT?
BUT WE AREN'T HEARTLESS. WE'RE GOING TO GIVE YOU SOME HELP.
ANYONE WHO'S EVER SEEN A COOKING COMPETITION ON TV KNOWS THIS PART. THIS IS WHERE WE GET TO BRING IN OUR SOUS CHEFS TO HELP US ON THIS NEXT CHALLENGE.
SURE, I COULD HAVE CALLED IN DINA STERN.
BUT THEN I HAD A BETTER IDEA.
THREE TWO ONE GO, ANGIE!

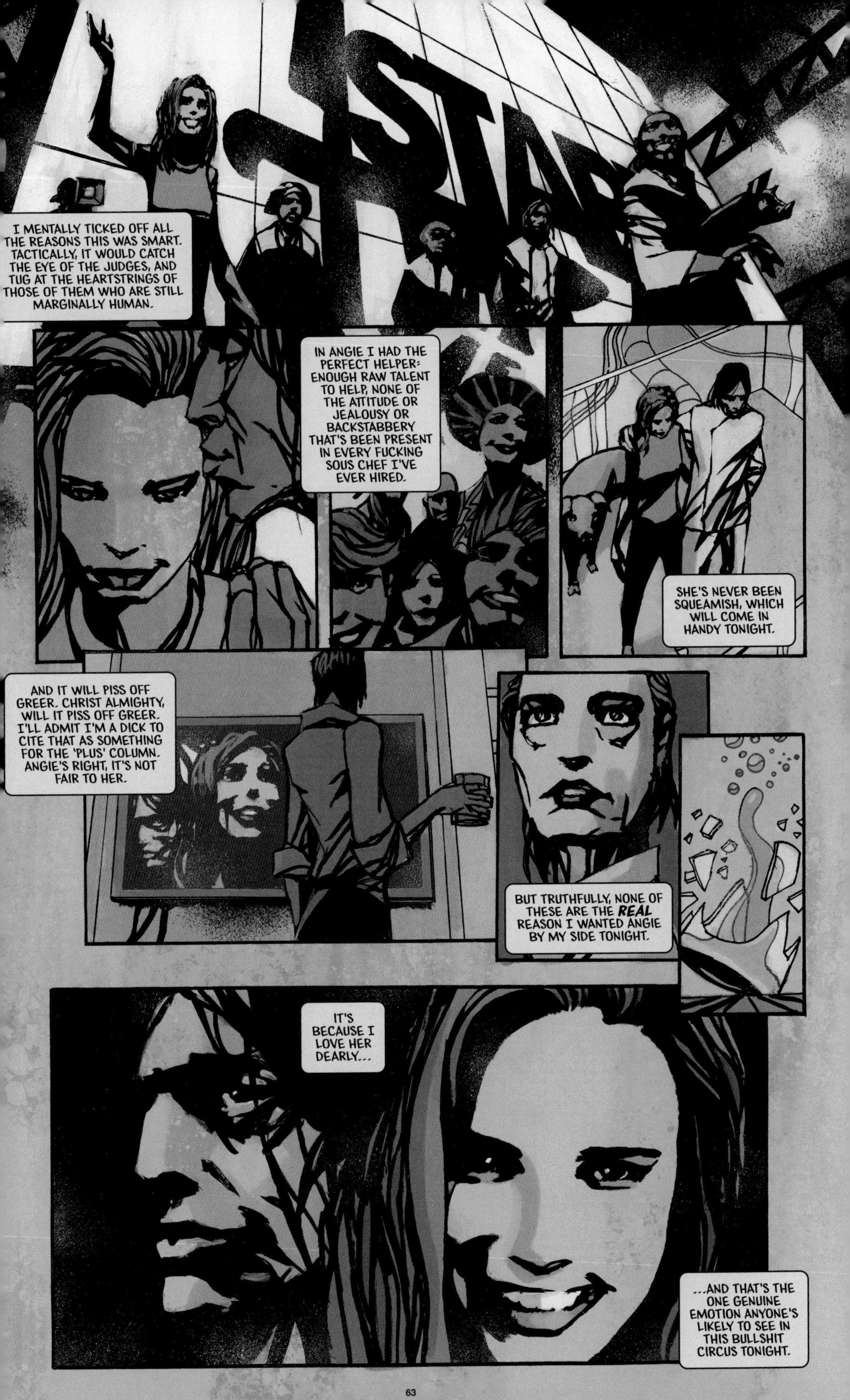

I MENTALLY TICKED OFF ALL THE REASONS THIS WAS SMART. TACTICALLY, IT WOULD CATCH THE EYE OF THE JUDGES, AND TUG AT THE HEARTSTRINGS OF THOSE OF THEM WHO ARE STILL MARGINALLY HUMAN.
STAR
IN ANGIE I HAD THE PERFECT HELPER: ENOUGH RAW TALENT TO HELP, NONE OF THE ATTITUDE OR JEALOUSY OR BACKSTABBERY THAT'S BEEN PRESENT IN EVERY FUCKING SOUS CHEF I'VE EVER HIRED.
SHE'S NEVER BEEN SQUEAMISH, WHICH WILL COME IN HANDY TONIGHT.
AND IT WILL PISS OFF GREER. CHRIST ALMIGHTY, WILL IT PISS OFF GREER. I'LL ADMIT I'M A DICK TO CITE THAT AS SOMETHING FOR THE 'PLUS' COLUMN. ANGIE'S RIGHT, IT'S NOT FAIR TO HER.
BUT TRUTHFULLY, NONE OF THESE ARE THE ***REAL*** REASON I WANTED ANGIE BY MY SIDE TONIGHT.
IT'S BECAUSE I LOVE HER DEARLY...
...AND THAT'S THE ONE GENUINE EMOTION ANYONE'S LIKELY TO SEE IN THIS BULLSHIT CIRCUS TONIGHT.

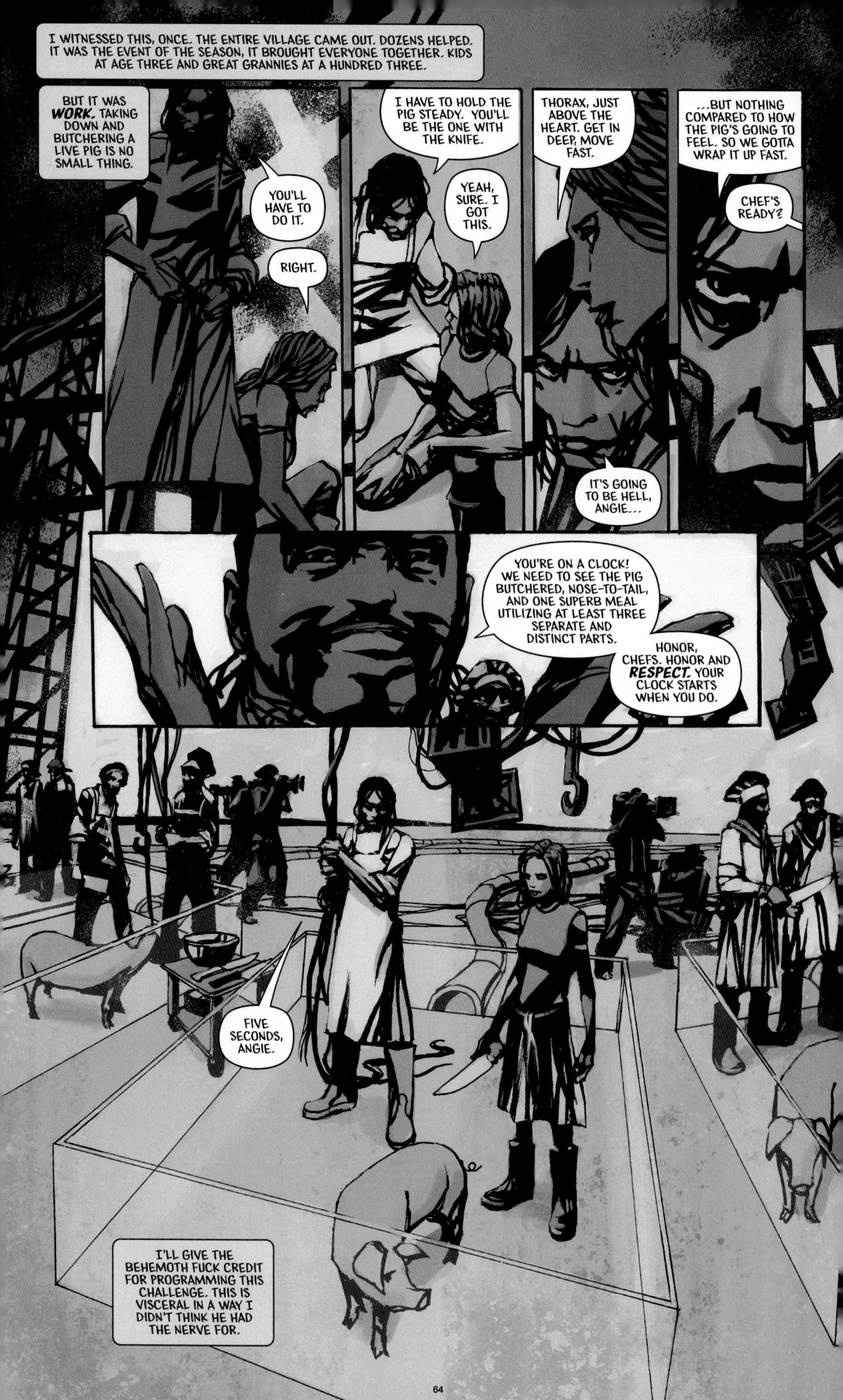

I WITNESSED THIS, ONCE. THE ENTIRE VILLAGE CAME OUT. DOZENS HELPED. IT WAS THE EVENT OF THE SEASON, IT BROUGHT EVERYONE TOGETHER. KIDS AT AGE THREE AND GREAT GRANNIES AT A HUNDRED THREE.
BUT IT WAS **WORK.** TAKING DOWN AND BUTCHERING A LIVE PIG IS NO SMALL THING.
YOU'LL HAVE TO DO IT.
RIGHT.
I HAVE TO HOLD THE PIG STEADY. YOU'LL BE THE ONE WITH THE KNIFE.
YEAH, SURE. I GOT THIS.
THORAX, JUST ABOVE THE HEART. GET IN DEEP, MOVE FAST.
IT'S GOING TO BE HELL, ANGIE...
...BUT NOTHING COMPARED TO HOW THE PIG'S GOING TO FEEL. SO WE GOTTA WRAP IT UP FAST.
CHEF'S READY?
YOU'RE ON A CLOCK! WE NEED TO SEE THE PIG BUTCHERED, NOSE-TO-TAIL, AND ONE SUPERB MEAL UTILIZING AT LEAST THREE SEPARATE AND DISTINCT PARTS.
HONOR, CHEFS. HONOR AND **RESPECT.** YOUR CLOCK STARTS WHEN YOU DO.
FIVE SECONDS, ANGIE.
I'LL GIVE THE BEHEMOTH FUCK CREDIT FOR PROGRAMMING THIS CHALLENGE. THIS IS VISCERAL IN A WAY I DIDN'T THINK HE HAD THE NERVE FOR.

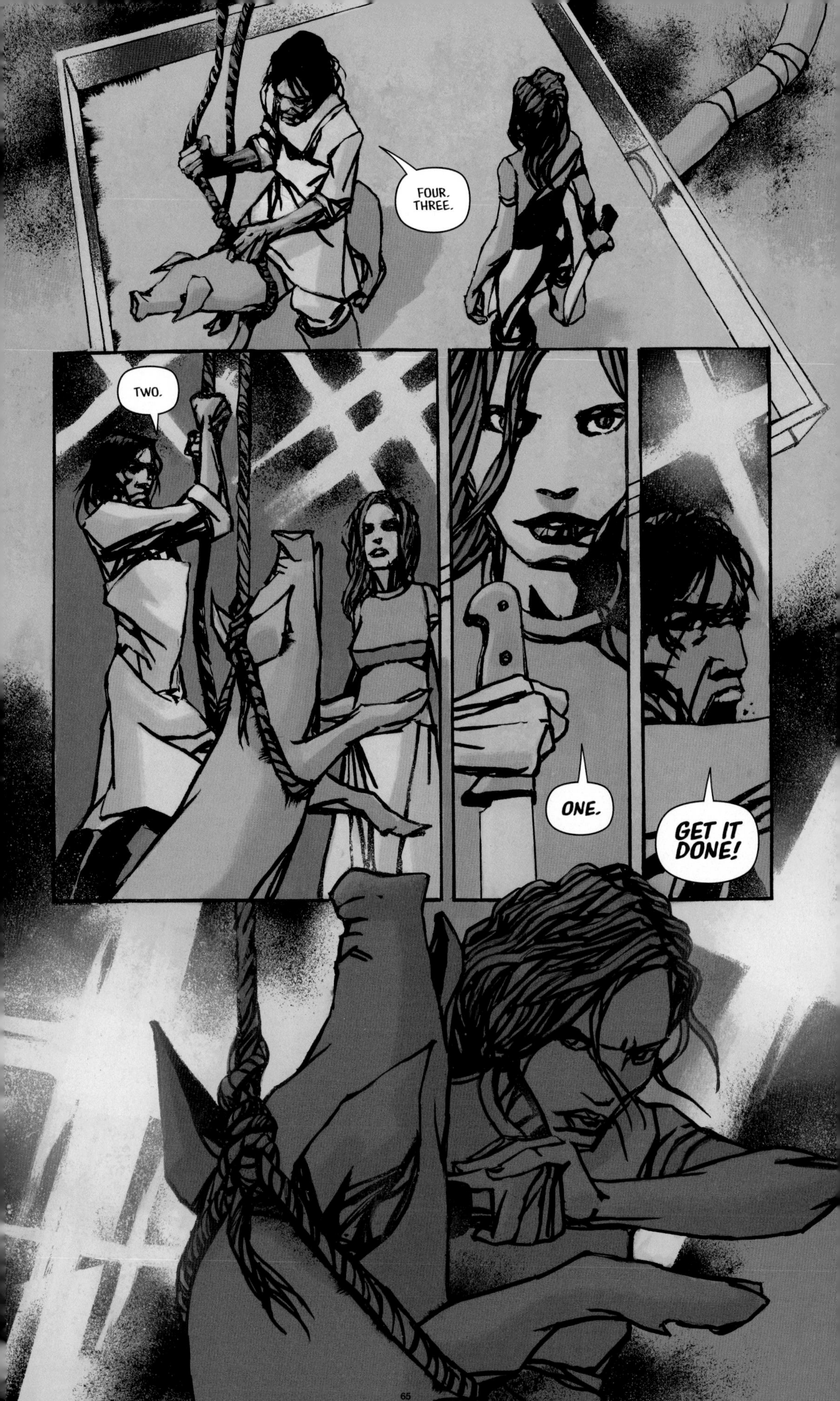
FOUR. THREE.
TWO.
ONE.
GET IT DONE!

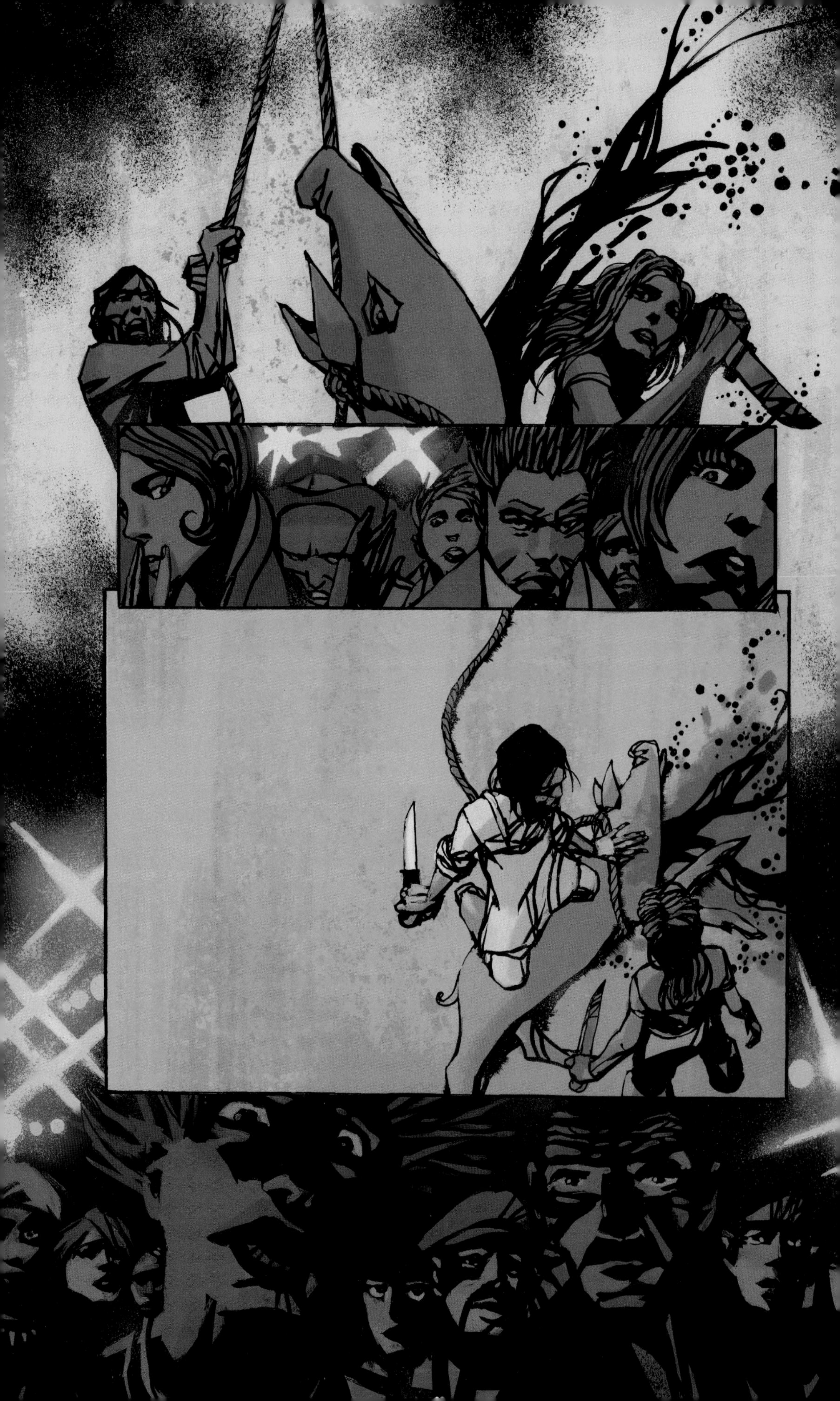

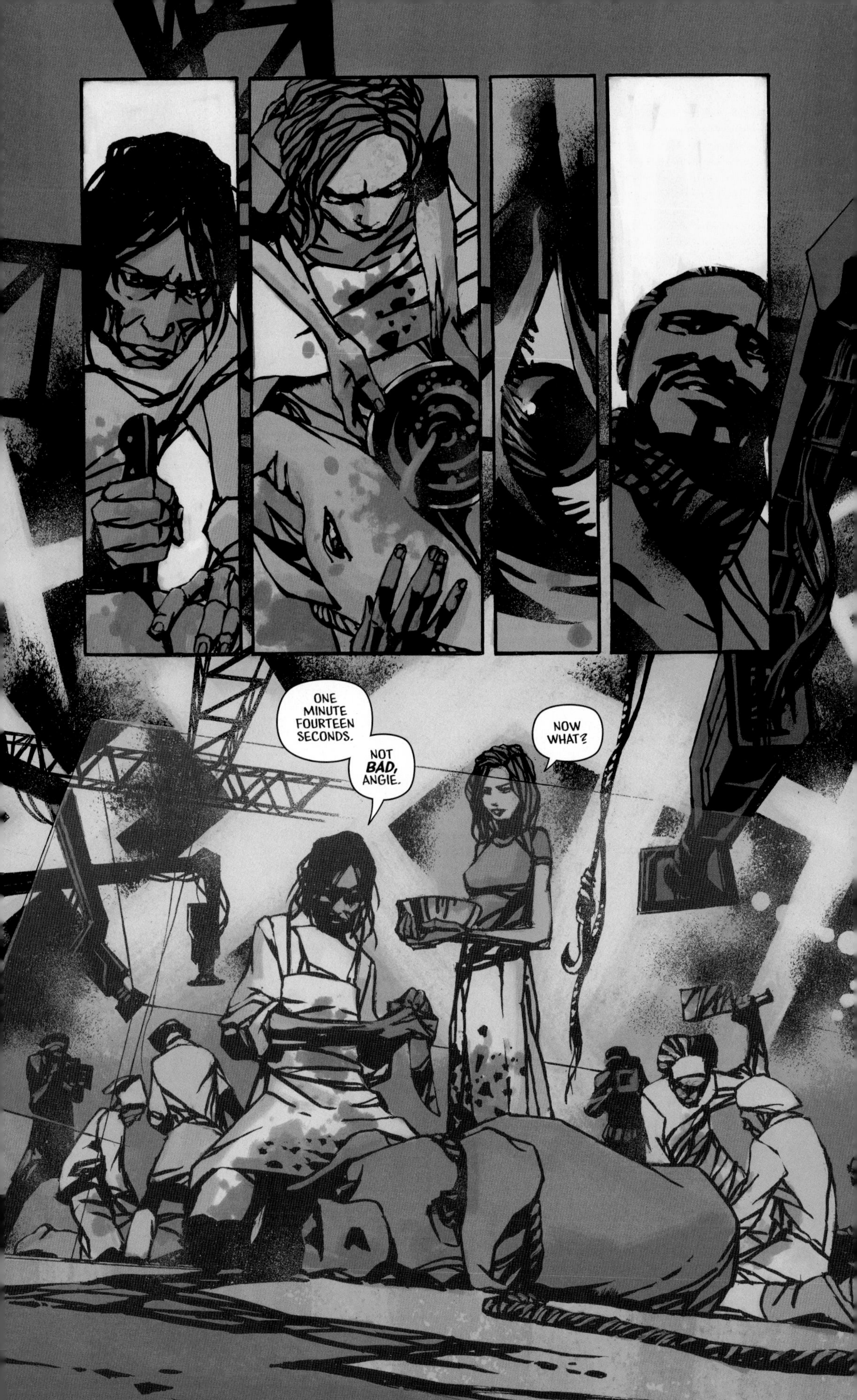
ONE MINUTE FOURTEEN SECONDS.
NOT BAD, ANGIE.
NOW WHAT?

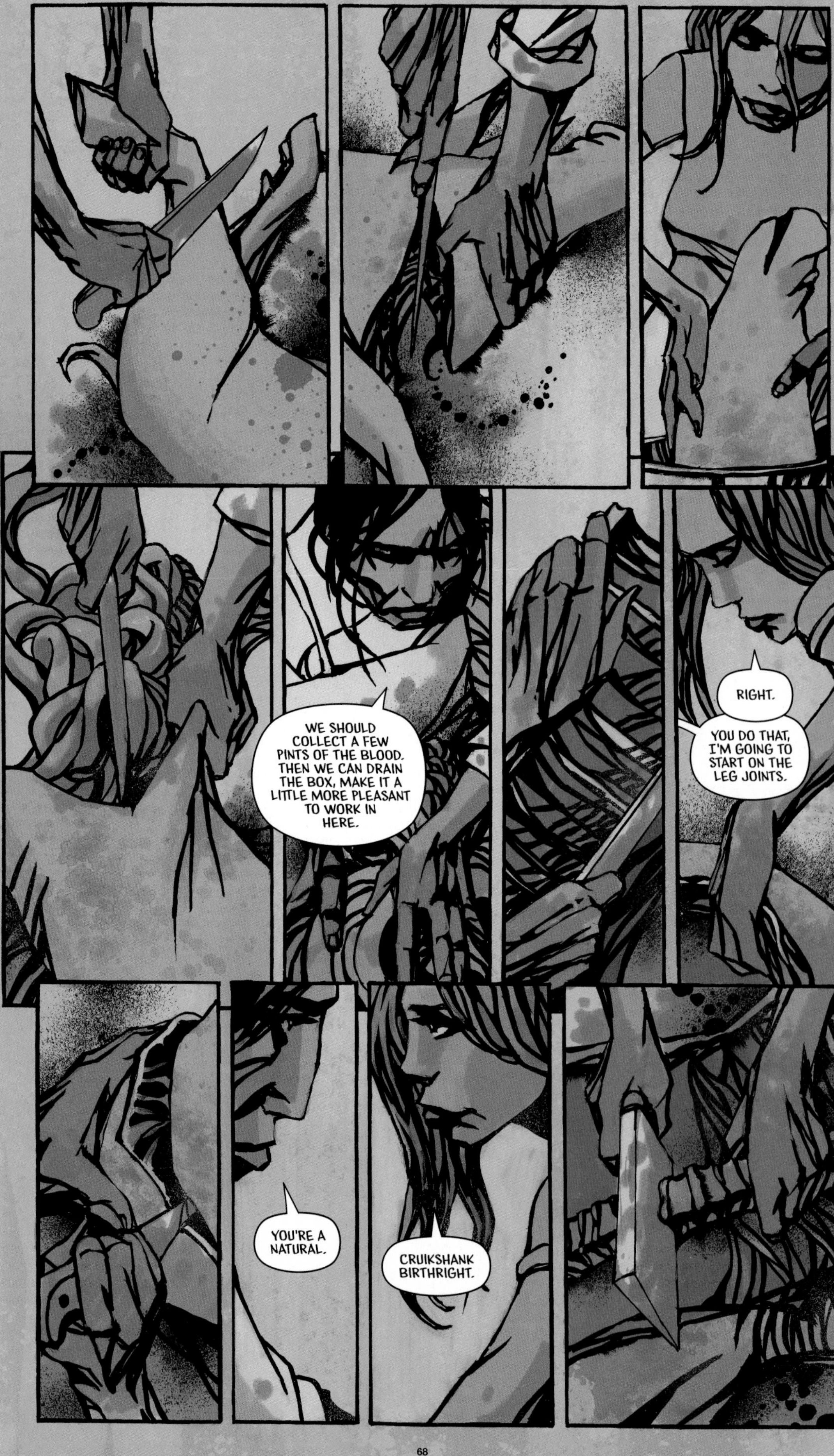
WE SHOULD COLLECT A FEW PINTS OF THE BLOOD. THEN WE CAN DRAIN THE BOX, MAKE IT A LITTLE MORE PLEASANT TO WORK IN HERE.
RIGHT.
YOU DO THAT, I'M GOING TO START ON THE LEG JOINTS.
YOU'RE A NATURAL.
CRUIKSHANK BIRTHRIGHT.

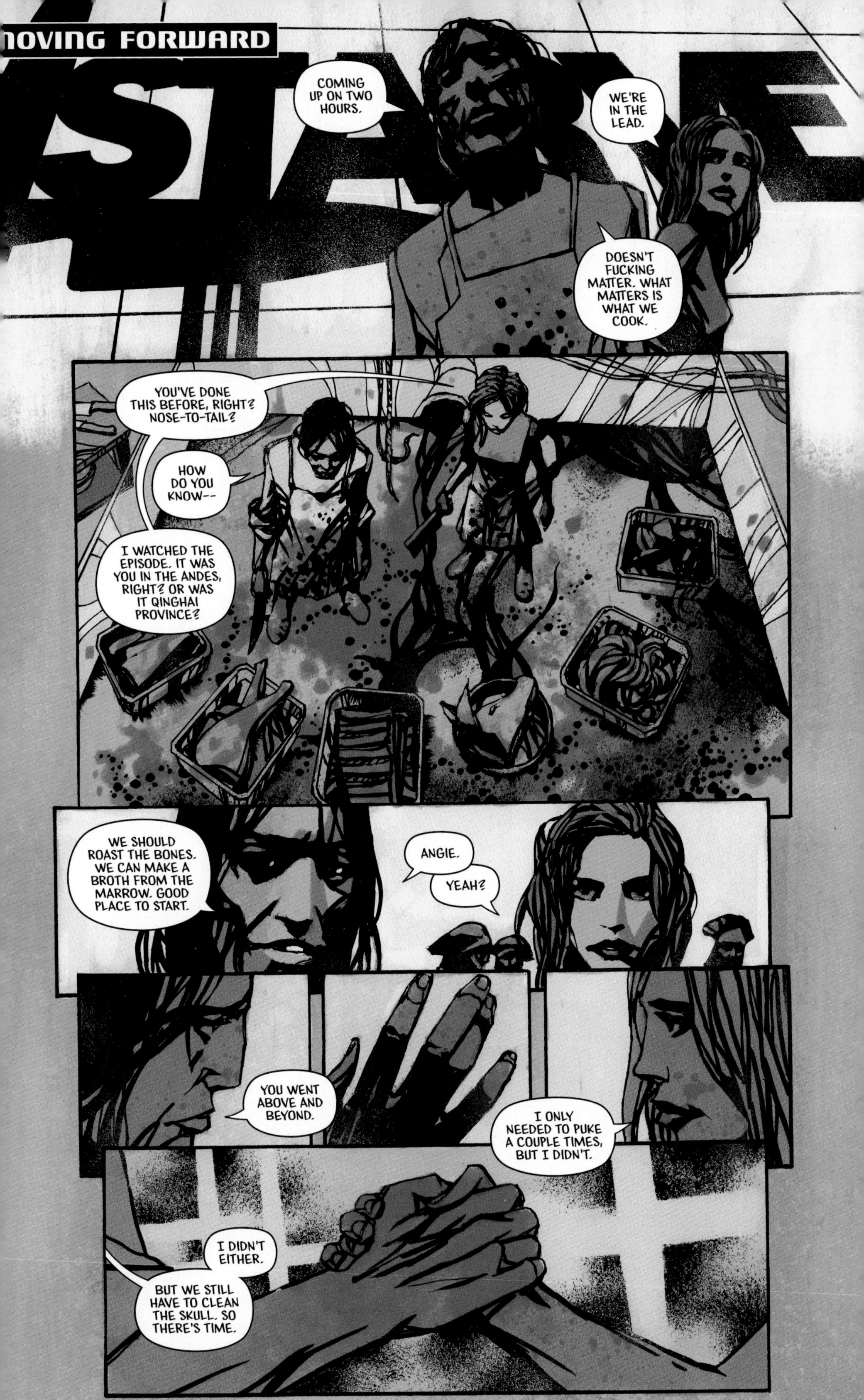
MOVING FORWARD
COMING UP ON TWO HOURS.
WE'RE IN THE LEAD.
DOESN'T FUCKING MATTER. WHAT MATTERS IS WHAT WE COOK.
YOU'VE DONE THIS BEFORE, RIGHT? NOSE-TO-TAIL?
HOW DO YOU KNOW--
I WATCHED THE EPISODE. IT WAS YOU IN THE ANDES, RIGHT? OR WAS IT QINGHAI PROVINCE?
WE SHOULD ROAST THE BONES. WE CAN MAKE A BROTH FROM THE MARROW. GOOD PLACE TO START.
ANGIE.
YEAH?
YOU WENT ABOVE AND BEYOND.
I ONLY NEEDED TO PUKE A COUPLE TIMES, BUT I DIDN'T.
I DIDN'T EITHER.
BUT WE STILL HAVE TO CLEAN THE SKULL. SO THERE'S TIME.

STARVE

PHASE TWO OF THE EVENING! EACH TEAM IS TASKED WITH A PERFECT THREE-COURSE MEAL FOR THE JUDGES.

TRUE NOSE-TO-TAIL COOKING IS *NOT* STUNT COOKING, NOR IS IT A SHOWCASE FOR THE BIZARRE AND RISKY. THIS IS HIGH-END FINE DINING, WORTHY OF *STARVE* AND ITS HONORED GUESTS.

YOU'VE HAD FIVE HOURS TO BUTCHER AND PREP. YOU NOW HAVE NINETY MINUTES TO PREPARE YOUR DISHES.

WHAT'S NEXT, DAD?

I'M THINKING.

I COULD THINK OF AT LEAST *THIRTY DISHES* I COULD EXECUTE IN MY SLEEP, BUT THEY ARE AL 'SAFE' DISHES, AND I WON'T WIN WITH THEM.

ON THE FLIPSIDE, THERE'S A DOZEN OR SO TRULY "EXTREM DISHES THAT I WOULD LOVE T CRAM DOWN THE JUDGES THROATS, BUT TONIGHT ISN'T T NIGHT TO MAKE A STATEMENT ANGIE'S RIGHT ABOUT THAT.

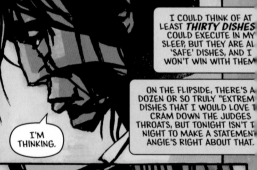

AT LEAST NOT A STATEMENT LIKE THE OTHER TIMES.

SHE'S WORKING TOO HARD FOR ME JUST TO MAKE A MOCKERY OF IT ALL.

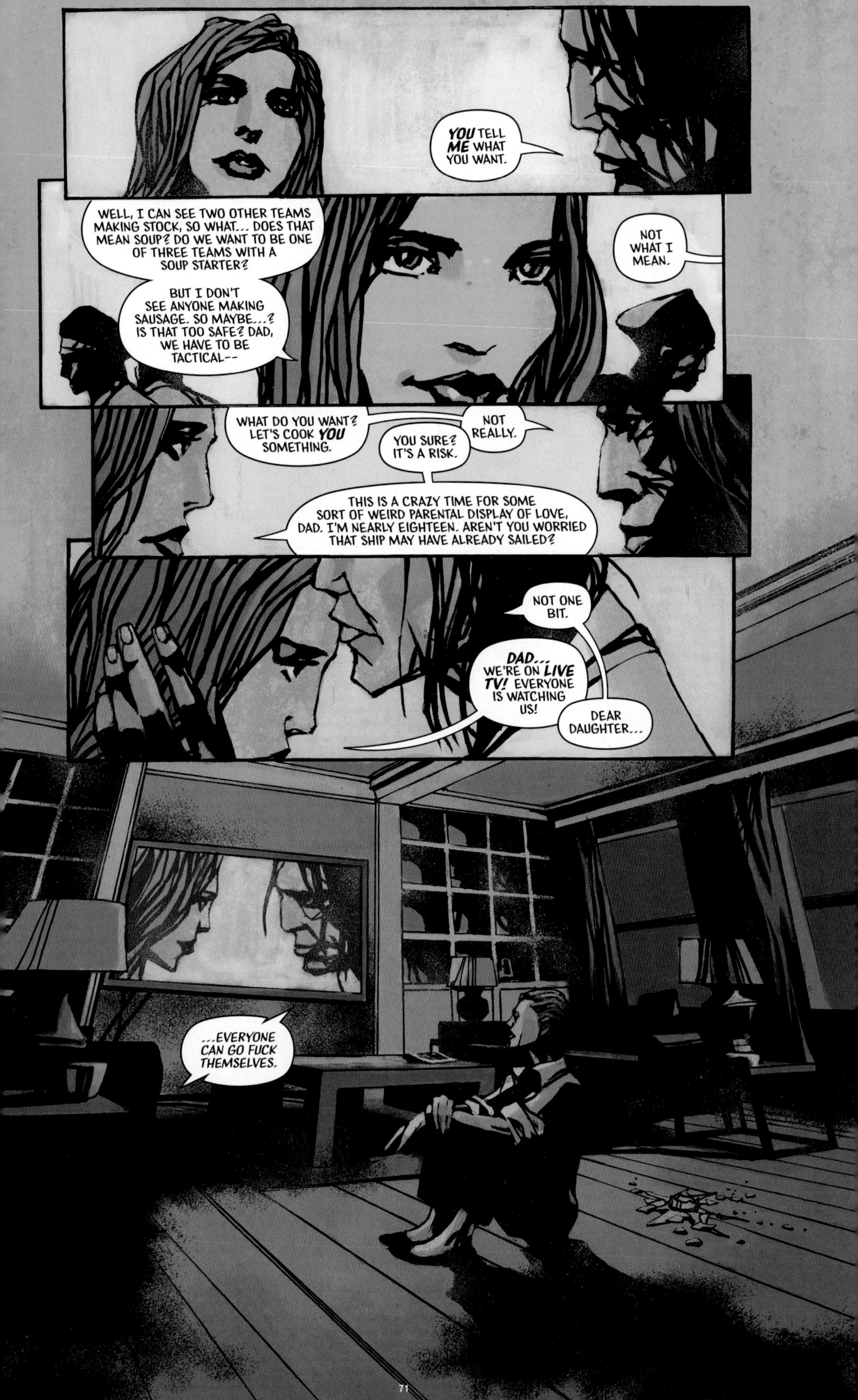
YOU TELL ME WHAT YOU WANT.
WELL, I CAN SEE TWO OTHER TEAMS MAKING STOCK, SO WHAT... DOES THAT MEAN SOUP? DO WE WANT TO BE ONE OF THREE TEAMS WITH A SOUP STARTER?
BUT I DON'T SEE ANYONE MAKING SAUSAGE. SO MAYBE...? IS THAT TOO SAFE? DAD, WE HAVE TO BE TACTICAL--
NOT WHAT I MEAN.
WHAT DO YOU WANT? LET'S COOK YOU SOMETHING.
NOT REALLY.
YOU SURE? IT'S A RISK.
THIS IS A CRAZY TIME FOR SOME SORT OF WEIRD PARENTAL DISPLAY OF LOVE, DAD. I'M NEARLY EIGHTEEN. AREN'T YOU WORRIED THAT SHIP MAY HAVE ALREADY SAILED?
NOT ONE BIT.
DAD... WE'RE ON LIVE TV! EVERYONE IS WATCHING US!
DEAR DAUGHTER...
...EVERYONE CAN GO FUCK THEMSELVES.

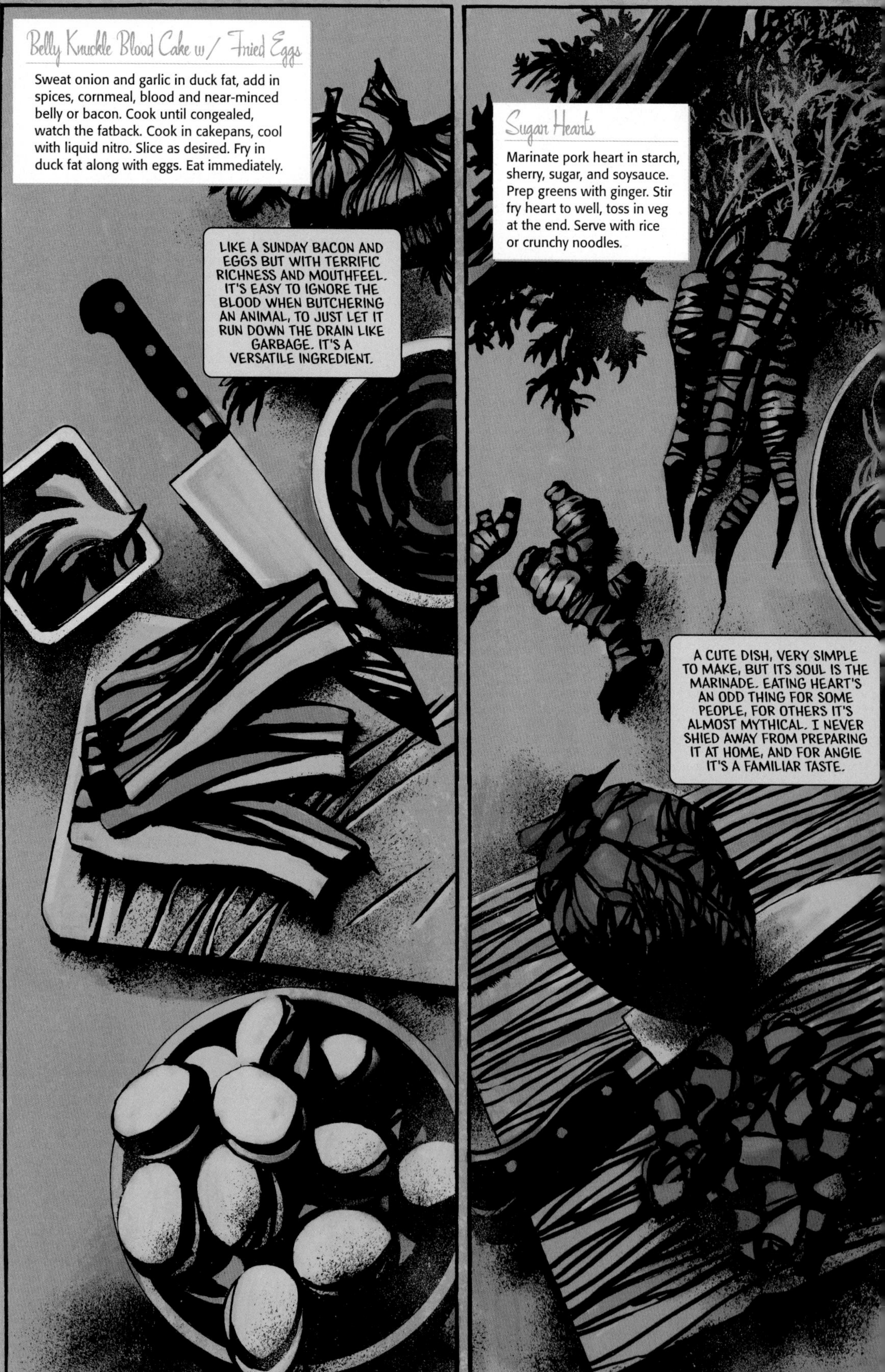
Belly Knuckle Blood Cake w/ Fried Eggs
Sweat onion and garlic in duck fat, add in spices, cornmeal, blood and near-minced belly or bacon. Cook until congealed, watch the fatback. Cook in cakepans, cool with liquid nitro. Slice as desired. Fry in duck fat along with eggs. Eat immediately.
LIKE A SUNDAY BACON AND EGGS BUT WITH TERRIFIC RICHNESS AND MOUTHFEEL. IT'S EASY TO IGNORE THE BLOOD WHEN BUTCHERING AN ANIMAL, TO JUST LET IT RUN DOWN THE DRAIN LIKE GARBAGE. IT'S A VERSATILE INGREDIENT.
Sugar Hearts
Marinate pork heart in starch, sherry, sugar, and soysauce. Prep greens with ginger. Stir fry heart to well, toss in veg at the end. Serve with rice or crunchy noodles.
A CUTE DISH, VERY SIMPLE TO MAKE, BUT ITS SOUL IS THE MARINADE. EATING HEART'S AN ODD THING FOR SOME PEOPLE, FOR OTHERS IT'S ALMOST MYTHICAL. I NEVER SHIED AWAY FROM PREPARING IT AT HOME, AND FOR ANGIE IT'S A FAMILIAR TASTE.

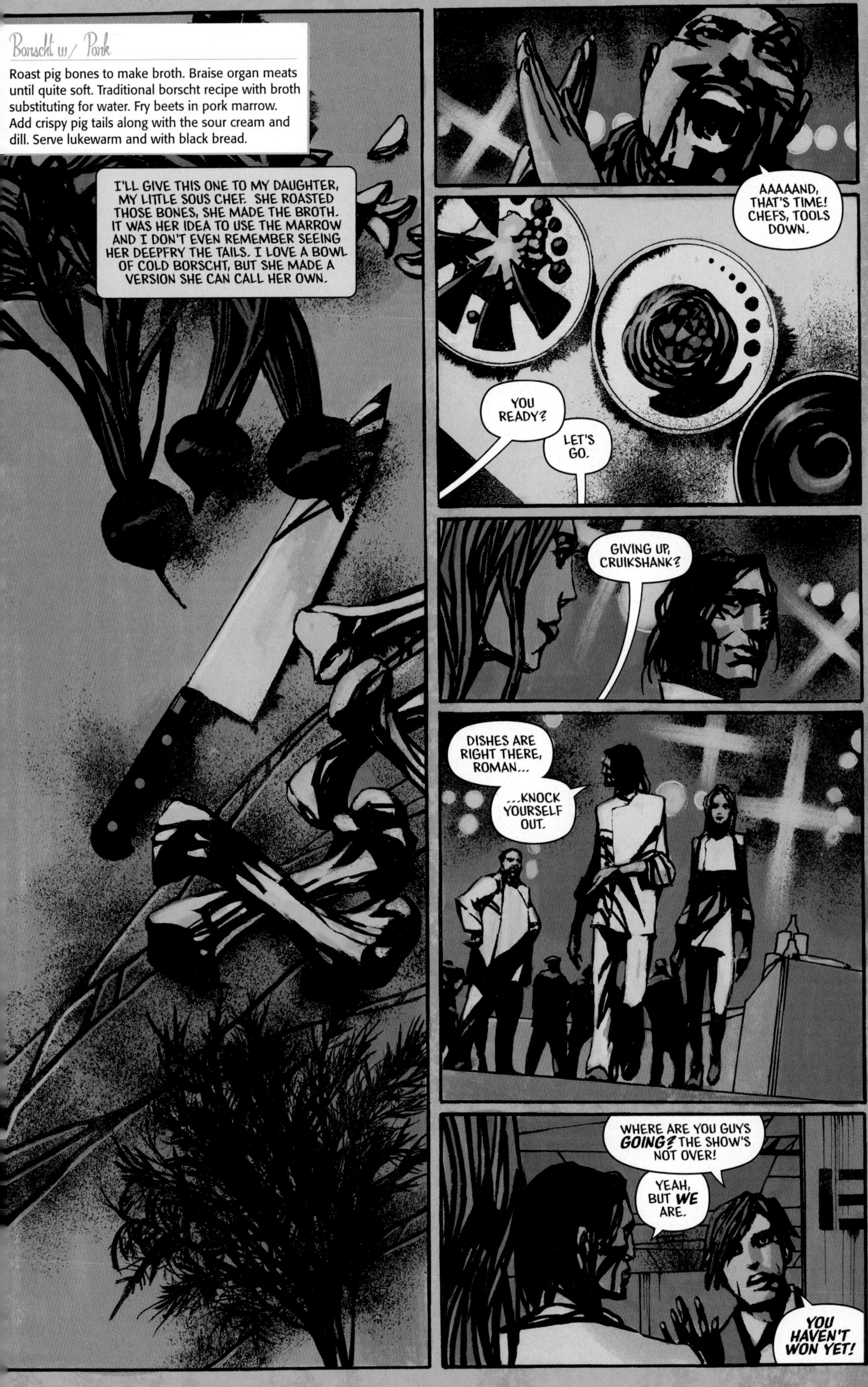
Borscht w/ Pork
Roast pig bones to make broth. Braise organ meats until quite soft. Traditional borscht recipe with broth substituting for water. Fry beets in pork marrow. Add crispy pig tails along with the sour cream and dill. Serve lukewarm and with black bread.
I'LL GIVE THIS ONE TO MY DAUGHTER, MY LITTLE SOUS CHEF. SHE ROASTED THOSE BONES, SHE MADE THE BROTH. IT WAS HER IDEA TO USE THE MARROW AND I DON'T EVEN REMEMBER SEEING HER DEEPFRY THE TAILS. I LOVE A BOWL OF COLD BORSCHT, BUT SHE MADE A VERSION SHE CAN CALL HER OWN.
AAAAAND, THAT'S TIME! CHEFS, TOOLS DOWN.
YOU READY?
LET'S GO.
GIVING UP, CRUIKSHANK?
DISHES ARE RIGHT THERE, ROMAN...
...KNOCK YOURSELF OUT.
WHERE ARE YOU GUYS GOING? THE SHOW'S NOT OVER!
YEAH, BUT WE ARE.
YOU HAVEN'T WON YET!

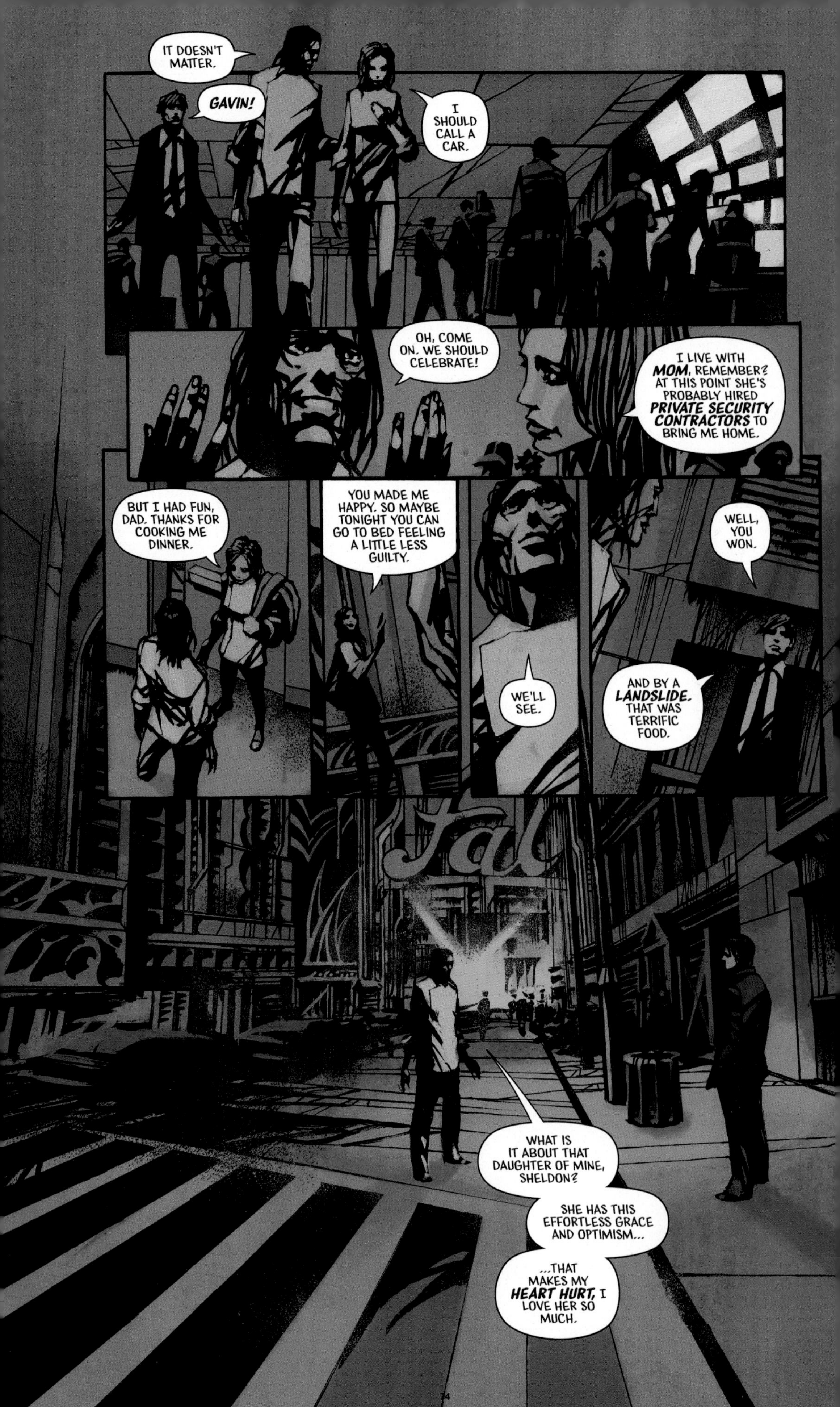
IT DOESN'T MATTER.
GAVIN!
I SHOULD CALL A CAR.
OH, COME ON. WE SHOULD CELEBRATE!
I LIVE WITH MOM, REMEMBER? AT THIS POINT SHE'S PROBABLY HIRED PRIVATE SECURITY CONTRACTORS TO BRING ME HOME.
BUT I HAD FUN, DAD. THANKS FOR COOKING ME DINNER.
YOU MADE ME HAPPY. SO MAYBE TONIGHT YOU CAN GO TO BED FEELING A LITTLE LESS GUILTY.
WE'LL SEE.
WELL, YOU WON.
AND BY A LANDSLIDE. THAT WAS TERRIFIC FOOD.
WHAT IS IT ABOUT THAT DAUGHTER OF MINE, SHELDON?
SHE HAS THIS EFFORTLESS GRACE AND OPTIMISM...
...THAT MAKES MY HEART HURT, I LOVE HER SO MUCH.

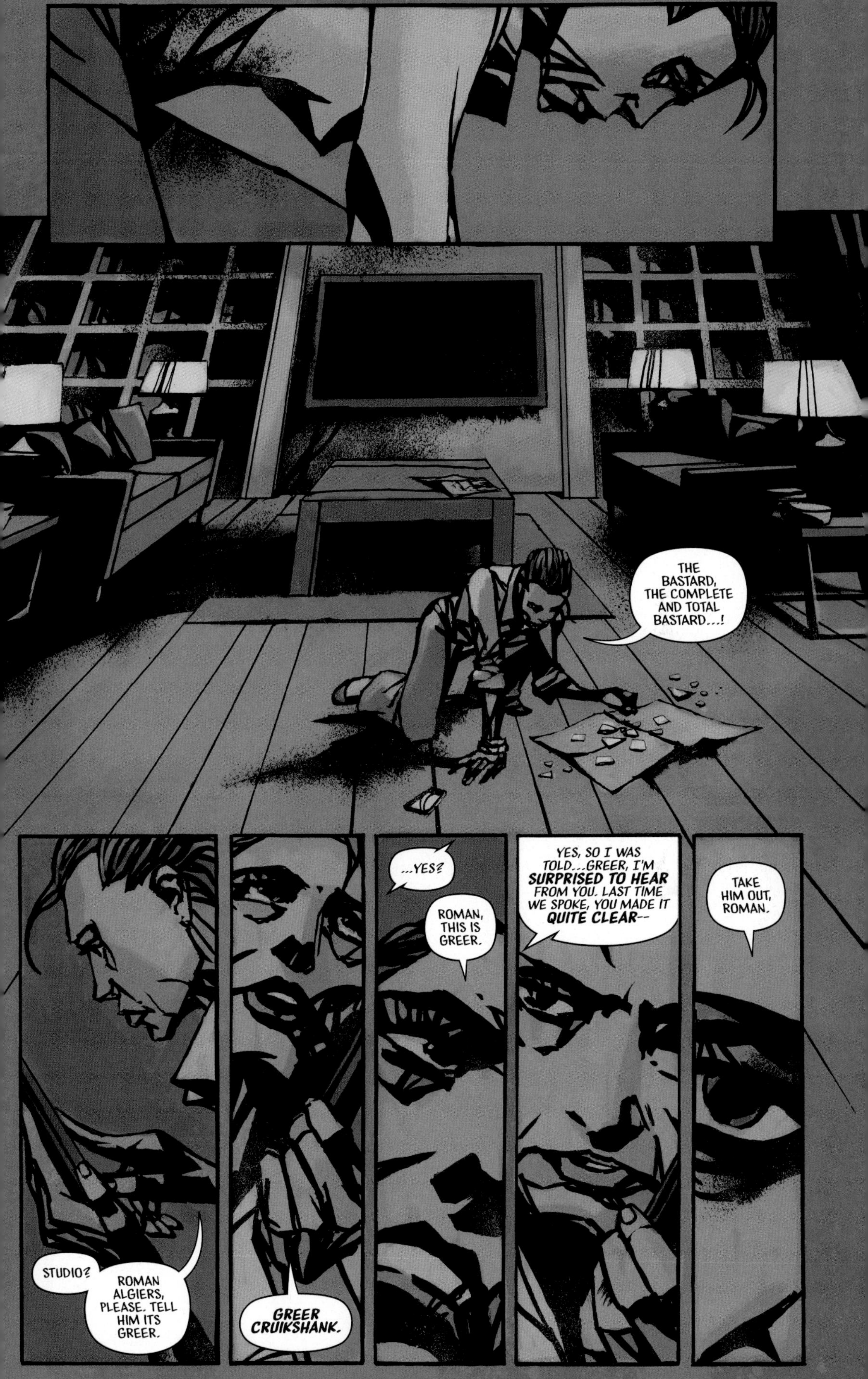
THE BASTARD, THE COMPLETE AND TOTAL BASTARD...!
STUDIO?
ROMAN ALGIERS, PLEASE. TELL HIM ITS GREER.
GREER CRUIKSHANK.
...YES?
ROMAN, THIS IS GREER.
YES, SO I WAS TOLD...GREER, I'M SURPRISED TO HEAR FROM YOU. LAST TIME WE SPOKE, YOU MADE IT QUITE CLEAR--
TAKE HIM OUT, ROMAN.

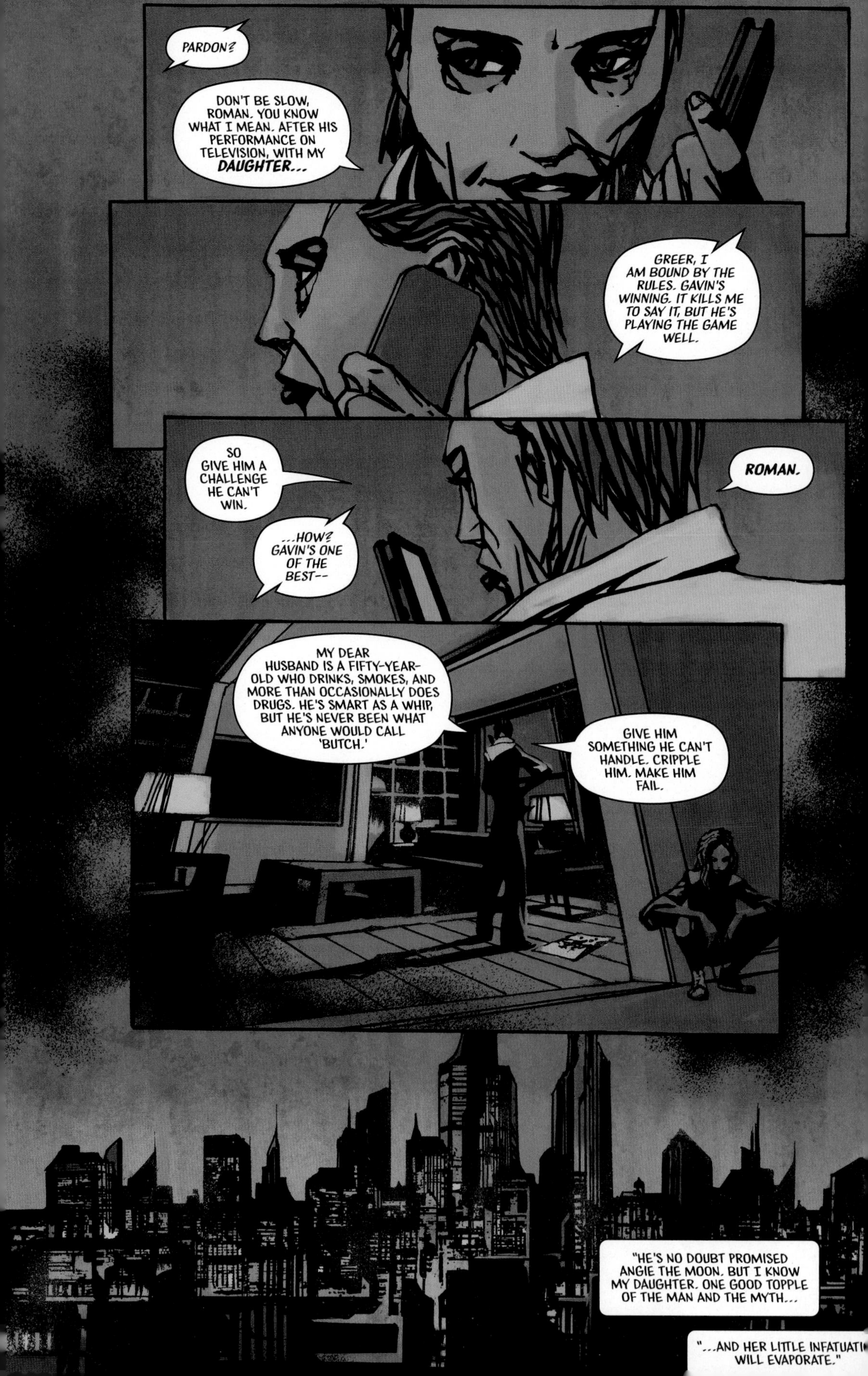
PARDON?
DON'T BE SLOW, ROMAN. YOU KNOW WHAT I MEAN. AFTER HIS PERFORMANCE ON TELEVISION, WITH MY DAUGHTER...
GREER, I AM BOUND BY THE RULES. GAVIN'S WINNING. IT KILLS ME TO SAY IT, BUT HE'S PLAYING THE GAME WELL.
SO GIVE HIM A CHALLENGE HE CAN'T WIN.
...HOW? GAVIN'S ONE OF THE BEST--
ROMAN.
MY DEAR HUSBAND IS A FIFTY-YEAR-OLD WHO DRINKS, SMOKES, AND MORE THAN OCCASIONALLY DOES DRUGS. HE'S SMART AS A WHIP, BUT HE'S NEVER BEEN WHAT ANYONE WOULD CALL 'BUTCH.'
GIVE HIM SOMETHING HE CAN'T HANDLE. CRIPPLE HIM. MAKE HIM FAIL.
"HE'S NO DOUBT PROMISED ANGIE THE MOON. BUT I KNOW MY DAUGHTER. ONE GOOD TOPPLE OF THE MAN AND THE MYTH...
"...AND HER LITTLE INFATUATI WILL EVAPORATE."

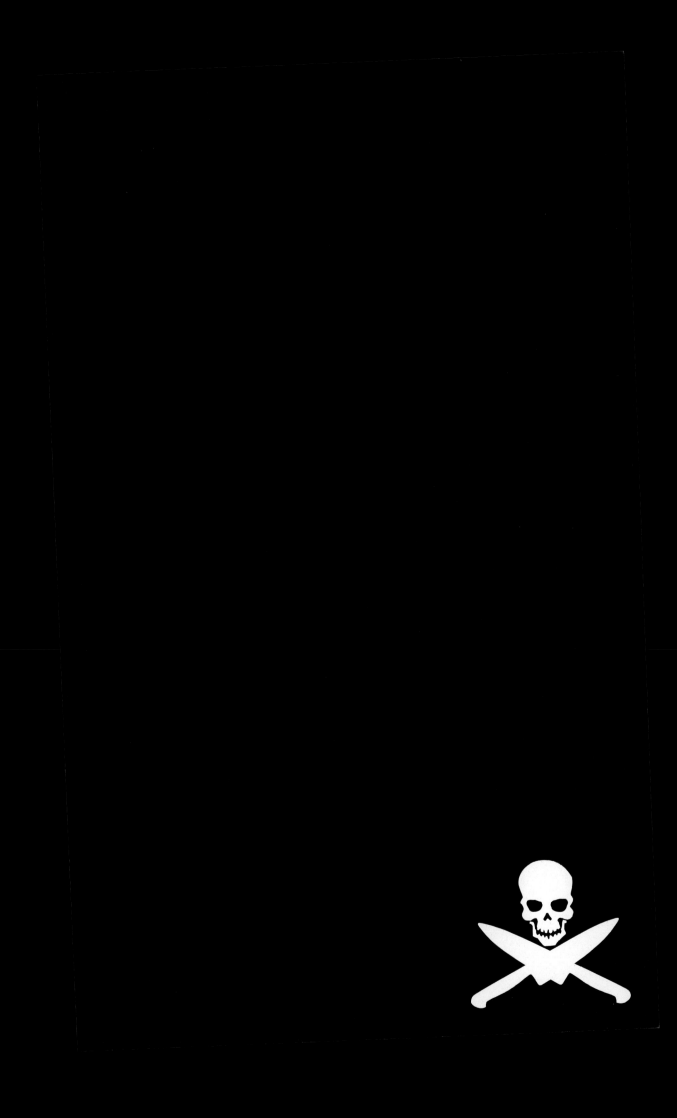

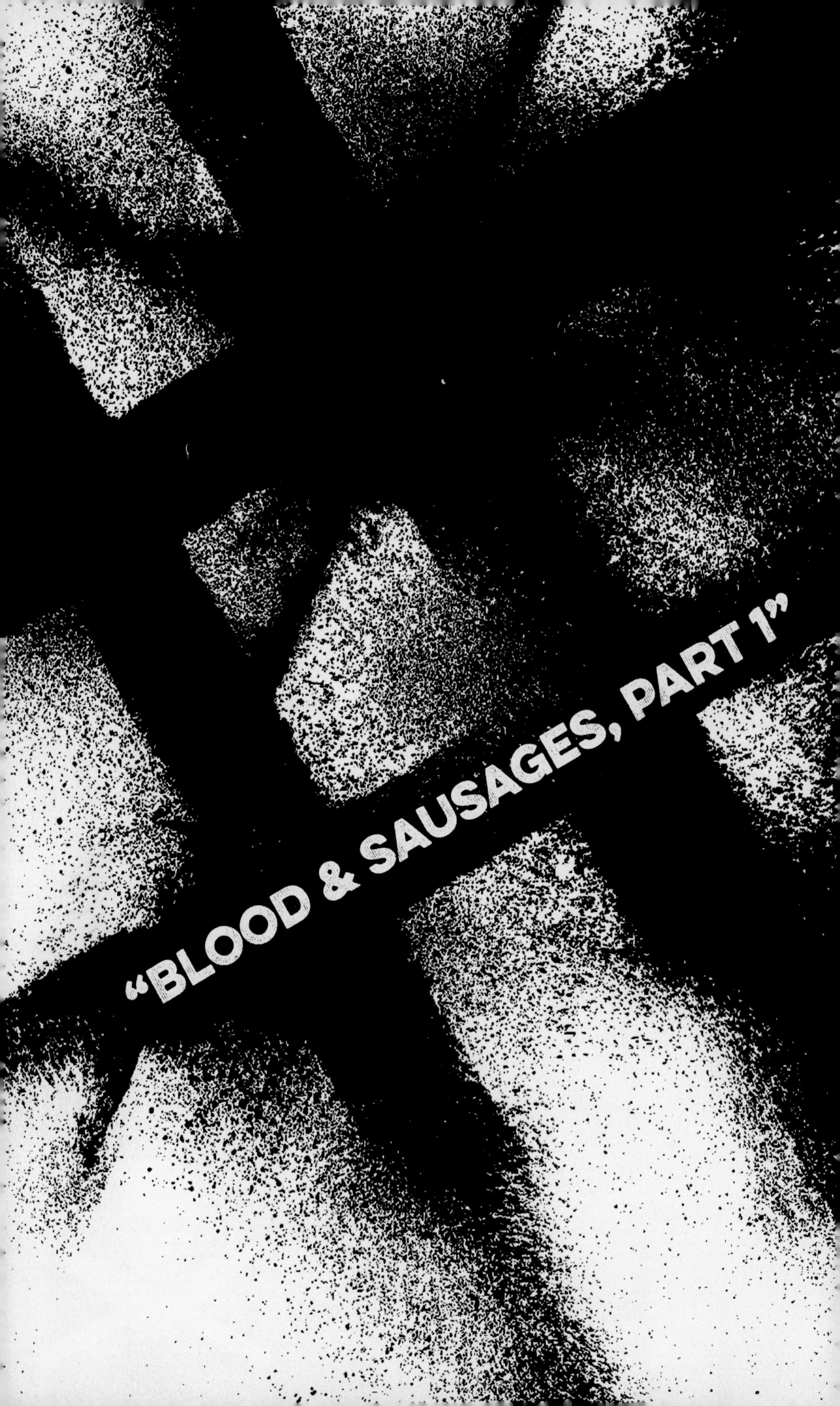

# "BLOOD & SAUSAGES, PART 1"

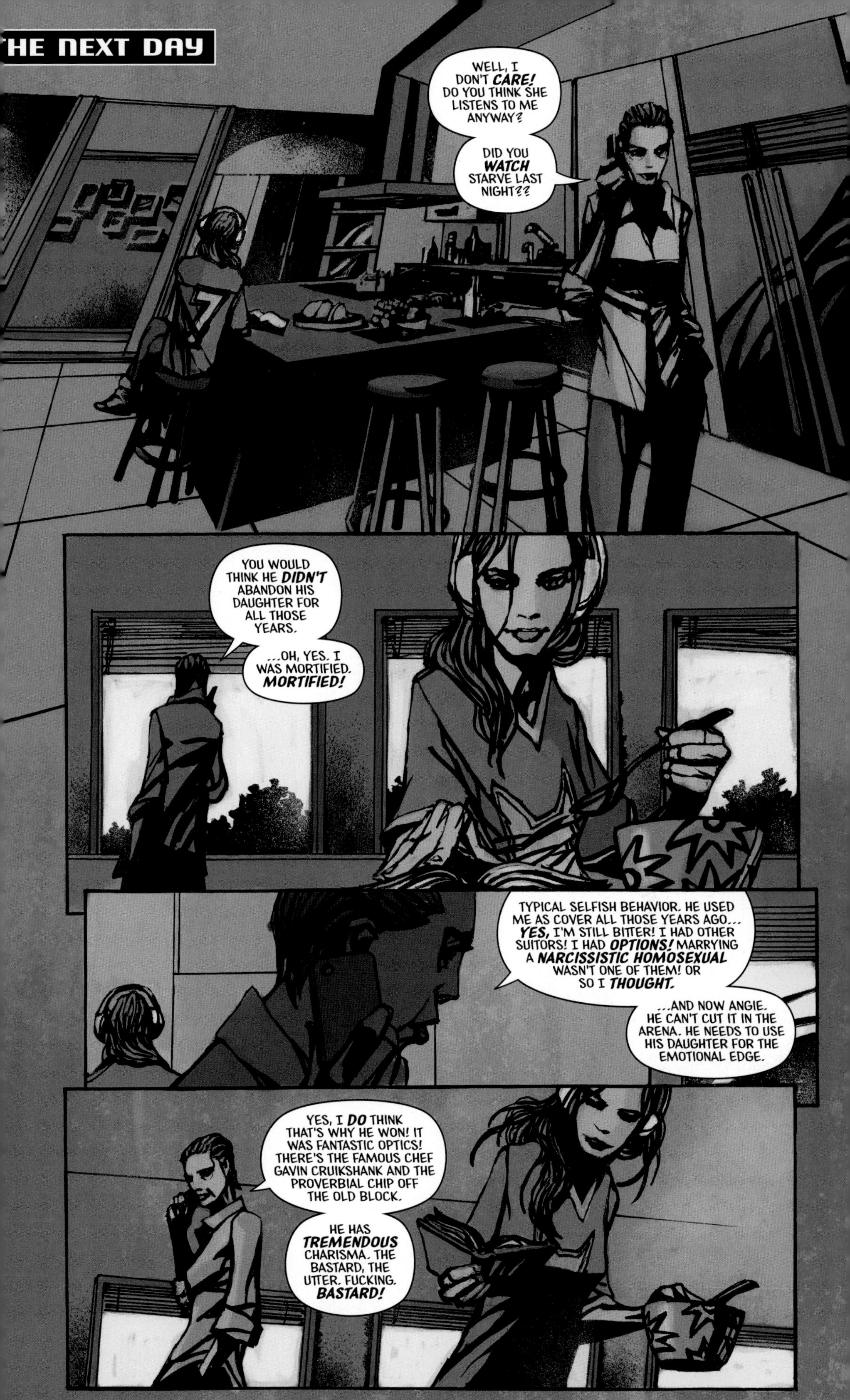

THE NEXT DAY
WELL, I DON'T CARE! DO YOU THINK SHE LISTENS TO ME ANYWAY?
DID YOU WATCH STARVE LAST NIGHT??
YOU WOULD THINK HE DIDN'T ABANDON HIS DAUGHTER FOR ALL THOSE YEARS.
...OH, YES. I WAS MORTIFIED. MORTIFIED!
TYPICAL SELFISH BEHAVIOR. HE USED ME AS COVER ALL THOSE YEARS AGO... YES, I'M STILL BITTER! I HAD OTHER SUITORS! I HAD OPTIONS! MARRYING A NARCISSISTIC HOMOSEXUAL WASN'T ONE OF THEM! OR SO I THOUGHT.
...AND NOW ANGIE. HE CAN'T CUT IT IN THE ARENA. HE NEEDS TO USE HIS DAUGHTER FOR THE EMOTIONAL EDGE.
YES, I DO THINK THAT'S WHY HE WON! IT WAS FANTASTIC OPTICS! THERE'S THE FAMOUS CHEF GAVIN CRUIKSHANK AND THE PROVERBIAL CHIP OFF THE OLD BLOCK.
HE HAS TREMENDOUS CHARISMA. THE BASTARD, THE UTTER. FUCKING. BASTARD!

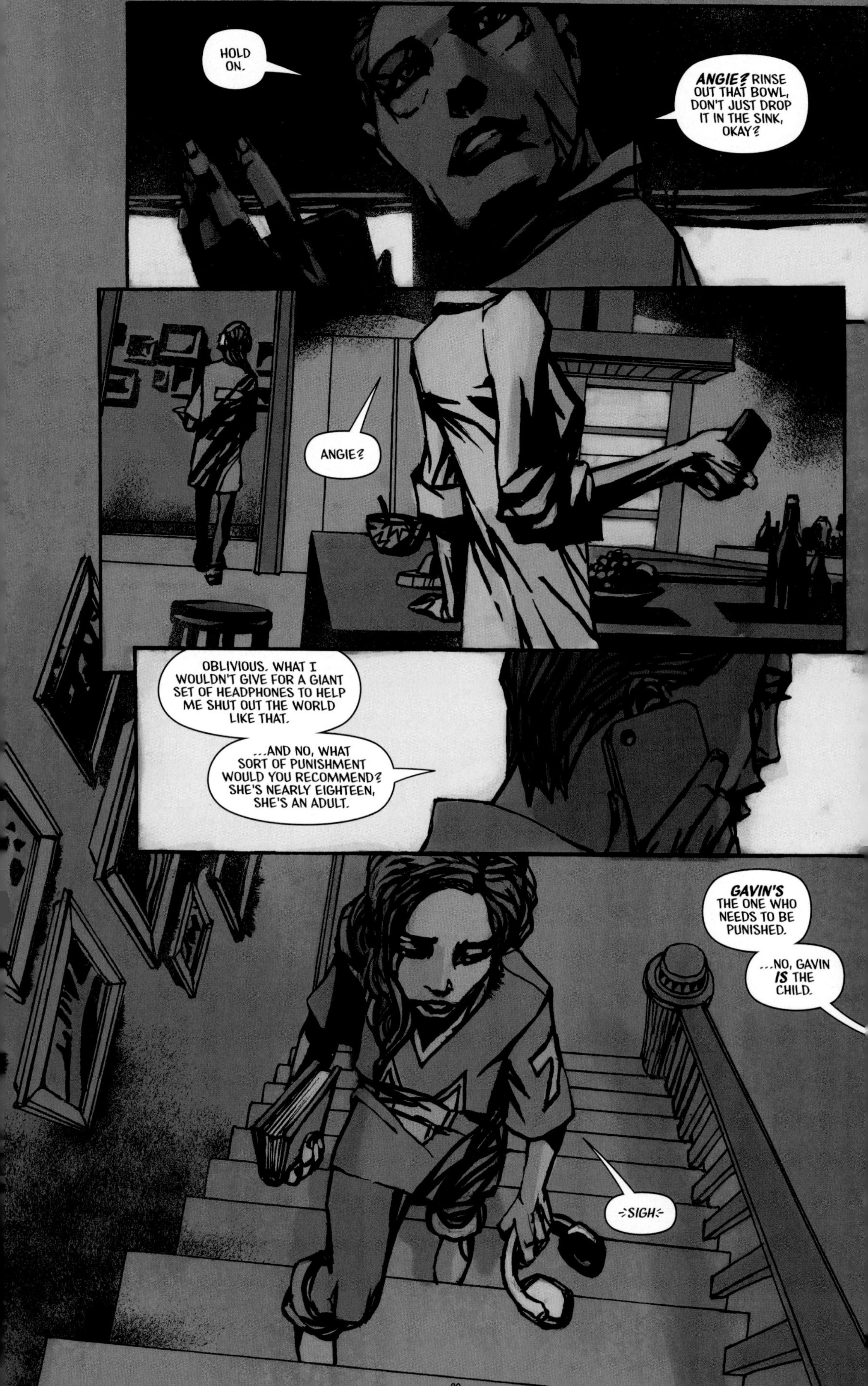
HOLD ON.
ANGIE? RINSE OUT THAT BOWL, DON'T JUST DROP IT IN THE SINK, OKAY?
ANGIE?
OBLIVIOUS. WHAT I WOULDN'T GIVE FOR A GIANT SET OF HEADPHONES TO HELP ME SHUT OUT THE WORLD LIKE THAT.
...AND NO, WHAT SORT OF PUNISHMENT WOULD YOU RECOMMEND? SHE'S NEARLY EIGHTEEN, SHE'S AN ADULT.
GAVIN'S THE ONE WHO NEEDS TO BE PUNISHED.
...NO, GAVIN IS THE CHILD.
SIGH

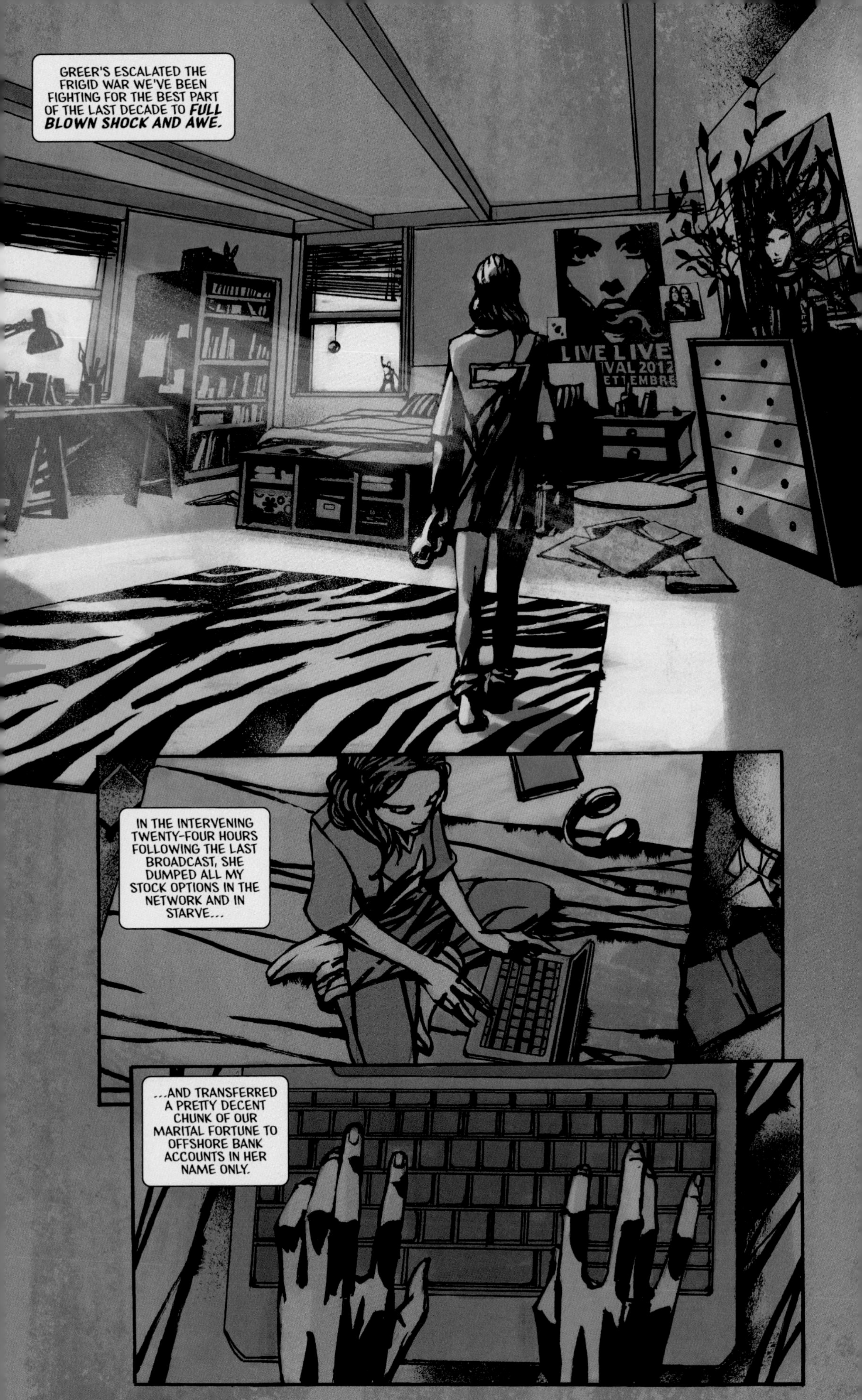
GREER'S ESCALATED THE FRIGID WAR WE'VE BEEN FIGHTING FOR THE BEST PART OF THE LAST DECADE TO FULL BLOWN SHOCK AND AWE.
LIVE LIVE
VAL 2012
ETTEMBRE
IN THE INTERVENING TWENTY-FOUR HOURS FOLLOWING THE LAST BROADCAST, SHE DUMPED ALL MY STOCK OPTIONS IN THE NETWORK AND IN STARVE...
...AND TRANSFERRED A PRETTY DECENT CHUNK OF OUR MARITAL FORTUNE TO OFFSHORE BANK ACCOUNTS IN HER NAME ONLY.

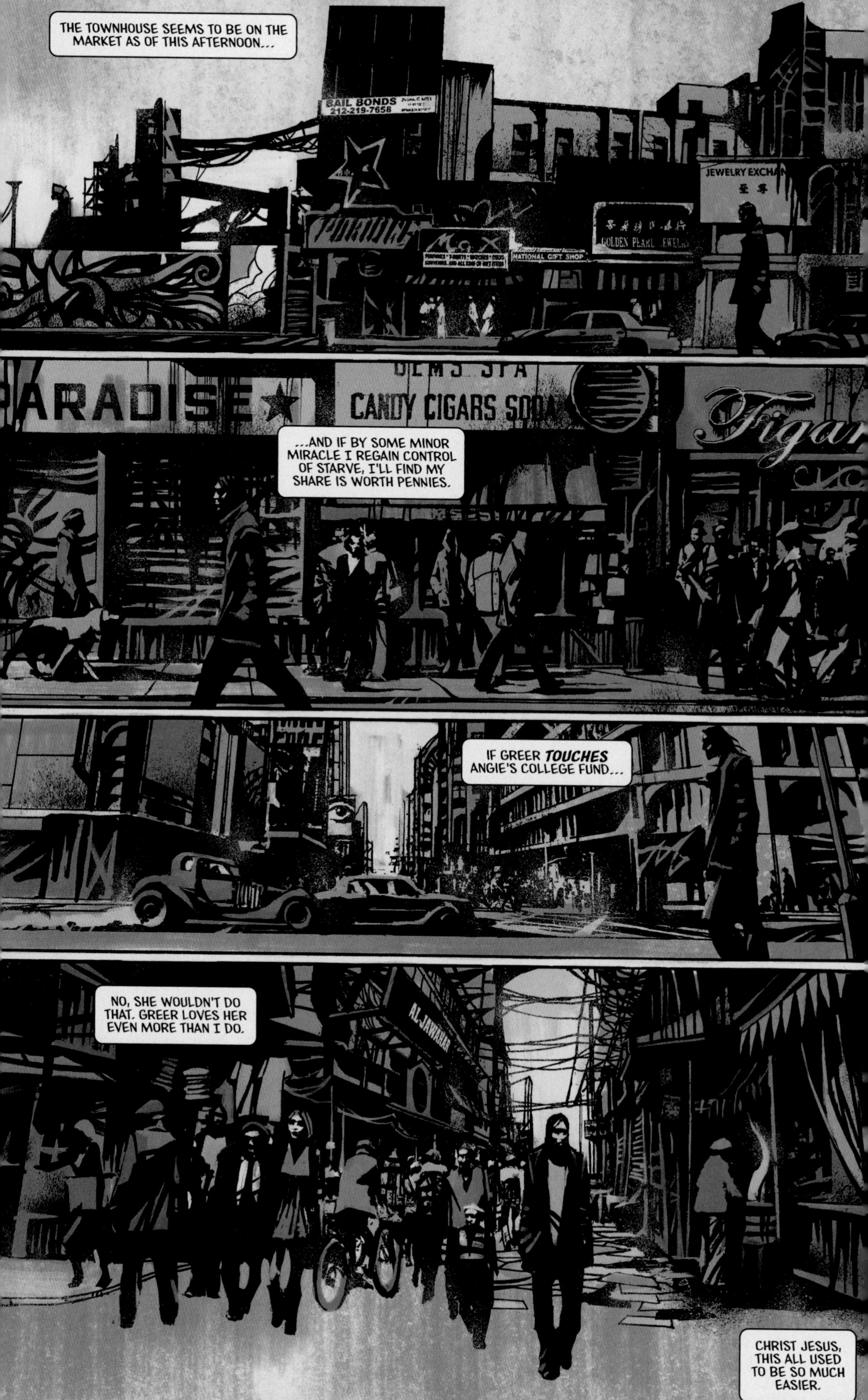

THE TOWNHOUSE SEEMS TO BE ON THE MARKET AS OF THIS AFTERNOON...
BAIL BONDS 212-219-7658
JEWELRY EXCHAN
NATIONAL GIFT SHOP
GOLDEN PEARL JEWELRY
PARADISE
CANDY CIGARS SODA
...AND IF BY SOME MINOR MIRACLE I REGAIN CONTROL OF STARVE, I'LL FIND MY SHARE IS WORTH PENNIES.
IF GREER *TOUCHES* ANGIE'S COLLEGE FUND...
NO, SHE WOULDN'T DO THAT. GREER LOVES HER EVEN MORE THAN I DO.
AL JAWAHAR
CHRIST JESUS, THIS ALL USED TO BE SO MUCH EASIER.

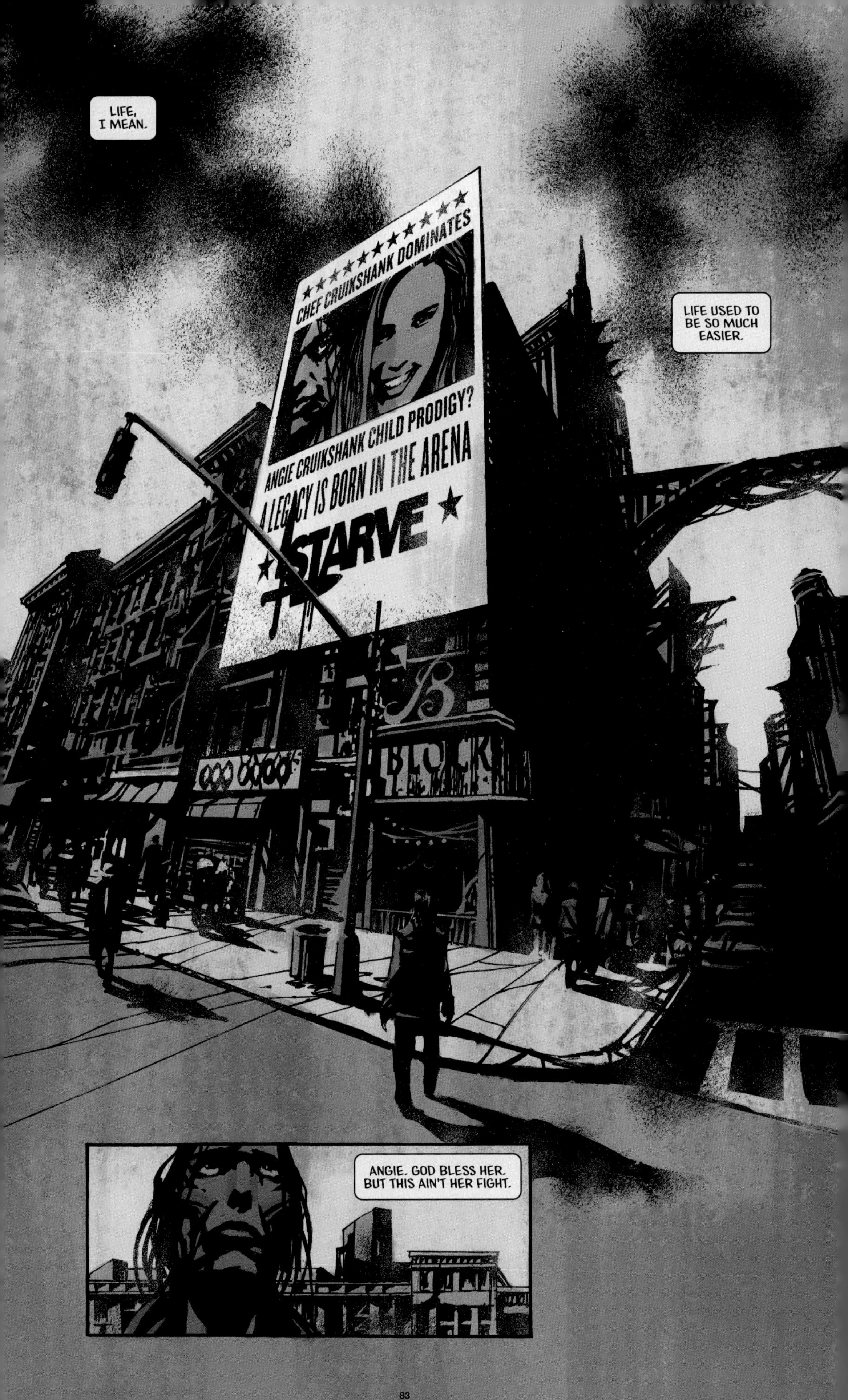

LIFE, I MEAN.
CHEF CRUIKSHANK DOMINATES
ANGIE CRUIKSHANK CHILD PRODIGY?
A LEGACY IS BORN IN THE ARENA
STARVE
LIFE USED TO BE SO MUCH EASIER.
ANGIE, GOD BLESS HER. BUT THIS AIN'T HER FIGHT.

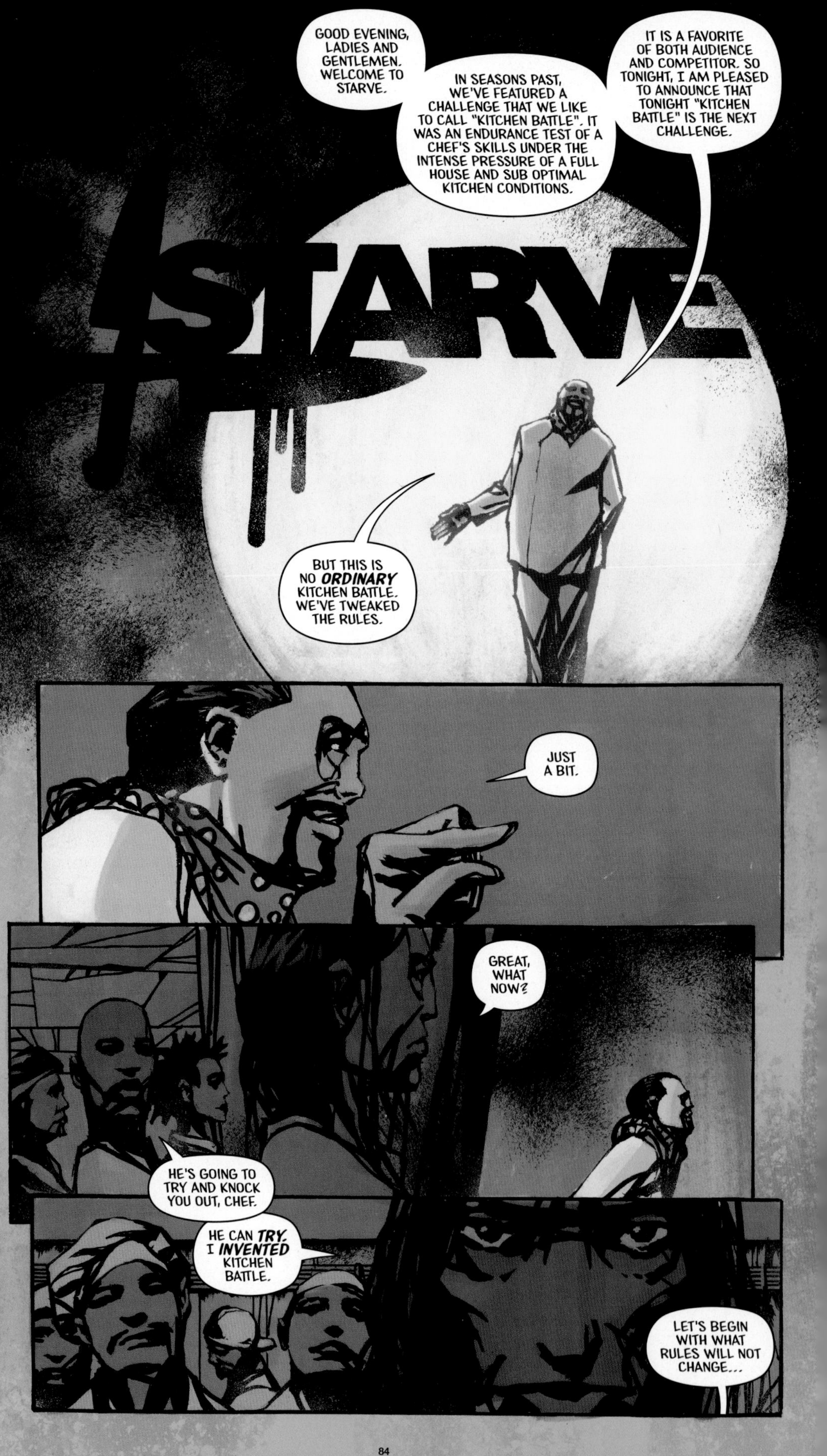

STARVE
GOOD EVENING, LADIES AND GENTLEMEN. WELCOME TO STARVE.
IN SEASONS PAST, WE'VE FEATURED A CHALLENGE THAT WE LIKE TO CALL "KITCHEN BATTLE". IT WAS AN ENDURANCE TEST OF A CHEF'S SKILLS UNDER THE INTENSE PRESSURE OF A FULL HOUSE AND SUB OPTIMAL KITCHEN CONDITIONS.
IT IS A FAVORITE OF BOTH AUDIENCE AND COMPETITOR. SO TONIGHT, I AM PLEASED TO ANNOUNCE THAT TONIGHT "KITCHEN BATTLE" IS THE NEXT CHALLENGE.
BUT THIS IS NO **ORDINARY** KITCHEN BATTLE. WE'VE TWEAKED THE RULES.
JUST A BIT.
GREAT, WHAT NOW?
HE'S GOING TO TRY AND KNOCK YOU OUT, CHEF.
HE CAN ***TRY.*** I ***INVENTED*** KITCHEN BATTLE.
LET'S BEGIN WITH WHAT RULES WILL NOT CHANGE...

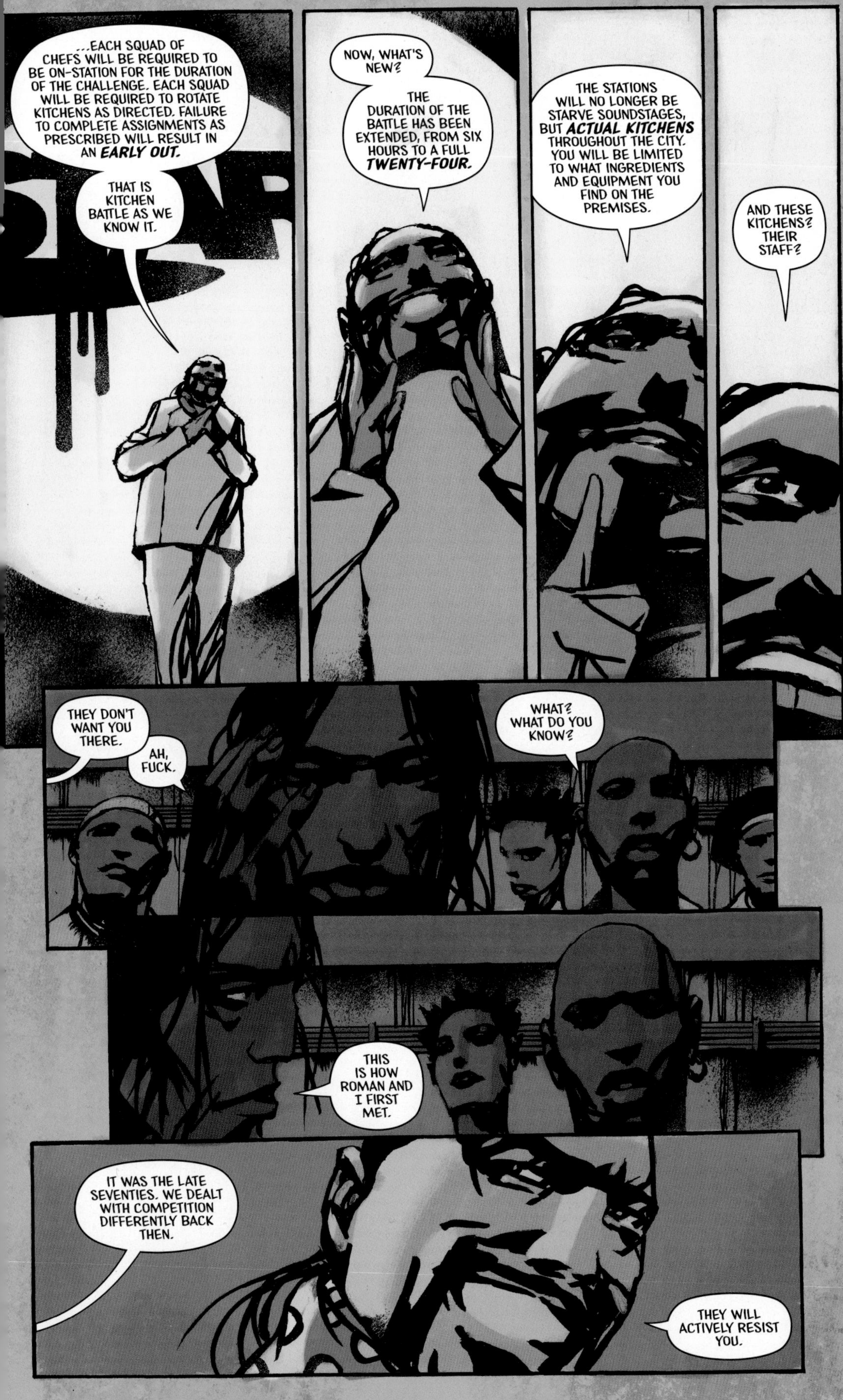

...EACH SQUAD OF CHEFS WILL BE REQUIRED TO BE ON-STATION FOR THE DURATION OF THE CHALLENGE. EACH SQUAD WILL BE REQUIRED TO ROTATE KITCHENS AS DIRECTED. FAILURE TO COMPLETE ASSIGNMENTS AS PRESCRIBED WILL RESULT IN AN EARLY OUT.
THAT IS KITCHEN BATTLE AS WE KNOW IT.
NOW, WHAT'S NEW?
THE DURATION OF THE BATTLE HAS BEEN EXTENDED, FROM SIX HOURS TO A FULL TWENTY-FOUR.
THE STATIONS WILL NO LONGER BE STARVE SOUNDSTAGES, BUT ACTUAL KITCHENS THROUGHOUT THE CITY. YOU WILL BE LIMITED TO WHAT INGREDIENTS AND EQUIPMENT YOU FIND ON THE PREMISES.
AND THESE KITCHENS? THEIR STAFF?
THEY DON'T WANT YOU THERE.
AH, FUCK.
WHAT? WHAT DO YOU KNOW?
THIS IS HOW ROMAN AND I FIRST MET.
IT WAS THE LATE SEVENTIES. WE DEALT WITH COMPETITION DIFFERENTLY BACK THEN.
THEY WILL ACTIVELY RESIST YOU.

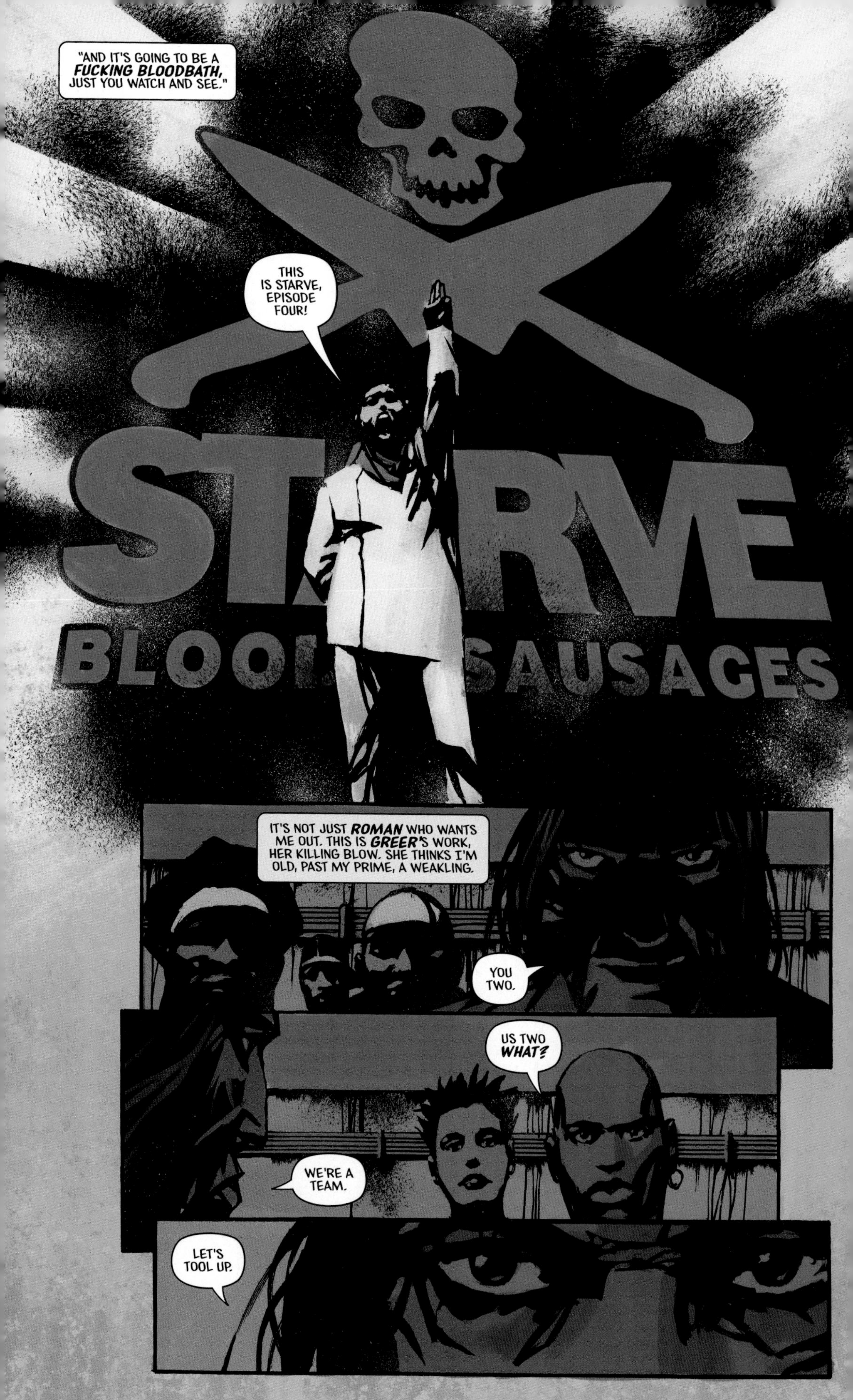
"AND IT'S GOING TO BE A ***FUCKING BLOODBATH,*** JUST YOU WATCH AND SEE."
THIS IS STARVE, EPISODE FOUR!
SAUSAGES
IT'S NOT JUST ***ROMAN*** WHO WANTS ME OUT. THIS IS ***GREER'S*** WORK, HER KILLING BLOW. SHE THINKS I'M OLD, PAST MY PRIME, A WEAKLING.
YOU TWO.
US TWO ***WHAT?***
WE'RE A TEAM.
LET'S TOOL UP.

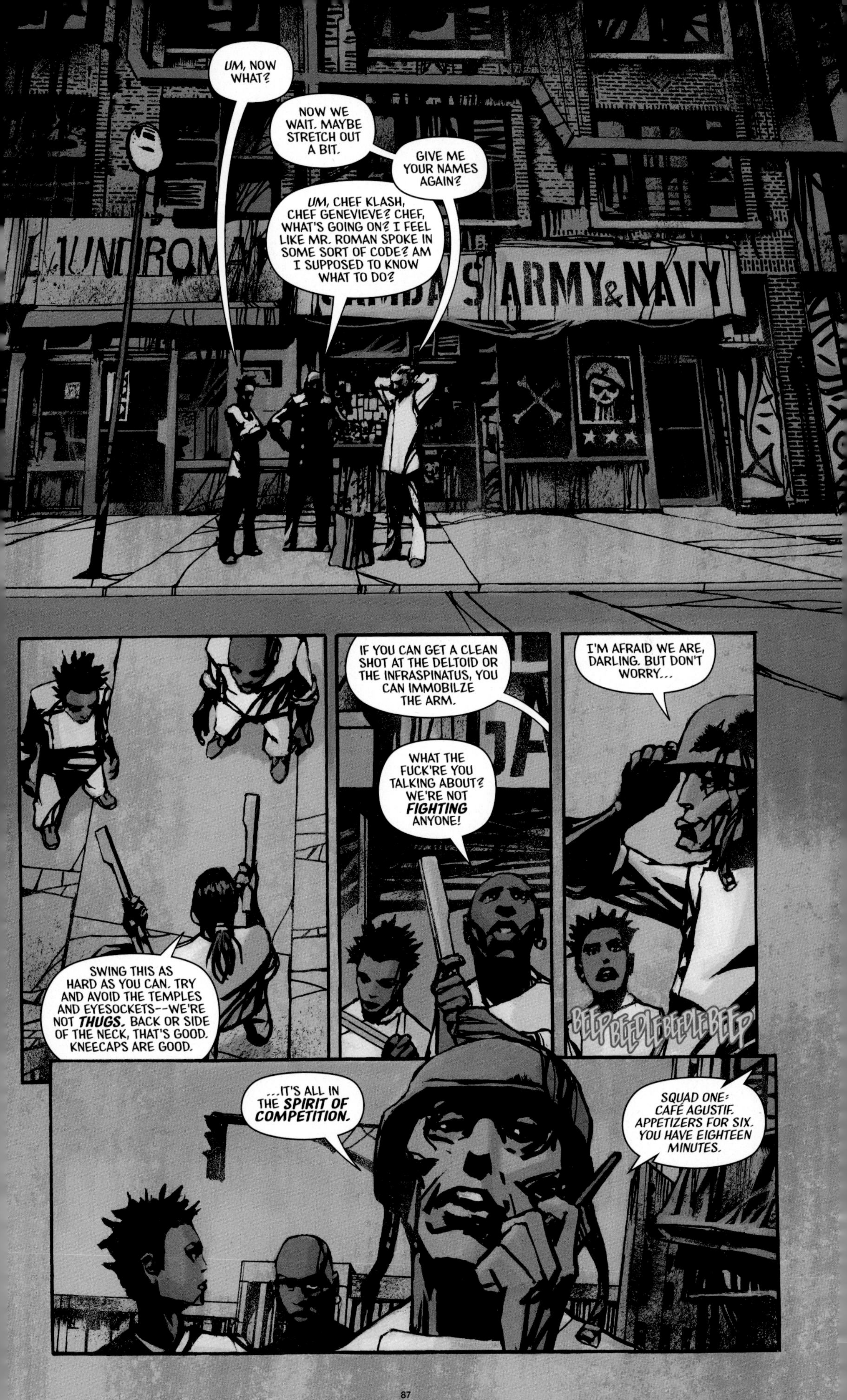
UM, NOW WHAT?
NOW WE WAIT. MAYBE STRETCH OUT A BIT.
GIVE ME YOUR NAMES AGAIN?
UM, CHEF KLASH, CHEF GENEVIEVE? CHEF, WHAT'S GOING ON? I FEEL LIKE MR. ROMAN SPOKE IN SOME SORT OF CODE? AM I SUPPOSED TO KNOW WHAT TO DO?
ARMY&NAVY
SWING THIS AS HARD AS YOU CAN. TRY AND AVOID THE TEMPLES AND EYESOCKETS--WE'RE NOT THUGS. BACK OR SIDE OF THE NECK, THAT'S GOOD. KNEECAPS ARE GOOD.
IF YOU CAN GET A CLEAN SHOT AT THE DELTOID OR THE INFRASPINATUS, YOU CAN IMMOBILZE THE ARM.
WHAT THE FUCK'RE YOU TALKING ABOUT? WE'RE NOT FIGHTING ANYONE!
I'M AFRAID WE ARE, DARLING. BUT DON'T WORRY...
BEEP BEEDLEBEEDLEBEEP
...IT'S ALL IN THE SPIRIT OF COMPETITION.
SQUAD ONE: CAFÉ AGUSTIF. APPETIZERS FOR SIX. YOU HAVE EIGHTEEN MINUTES.

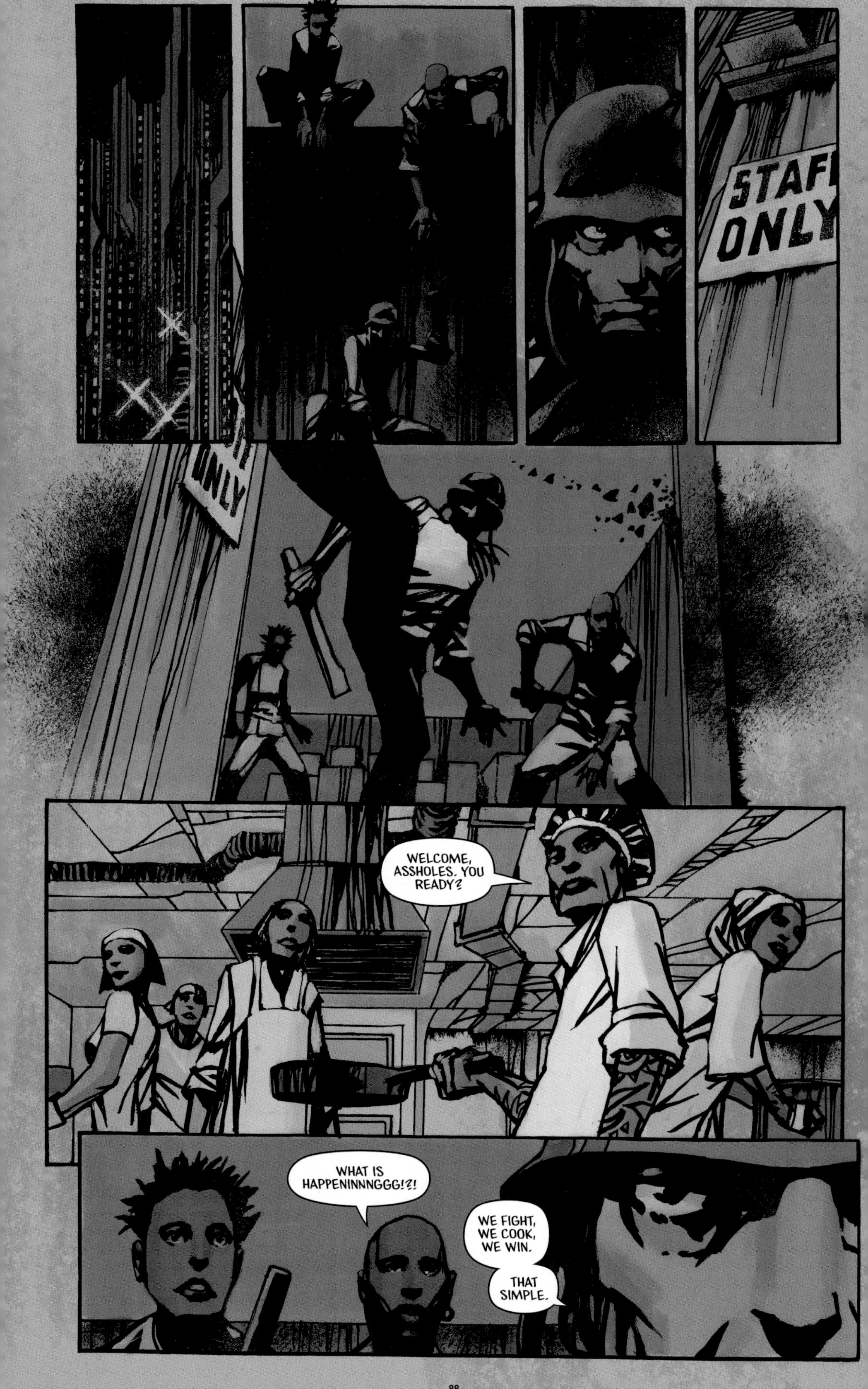
STAFF ONLY
ONLY
WELCOME, ASSHOLES. YOU READY?
WHAT IS HAPPENINNNGGG!?!
WE FIGHT, WE COOK, WE WIN.
THAT SIMPLE.

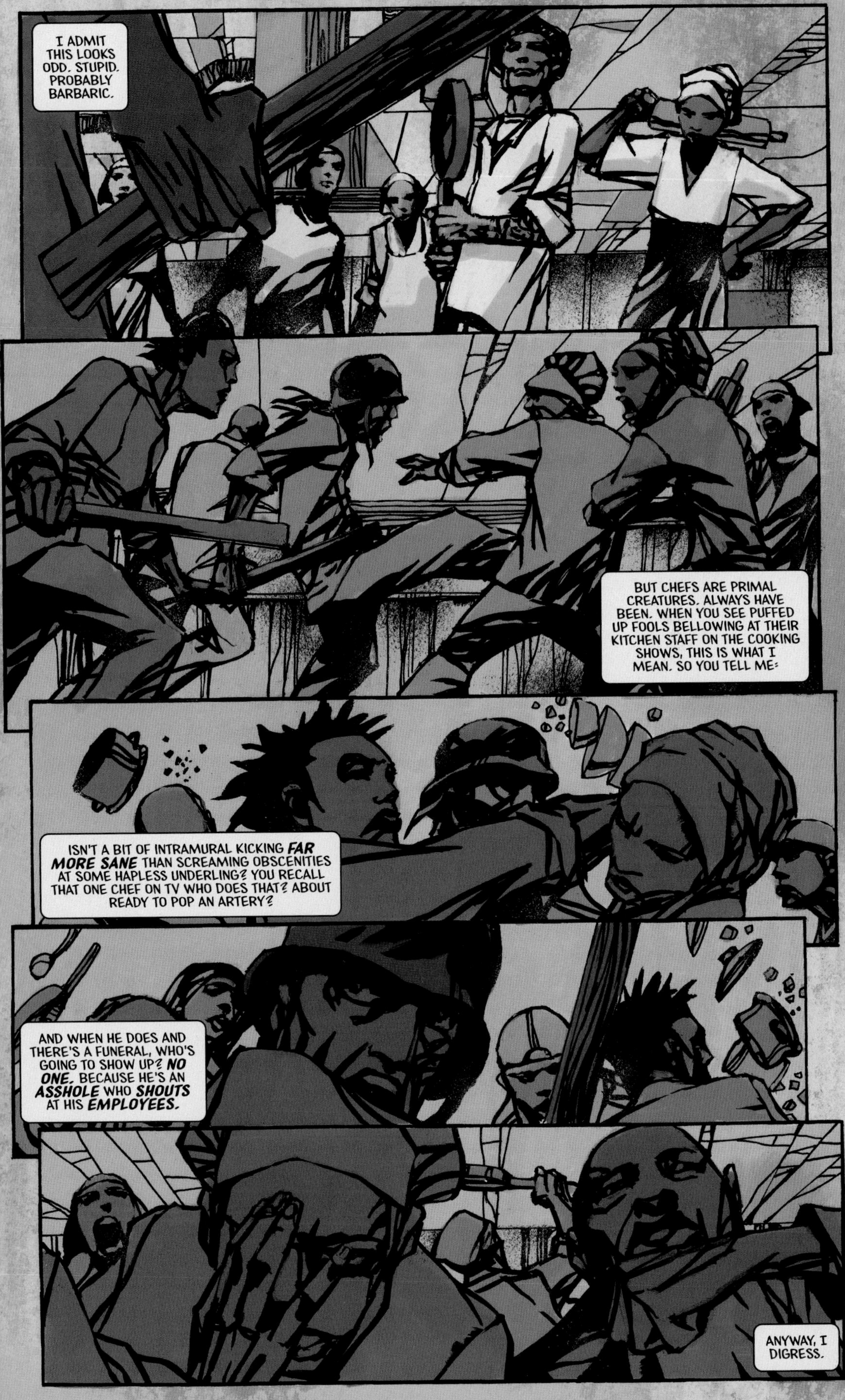
I ADMIT THIS LOOKS ODD. STUPID. PROBABLY BARBARIC.
BUT CHEFS ARE PRIMAL CREATURES. ALWAYS HAVE BEEN. WHEN YOU SEE PUFFED UP FOOLS BELLOWING AT THEIR KITCHEN STAFF ON THE COOKING SHOWS, THIS IS WHAT I MEAN. SO YOU TELL ME:
ISN'T A BIT OF INTRAMURAL KICKING FAR MORE SANE THAN SCREAMING OBSCENITIES AT SOME HAPLESS UNDERLING? YOU RECALL THAT ONE CHEF ON TV WHO DOES THAT? ABOUT READY TO POP AN ARTERY?
AND WHEN HE DOES AND THERE'S A FUNERAL, WHO'S GOING TO SHOW UP? NO ONE. BECAUSE HE'S AN ASSHOLE WHO SHOUTS AT HIS EMPLOYEES.
ANYWAY, I DIGRESS.

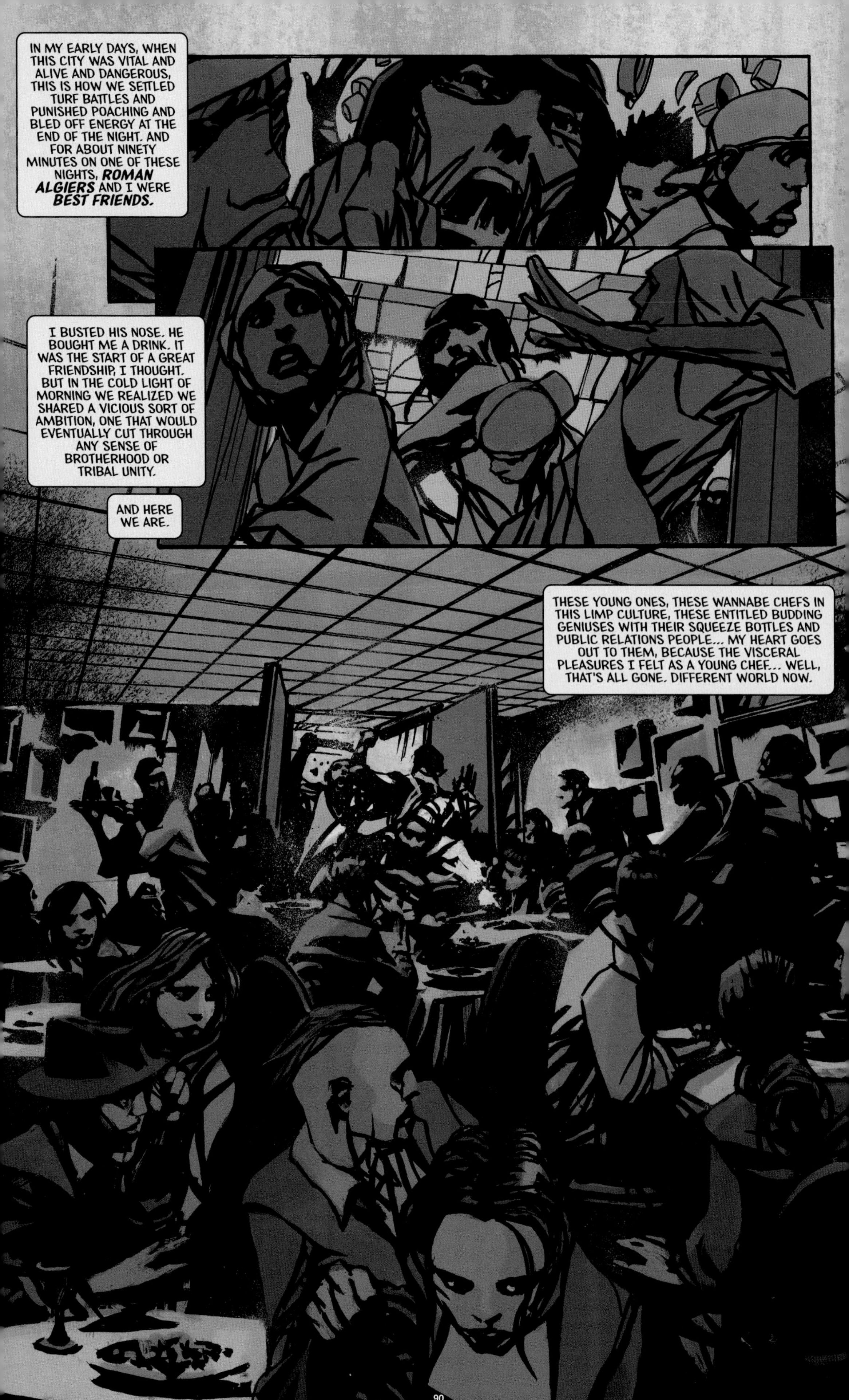
IN MY EARLY DAYS, WHEN THIS CITY WAS VITAL AND ALIVE AND DANGEROUS, THIS IS HOW WE SETTLED TURF BATTLES AND PUNISHED POACHING AND BLED OFF ENERGY AT THE END OF THE NIGHT. AND FOR ABOUT NINETY MINUTES ON ONE OF THESE NIGHTS, ROMAN ALGIERS AND I WERE BEST FRIENDS.
I BUSTED HIS NOSE. HE BOUGHT ME A DRINK. IT WAS THE START OF A GREAT FRIENDSHIP, I THOUGHT. BUT IN THE COLD LIGHT OF MORNING WE REALIZED WE SHARED A VICIOUS SORT OF AMBITION, ONE THAT WOULD EVENTUALLY CUT THROUGH ANY SENSE OF BROTHERHOOD OR TRIBAL UNITY.
AND HERE WE ARE.
THESE YOUNG ONES, THESE WANNABE CHEFS IN THIS LIMP CULTURE, THESE ENTITLED BUDDING GENIUSES WITH THEIR SQUEEZE BOTTLES AND PUBLIC RELATIONS PEOPLE... MY HEART GOES OUT TO THEM, BECAUSE THE VISCERAL PLEASURES I FELT AS A YOUNG CHEF... WELL, THAT'S ALL GONE. DIFFERENT WORLD NOW.

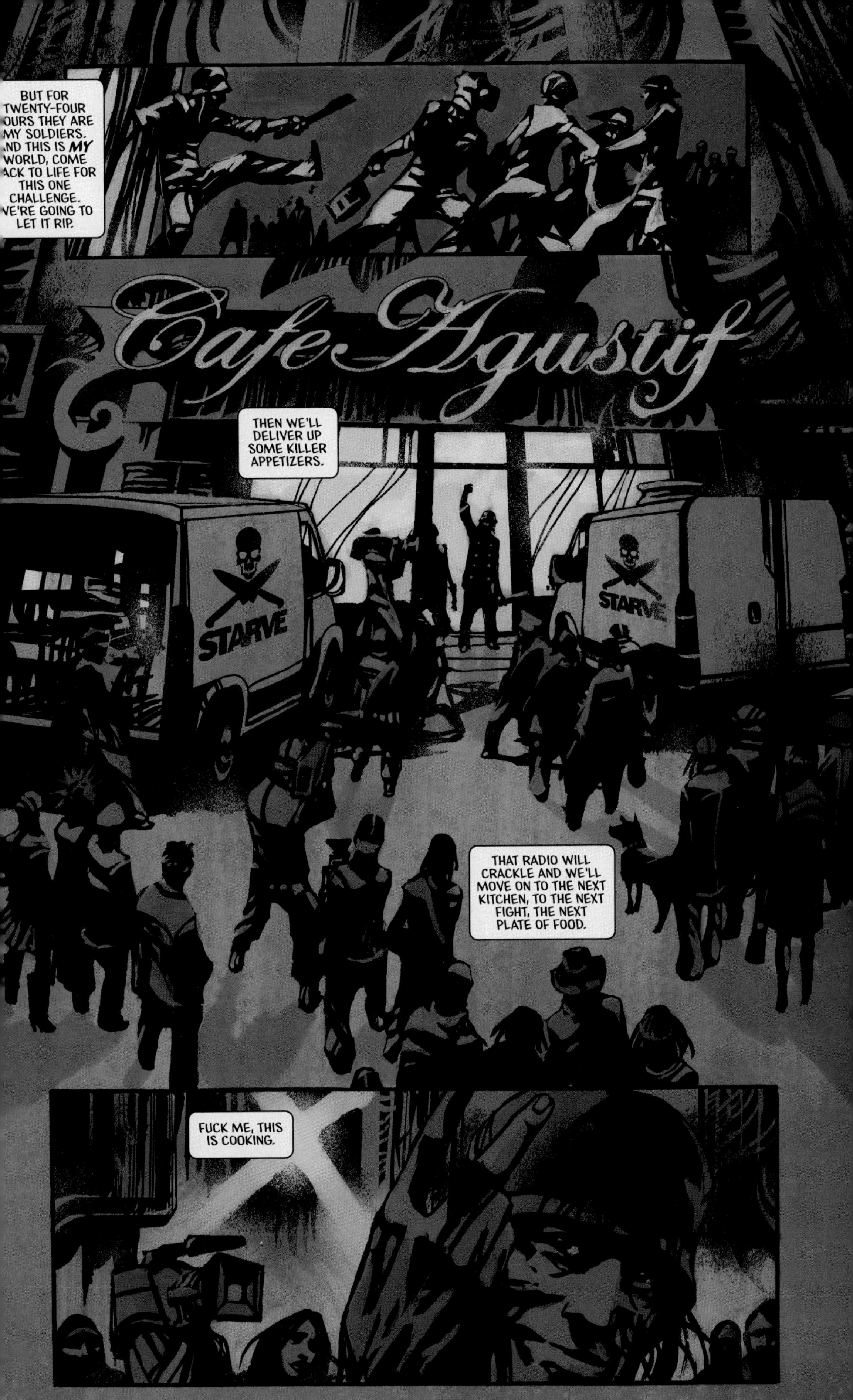
BUT FOR TWENTY-FOUR OURS THEY ARE MY SOLDIERS. ND THIS IS MY WORLD, COME ACK TO LIFE FOR THIS ONE CHALLENGE. VE'RE GOING TO LET IT RIP.
Cafe Agustif
THEN WE'LL DELIVER UP SOME KILLER APPETIZERS.
STARVE
STARVE
THAT RADIO WILL CRACKLE AND WE'LL MOVE ON TO THE NEXT KITCHEN, TO THE NEXT FIGHT, THE NEXT PLATE OF FOOD.
FUCK ME, THIS IS COOKING.

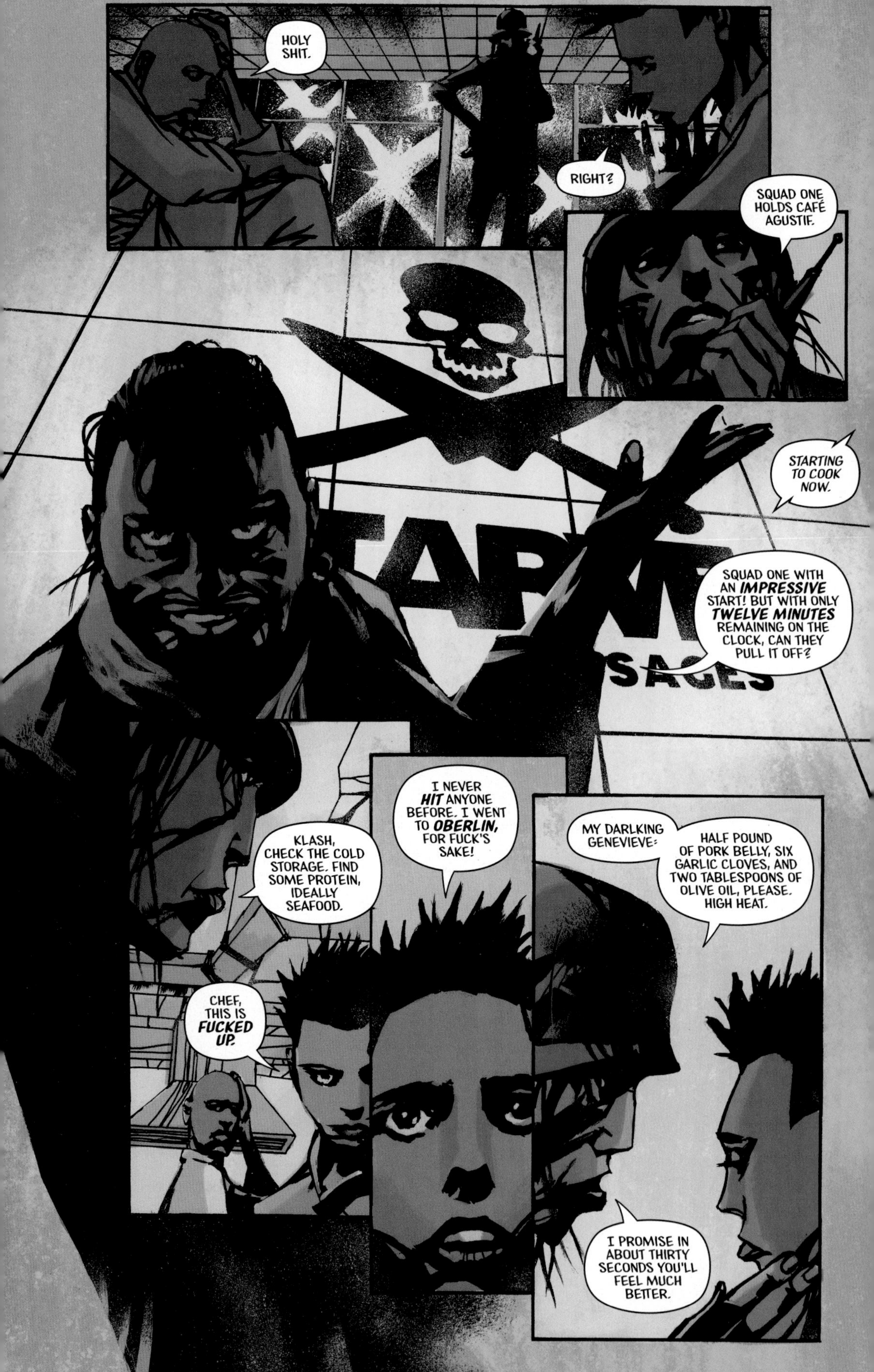
HOLY SHIT.
RIGHT?
SQUAD ONE HOLDS CAFÉ AGUSTIF.
STARTING TO COOK NOW.
SQUAD ONE WITH AN IMPRESSIVE START! BUT WITH ONLY TWELVE MINUTES REMAINING ON THE CLOCK, CAN THEY PULL IT OFF?
KLASH, CHECK THE COLD STORAGE. FIND SOME PROTEIN, IDEALLY SEAFOOD.
I NEVER HIT ANYONE BEFORE. I WENT TO OBERLIN, FOR FUCK'S SAKE!
MY DARLKING GENEVIEVE:
HALF POUND OF PORK BELLY, SIX GARLIC CLOVES, AND TWO TABLESPOONS OF OLIVE OIL, PLEASE. HIGH HEAT.
CHEF, THIS IS FUCKED UP.
I PROMISE IN ABOUT THIRTY SECONDS YOU'LL FEEL MUCH BETTER.

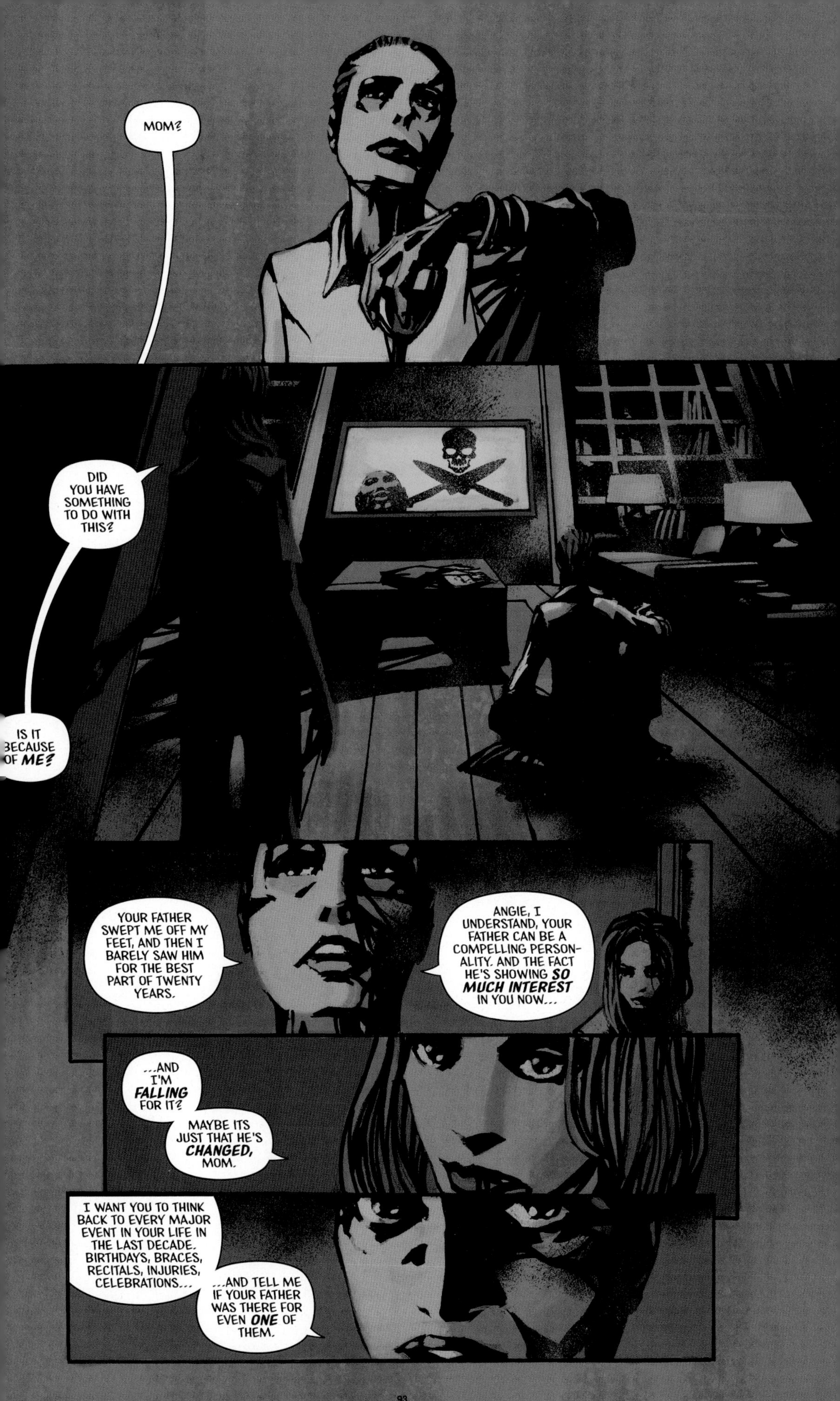

MOM?
DID YOU HAVE SOMETHING TO DO WITH THIS?
IS IT BECAUSE OF ME?
YOUR FATHER SWEPT ME OFF MY FEET, AND THEN I BARELY SAW HIM FOR THE BEST PART OF TWENTY YEARS.
ANGIE, I UNDERSTAND, YOUR FATHER CAN BE A COMPELLING PERSONALITY. AND THE FACT HE'S SHOWING SO MUCH INTEREST IN YOU NOW...
...AND I'M FALLING FOR IT?
MAYBE ITS JUST THAT HE'S CHANGED, MOM.
I WANT YOU TO THINK BACK TO EVERY MAJOR EVENT IN YOUR LIFE IN THE LAST DECADE. BIRTHDAYS, BRACES, RECITALS, INJURIES, CELEBRATIONS...
...AND TELL ME IF YOUR FATHER WAS THERE FOR EVEN ONE OF THEM.

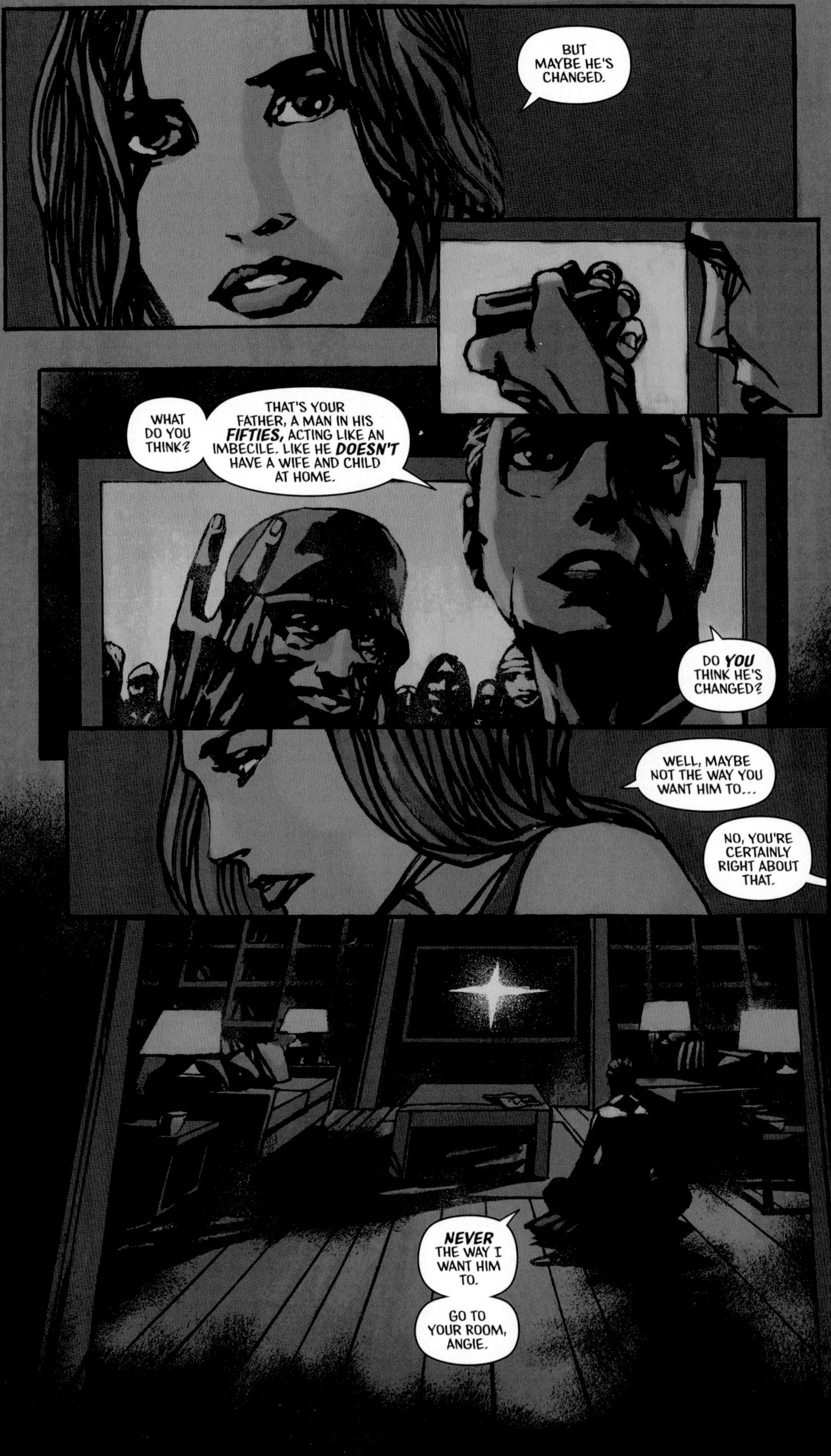
BUT MAYBE HE'S CHANGED.
WHAT DO YOU THINK?
THAT'S YOUR FATHER, A MAN IN HIS FIFTIES, ACTING LIKE AN IMBECILE. LIKE HE DOESN'T HAVE A WIFE AND CHILD AT HOME.
DO YOU THINK HE'S CHANGED?
WELL, MAYBE NOT THE WAY YOU WANT HIM TO...
NO, YOU'RE CERTAINLY RIGHT ABOUT THAT.
NEVER THE WAY I WANT HIM TO.
GO TO YOUR ROOM, ANGIE.

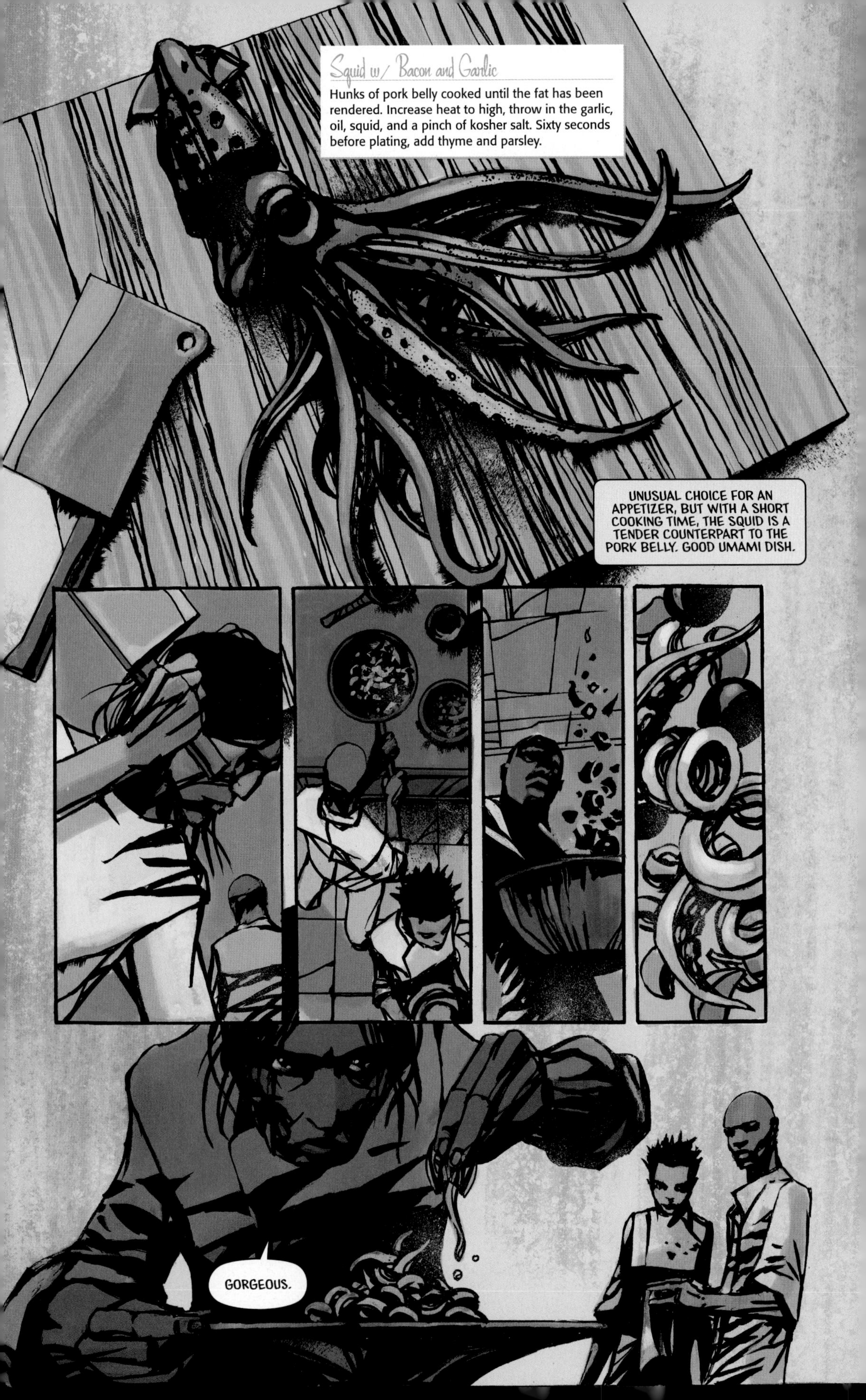

Squid w/ Bacon and Garlic
Hunks of pork belly cooked until the fat has been rendered. Increase heat to high, throw in the garlic, oil, squid, and a pinch of kosher salt. Sixty seconds before plating, add thyme and parsley.
UNUSUAL CHOICE FOR AN APPETIZER, BUT WITH A SHORT COOKING TIME, THE SQUID IS A TENDER COUNTERPART TO THE PORK BELLY. GOOD UMAMI DISH.
GORGEOUS.

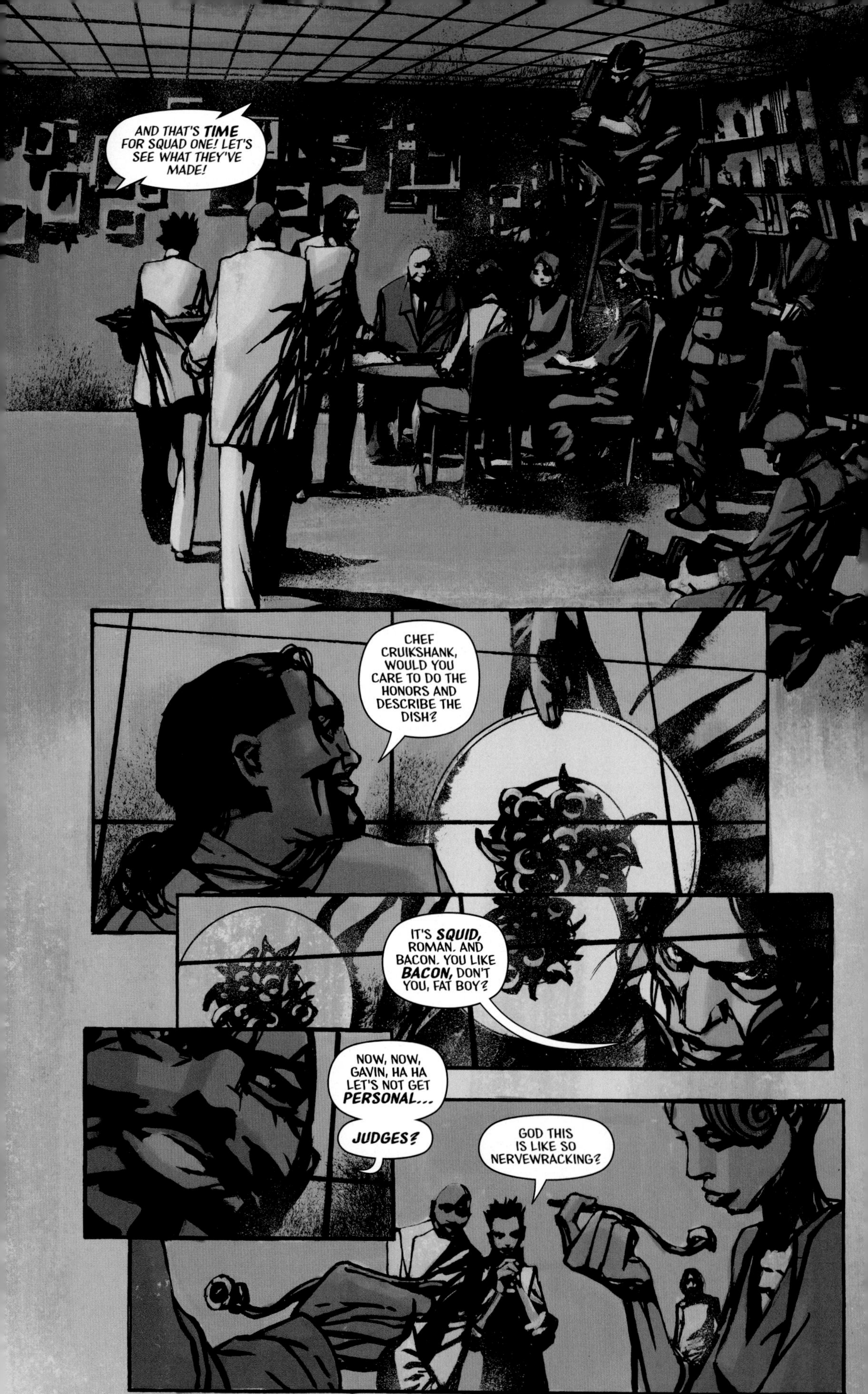
AND THAT'S TIME FOR SQUAD ONE! LET'S SEE WHAT THEY'VE MADE!
CHEF CRUIKSHANK, WOULD YOU CARE TO DO THE HONORS AND DESCRIBE THE DISH?
IT'S SQUID, ROMAN. AND BACON. YOU LIKE BACON, DON'T YOU, FAT BOY?
NOW, NOW, GAVIN, HA HA LET'S NOT GET PERSONAL...
JUDGES?
GOD THIS IS LIKE SO NERVEWRACKING?

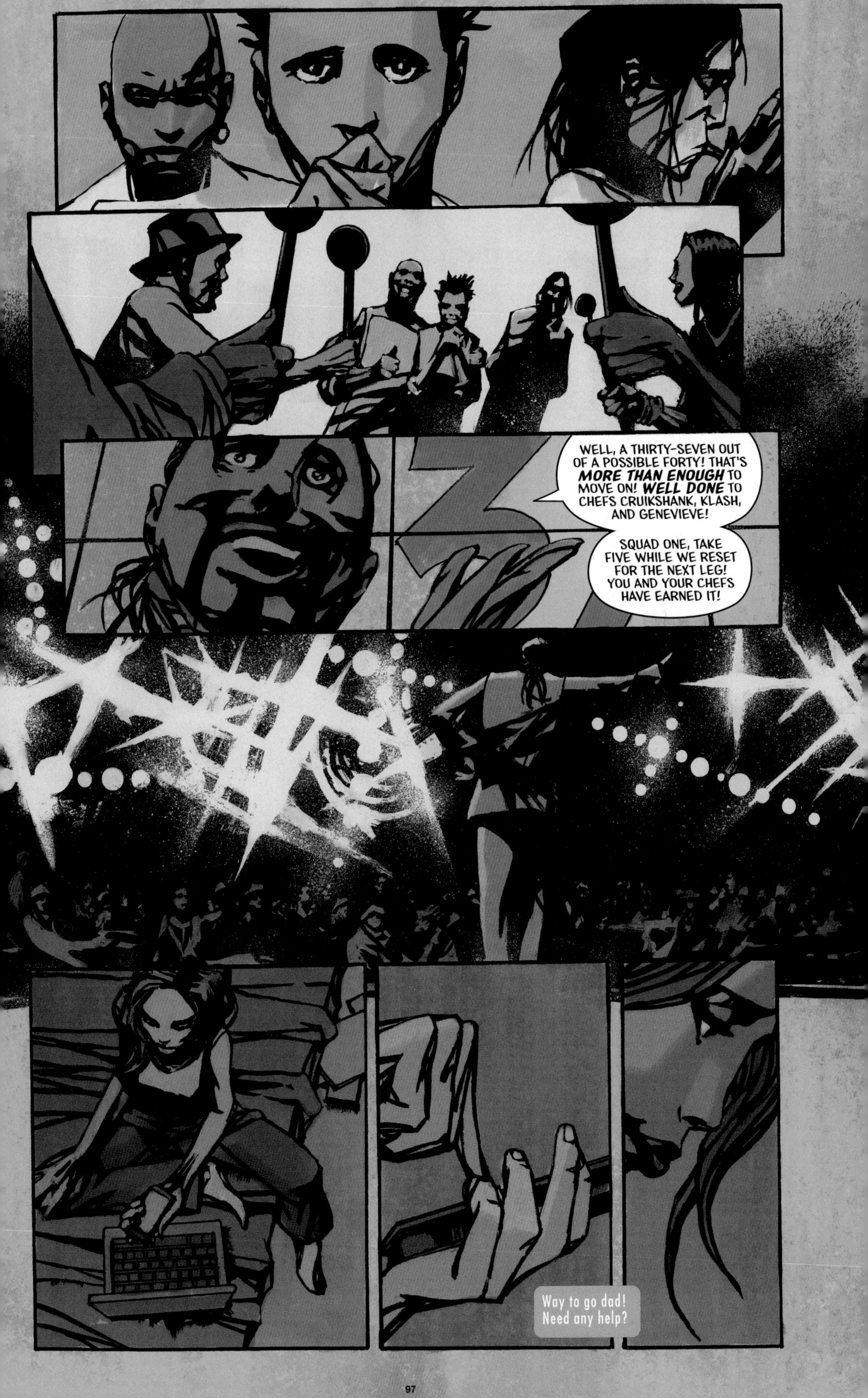
WELL, A THIRTY-SEVEN OUT OF A POSSIBLE FORTY! THAT'S **MORE THAN ENOUGH** TO MOVE ON! **WELL DONE** TO CHEFS CRUIKSHANK, KLASH, AND GENEVIEVE!
SQUAD ONE, TAKE FIVE WHILE WE RESET FOR THE NEXT LEG! YOU AND YOUR CHEFS HAVE EARNED IT!
Way to go dad! Need any help?

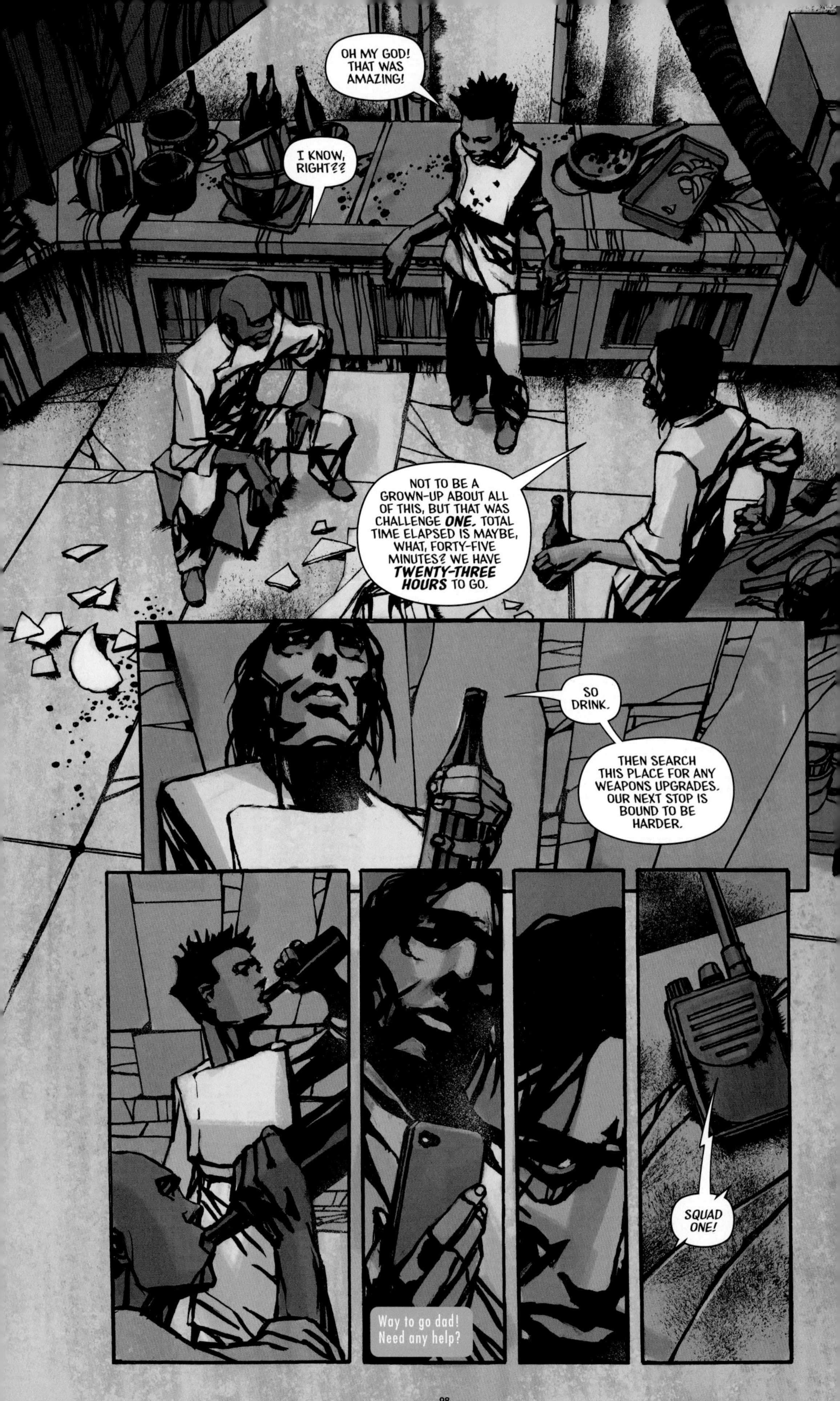
OH MY GOD! THAT WAS AMAZING!
I KNOW, RIGHT⁈
NOT TO BE A GROWN-UP ABOUT ALL OF THIS, BUT THAT WAS CHALLENGE ONE. TOTAL TIME ELAPSED IS MAYBE, WHAT, FORTY-FIVE MINUTES? WE HAVE TWENTY-THREE HOURS TO GO.
SO DRINK.
THEN SEARCH THIS PLACE FOR ANY WEAPONS UPGRADES. OUR NEXT STOP IS BOUND TO BE HARDER.
Way to go dad! Need any help?
SQUAD ONE!

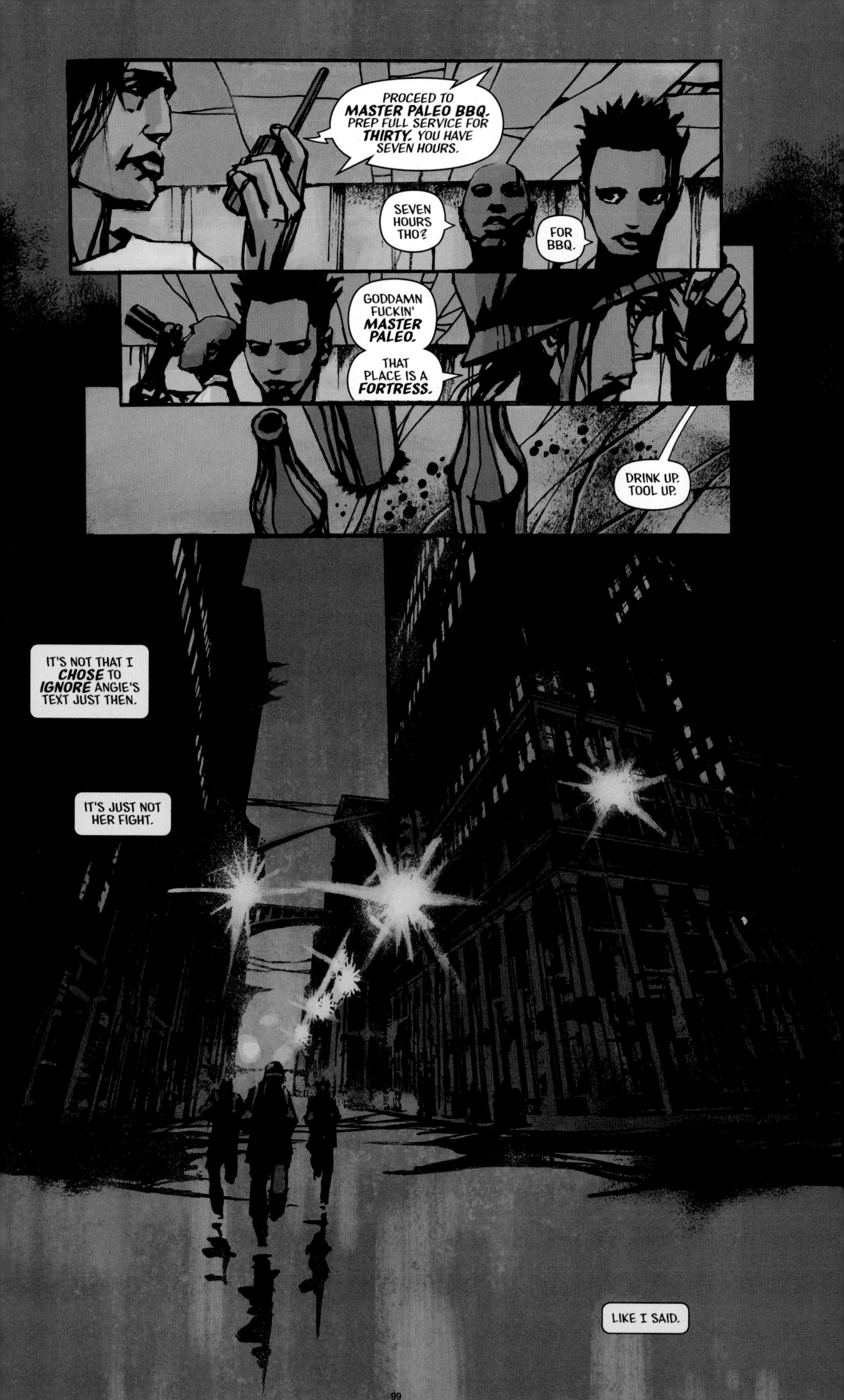
PROCEED TO MASTER PALEO BBQ. PREP FULL SERVICE FOR THIRTY. YOU HAVE SEVEN HOURS.
SEVEN HOURS THO?
FOR BBQ.
GODDAMN FUCKIN' MASTER PALEO.
THAT PLACE IS A FORTRESS.
DRINK UP. TOOL UP.
IT'S NOT THAT I CHOSE TO IGNORE ANGIE'S TEXT JUST THEN.
IT'S JUST NOT HER FIGHT.
LIKE I SAID.

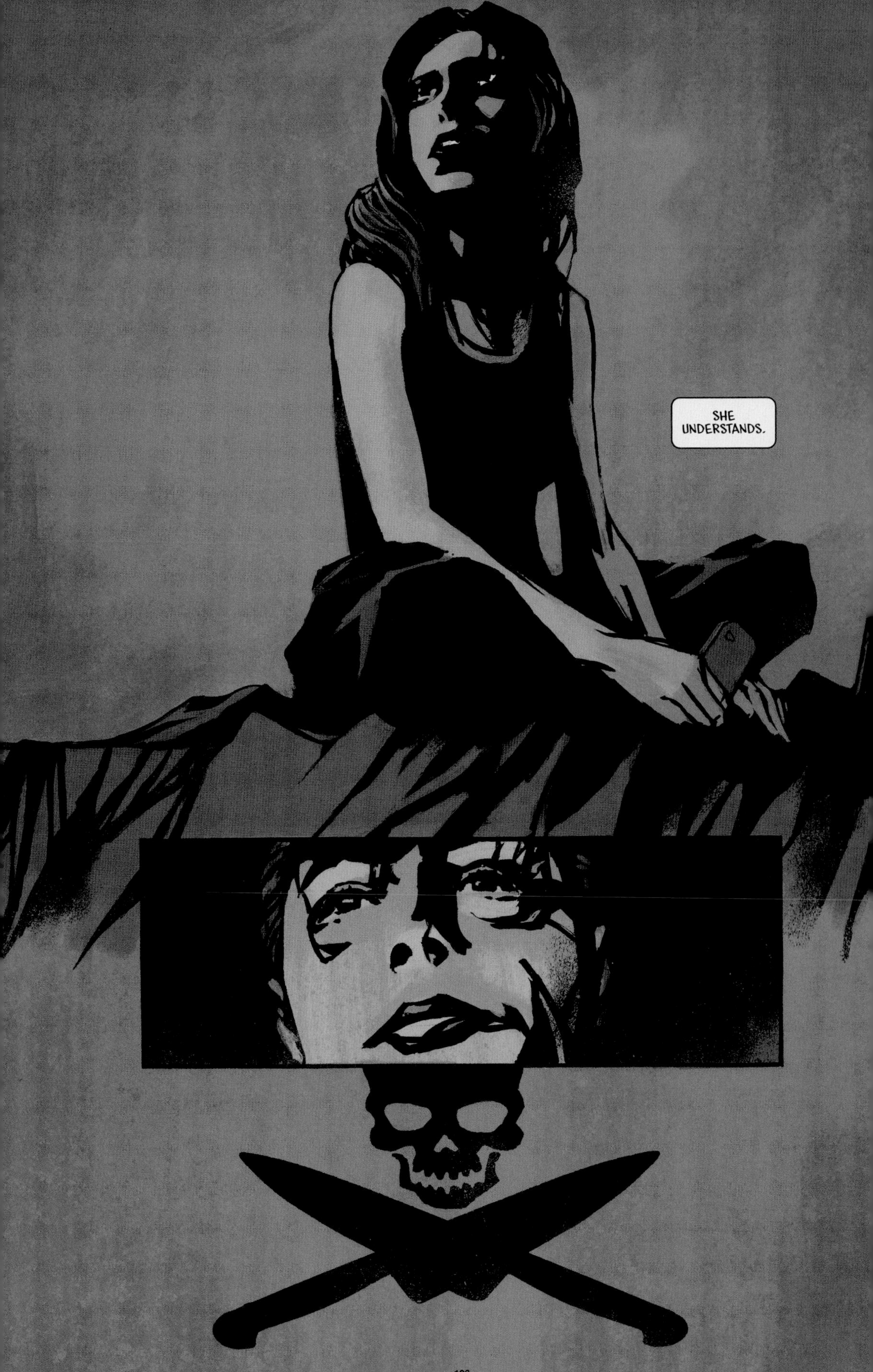
SHE UNDERSTANDS.

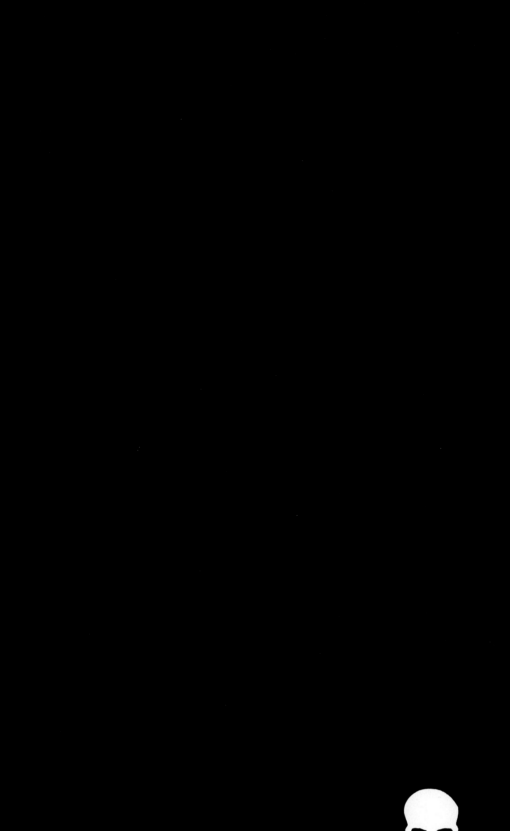

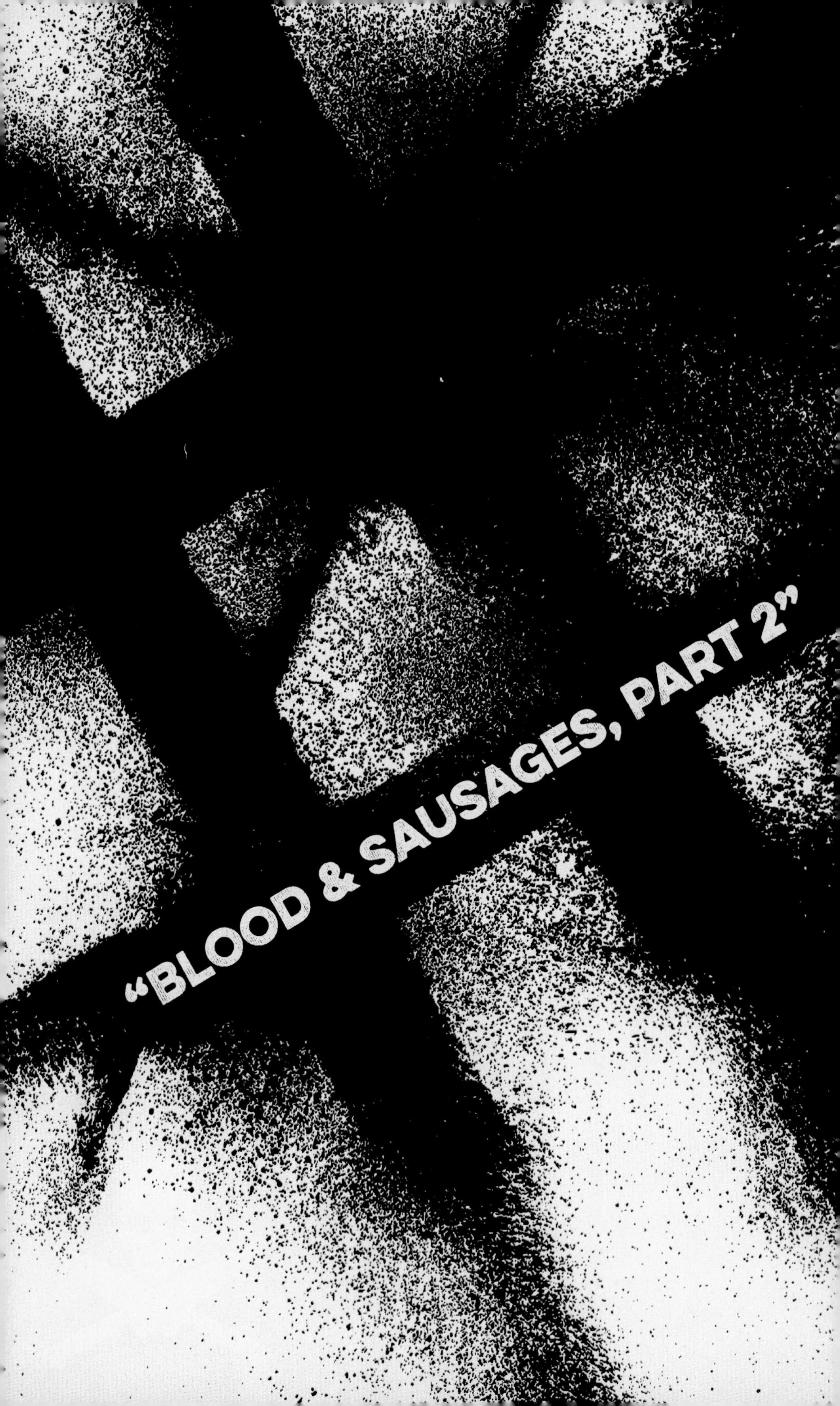

# "BLOOD & SAUSAGES, PART 2"

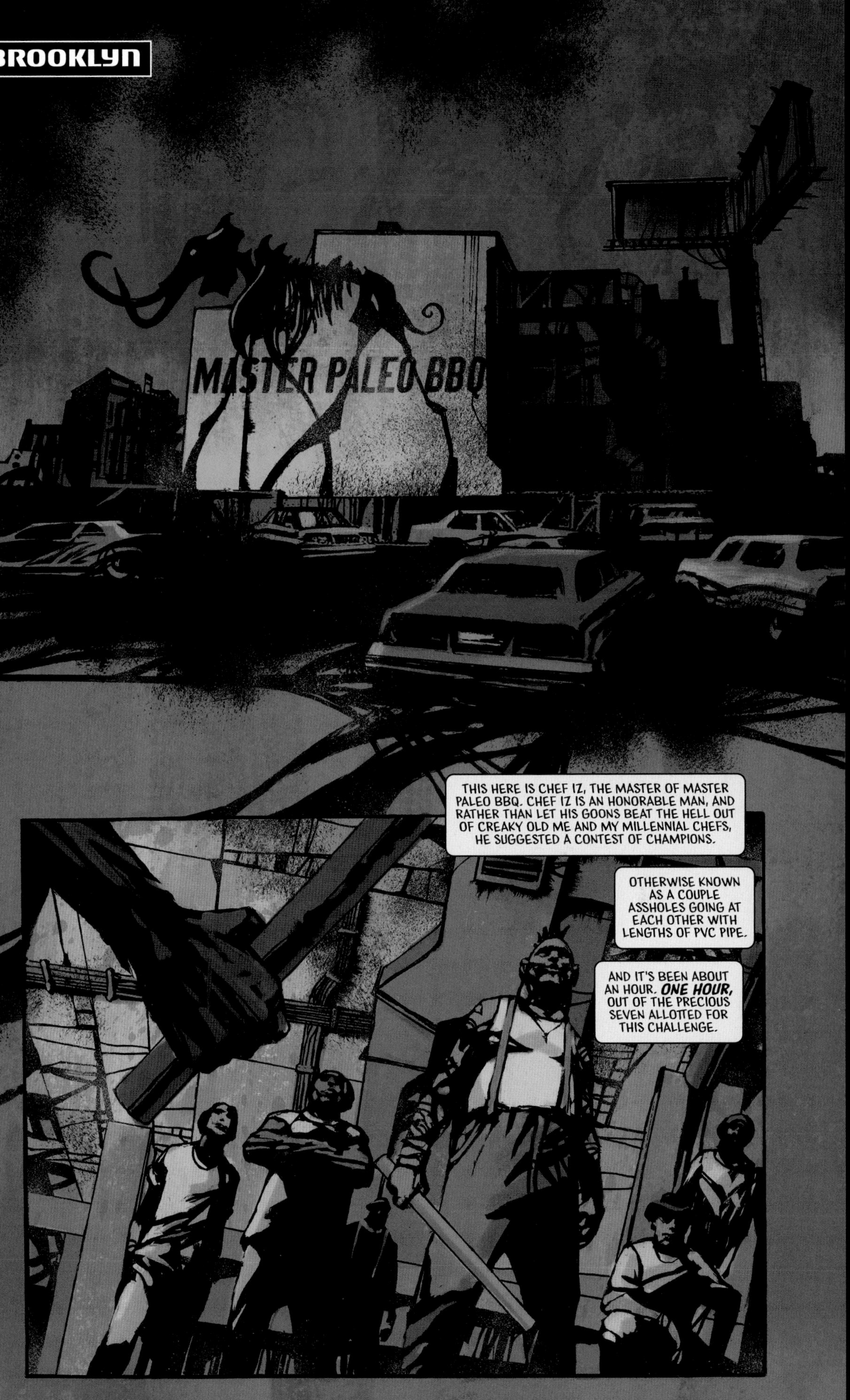

BROOKLYN
MASTER PALEO BBQ
THIS HERE IS CHEF IZ, THE MASTER OF MASTER PALEO BBQ. CHEF IZ IS AN HONORABLE MAN, AND RATHER THAN LET HIS GOONS BEAT THE HELL OUT OF CREAKY OLD ME AND MY MILLENNIAL CHEFS, HE SUGGESTED A CONTEST OF CHAMPIONS.
OTHERWISE KNOWN AS A COUPLE ASSHOLES GOING AT EACH OTHER WITH LENGTHS OF PVC PIPE.
AND IT'S BEEN ABOUT AN HOUR. ***ONE HOUR,*** OUT OF THE PRECIOUS SEVEN ALLOTTED FOR THIS CHALLENGE.

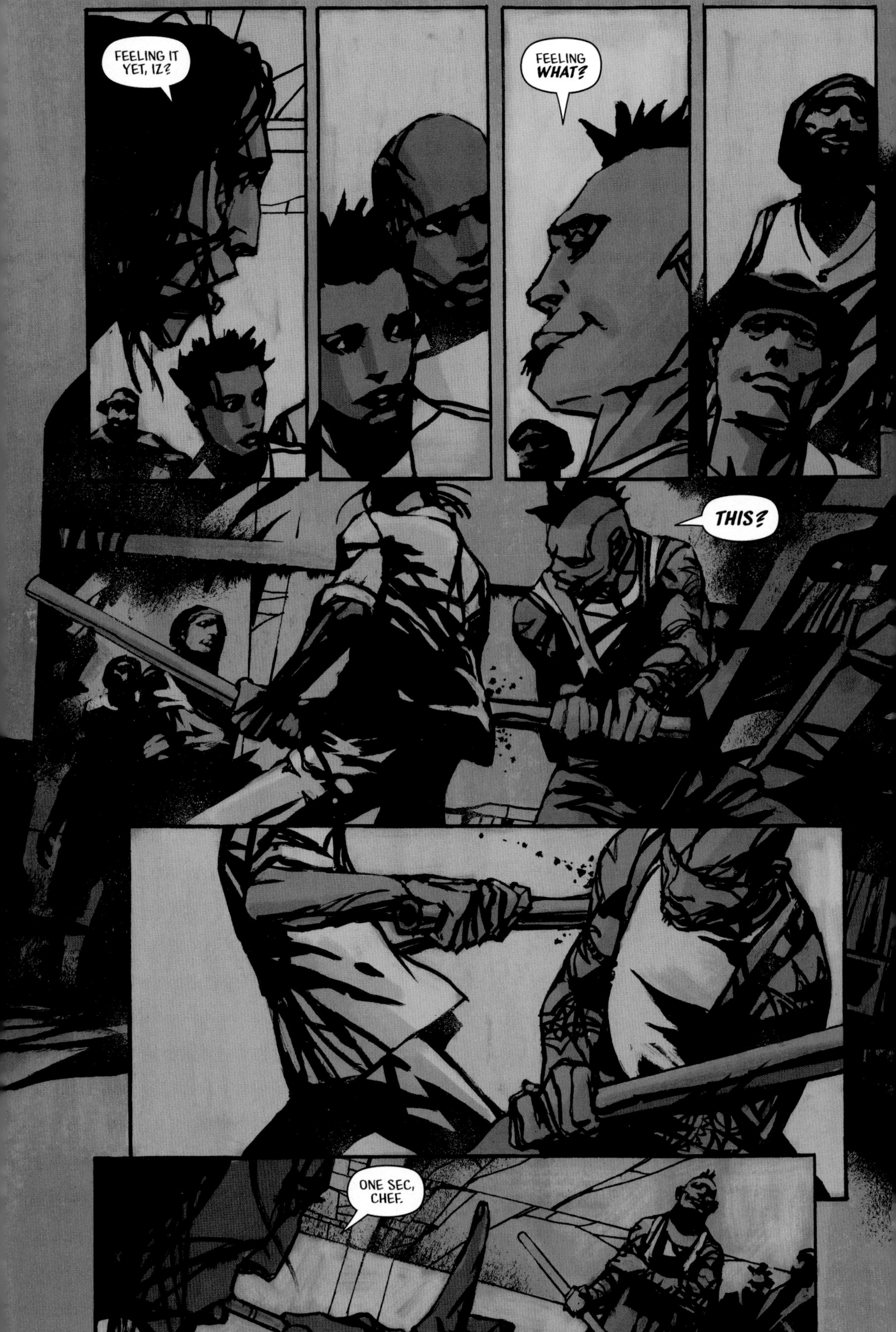
FEELING IT YET, IZ?
FEELING WHAT?
THIS?
ONE SEC, CHEF.
NO REASON THIS CAN'T BE CIVLIZED.

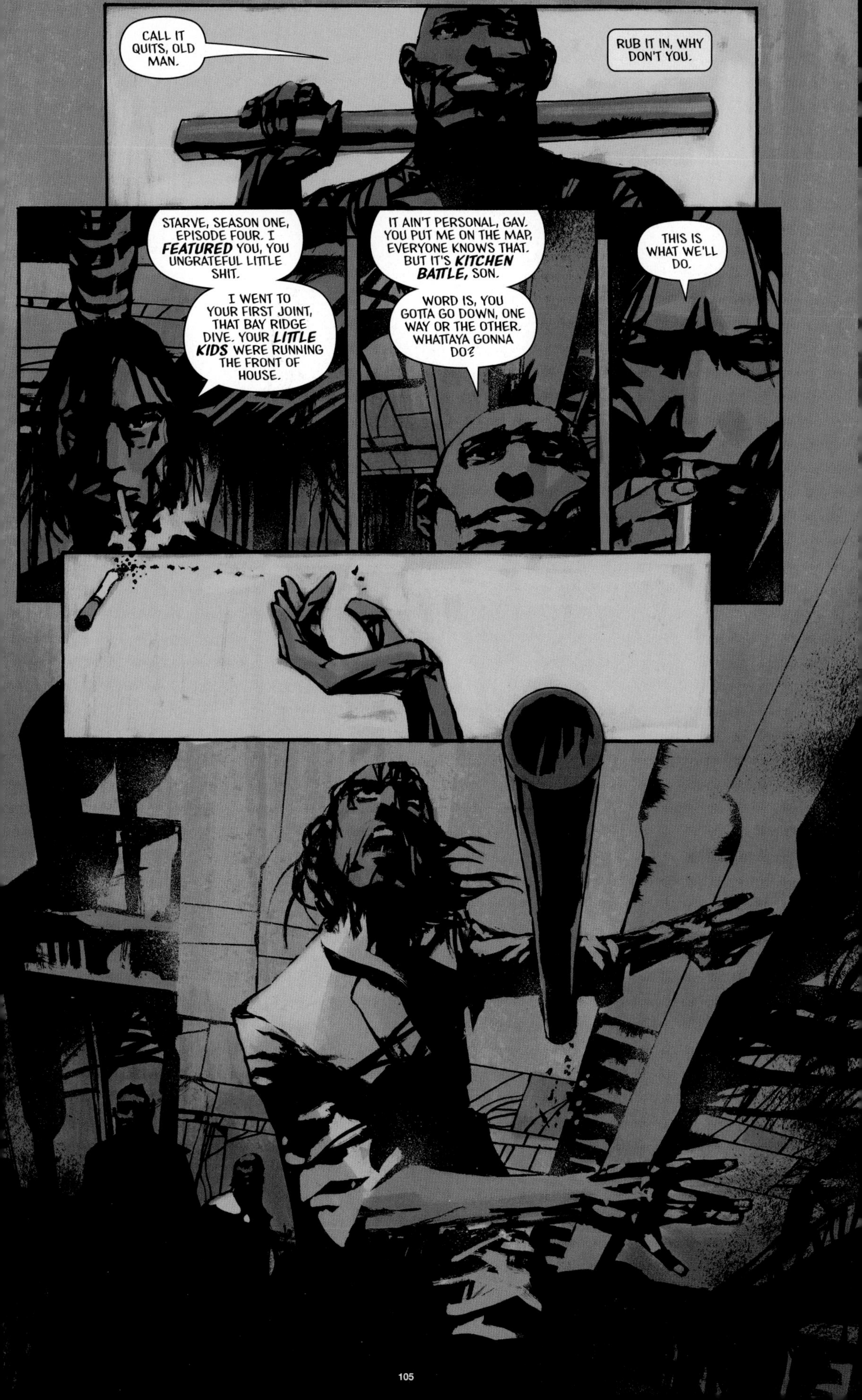
CALL IT QUITS, OLD MAN.
RUB IT IN, WHY DON'T YOU.
STARVE, SEASON ONE, EPISODE FOUR. I **FEATURED** YOU, YOU UNGRATEFUL LITTLE SHIT.
I WENT TO YOUR FIRST JOINT, THAT BAY RIDGE DIVE. YOUR **LITTLE KIDS** WERE RUNNING THE FRONT OF HOUSE.
IT AIN'T PERSONAL, GAV. YOU PUT ME ON THE MAP, EVERYONE KNOWS THAT. BUT IT'S **KITCHEN BATTLE,** SON.
WORD IS, YOU GOTTA GO DOWN, ONE WAY OR THE OTHER. WHATTAYA GONNA DO?
THIS IS WHAT WE'LL DO.

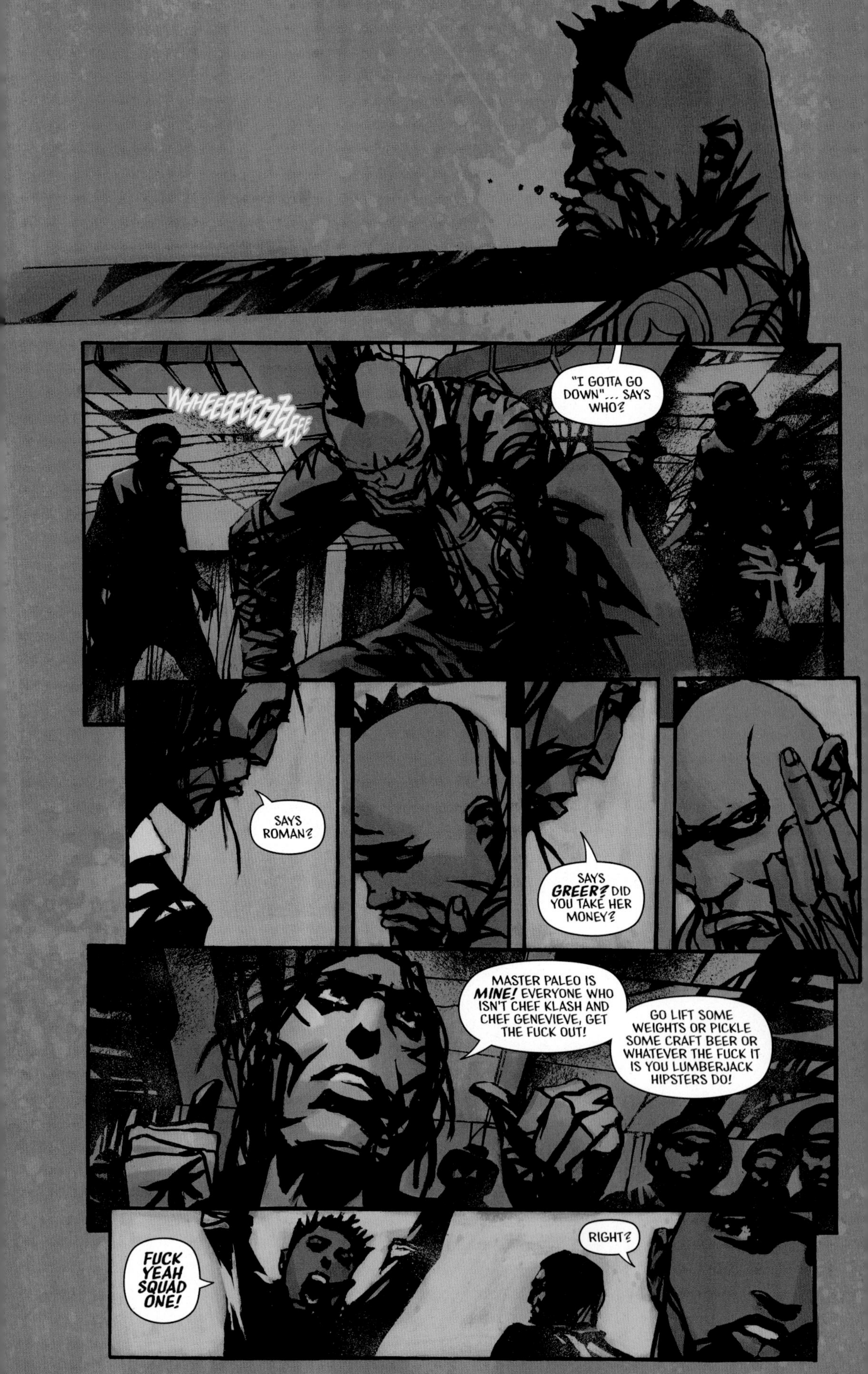
WHHEEEEEEZZZZEEE
"I GOTTA GO DOWN"... SAYS WHO?
SAYS ROMAN?
SAYS GREER? DID YOU TAKE HER MONEY?
MASTER PALEO IS MINE! EVERYONE WHO ISN'T CHEF KLASH AND CHEF GENEVIEVE, GET THE FUCK OUT!
GO LIFT SOME WEIGHTS OR PICKLE SOME CRAFT BEER OR WHATEVER THE FUCK IT IS YOU LUMBERJACK HIPSTERS DO!
FUCK YEAH SQUAD ONE!
RIGHT?

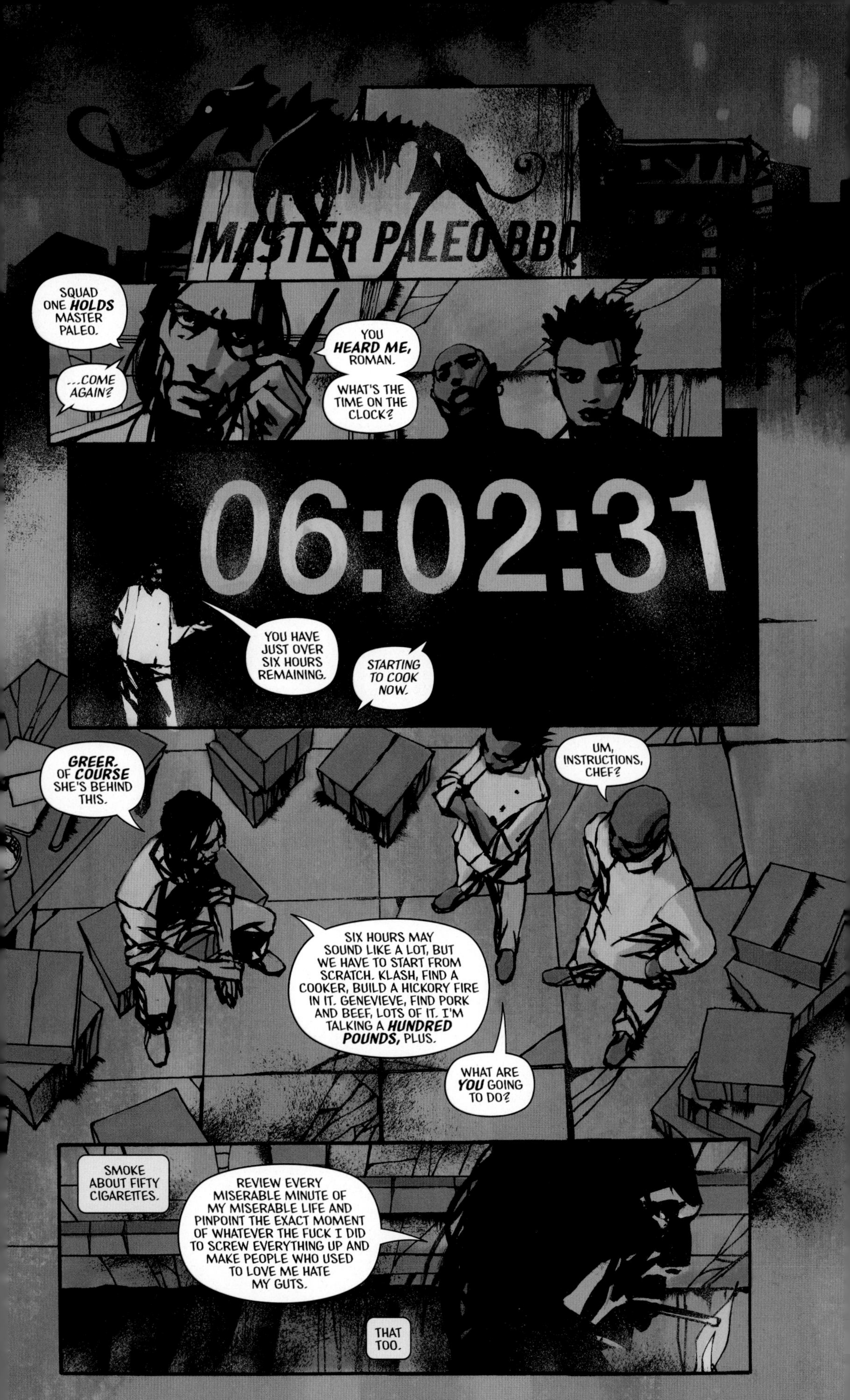
MASTER PALEO BBQ
SQUAD ONE HOLDS MASTER PALEO.
...COME AGAIN?
YOU HEARD ME, ROMAN.
WHAT'S THE TIME ON THE CLOCK?
06:02:31
YOU HAVE JUST OVER SIX HOURS REMAINING.
STARTING TO COOK NOW.
GREER. OF COURSE SHE'S BEHIND THIS.
UM, INSTRUCTIONS, CHEF?
SIX HOURS MAY SOUND LIKE A LOT, BUT WE HAVE TO START FROM SCRATCH. KLASH, FIND A COOKER, BUILD A HICKORY FIRE IN IT. GENEVIEVE, FIND PORK AND BEEF, LOTS OF IT. I'M TALKING A HUNDRED POUNDS, PLUS.
WHAT ARE YOU GOING TO DO?
SMOKE ABOUT FIFTY CIGARETTES.
REVIEW EVERY MISERABLE MINUTE OF MY MISERABLE LIFE AND PINPOINT THE EXACT MOMENT OF WHATEVER THE FUCK I DID TO SCREW EVERYTHING UP AND MAKE PEOPLE WHO USED TO LOVE ME HATE MY GUTS.
THAT TOO.

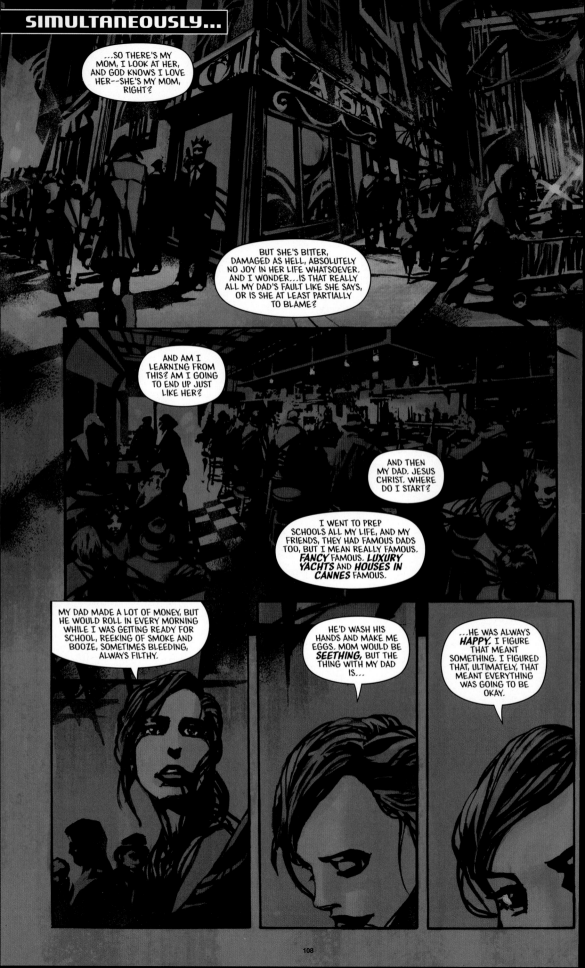

...SO THERE'S MY MOM, I LOOK AT HER, AND GOD KNOWS I LOVE HER--SHE'S MY MOM, RIGHT?

BUT SHE'S BITTER, DAMAGED AS HELL, ABSOLUTELY NO JOY IN HER LIFE WHATSOEVER. AND I WONDER...IS THAT REALLY ALL MY DAD'S FAULT LIKE SHE SAYS, OR IS SHE AT LEAST PARTIALLY TO BLAME?

AND AM I LEARNING FROM THIS? AM I GOING TO END UP JUST LIKE HER?

AND THEN MY DAD. JESUS CHRIST. WHERE DO I START?

I WENT TO PREP SCHOOLS ALL MY LIFE, AND MY FRIENDS, THEY HAD FAMOUS DADS TOO, BUT I MEAN REALLY FAMOUS. *FANCY* FAMOUS. *LUXURY YACHTS* AND *HOUSES IN CANNES* FAMOUS.

MY DAD MADE A LOT OF MONEY, BUT HE WOULD ROLL IN EVERY MORNING WHILE I WAS GETTING READY FOR SCHOOL, REEKING OF SMOKE AND BOOZE, SOMETIMES BLEEDING, ALWAYS FILTHY.

HE'D WASH HIS HANDS AND MAKE ME EGGS. MOM WOULD BE *SEETHING*, BUT THE THING WITH MY DAD IS...

...HE WAS ALWAYS *HAPPY.* I FIGURE THAT MEANT SOMETHING. I FIGURED THAT, ULTIMATELY, THAT MEANT EVERYTHING WAS GOING TO BE OKAY.

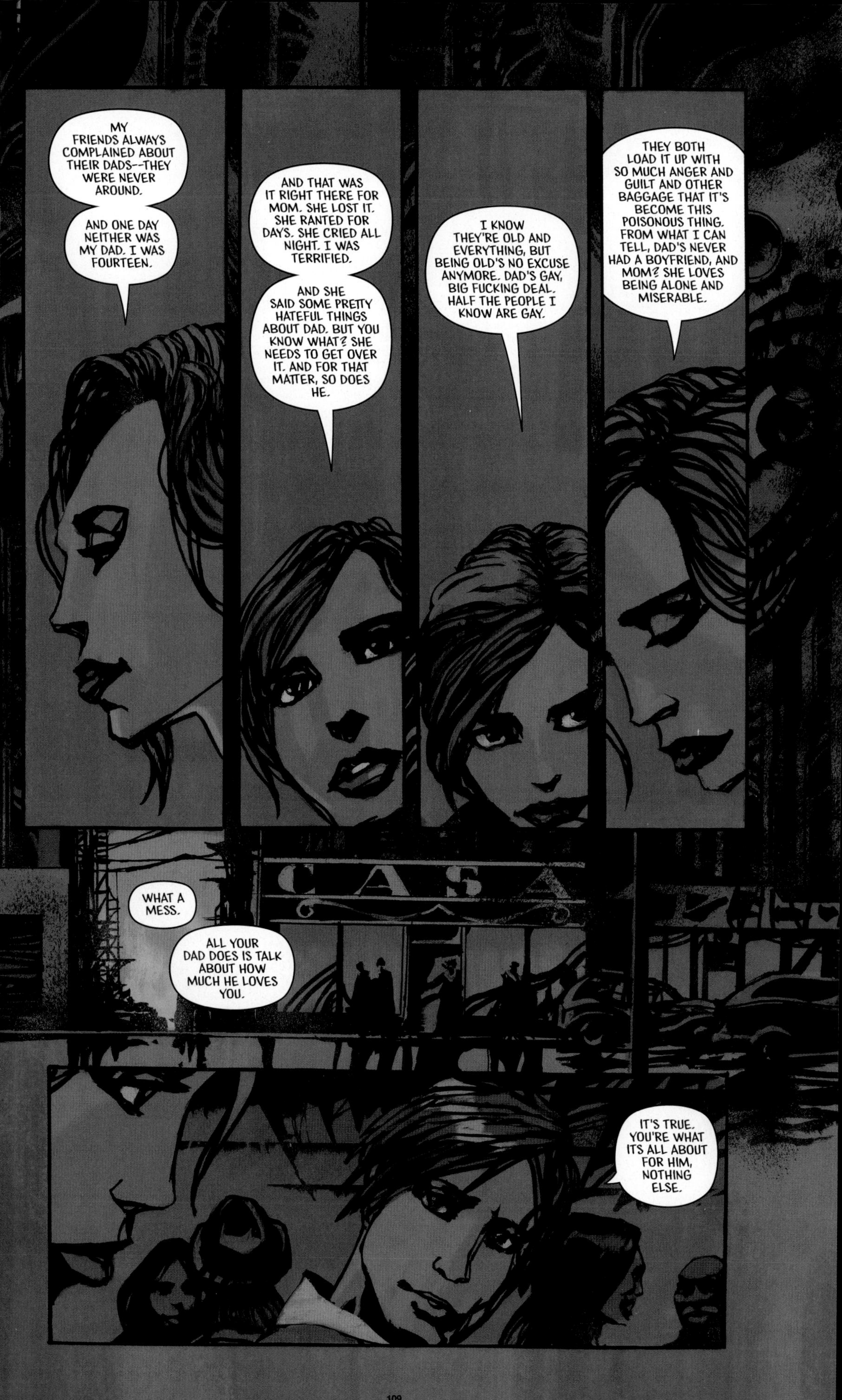

MY FRIENDS ALWAYS COMPLAINED ABOUT THEIR DADS--THEY WERE NEVER AROUND.
AND ONE DAY NEITHER WAS MY DAD. I WAS FOURTEEN.
AND THAT WAS IT RIGHT THERE FOR MOM. SHE LOST IT. SHE RANTED FOR DAYS. SHE CRIED ALL NIGHT. I WAS TERRIFIED.
AND SHE SAID SOME PRETTY HATEFUL THINGS ABOUT DAD. BUT YOU KNOW WHAT? SHE NEEDS TO GET OVER IT. AND FOR THAT MATTER, SO DOES HE.
I KNOW THEY'RE OLD AND EVERYTHING, BUT BEING OLD'S NO EXCUSE ANYMORE. DAD'S GAY, BIG FUCKING DEAL. HALF THE PEOPLE I KNOW ARE GAY.
THEY BOTH LOAD IT UP WITH SO MUCH ANGER AND GUILT AND OTHER BAGGAGE THAT IT'S BECOME THIS POISONOUS THING. FROM WHAT I CAN TELL, DAD'S NEVER HAD A BOYFRIEND, AND MOM? SHE LOVES BEING ALONE AND MISERABLE.
CASA
WHAT A MESS.
ALL YOUR DAD DOES IS TALK ABOUT HOW MUCH HE LOVES YOU.
IT'S TRUE. YOU'RE WHAT ITS ALL ABOUT FOR HIM, NOTHING ELSE.

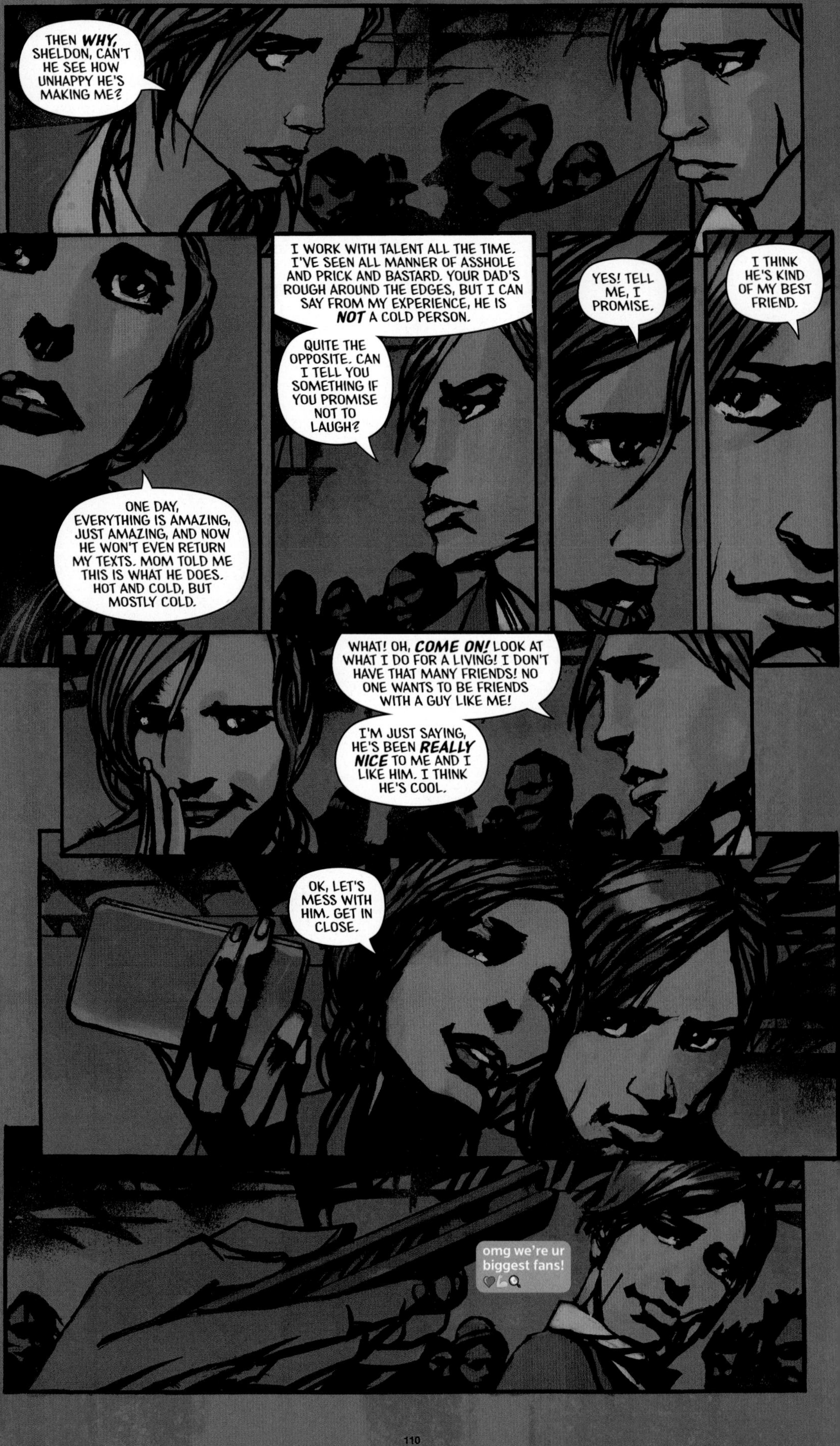
THEN WHY, SHELDON, CAN'T HE SEE HOW UNHAPPY HE'S MAKING ME?
ONE DAY, EVERYTHING IS AMAZING, JUST AMAZING, AND NOW HE WON'T EVEN RETURN MY TEXTS. MOM TOLD ME THIS IS WHAT HE DOES. HOT AND COLD, BUT MOSTLY COLD.
I WORK WITH TALENT ALL THE TIME. I'VE SEEN ALL MANNER OF ASSHOLE AND PRICK AND BASTARD. YOUR DAD'S ROUGH AROUND THE EDGES, BUT I CAN SAY FROM MY EXPERIENCE, HE IS NOT A COLD PERSON.
QUITE THE OPPOSITE. CAN I TELL YOU SOMETHING IF YOU PROMISE NOT TO LAUGH?
YES! TELL ME, I PROMISE.
I THINK HE'S KIND OF MY BEST FRIEND.
WHAT! OH, COME ON! LOOK AT WHAT I DO FOR A LIVING! I DON'T HAVE THAT MANY FRIENDS! NO ONE WANTS TO BE FRIENDS WITH A GUY LIKE ME!
I'M JUST SAYING, HE'S BEEN REALLY NICE TO ME AND I LIKE HIM. I THINK HE'S COOL.
OK, LET'S MESS WITH HIM. GET IN CLOSE.
omg we're ur biggest fans!

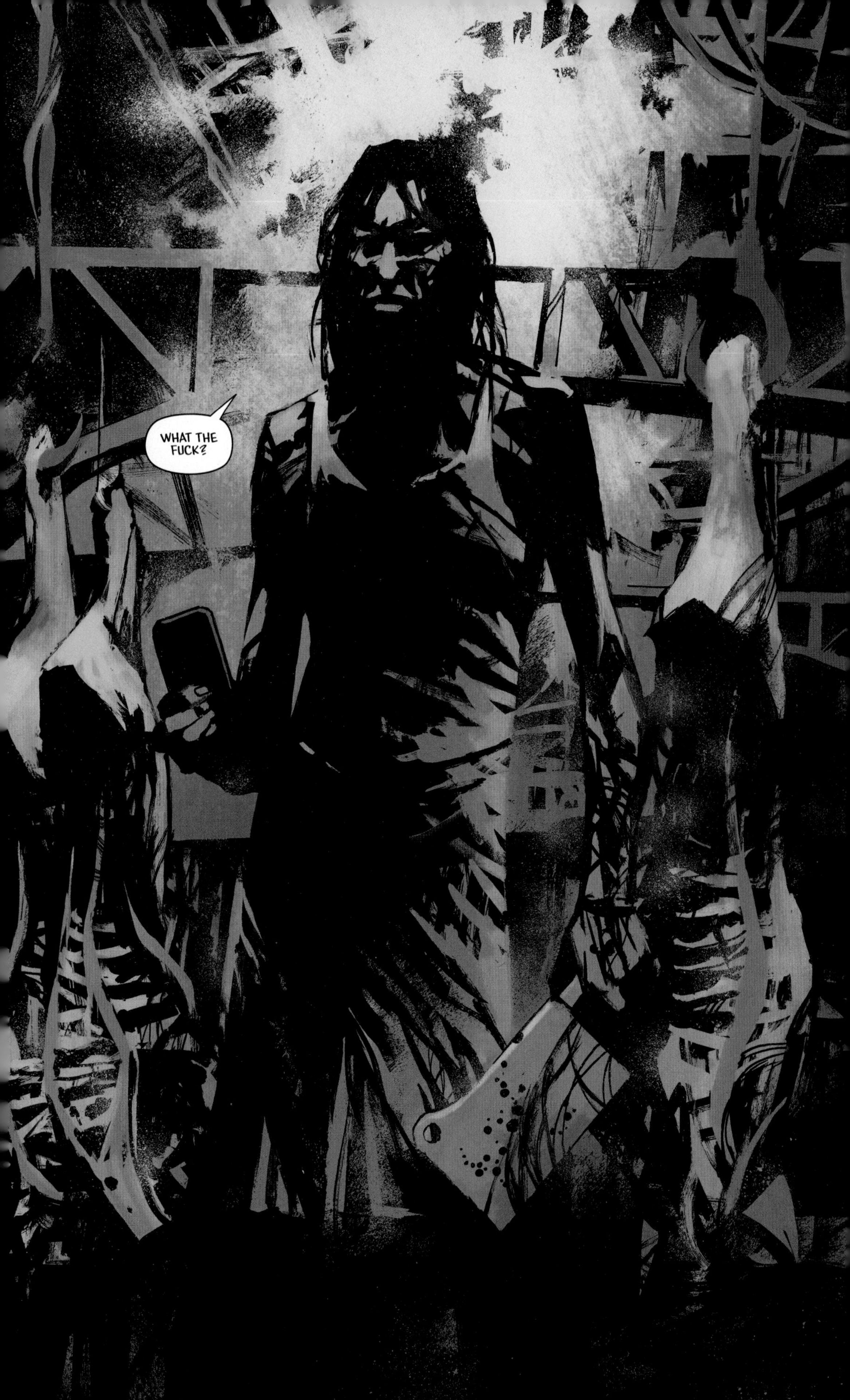
WHAT THE
FUCK?

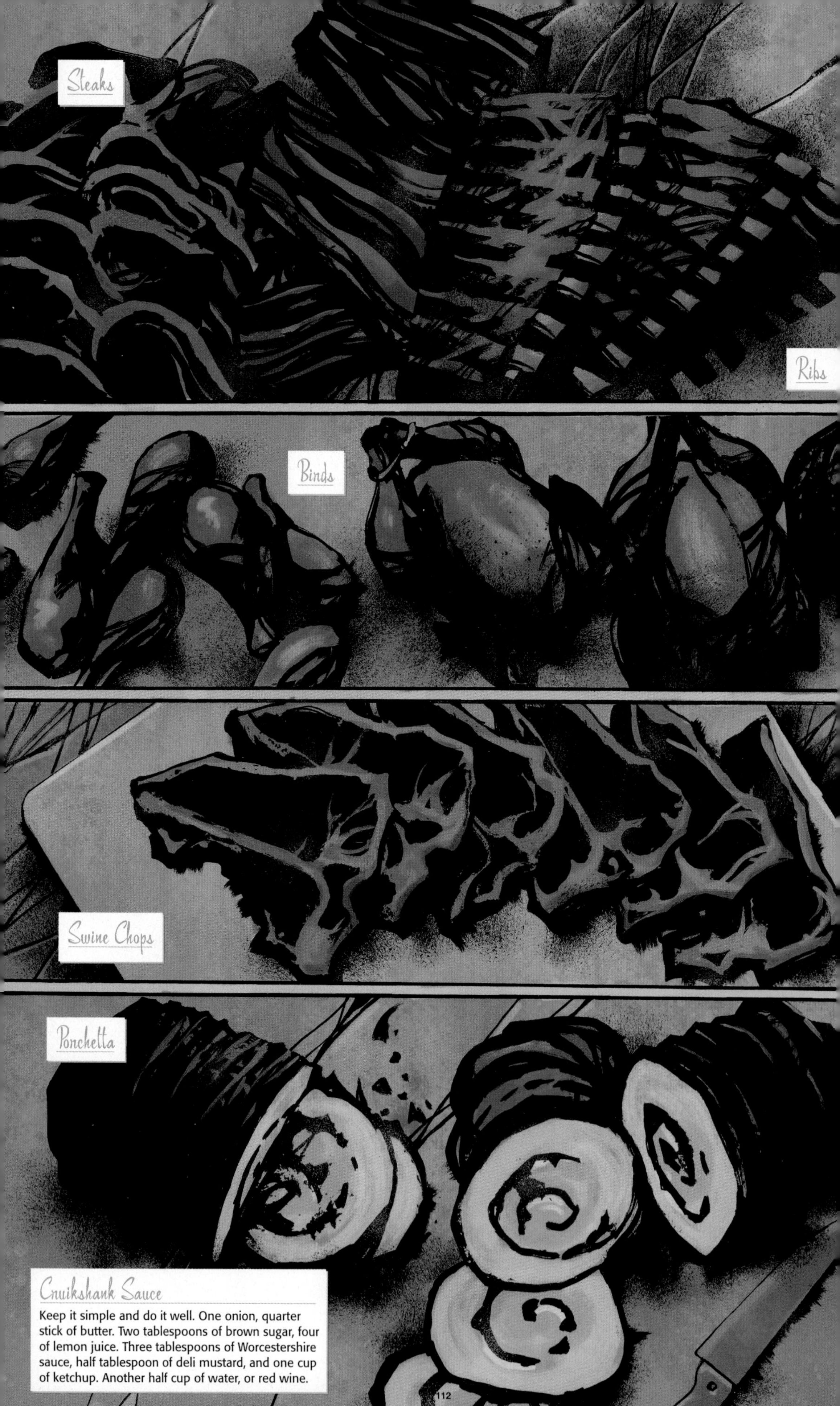
Steaks
Ribs
Birds
Swine Chops
Porchetta
Cruikshank Sauce
Keep it simple and do it well. One onion, quarter stick of butter. Two tablespoons of brown sugar, four of lemon juice. Three tablespoons of Worcestershire sauce, half tablespoon of deli mustard, and one cup of ketchup. Another half cup of water, or red wine.

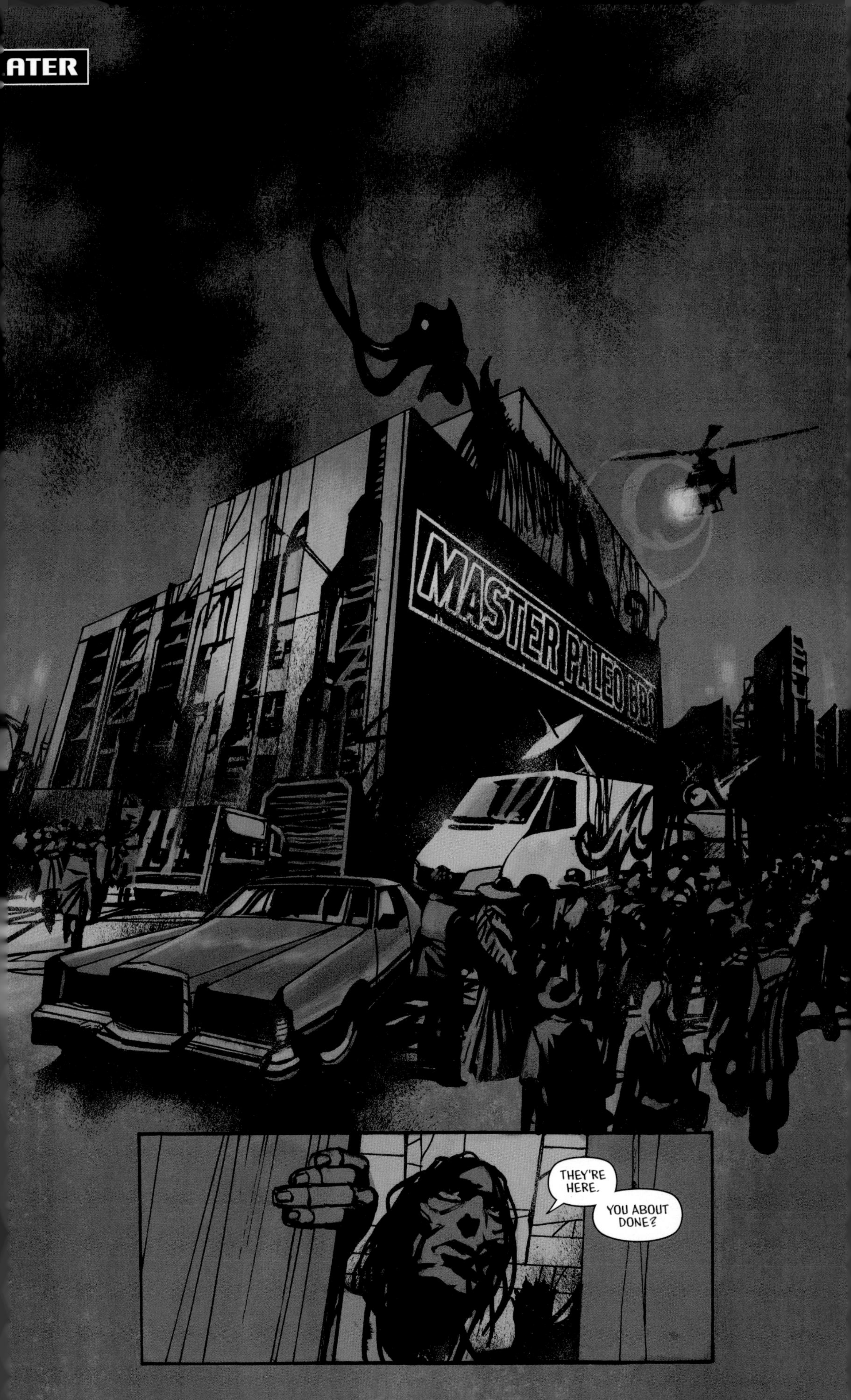
LATER
MASTER PALEO BBQ
THEY'RE HERE.
YOU ABOUT DONE?

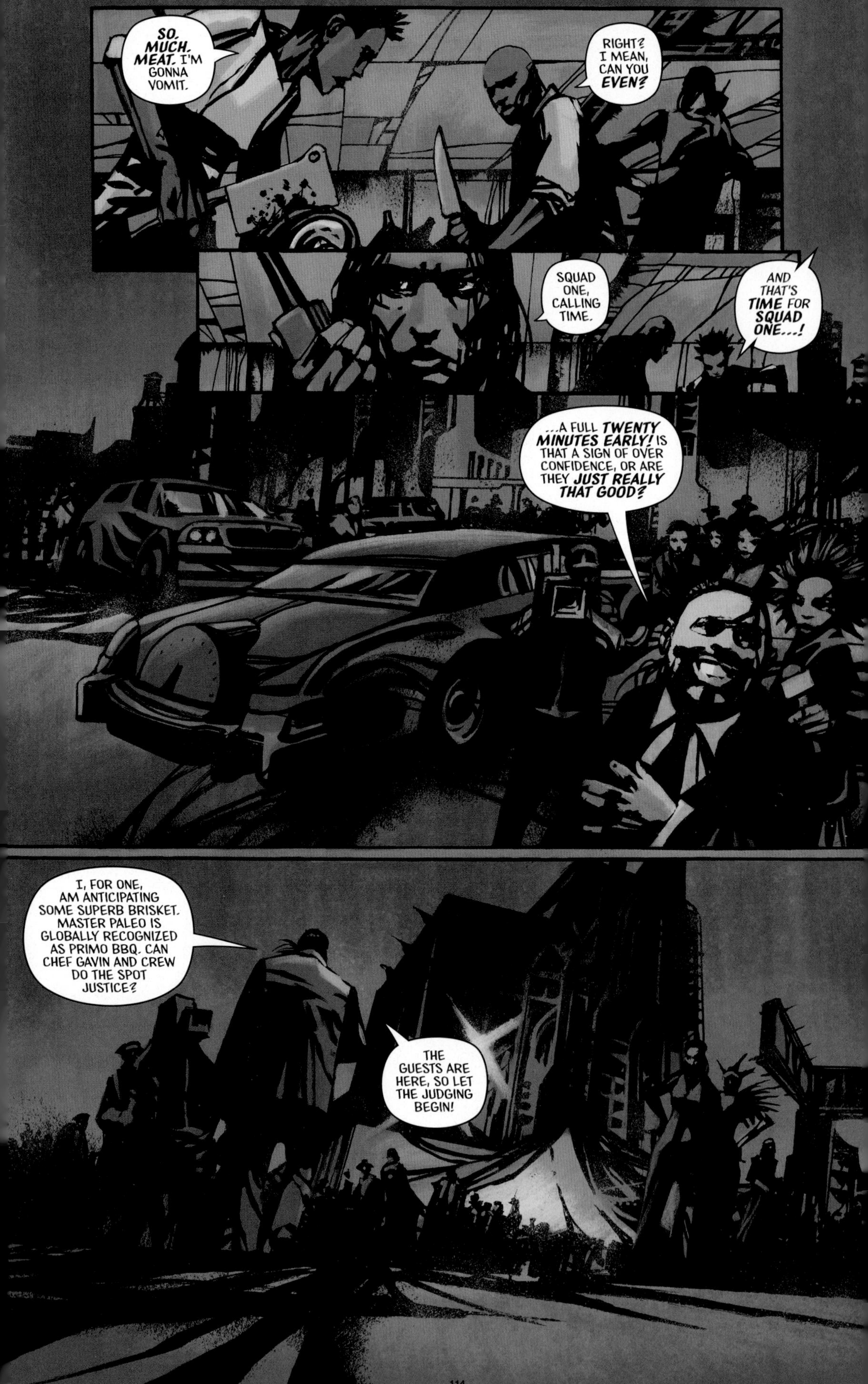
SO. MUCH. MEAT. I'M GONNA VOMIT.
RIGHT? I MEAN, CAN YOU EVEN?
SQUAD ONE, CALLING TIME.
AND THAT'S TIME FOR SQUAD ONE...!
...A FULL TWENTY MINUTES EARLY! IS THAT A SIGN OF OVER CONFIDENCE, OR ARE THEY JUST REALLY THAT GOOD?
I, FOR ONE, AM ANTICIPATING SOME SUPERB BRISKET. MASTER PALEO IS GLOBALLY RECOGNIZED AS PRIMO BBQ. CAN CHEF GAVIN AND CREW DO THE SPOT JUSTICE?
THE GUESTS ARE HERE, SO LET THE JUDGING BEGIN!

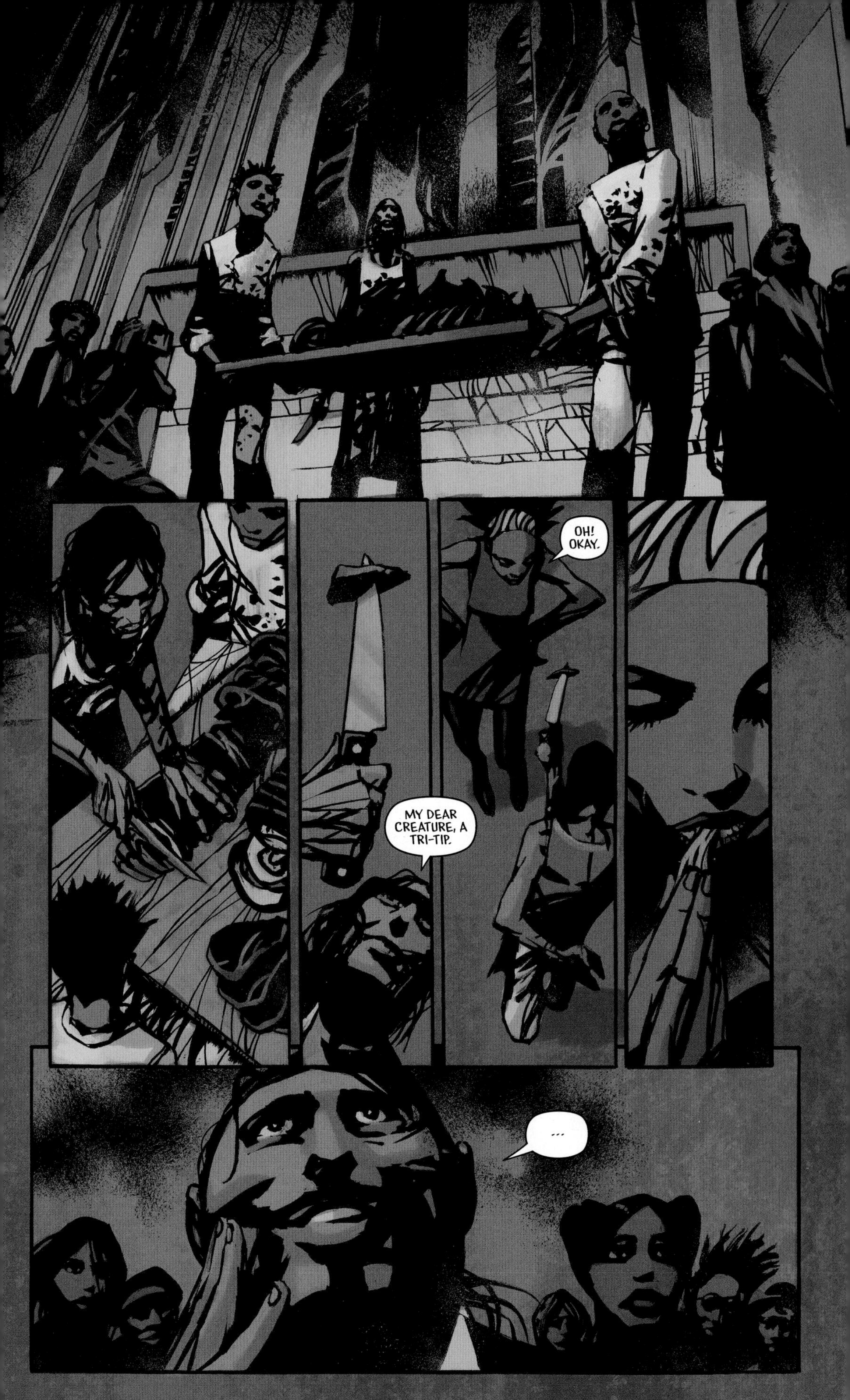
MY DEAR CREATURE, A TRI-TIP.
OH! OKAY.
...

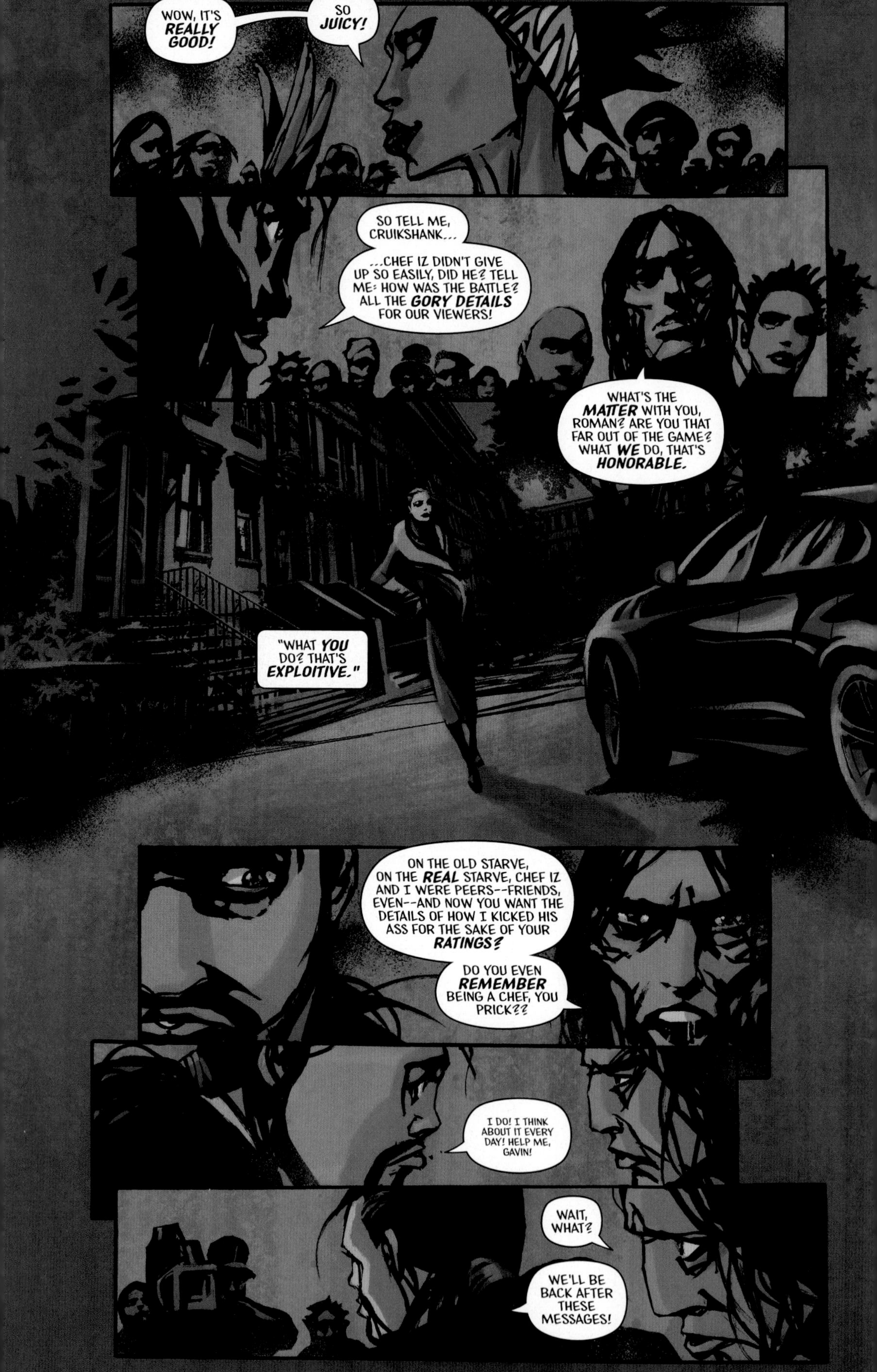
WOW, IT'S REALLY GOOD!
SO JUICY!
SO TELL ME, CRUIKSHANK...
...CHEF IZ DIDN'T GIVE UP SO EASILY, DID HE? TELL ME: HOW WAS THE BATTLE? ALL THE GORY DETAILS FOR OUR VIEWERS!
WHAT'S THE MATTER WITH YOU, ROMAN? ARE YOU THAT FAR OUT OF THE GAME? WHAT WE DO, THAT'S HONORABLE.
"WHAT YOU DO? THAT'S EXPLOITIVE."
ON THE OLD STARVE, ON THE REAL STARVE, CHEF IZ AND I WERE PEERS--FRIENDS, EVEN--AND NOW YOU WANT THE DETAILS OF HOW I KICKED HIS ASS FOR THE SAKE OF YOUR RATINGS?
DO YOU EVEN REMEMBER BEING A CHEF, YOU PRICK??
I DO! I THINK ABOUT IT EVERY DAY! HELP ME, GAVIN!
WAIT, WHAT?
WE'LL BE BACK AFTER THESE MESSAGES!

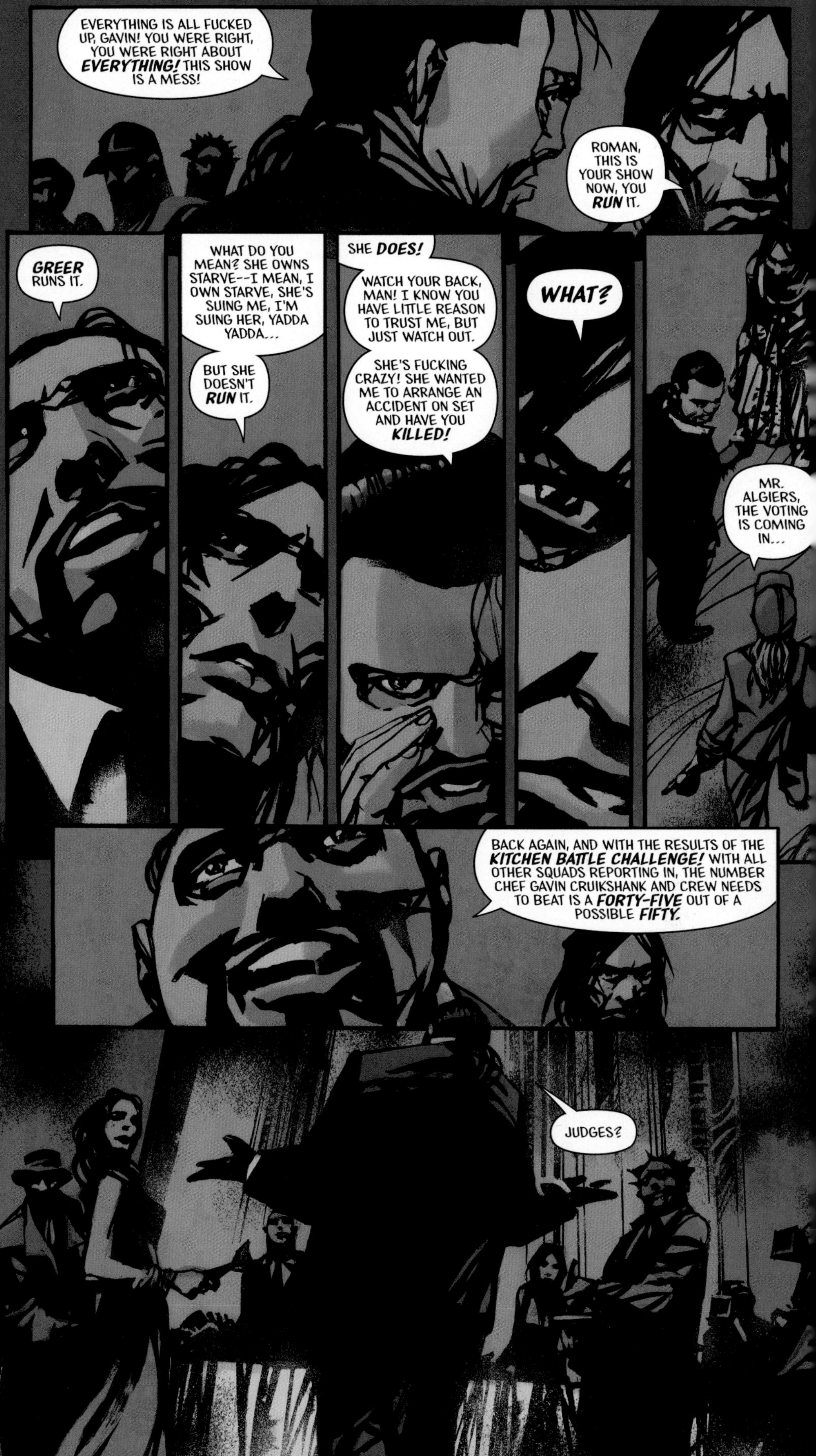
EVERYTHING IS ALL FUCKED UP, GAVIN! YOU WERE RIGHT, YOU WERE RIGHT ABOUT EVERYTHING! THIS SHOW IS A MESS!
ROMAN, THIS IS YOUR SHOW NOW, YOU RUN IT.
GREER RUNS IT.
WHAT DO YOU MEAN? SHE OWNS STARVE--I MEAN, I OWN STARVE, SHE'S SUING ME, I'M SUING HER, YADDA YADDA...
BUT SHE DOESN'T RUN IT.
SHE DOES!
WATCH YOUR BACK, MAN! I KNOW YOU HAVE LITTLE REASON TO TRUST ME, BUT JUST WATCH OUT.
SHE'S FUCKING CRAZY! SHE WANTED ME TO ARRANGE AN ACCIDENT ON SET AND HAVE YOU KILLED!
WHAT?
MR. ALGIERS, THE VOTING IS COMING IN...
BACK AGAIN, AND WITH THE RESULTS OF THE KITCHEN BATTLE CHALLENGE! WITH ALL OTHER SQUADS REPORTING IN, THE NUMBER CHEF GAVIN CRUIKSHANK AND CREW NEEDS TO BEAT IS A FORTY-FIVE OUT OF A POSSIBLE FIFTY.
JUDGES?

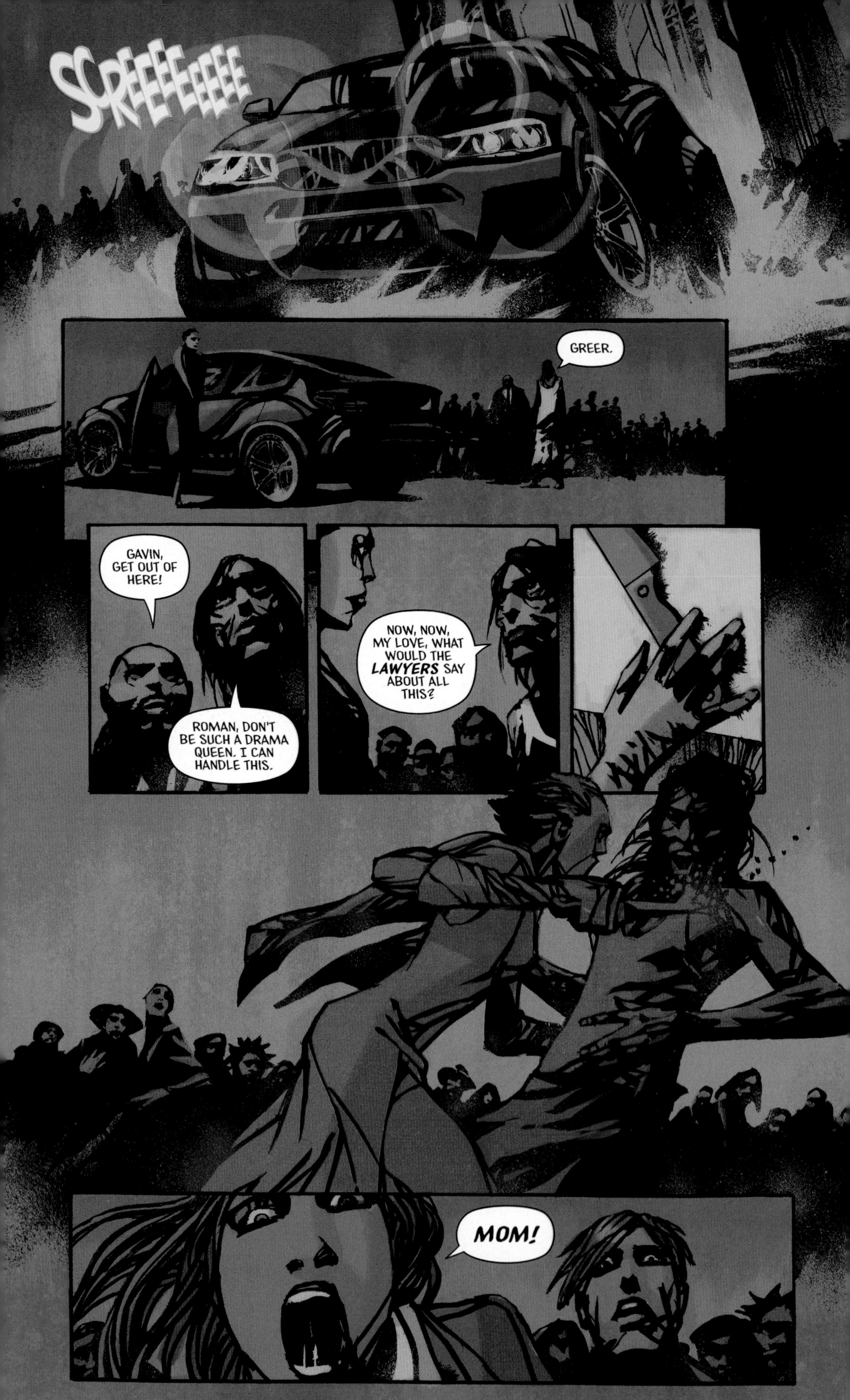
SCREEEEEEEE
GREER.
GAVIN, GET OUT OF HERE!
ROMAN, DON'T BE SUCH A DRAMA QUEEN. I CAN HANDLE THIS.
NOW, NOW, MY LOVE, WHAT WOULD THE LAWYERS SAY ABOUT ALL THIS?
MOM!

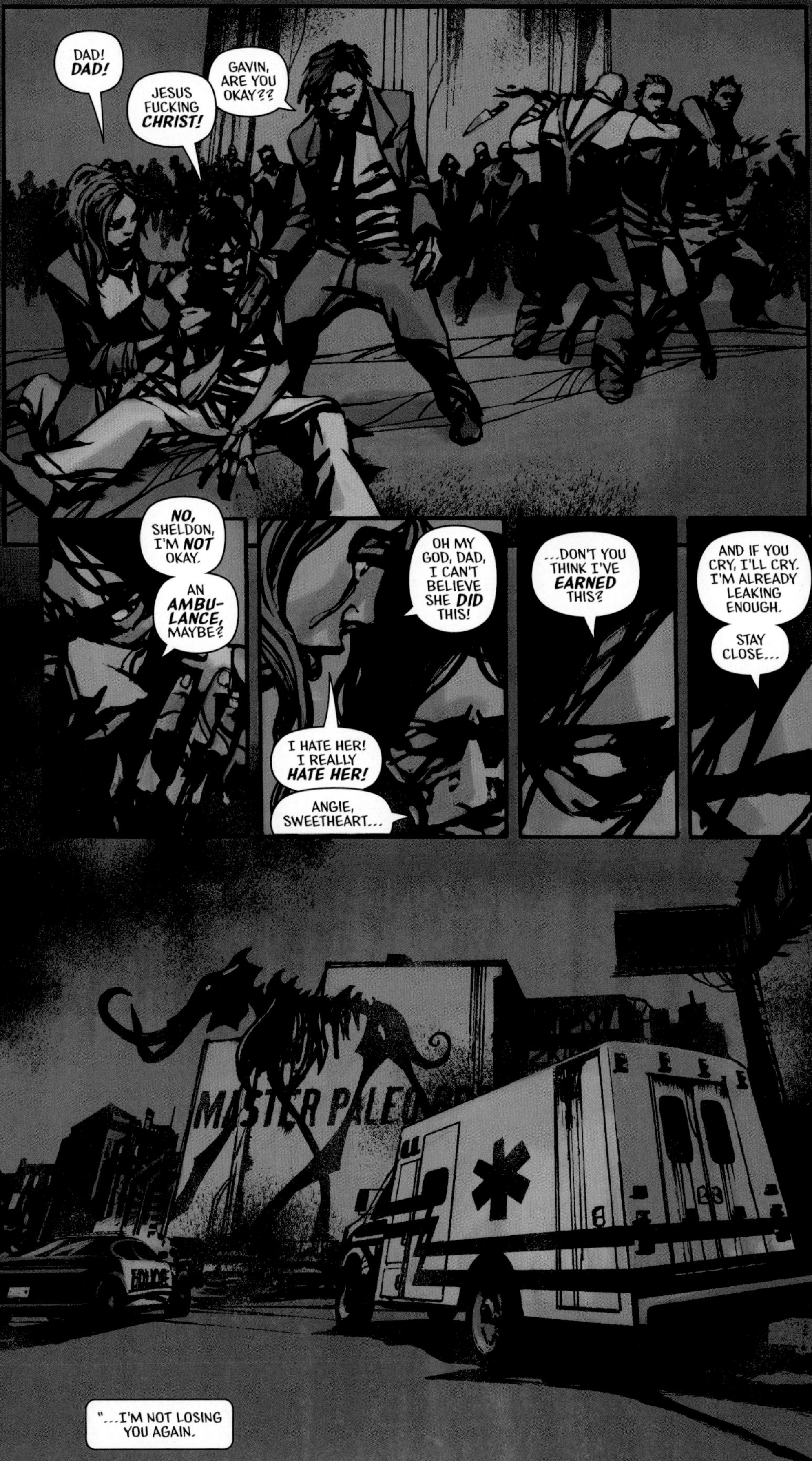
DAD! DAD!
JESUS FUCKING CHRIST!
GAVIN, ARE YOU OKAY??
NO, SHELDON, I'M NOT OKAY.
AN AMBULANCE, MAYBE?
OH MY GOD, DAD, I CAN'T BELIEVE SHE DID THIS!
I HATE HER! I REALLY HATE HER!
ANGIE, SWEETHEART...
...DON'T YOU THINK I'VE EARNED THIS?
AND IF YOU CRY, I'LL CRY. I'M ALREADY LEAKING ENOUGH.
STAY CLOSE...
MASTER PALEO
POLICE
"...I'M NOT LOSING YOU AGAIN.

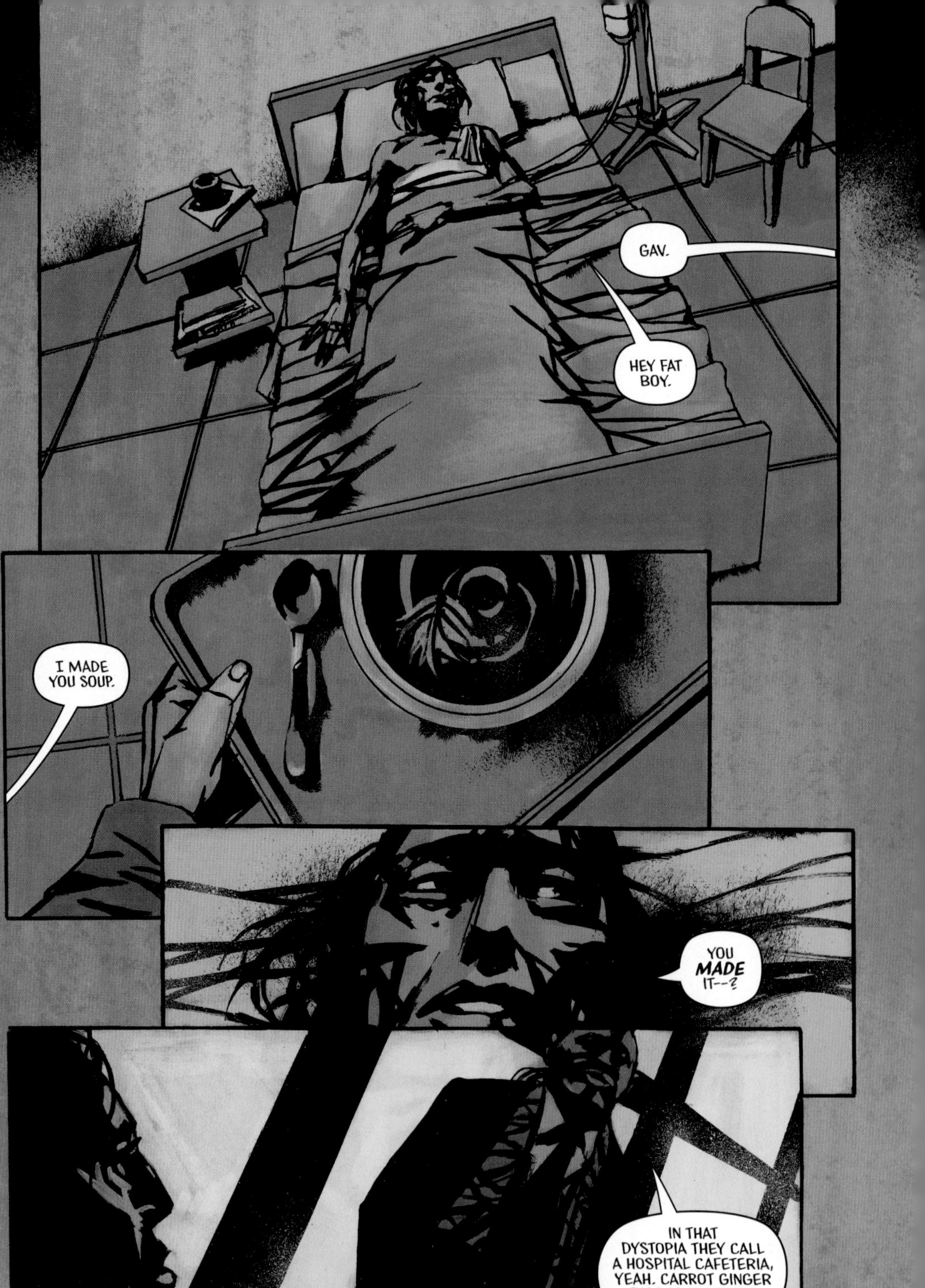
GAV.
HEY FAT BOY.
I MADE YOU SOUP.
YOU MADE IT--?
IN THAT DYSTOPIA THEY CALL A HOSPITAL CAFETERIA, YEAH. CARROT GINGER BISQUE. I KEPT IT SIMPLE.

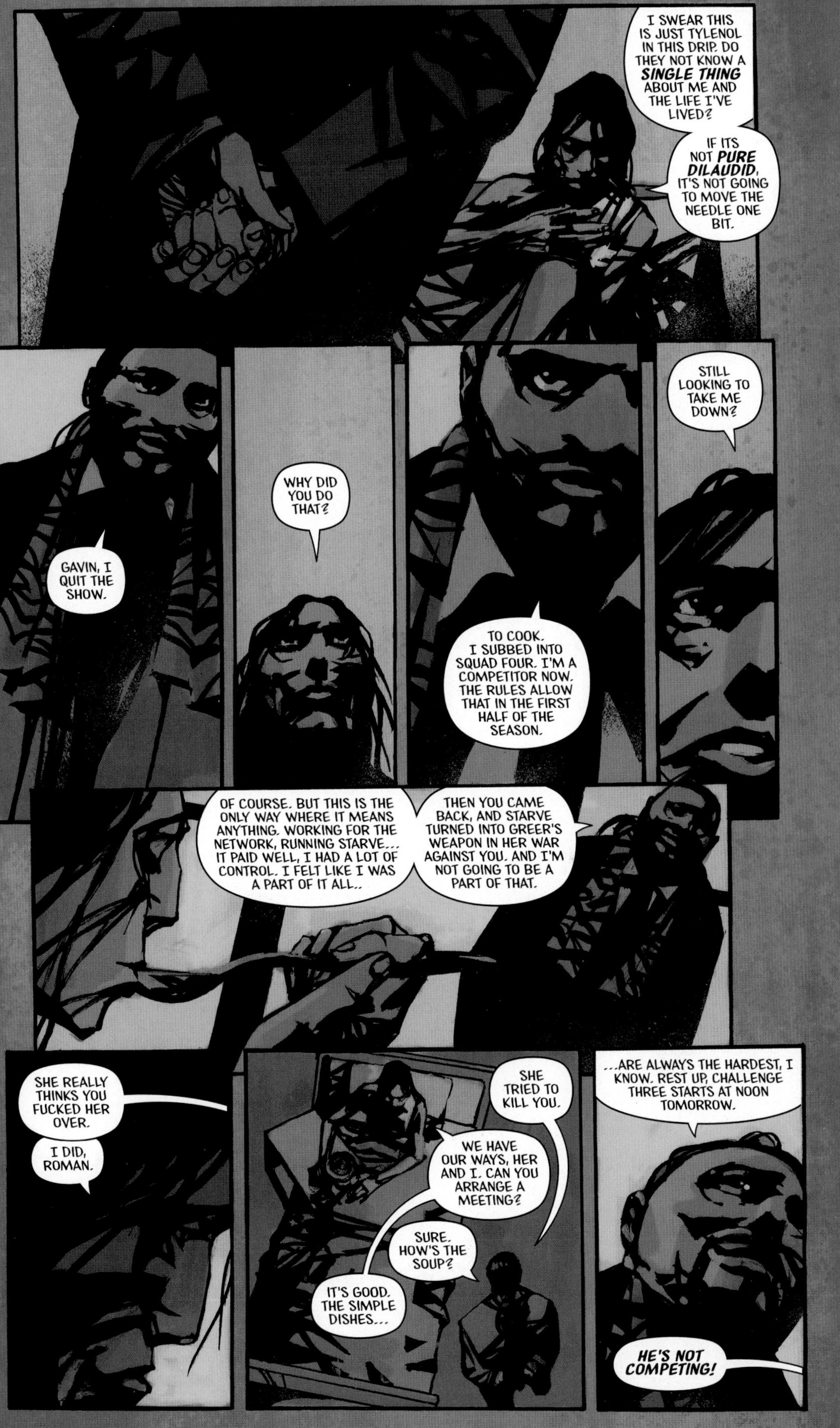
I SWEAR THIS IS JUST TYLENOL IN THIS DRIP. DO THEY NOT KNOW A SINGLE THING ABOUT ME AND THE LIFE I'VE LIVED?
IF ITS NOT PURE DILAUDID, IT'S NOT GOING TO MOVE THE NEEDLE ONE BIT.
GAVIN, I QUIT THE SHOW.
WHY DID YOU DO THAT?
TO COOK. I SUBBED INTO SQUAD FOUR. I'M A COMPETITOR NOW. THE RULES ALLOW THAT IN THE FIRST HALF OF THE SEASON.
STILL LOOKING TO TAKE ME DOWN?
OF COURSE. BUT THIS IS THE ONLY WAY WHERE IT MEANS ANYTHING. WORKING FOR THE NETWORK, RUNNING STARVE... IT PAID WELL, I HAD A LOT OF CONTROL. I FELT LIKE I WAS A PART OF IT ALL..
THEN YOU CAME BACK, AND STARVE TURNED INTO GREER'S WEAPON IN HER WAR AGAINST YOU. AND I'M NOT GOING TO BE A PART OF THAT.
SHE REALLY THINKS YOU FUCKED HER OVER.
I DID, ROMAN.
SHE TRIED TO KILL YOU.
WE HAVE OUR WAYS, HER AND I. CAN YOU ARRANGE A MEETING?
SURE. HOW'S THE SOUP?
IT'S GOOD. THE SIMPLE DISHES...
...ARE ALWAYS THE HARDEST, I KNOW. REST UP, CHALLENGE THREE STARTS AT NOON TOMORROW.
HE'S NOT COMPETING!

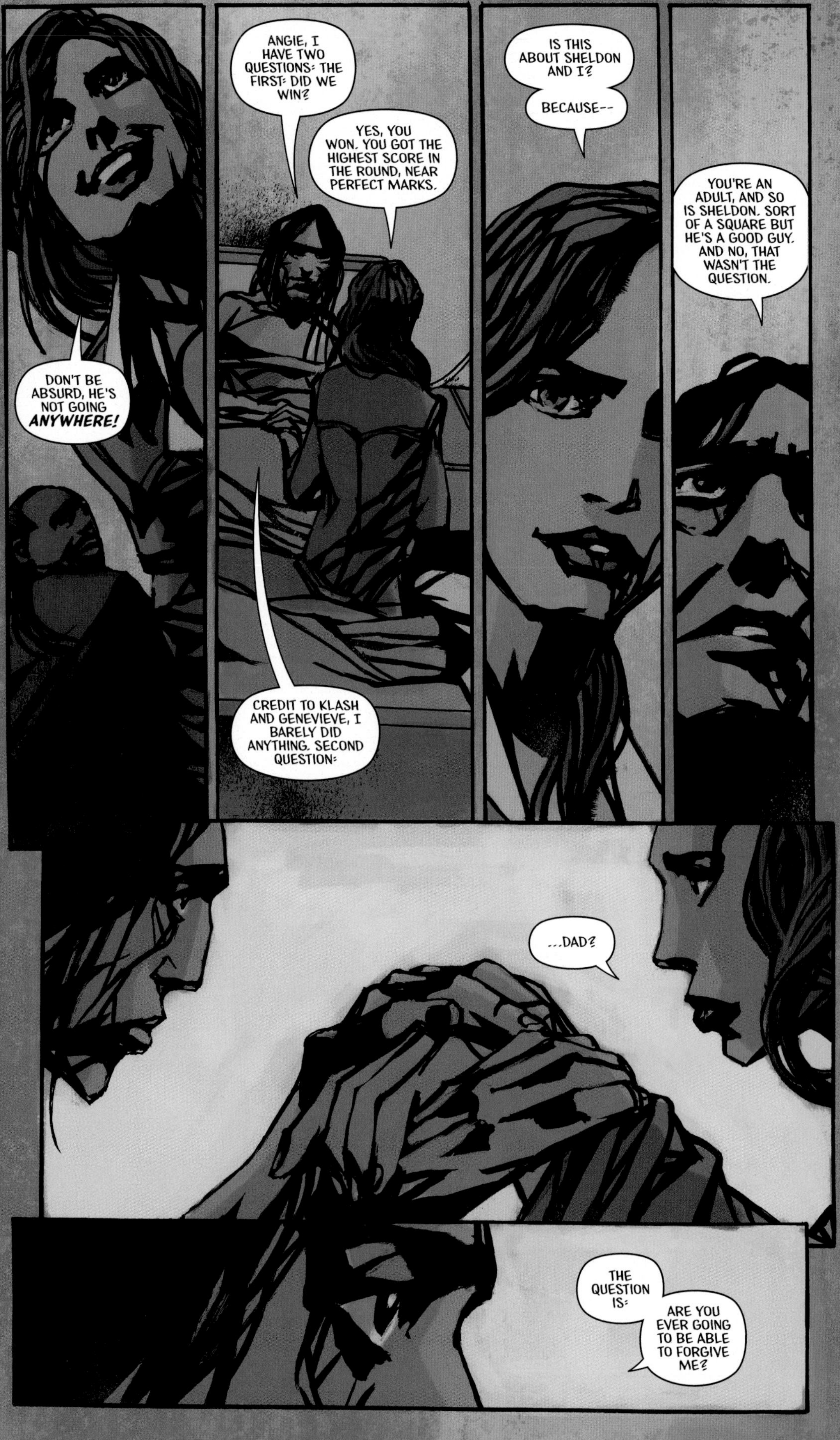
DON'T BE ABSURD, HE'S NOT GOING *ANYWHERE!*
ANGIE, I HAVE TWO QUESTIONS: THE FIRST: DID WE WIN?
YES, YOU WON. YOU GOT THE HIGHEST SCORE IN THE ROUND, NEAR PERFECT MARKS.
CREDIT TO KLASH AND GENEVIEVE, I BARELY DID ANYTHING. SECOND QUESTION:
IS THIS ABOUT SHELDON AND I?
BECAUSE--
YOU'RE AN ADULT, AND SO IS SHELDON. SORT OF A SQUARE BUT HE'S A GOOD GUY. AND NO, THAT WASN'T THE QUESTION.
...DAD?
THE QUESTION IS:
ARE YOU EVER GOING TO BE ABLE TO FORGIVE ME?

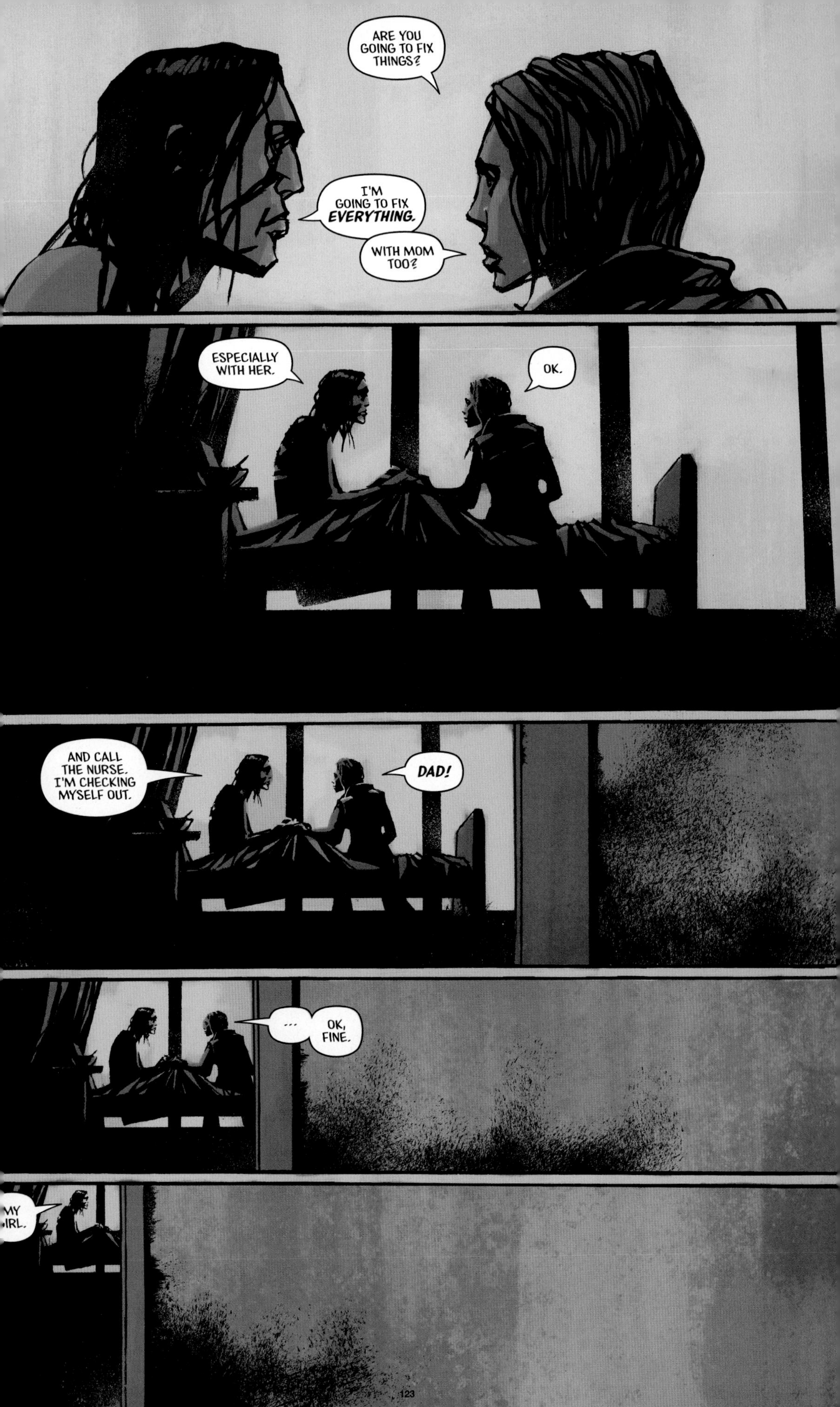

ARE YOU GOING TO FIX THINGS?
I'M GOING TO FIX EVERYTHING.
WITH MOM TOO?
ESPECIALLY WITH HER.
OK.
AND CALL THE NURSE. I'M CHECKING MYSELF OUT.
DAD!
...
OK, FINE.
MY
IRL.

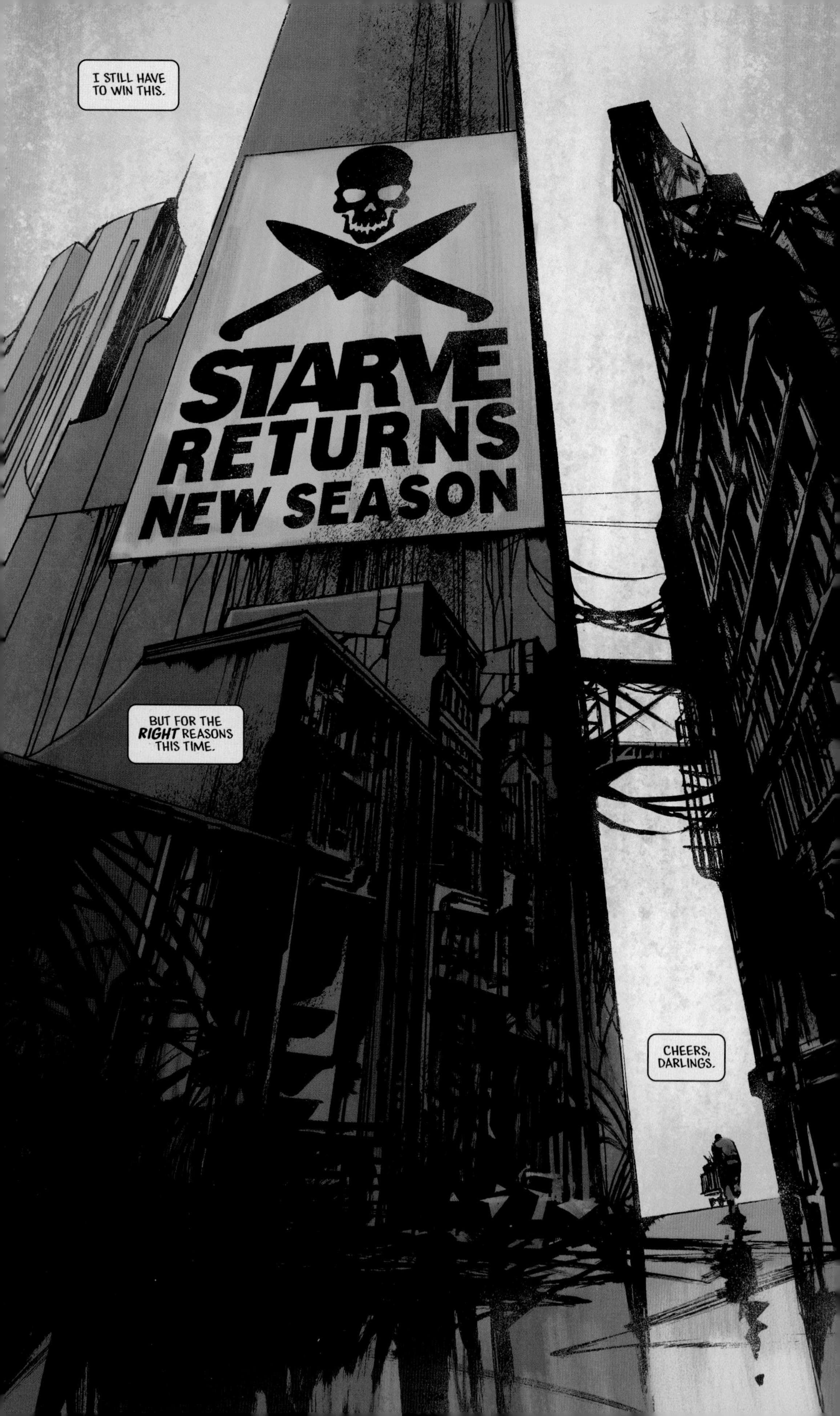
I STILL HAVE TO WIN THIS.
STARVE RETURNS NEW SEASON
BUT FOR THE RIGHT REASONS THIS TIME.
CHEERS, DARLINGS.

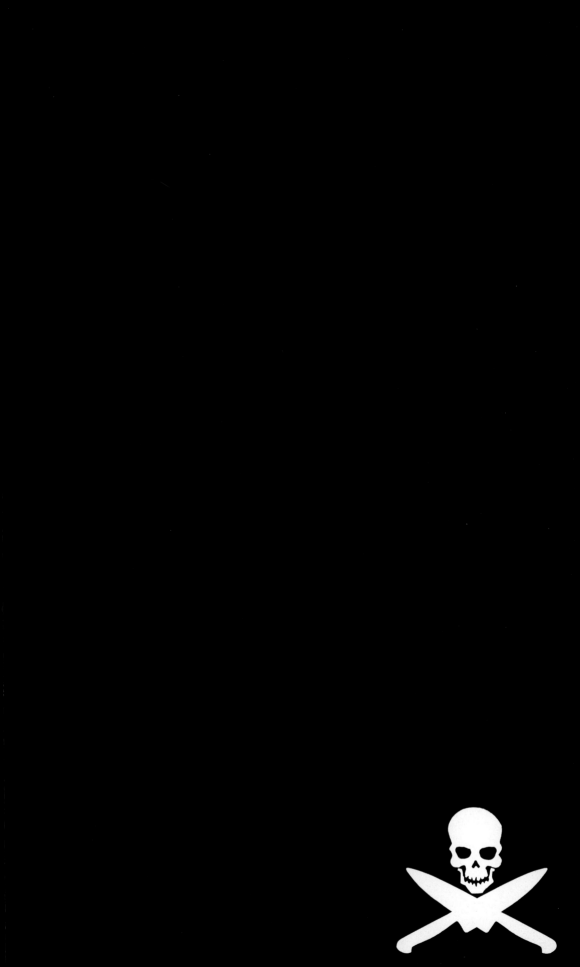

COVER GALLERY

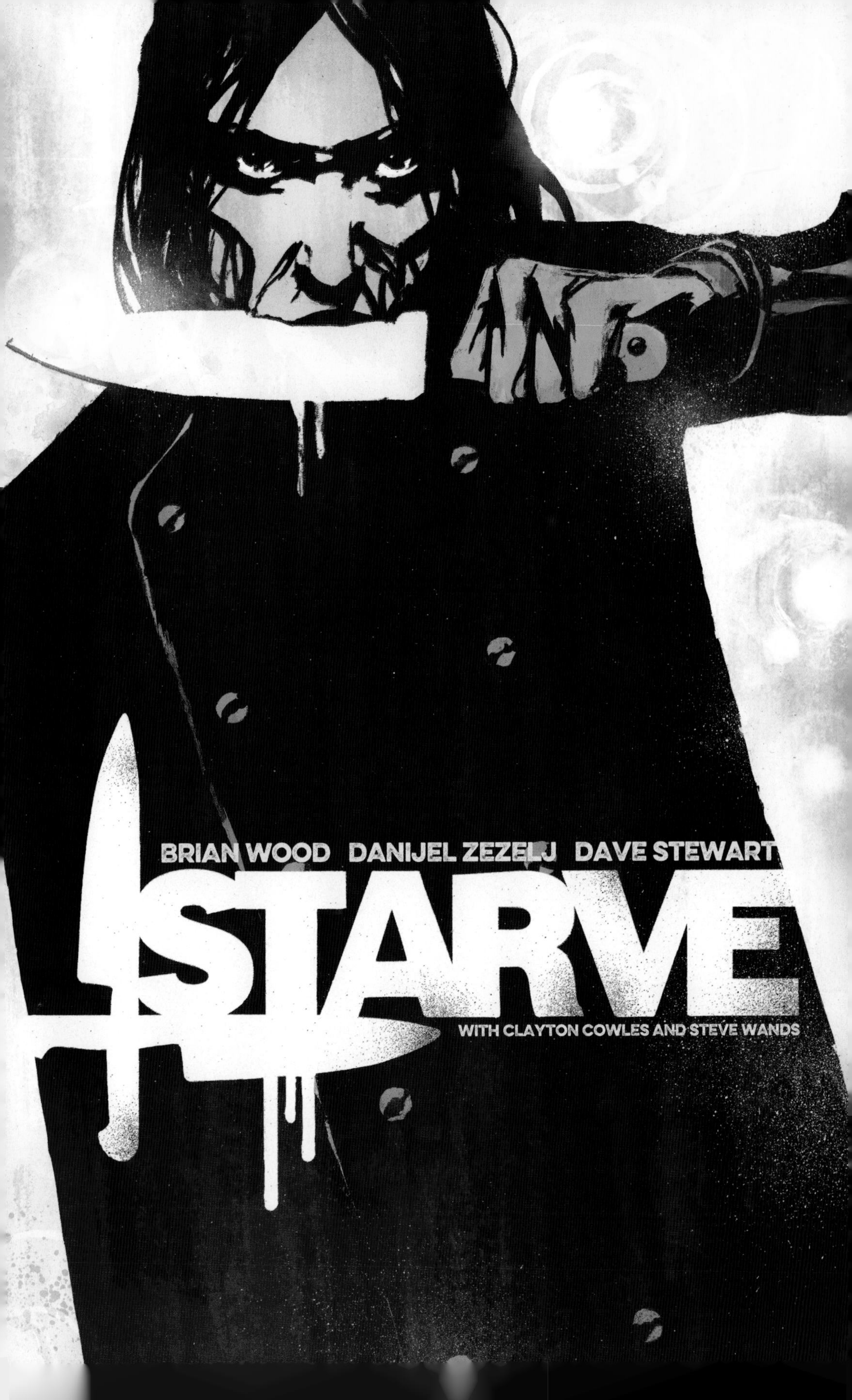
BRIAN WOOD DANIJEL ZEZELJ DAVE STEWART
STARVE
WITH CLAYTON COWLES AND STEVE WANDS

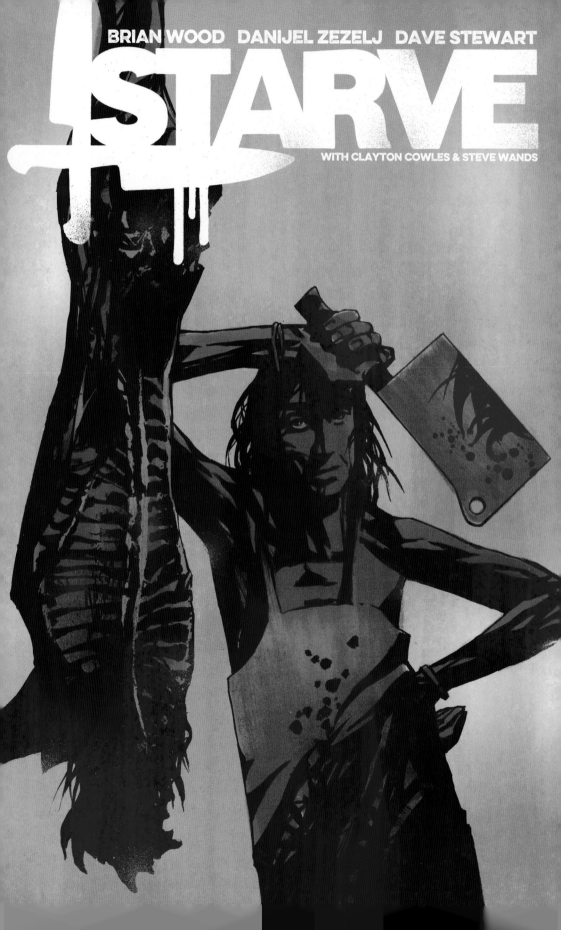

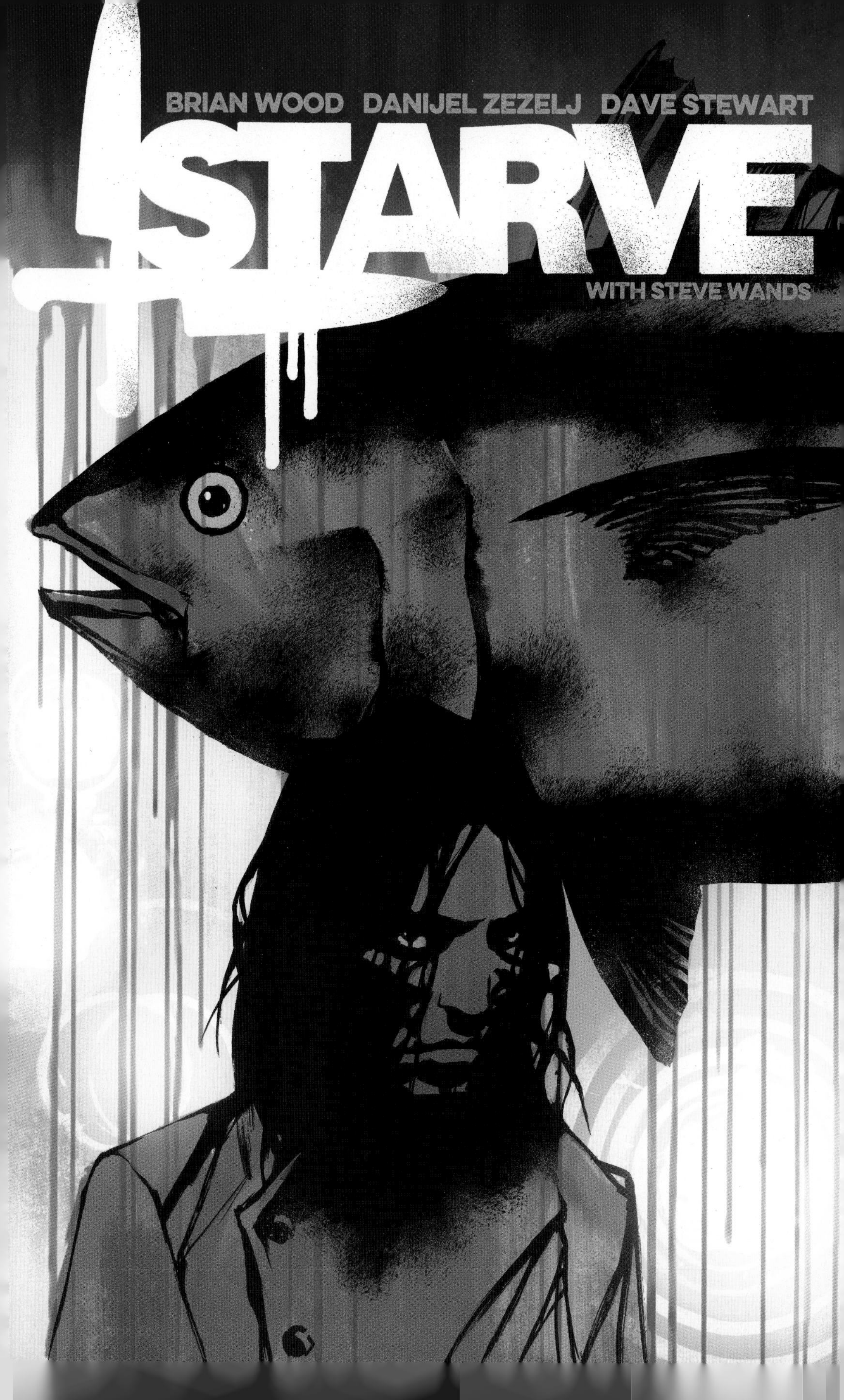
BRIAN WOOD DANIJEL ZEZELJ DAVE STEWART
STARVE
WITH STEVE WANDS

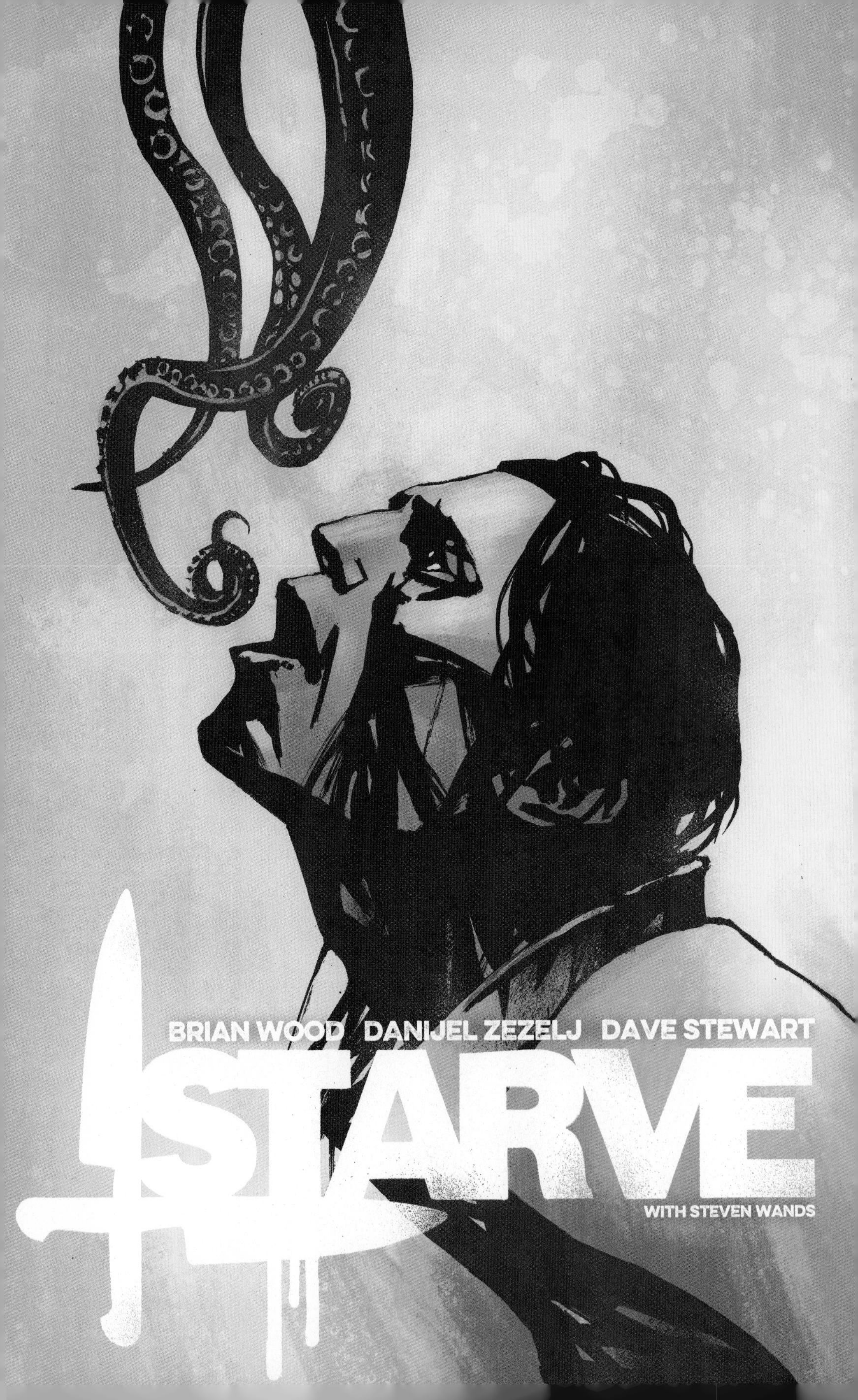

BRIAN WOOD
DANIJEL ZEZELJ
DAVE STEWART
STARVE
WITH STEVEN WANDS

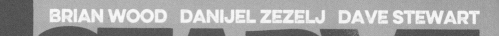

BRIAN WOOD    DANIJEL ZEZELJ    DAVE STEWART

# STARVE

WITH STEVEN WANDS

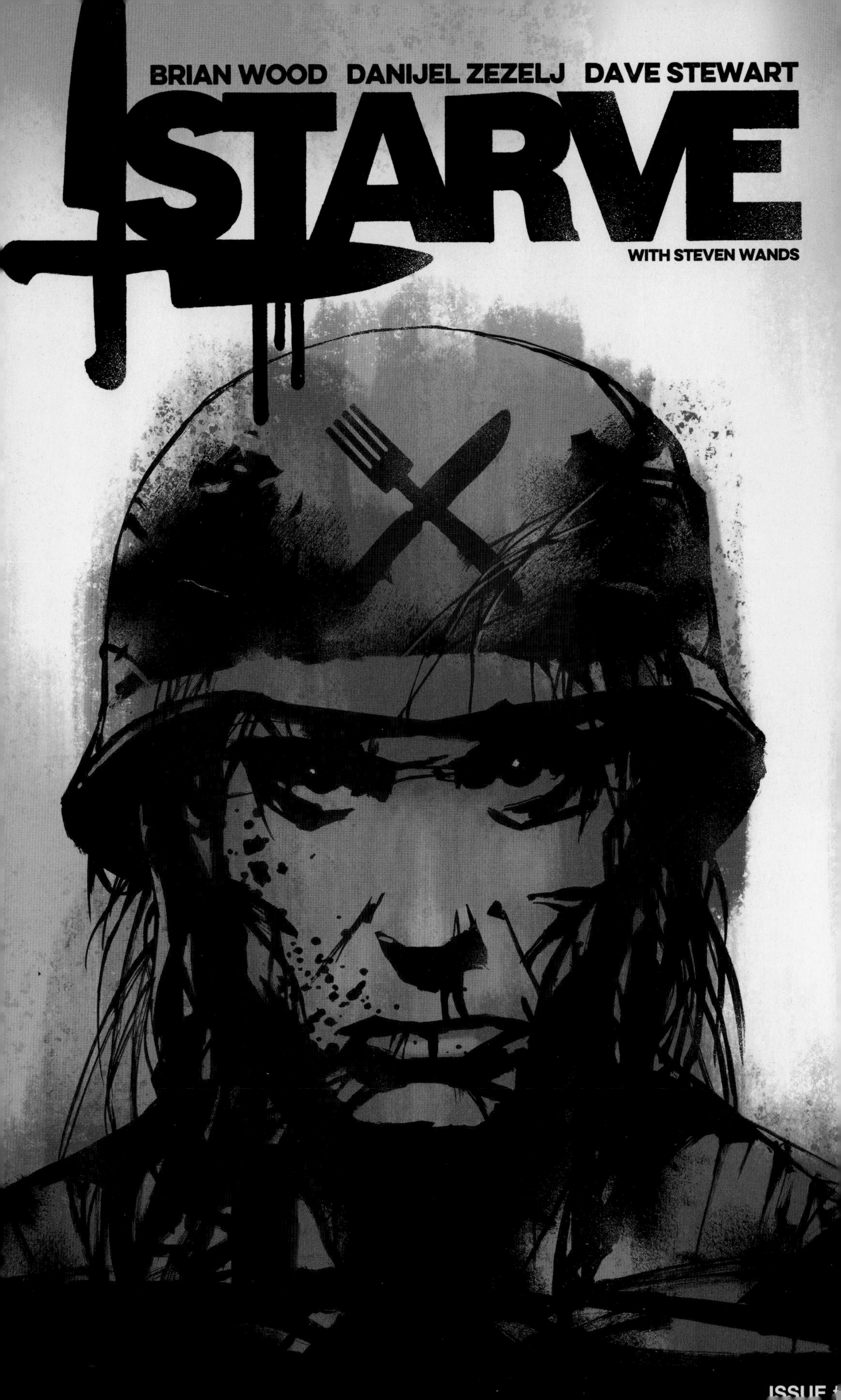
BRIAN WOOD DANIJEL ZEZELJ DAVE STEWART
STARVE
WITH STEVEN WANDS
ISSUE

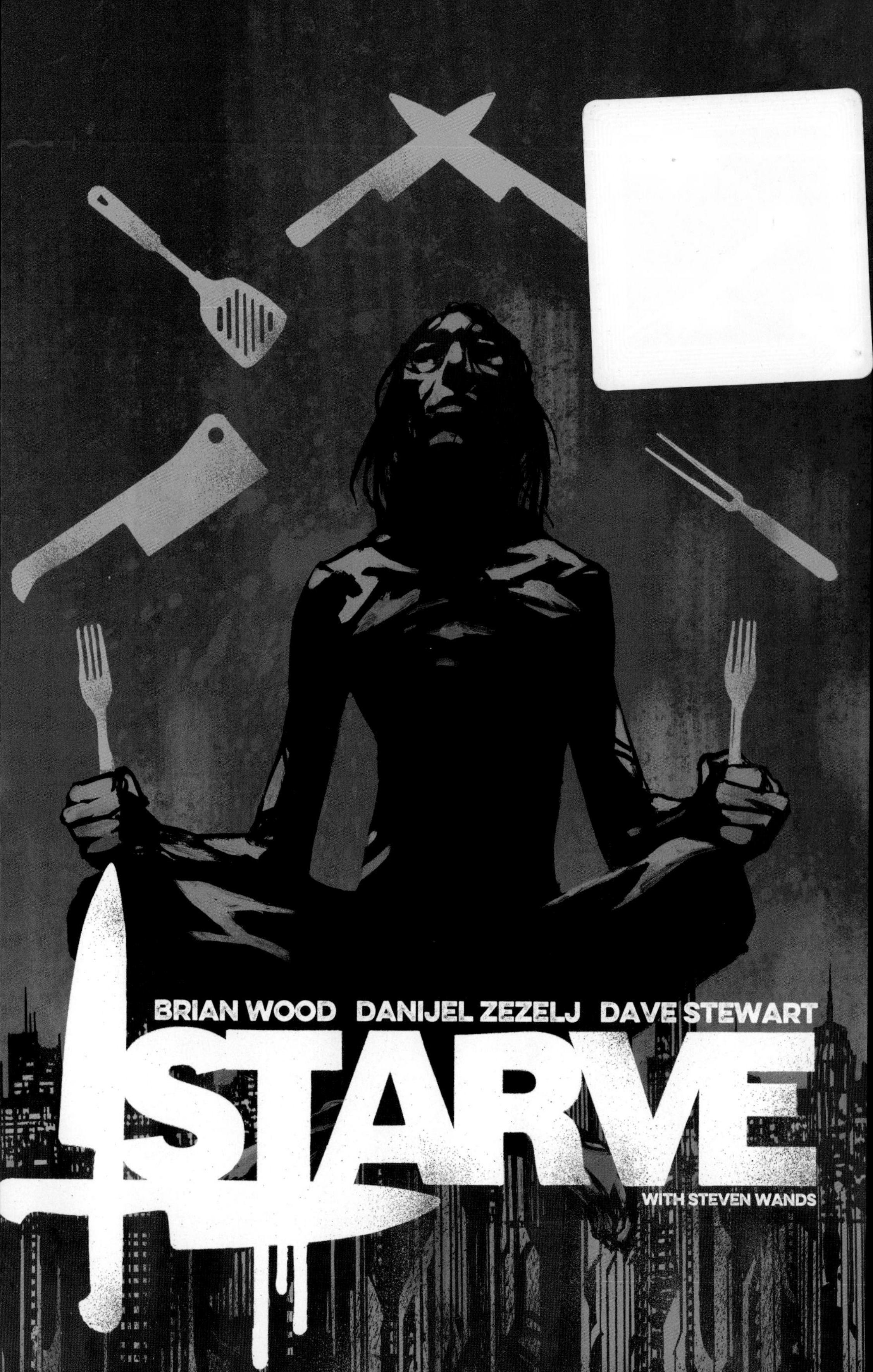
BRIAN WOOD DANIJEL ZEZELJ DAVE STEWART
STARVE
WITH STEVEN WANDS

ISSUE #5

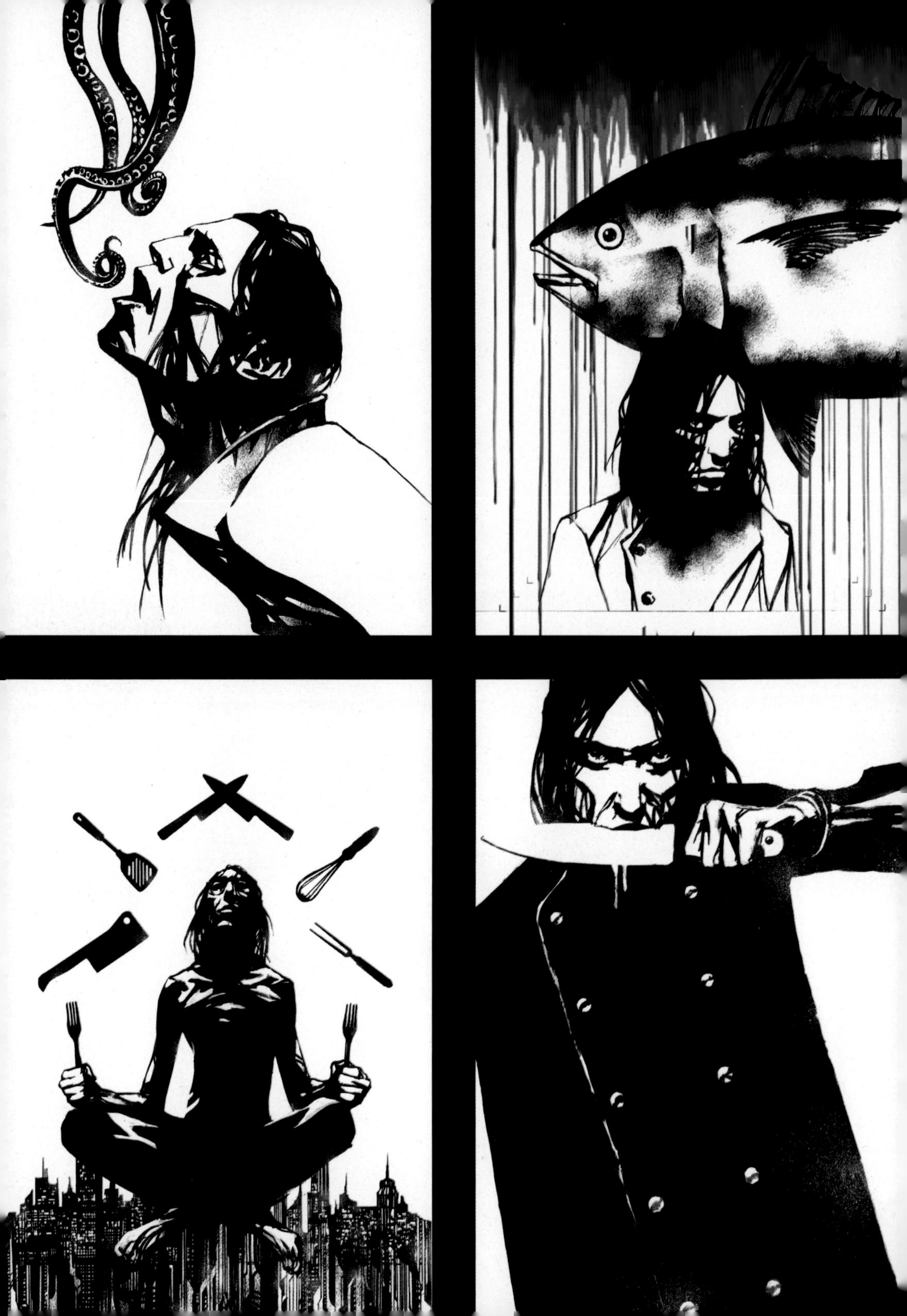

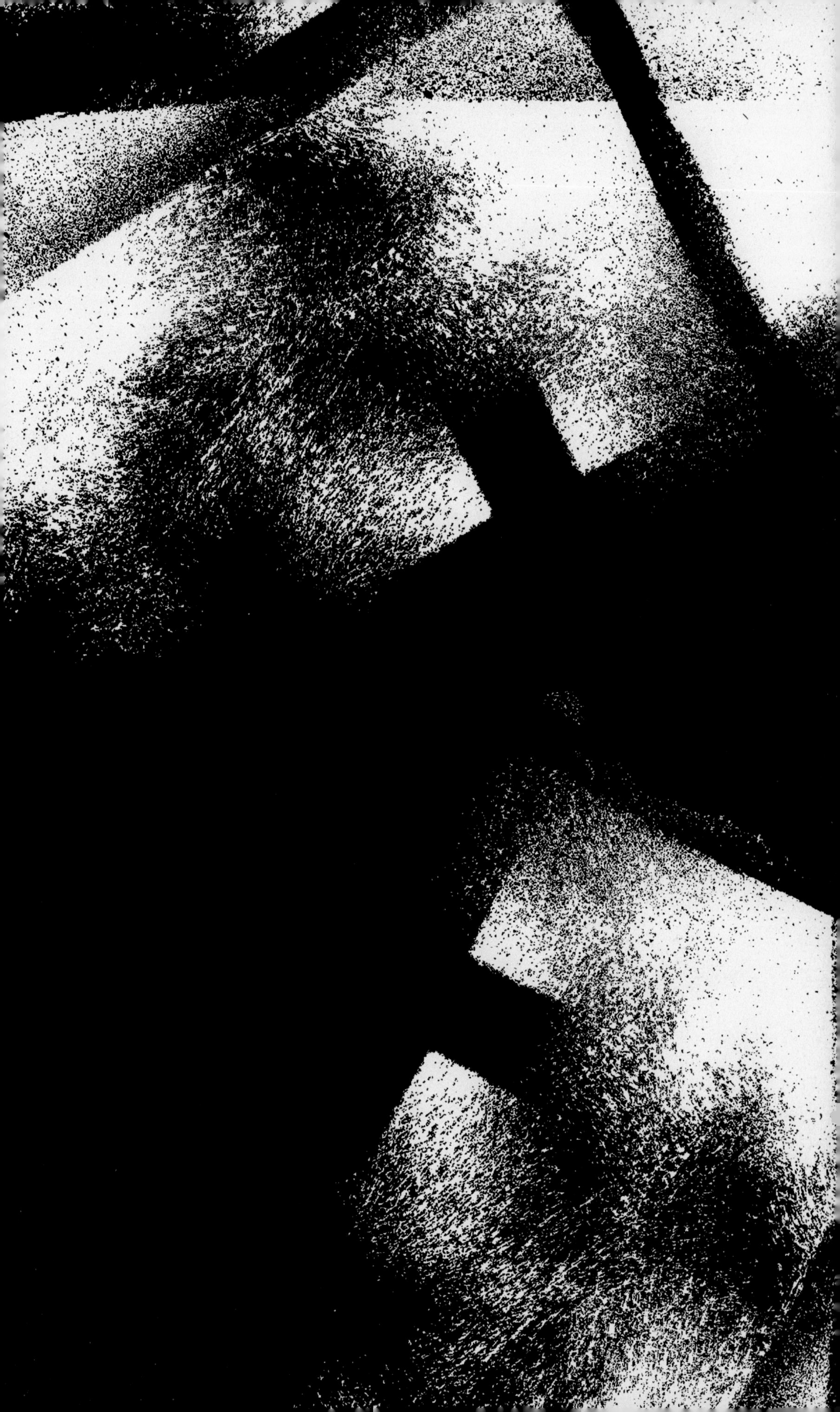

STARVE

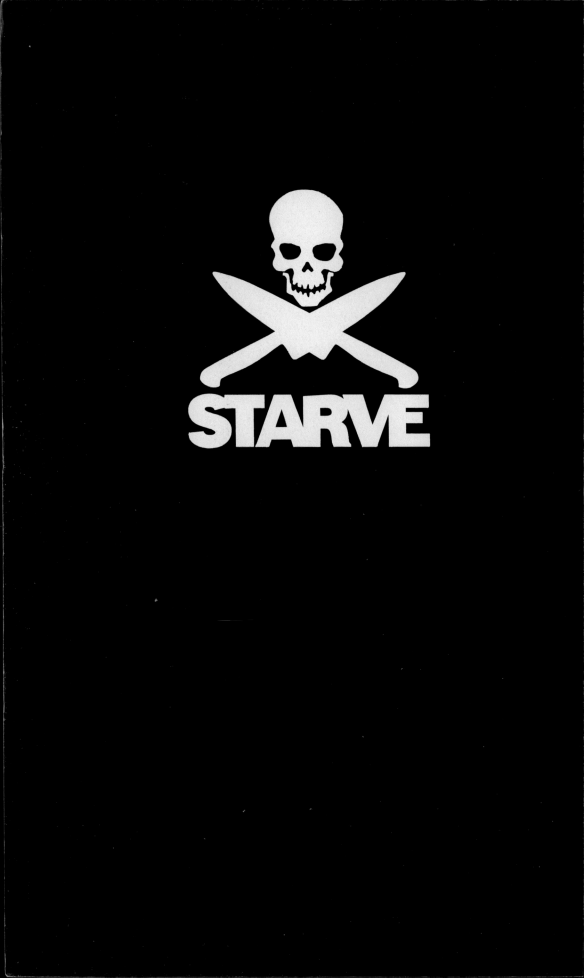